TOURING KELLY'S POEM

Kieran York

Scarlet Clover Publishers, LLC
Littleton, Colorado

Cover Art, Design, and Technical Director—Beth Mitchum
Photography by Kieran York

Editor/Formatter—Rogena Mitchell-Jones, Literary Editor
www.rogenamitchell.com

Published by Scarlet Clover Publishers LLC
www.kieranyork.com and www.scarletcloverpublishers.com
P.O. Box 621002; Littleton, Colorado 80162

Printed and bound in the United States of America, UK, and Europe

ISBN-13: 978-0692389751
ISBN-10: 069238975X

TOURING KELLY'S POEM

Kieran York

TABLE OF CONTENTS

BOOK TWO: As Mexico As a Journey's End

OTHER BOOKS BY KIERAN YORK

Loitering on the Frontier
Night Without Time
Earthen Trinkets
Careful Flowers
Appointment with a Smile

Crystal Mountain Veils (A Royce Madison Mystery)
First and Second Editions

Timber City Masks (A Royce Madison Mystery)
First and Second Editions

Sugar With Spice (Short Fiction)
Blushing Aspen (Poetry)

Within Our Celebration (Forthcoming Short Fiction)
Shinney Forest Cloaks (A Royce Madison Mystery)

Poetry Contributor to Sappho's Corner Poetry Series:
Wet Violets, Volume 2
Roses Read, Volume 3
Delectable Daisies, Volume 4

Dedicated to the memory of
Coley Banks Taylor
My Calvin Thurston

And to all of the other teachers,
tutors, professors, and mentors
who educate us, guide us,
and enlighten our lives.

ACKNOWLEDGMENTS

I want to acknowledge Beth Mitchum—my mentor and friend. I thank her for her encouragement and collaboration. I also thank her for being my 'publishing' guide through the maze that is creating a book.

I thank my editor, Rogena Mitchell-Jones—a gifted grammarian. This book is a huge book and a huge challenge. So I thank my editor and friend for taking the challenge. She treated my words with tenderness and brilliance.

I thank my friend, Shawn Marie Bryan, for building my website. I'm fortunate she's my friend.

We invite you to check out the Scarlet Clover website at:
www.scarletcloverpublishers.com

And as always, I thank my family and friends—ever supportive of this 'writing' journey. I'm indebted to each of you for kindness and love.

I want to also thank the readers for lending me your time. Thank you for traveling with my words and with my heart.

I hope you all enjoy this tour!

BOOK ONE
WHEN ALL THE WORLD WAS MEXICO

Part I—All Are Naked, None Is Safe
Part II—All That We Played With Here
Part III—All Lovely Things

BOOK TWO
AS MEXICO AS A JOURNEY'S END

Part IV—Help Us to Bring Darkness Into the Light
Part V—In Masks Outrageous and Austere

BOOK ONE: WHEN ALL THE WORLD WAS MEXICO

PART I—ALL ARE NAKED, NONE IS SAFE

What is our innocence, what is our guilt?
All are naked, none is safe.
And whence is courage: the unanswered question,
the resolute doubt -
dumbly calling, deftly listening -
that in misfortune even death,
encourages others and in its defeat,
stirs the soul to be strong.
Marianne More "What Are Years?"
(MacMillan Co. *What Are Years?*)

PROLOGUE

THE EARLY NINETEEN-SIXTIES *were a different era—entirely.*
Dress was more formal and much less revealing. The mores,
the values, and the language of the time were very different
from the world of the 2000s. There were enormous
inconsistencies. Car doors would be opened for a woman, yet
career entryways would be locked.

It was inappropriate language to use a minority slur, yet
some bigots used jokes and innuendos to characterize
minorities. To capture the timeline, I have used terms today
are not permissible in our everyday conversation. Thanks to
most people wanting to be politically correct—kind and
tolerant, we've become much more considerate of those with
whom we share the planet.

Although hatred and bigotry remains, it has diminished in
our speech, hiring practices, and many other areas where
persecution once ruled. Americans are still sifting through the
concept of tolerance. Perhaps bias and prejudice will never be
excluded from our hearts. But it is my hope the concept of
eradicating hatred will continue.

It's important to us and to our future for love to prevail.

Kieran York

ONE

AUTUMN, 1963

I WANT TO become a poet. Well, I need to become a poet because I've always been one. I've heard life is a poem. If life is a poem—I hope my poetry is always on tour.

These thoughts began when all the truly energetic contemplations began.

Beginning! Perhaps the most arduous, important tour of my life did begin with a concept vital to a poem.

I can remember the thoughts as they scooted through my brain. I am convinced the Creator has mousetraps set for us. I learned this after a skiing accident when I was nineteen-years-old. I'd always debated the bromides about living to the fullest. We tease ourselves with mortality. This is the joke played on those coming of age. Indeed, life's most difficult journey must be youth.

For many years, we expect to live forever. So what if it has never been done before. We are immune to death. We are organic promise and invincible star stuff. And life seemed particularly secure in 1963's New Frontier. The time was magnificent. It was magic, and magic could save me; it could save us all.

However, last winter froze reality into my brain. My skis were aimed at a dense forest of trees. With no escape, and out of control, I broad-sided a row of trees. My carnage had been grated through those unyielding pines. Magic could not and did not save me. I was too careful to trust my instinct.

Although I had survived, I'd been physically battered. But the truest change was now in my mind. Life became a process of working without a net. I was now prepared for the eventuality of the grim reaper. Death was being cheated a moment at a time. Now I knew living's secret.

Exploration was to become my holy assignment. I was gliding on the wings of my spare life. There was a trip that needed taking. I recall the ancient term for journey is *journe*. I was to go on a *journe* out of myself, and into my heart.

I would be touring my poem.

* * * * *

GLANCING AT THE swirling background lines on my passport was a reminder my journey had begun. All the details of me were listed: Kelly Anne Benjamin; September 1943; Kansas; Female; 5'5"; 105 pounds; Blond; Hazel eyes. Actually, I gave a hasty self-description: medium-long, maize-colored hair with eyes more gold-flecked. They take on a blue or a green depending on the lighting. I smiled at my constant rewriting.

Visiting Mexico on business? Not really—unless it is the business of seeking adventure. Again, a correction—hungering for adventure. On and on to Rouen. Adventure, it is said, teaches life's balancing act: Tangles and tingles, passion, punishment, pleasure, and pain. Some of the sidebars of living have mixtures of the above. There is great bewilderment juxtaposing youth.

One thing is certainly true. Gusto for living and experiencing is crucial. And this requires dismantling fear. South of the border was near enough. It was a mere hop through Kansas, a skip past Oklahoma and a jump over Texas. My destination had been decided. Studying in Mexico City was to become my odyssey. Many keyboards have been filled with stories from beneath our southern border.

Escapism is one's ultimate goal for novelists. The *norm* is much less complicated. Norm? I should stay as sweet as I am, snag a promising husband, and populate the world. I'd already seen my mother tacked down—nailed to the cross of matrimony. The prospect couldn't have interested me less.

Finding a roadmap to becoming an infant prodigy of *The Letters* is difficult. Searching out those true contents had taken me through all of the writing courses offered at the small university in the center of Kansas. There was more of a requirement, I assumed. I needed to stop rationing life and begin to pour excitement from a hot, erotic decanter of exploration.

With relish, the same hunger of Proust's boyhood need for his spirit kiss, I must scout out my own estranged, awakening kiss. That is, break the shell, poke my head out, and kiss the daylight.

My Gran was certain I'd get dysentery. My sister, Kris, was certain I'd be attacked by bandits. My father was certain I'd be arrested. Mother was certain I'd get pregnant. Friends were certain I'd become a drug addict, never to return to Kansas. I was certain I'd make every attempt at being authenticated. Nothing more.

Mexico City would fill my agenda.

* * * * *

ARRIVING, I KNEW instinctively Mexico City would become my personal Getaway University. As I surveyed the city streets from the backseat of a cab, I realized life often speaks a strange language. I was meant to be here. This was fate's answer and was no generic long-shot. It was my legitimate calling. Adventures could be accrued.

I had no idea how the stocky-*torsoed* taxi driver could make it through the *glorietas* while turned around talking with me. I encouraged him to turn back around and face the traffic. Most accidents, he responded, happen from the rear. Between healthy skepticism and recollections of my recent skirmish with the skis, I motioned for him to glance ahead.

It was my first lesson in logic and practicality not being married. Nor need they be in Mexico. I reopened my eyes in time to see the pulsating cars pass by as we sped. Palm trees and statues lined the *Paseo de la Reforma*. The Diana Fountain with her bow drawn blinked by. I half saluted her hunt.

After turning onto a side street, I saw the apartment building come into view. I hauled my suitcase up the circular flight of stairs to the fifth landing. I wasn't certain if the slight tremble from within was one of anticipation or of trepidation.

"House of Sanchez," a small voice from a diminutive woman announced. She was an American in her early seventies. *Señora* Edith Sanchez was wearing the pinkest, fluffiest bedroom slippers I'd ever seen. Her gray hair was piled up into a tower on her head. Pin-point, blue-gray eyes squinted at me as she ushered me into her sitting room. Filled with a density of plant life, the room's elaborate draperies dulled the light. Oval-backed, imitation Hepplewhite chairs were lined up against one wall of the parlor. A china cabinet was filled with bone-colored decorative cups, souvenirs, and figurines. A Grieg piano concerto would have been a perfect touch. I could have been in the middle of Goeth's *Wilhelm Meister's Apprenticeship* and I knew it.

After warmly welcoming me, Edith Sanchez nodded for me to be seated. Carefully, she poured tea. "Do you take lemon or cream?"

"No, thank you." I sipped the strong tea. "It was nice of you to fix tea," I commented with a polite smile.

"After such a long trip, you need refreshment." She slid a tray toward me. "Try a biscuit, dear."

"Thank you." I tasted the wafer-thin cookie. "Have you been in Mexico City long?"

"My dear friend, Belle and I were visiting from Chicago. When we met our husbands, we decided to marry and stayed on. My husband departed."

"Departed?"

"Twenty-two years ago, I lost him to a stroke. Señor Sanchez was a fine gentleman. Not at all like the brash young men of today." She sipped gingerly at her tea. "He left me with a sizable bank account, but the years have dwindled my income. I must now take roomers. Four women are my lodgers. Three of you are university women. Erika is a working girl."

"I'm glad there are others going to the university. I won't feel alone when I go the first time."

She began her rundown. It was meant to be an abbreviated full disclosure. "Nora is from a small town outside Portland. A lovely young woman. She studies political science. She is also a Christian Scientist. As am I." Her head elevated. "Leigh is from Colorado. A graduate student. She's older. As is Erika. Erika is a European and more worldly. She steals my cheese. And she's behind on her rent payments," she tattled.

My lips churned as I attempted not to laugh. I hadn't expected an inventory on poor Erika. "Which woman will I be rooming with?"

"Nora. And there will be someone coming in every day to clean. Light cleaning only, you know. Dusting, vacuuming, and the like. If you have anything special for the maid to do, there will be an extra charge. Let me know and I'll make the arrangements. Also," she rushed her sentence, "you'll have your own shelf in the kitchen. And I must warn you to watch Erika. She's untrustworthy. You know the type." Her words were fringed with heavy-gauge honey.

"Type?"

"Yes. I have a cupboard I keep under lock and key. Erika is Austrian with a very wild background. I'm certain you're from a good family. And you're aware of the dangers of too closely associating with such a type. But Nora Lawrence is a fine, young woman."

I placed the cup delicately back onto the saucer. The señora would be a delight. When the inquiry was finally shut down, she led me to my room—Nora and my room. Old walnut highboys, student desks, shelves, and cot-sized beds were strategically placed on opposite sides of the room. The señora opened the drawers to show me the fresh paper lining. She then concluded her tour. I pitched my luggage onto the bed without stuffed animals residing on it.

"Kelly, I'll be keeping some of my plants in here for you. It's a very sunny room. Do be careful of my violets. One of my roomers placed a pot on the window ledge and burned them beyond recognition."

"I'll be very careful," I assured her with a wide smile. At this time, there were only two potted plants in the room. Assuming the plants were checked in and out of different rooms, like a horticultural library, I hoped none of them would expire while in my safeguard.

In Frazer's *Golden Bough*, I had read the Indians of Guayaquil, Equador, used human blood, and sacrificed human hearts when they sowed their fields. In Cuenca, they used up hundreds of evildoers, and even little children, per harvest. After the señora's comments about rude young men, I wondered if she might have revitalized the violet's soil with their bodies. She had been in Mexico for years, and it wasn't all that long ago Mexican harvest festivals placed criminals against two immense stones and crushed them. The remains were buried. It was called meeting the stones.

The violets looked absolutely vigorous.

I dispensed my belongings. I couldn't help noticing Nora's side of the bulletin board had an assortment of photographs. One was of a young woman standing next to a handsome guy. They were obviously related. The similarities were great. Round faces, blue eyes, freckles, and great white smiles. The woman's sable hair was medium length while the young man sported a flattop.

Beneath the board was a set of shelves. I looked at the books piled up. Nothing about the Lake Poets for Nora Lawrence. Not a single line of poetry could be found. I'd attempt for a literary balance. Upon my shelf, I placed a few poetry and literature books. Lifting to place a paperback copy of Hamilton's *Mythology*, I smiled.

I recalled my Gran's commentary when she'd seen it. She did a double-take as she picked it up. On the cover was the photo of a nude god statue. She thumbed through it as though she were handling last week's garbage. She read out loud one of the 'limb from limb' speeches.

"Well," she raged, "you bein' in college and studying such things! In my day, there was no such nonsense," she snorted. "And you best get this writing business out of your head if it's those sorts of books you'll be reading. Cease, before it's too late and you come to no good."

"Gran, it is literature."

Her enormous dewlap bobbed as she nervously rocked her wheelchair. She threatened, "I won't be leaving any of my money for such a thing. Well?" she demanded my acknowledgment and my agreement.

"Gran," I argued, "mythology is needed in order to have a base for studying literature. The classics. Latin...."

"Latin!" She squinted. "The Holy Mass is in Latin."

"So is some of mythology," I timidly replied. "I'm learning about it in school."

"Not in my school," she retorted. Then she shifted positions, tacking her eyes to the window. "I don't believe they teach such things here. Not in Kansas."

* * * * *

"I MEAN *REALLY*!" Leigh James, a tall blonde with a magnificent tan stood in the bedroom's doorway. "Sanchez told me you're as sweet as Nora Lawrence. I said to myself, *a true bitch brigade if ever I saw one.*"

"Pardon," I looked up with stupefied perplexity.

"Priceless! Two Nora Lawrences." She pushed back straggles of hair from her attractive, oblong face. She draped her long body across the opposite bed. "So," she inventoried, "you sweet or no?"

"Probably not."

"I'm Leigh James from Colorado Springs. Not sweet at all."

"Kelly Benjamin. I'm from Kansas City. Actually, it's a suburb. I used to go skiing in Colorado."

"I lived there and hated cold-weather sports. That's why I'm here. Why are you here?"

"I like the sun. I've given up skiing."

"So why were you checking out the violets?"

"Thinking about how the Mexicans used to sacrifice men for their crops."

Leigh's laugh snapped. "*No me parece mala idea.*"

"Sorry, I don't know much Spanish."

"I commented it isn't such a bad idea. Sacrificing men. Anyway, I'm a grad student. Archeology." Leigh stretched. "But I suppose Sanchez filled you in. I study shard. And you study creative writing?"

"Right. Poetry mostly."

"I suppose Sanchez gave you her censorious tour." Leigh periodically, ritualistically, pushed her hair from her low forehead. Dark eyes darted, then stapled to her subject, me, as she asked each question. Her long hair was wound into a bun at the back of her head. A large pair of eyeglasses acted as her prop. She bit the fawn-colored plastic ends when the glasses were off. When on, they slipped down the bridge of her nose. "So welcome to the ribald group."

"Sanchez did mention Erika is worldly. And steals cheese."

"She's still on the fucking cheese trip." Leigh sighed. "I mean *really*. She does her cheese moan when Erika gets behind on her rent. You'll like Erika. Nora's okay. She's damned inhibited. And she repents when she's not."

"I'm not exactly the worldly type myself."

Leigh's laugh exploded. "Don't tell me you're a *cupcake*?"

"Cupcake?" I inquired.

Stuttering, she decoded, "Virgin."

"Naw," I lied. "Know any available men?"

"Only a gay playwright. Paul," she reported.

"I don't suppose he'd be interested." I fished in my handbag for a package of gum. "Gum?" I offered.

"Sure. So you're looking for available men?"

"Searching excitement. Experience." I unwrapped a stick of gum, folded it and slipped it into my mouth.

"Experience?" she queried.

"Adventure."

"I mean really." Leigh stood and then ambled toward the doorway. "Did you ever come to the right apartment!"

I quit chewing gum. "Leigh, what did you mean by that?"

Leigh turned. She winked back over her shoulder.

* * * * *

"GLAD TO SEE I finally have a roommate," Nora Lawrence greeted me. She plopped on her bed. Her large, blue eyes, with a contact-lens-blink boomed out of her circular, all-American, freshly scrubbed face. She was about my height and was a few curvy, well-placed pounds heavier. With a huge grin, she questioned, "Met the others yet?"

Closing my notebook, I answered, "I've met Leigh. Erika hasn't arrived yet."

"Erika is Austrian. A working girl." Nora's thin eyebrows bounced. "Honestly, a *working* girl."

"You mean like…." I searched a word, "a hooker?"

"Exactly." Nora slid off her pumps and immediately wiggled her toes. "Between Erika's *dates* and Leigh's pretense! We know she's a lesbian. She never denies it but never admits it. I have it on authority she likes women. As lovers."

"It must be why she knows a gay playwright," I mulled. "Wow. A diverse group."

"You mean it doesn't bother you?"

I was enthralled. "Nope. To each her own." I shrugged. I wasn't going to give a *falling off the face of earth* expression over the revelation.

"I always keep a robe on when she's around," Nora disclosed. Her glance snagged on my bookshelf. "You brought a library?"

"Only a few books. What I need is a good learner's guide

to Spanish." I issued a limp laugh. "I studied French and then decided to spend my final two years of college in Mexico. I'd say it was a complete educational afterthought."

"French?"

"My grandmother, I call her Gran, speaks a little French. It was easy, so it became my elected language."

"It's my second year down here. Spanish is my minor." She leaned back against the wall. "Don't say *yes* if you don't completely understand the question."

"I'll take a crash course in Spanish before committing to heavy petting. So what's there to do around here?" I began placing my clothing in the drawers.

"We could go out for coffee later."

"Work our way up the ladder of degeneracy, one rung at a time?"

Nora frowned. "It's only your first night here."

"Exactly. And I am anxious for some excitement," I stressed.

"Is everyone from Kansas as impatient as you are?"

Smiling, I replied, "No. Only my Gran."

* * * * *

NORA WORKED OUT the details as if she were CEO of a dating agency. She had been dating a Frenchman named Michel Evremond. She called him attempting to fix up a blind date for me. There was more than a slight hint of her domineering capabilities when she instructed Michel to get back with her quickly. She didn't have all night. I figured with my normal propensity to fossilize until life moved me on to the next square, I'd get along fine with her. Her proclivity for sliding players across a game board wouldn't meet with my resistance. Friends supplemented me.

Nora's eyes hissed at the phone as she awaited Michel's call. "He'd better call back," she admonished.

"Not everyone is willing to risk a blind date."

She tugged at her skirt as she crossed her legs. Examining her fingernails, she pronounced, "I'm recommending you. Of course, you're all right."

When the phone rang, she rushed into the hall to set our social agenda. I sorted my ledge of books. When she returned, I quizzed, "So do I have a date?"

"His name is Eduardo Rivera. Latin handsome. Five-ten, thin build, nice eyes, and quiet." Nora searched her memory as her eyelids batted. "He's an architect. Dreamy smile. Studied philosophy. Shy. Golly, that's about it."

I knew I could sneak a little poetry into any discussion of philosophy. I hoped a shy philosopher-architect didn't offer an appetizer of stoicism. Fun was a wonderful ingredient for a date.

Life is a grab-bag.

* * * * *

MY THOUGHTS WERE of home when I fanned through a rhyming dictionary my kid sister, Kris, had given me. My mother had objected to my picking up and rushing off to a foreign country. My desire to write was another true cross for her to shoulder. She realized most poetry had a beatnik influence.

Certainly, old poets in ruffled shirts were saints, for all Mom knew. I wasn't about to tell her Coleridge lapped up his laudanum. Rumors had Wordsworth alarmingly *near* his sister, Dorothy. And Proust was running around checking public latrines for dangling parts. Pope was not one. Dylan was a true dipsomaniac. And Whitman was certainly tooty-fruity—

according to the norm.

But I was tightly affixed to their corner. I understood their great old poet souls were scorched as they sculpted those sonnets. I loved each and every one of them for they never quit to me—which goes to prove, in or out of the loony bin, gutter, or grave, the heart of poetry never stops beating. It never ceases to beat and tick word messages. Mom was, however, correct about modern poetry not even rhyming. That, she contended, had been brought forth by the beat generation. They, with all their filth and curse words, were the fallen angels.

* * * * *

NORA DIRECTED US to a corner table. The piano bar at Chipp's was famous, she commented as we were settling in to await the arrival of Michel and Eduardo. I inspected the swank setting. Then I caught a first glimpse of my blind date. With his soft, absorptive eyes, his authentic smile, and handsome face, he definitely passed inspection.

I hoped I'd made a similar good grade.

With a shy stammer, he welcomed me to Mexico City. Most men had never beckoned me with Pan's pipes. I'd never been a part of the flock on my way to Mount Arcadia. But Eduardo was different. Perhaps, I thought, he might be the one to enlighten my sexual curiosity.

We spent the early portion of the evening dancing. Then we took an excursion around the city. Eduardo had driven his family's Citron so there would be room enough for the four of us. Michel and Nora barely needed any room at all at first. Then I noticed they began doing some fairly acrobatic sprawling. They weren't aware of anything as we circled the monuments that I was finding enthralling. There was the

Palacio National, La Plaza de la Constitución, Bellas Artes, Columna de la Independencia, and the *Monumento a la Revolución.* Guess Nora and Michel had those amazing sights memorized.

I, however, felt the night's energy with its flushing bubbles of light. They were the colors of Modigliani and Kandinsky. The *Avenida Juarez* was the blazing watercolors of night. Eduardo beamed when he saw how I appreciated his city.

We're all basically classmates of the planet, but our homelands usually have us by the heart. I didn't attempt to explain; there was no parable to fit my special motif of the world. Exciting parts of the world make adrenaline junkies of us.

After the tour, we returned to our apartment. Eduardo walked me to the door. When we reached the final step onto the apartment landing, Eduardo leaned into my kiss. As we pressed against the door's frame, the doorbell rang. We met Erika. She flung open the door. Wearing only a skimpy bra and matching hot pink bikini panties, she frowned. Eduardo politely contained his sated desires and left.

"So. Vat iz et zat you vant?" Erika's curt words snapped.

"I want in. I'm Kelly. The new roommate. And you must be Erika."

"Yah." She half bowed. Erika could have been Sophia Loren's kid sister. With cinnamon-tinted, auburn, shoulder-length hair, and flashing dark eyes, she was a duplicate of the star. Her fiery expression and sultry voice matched with those pouty lips. "You vant zome cookies?"

"No thanks." I wondered when she would pull out the stolen brick of cheese. She gave a lush belly laugh when I told her Nora and Michel were saying their goodbyes. When we arrived at the dining room table, we sat.

Her life and times were then elaborated upon. She'd arrived in Mexico City poised to marry a famous bullfighter. He was more of a bullshitter, for he impregnated her, so she then took off for Spain. *His* ticket to Mexico had not been a one-way ticket. Erika went through a botched abortion. Five years later, still single, she remained in Mexico. Her eyes batted wildly. She crossed her arms and her boobs poured out over her bra. That was her storytelling for the night. She was ready to sleep. I tucked myself into bed. I couldn't, I realized, have selected a more diversified group. And even if Erika stole an entire vat of cheese, I found her charming. I wanted to tap back into her Mozart-cantata sentences soon, I mused.

As luck would have it, I bordered on being an insomniac. Unless Hypnos would touch me with his magic wand, or fan me with his dark wing and team up with Morpheus, I probably wouldn't sleep my first night in D.F. So Nora's sawing snores wouldn't keep me awake. Her nasal, twanging snorts would only become my background music. I would sort out Bach's 'Taccata and Fugue in D Minor' as she sputtered away.

Garbled with my jetlag, the city noises, and Nora, a whimsical addition to my dreams was provided. Nights brought pirate battles for my soul, mob funerals, a pit of crazed bats, a slippery cloud climb, pounding gavels, Whitman's heartbeat, Hitler's squeal, a cave of hairy ancestors, space ships, Jesus removing his sandals, and the colors of Mexico City. Dreams would whip me like the tail of a kite.

But, for whatever reason, in this city, I felt less crowded by time's programming.

This moment could never be replicated. Truth is so simple.

TWO

AN ADVENTURE-SEEKING SPIRIT flung out of bed. It belonged to me and to my first morning in Mexico. Ghost-wrestling was saved for another night. Morning's light was my starting bell. After I had galloped through a quick shower, I was ready to stuff myself on life's banquet.

Dressed in a printed, cotton blouse with a matching skirt, and sandals, I decided to set out. I picked up a key Sanchez had left on my desk. After scribbling a note saying I intended to go for a walk, I left the apartment.

My purse was crammed with a blank notebook, a ballpoint pen, a very limited Spanish dictionary, a few pesos, and my passport. I would get a five dollar bill converted to pesos first off. Currency considerations were usually not my mainstay, but I hated to be without funds in a foreign land.

I inhaled the fragrance of steaming loaves of bread as I passed the bakery on the corner. A fruit stand with geometrically stacked fruits was directly across the street. Multiple aromas hung in the air. Cantaloupes, pears, melons, pineapples, and other assortments of fruits and vegetables were colorful pyramids.

Corner vendors with bowknot knees, squatted beside small makeshift ovens. They turned the steaming corn on the cob and flipped tortillas. I wondered what they thought of Mexico's social diversity. I wondered what they thought of the men in tailored suits who rushed from one sales pitch to another. I wondered what they thought of me as they prattled amongst themselves. Probably, I conceded, they figured I was a crazy American, lost and searching.

Maybe they did know my secret.

My ambling finally stopped when I reached another bakery a couple of blocks from the apartment. My stomach was on empty, so the bin of rolls and line of pastries tempted me. My plan was to purchase a breakfast picnic, then stroll over to Chapultepec Park. I recalled from last night's tour, the magnificent park was only a couple of blocks away. The *Fuente de Diana* became my location's base marker. After purchasing a massive disc of pastry, I stopped by the small market shop for a bottle of orange juice.

It was on to the park once the shopping was complete. I loved climbing the adventure bean-stock. What I didn't like, I realized after finding a vacant concrete plank bench in the park, were the constant stares and side-glances from passersby. Granted, I was wicker-white. My pale skin and blond hair, mixed with having an early morning picnic in the park, might have enticed a joke or two.

Constant smiles were issued for I was determined it was fine if these folks figured I was a nut case. I was determined to make this park my own poetry factory. Many great artists were ridiculed for being off-kilter. Goldsmith sold *Vicar* for sixty pounds to pay his rent. Village children stoned Vincent's canvases. So what the heck was a few moments of mockery to me? Nothing, if I could wean a few lines of poetry onto the journal I carried.

Teaching myself to live without blushing might take some doing. But at least I had started early in the day.

* * * * *

ON MY WAY back to the apartment, I determined Mexico was the right choice. I needed this country's charm. I tried to understand its draw. I had worked last summer within Kansas City's hub of excitement. I was an intern at the daily newspaper. K.C. was a pounding, bellowing, stone-faced matriarch. Mexico City was a mystical enchantress. K.C. had an excitement because it was an adjoining playground to my small town/suburban life. But Mexico was a true wonderland. With its population of six million, it remained *almost* six million more than my small community had been. In my heart, it meant many more friendship opportunities.

As I tugged with my reasoning for selecting Mexico, I crossed the street. After purchasing a few grocery items for my shelf, I headed back to the apartment. I'd written in my note to Nora, I'd be about an hour and the hour was nearly up. I was aware, after having only known her a day, she didn't like miscalculation.

Everyone was circled around the table. Leigh, clad in pajamas, sans slippers, wiggled her toes in waves. Erika was absorbed in the astrology section of the morning paper. Nora was miffed I'd gone out on my own. Sanchez stabbed a wedge of melon and complained about the problems of getting good help.

Nora ruffled the collar of her Prussian-blue terry robe. She huddled. "Kelly, there's a way to see this city and a way *not* to see it. If you get my drift."

Leigh chuckled. "You tell her, Nora."

Countering indignantly, Nora spewed, "I'm trying to explain women aren't to go out alone in this city. I'm trying to be helpful. Not bossy."

"And I appreciate it," I said. "And thanks for fixing me up with Eduardo. He's adorable."

"You must," Sanchez cautioned, "see only young men

with the same fine background as yours."

A semi-smile crossed my mouth. I had no idea where Sanchez got my background check, but *fine* wasn't exactly a part of my past. My father was an alcoholic. He shifted from job to job. My mother, a nurse, held the family together. And the only stories I'd ever sold were to confession magazines. Although it was a literary prostitution commingled with my lofty goals, I didn't mind. It did supplement my part-time jobs and kept me in college. Being a pauper appealed to me. Poets must not look affluent.

"This Eduardo," Sanchez delved, "does his family have position?"

"He's an architect. Studied philosophy, as well," I reported.

"He's not an unhealthy influence?" she cross-examined.

Nora answered for me. "He's Michel's friend. They're on the same fencing team. So I can vouch for him."

Erika looked up from her newspaper. Her eyebrows bobbed. She giggled. "Zome of the menz, zhey are King Kong. Zhey take what they vant. Kelly, you vant to go to ze *Rincon de Goya* tonight for dinner? We go. Et vil be fun, no? And no one takez advantage. We go if I don't get ze appointment?"

"Appointment!" Leigh howled. "I mean, really."

"This Eduardo—" Sanchez began.

"Señora," Nora confirmed, redirecting Sanchez's objections, "Eduardo is a gentleman. And his family is terribly prominent. They own a machine factory. Now then, about the *Rincon* tonight?"

"Nora's being the chief tamale," Leigh accused. To me, she then disclosed, "You'll like the *Rincon*. A couple blocks away. Spanish Flamenco gypsy shows. Good clean fun," she stressed as Sanchez exited to the kitchen. Leigh then leaned into her whisper. "She wants to raise our rents because her food keeps missing. I mean, really! Who wants those *goddamn, sugary* cakes she gobbles up? Enough to gag you."

Erika pointed to her head and gave a couple of swirls. "She iz inzane. I don't take her cheeze. What she thinkz I am, a mouze?"

"Maybe it *is* a goddamn mouse," Leigh powwowed. "Let's tell her to set a fucking trap." She leaned back, tipping her chair. "She hates it when I lean like this." With a laugh, Leigh recalled, "One time back home a mouse got into the toaster. I was real little and thought it was dancing bread."

"What happenz wiz ze mouze?"

"Fried the little sonofabitch," Leigh reported with a roar.

"Back to the problem," Nora directed. "Sanchez hires and fires too many maids. So it might be the hired help. Or she might forget what groceries she's actually got."

Leigh was still cackling. "Maids. Elena was trying to water the plants with my douche bag last week. If that gives you any idea about what kind of a sophisticated criminal she would make."

Chuckling, I quizzed, "So how are the plants doing? Did you infect the violets?"

"Hell no," Leigh said with a snicker. "After last week, it's a jungle in there."

"Honestly," Nora scolded. "You're terrible, Leigh."

"Nora, you could help Sanchez with her lists." As an aside to me, Leigh explained, "Sanchez tacks up lists every time she gets pissed." When Sanchez entered, Leigh sighed. "Well, Señora, I hear you're missing supplies again. Guess you'll have a busy morning taking pen to paper."

* * * * *

AFTER ORDERING A round of *Cuba Libres*, I was cautioned

about booze and high altitude. They weren't the first admonitory words I'd heard. I was also cautioned to hold onto my purse and to count all my fingers and toes after doing business with the locals. But days of caution seemed a thing of the past. I didn't object when Nora, after one drink, ordered a round of tequilas. She salted the flesh valley between her thumb and forefinger, gulped a shot glass of tequila, and then sucked hard on a slice of lime. Her face screwed, and she exhaled a blast of air. "Fun, isn't it?" she questioned.

Leigh chided, "If it were fun, Nora, you wouldn't be doing it."

"Oh, Leigh, honestly!" Nora glared.

I pitched the tequila into my mouth. Sputtering, I felt the sting as it went down. "Fire," I exclaimed.

"It's from a cactus plant. Maguey. They roast the leaves, crush them, and put the juices into casks to ferment," Nora lectured. "Then they distil it and have tequila."

"Sorry, Erika isn't here," I commented as I cleared my vocal chords.

"Her appointment is taking longer than she'd expected. Bet she's getting a terrific *tip*," Leigh said with a giggle.

"Doesn't Sanchez catch on?" I inquired.

"She thinks men are grandfatherly toward Erika. Pay her rent, buy her clothes, give her cash, all for the hell of it," Leigh summarized.

By the time we were on our third drink, I had decided to find the restroom. When I stood, I felt my feet firmly planted on rockers. As if the projector was going in reverse, I sat back down. "Whew! I'm not used to drinking. I think my feet are tricking me and my eyes are crossing."

"The Mayan thought looking cross-eyed was beautiful. They even dangled bits of pitch between baby's eyes," Leigh mentioned. "They might have given the little shits some tequila instead."

I was blindsided and my brain was a cage of squirrels. There was no doubt my eyes had indeed crossed. My legs, too.

The swirling scarlet, vermilion, lemon, tangerine, and plum colors were actually Spanish dancers. To me, they were the inside of an elaborate kaleidoscope.

We were all semi-anesthetized by the time we walked back across the *Reforma*. I attempted to maintain my balance as I walked. I even glanced up at the evening skies and felt an indestructibility overtaking me. But I knew better. Death was inevitable and the rest was self-hoodwinking. Having been near death is a ransom of sorts.

I'm glad I'm not the world's Creator. For how could any loving entity give precious life and then so callously rescind it? This question is probably formulated by everyone as we go through adolescence to adulthood.

Naturally, the real test was to see if I could contain my anger. Spitting pabulum at the Great Executioner never bought anyone a spare lifetime.

THREE

So MUCH FOR Polly Pureheart at the gin mill.

I was participating in a hangover. I dismounted from my bed and proclaimed myself truly wounded but basically sound. The Señora was sipping tea at the table as my body sagged into a chair.

"Late," she accused.

"Sorry if we woke you."

"My girlies should be home at night. A city of sin is out there." Her eyes dipped as she took chipmunk bites of the toast.

"With school beginning, we'll certainly need to be in earlier," I conceded.

Leigh staggered to the table. "What a night," she moaned.

"You girlies shouldn't be drinking. What will decent men think?"

Leigh glanced back at Sanchez. Her eyebrows lifted nearly to her hairline. "Nothing, I hope."

Nora exited the bathroom, towel-drying her thick hair. "That's better," she chirped.

While Nora and Leigh bantered, I studied Sanchez's morning skin. It had the same transparency of caked milk. That bit of aging reminded me of my grandmother. Gran was in her mid-eighties and had been confined to a wheelchair for over four years. Before that, it was a walker or cane. Gran was a fighter throughout her invalid state. She always had stories of the wild Kansas frontier. Settlers needed grit, she'd told me. And my pilgrimage into the past was taken at her side, through her memories. I was intrigued with tales of pioneer ingenuity, and also with my Gran.

It was natural to me to study all the sags in Gran's eyelids. Every crevasse and crease in her face was bolted to my memory. Her wispy eyebrows and sprays of gray hair were memorized. The blueness of her eyes held me captive when she issued yarns of pioneer life.

When Leigh turned her vituperation on me, I was thrilled. It kept me from becoming homesick. "Kelly is an undercover cupcake, it turns out," she blasted.

I had let my chastity secret slip. Although I was not in a coven of hedonists, I was probably the only remaining virgin on campus. "Leigh, how are the plants in your room doing? Have enough marl?" I questioned.

"I'd call you faux erotic."

"About your plants. And the additives…." I continued

"They've got great loam," she replied. "But then, I'm into archeology. Not biology, so like you."

I jabbed, "You must tell me more about your field of study."

"Kelly," she explained, "I'm not into the typical bullshit of literature. My profession is one of greatness. The study of *truth*. The bullshit I study is actual." She broke to laugh a few moments and then she continued. "I don't work with made-up crap like you do. I work with a hand-ax, trowel, and whiskbroom."

"Whiskbroom," I howled. "What do you need that for? Planning to take short rides?"

* * * * *

WEKWOM TEKSOS. I pondered the words on my way to enroll at the University of the Americas. *Wekwom teksos.*

The snaking motion of the lifting bus, as it chugged up the mountainside toward the university campus, created a wobbly moment or two within my stomach. During the sixteen kilometer trip, I gorged myself on the view of profusely verdant foliage. The twenty-minute ride went by too rapidly.

I carefully scanned the main entrance of the campus that was to become my home of higher learning for this, my junior year. To one side was the College Theatre with stalks of leaves twining around the columns. There was also a student center, sun terrace, library, the Foreign Trade Center Quadrangle, post office, and various classrooms

The Creative Writing Center held my immediate attention. Splashed with mosaics, the building was colorful and free-flow, just the way I wanted my poems to be. Stone-lined paths routed me from center to center during my first tour. I ended my expedition under a stone archway that descended a grassy hill. Students were relaxing as the bright sun shone down on them and their stacks of newly purchased books.

Although I'd enrolled late, the classes were exactly what I'd planned. They were: Analysis of Poetry; Techniques of Fiction Writing; English Literature to 1750; and a beginning Spanish course. On Leigh's behalf, I'd looked for a program called Analysis of Cupcake 101 and hadn't found it offered this term. But I was encouraged by the schedule of the next two quarters. I would take Short Story, Playwriting, Poetry, and Whitman. And more.

There always seemed some hidden bond between Whitman and me. Maybe, I considered, my journey had brought me to this resplendent land with its ornamental symbolism and pastoral involvement in order for me to study Whitman.

Scripting a high heart, my being a scrivener would do honor to Walt. I could visualize Walt standing on a corner selling *Leaves* from a basket. Rude passersby would not even see him. I could cry when thinking about his love letters, his legacy to modern poetry. His passionate, androgynous poetry moved me deeply.

There were additional similarities between Walt and me. His great-grandmother, Sarah White, was a rugged individualist. She chewed tobacco, swore, and was later confined as an invalid. My Gran was always her own person, too. Whitman loved Lincoln, Caravaggio and was a 'life visitor' and wound-dresser.

After Whitman had died, they removed his brain and sent it to be measured and weighed at the American Anthropometrics Society. His brain was destroyed when a lab worker accidentally dropped it on the floor. When I told Nora about Whitman's brain, she commented students aren't the only ones who lose their minds at the academies. For Nora, it was a very good line.

I purchased an armload of books. Glancing down at the spines of each text, I congratulated myself on opting for such a great word stash. These would integrate with my mind to ultimately produce a word weaver—*wekwom teksos.* I hoped.

Leigh caught up with me. She was carrying her own load of books. I grumbled, "I'd save money if I could purchase these books by the pound."

"I have no goddamn idea why an archeology grad student needs to be encumbered by all this shit. My mission is to become an expert on dendrochronology, obsidian dating, and the Teotihuacan culture."

"I thought your mission was to become the lesbian greeting committee."

"Whew! I wondered when you'd come out with something

like that." She grinned perversely. "Or come out. But then you haven't admitted to yourself lesbians aren't from Lisbon." When I didn't rile, she continued. "I thought I was a bitch, but next to you, I'm practicing."

"I find archeology interesting," I murmured, changing the conversation.

"As in Lesbos?"

"As in the cave paintings in Lascaux, France. That, I read, was discovered by a dog named Robot."

"Trying to debase dogs or the French?" she questioned with a wink.

I hugged my books as we sauntered toward the bus stop. "Did you know *wekwom teksos* means 'word weaver' in Greek?"

"Now you're getting out of your depth, cupcake." She smiled with her words, but the smile was nearer the baring of teeth.

My return grin was that of a fake leprechaun.

* * * * *

WITH A FLURRY of words, Erika told me Eduardo had called and would call back later. She had also sorted my mail. A letter, jammed with family news, was the first I opened. My mother tattled about Kris having been caught going on a 'date' without permission. It couldn't have been *with* permission, as Kris was considered too young to date. When caught, Kris was grounded. Can punishment be far behind, I questioned. A note written by Kris refuted the allegation. She was innocent, for it was not a 'date' at all. An immaculate date.

As I unfolded Gran's well-creased letter, I knew now I would get the true scoop. A dollar bill flew out, and like a leaf to the ground, fluttered to my feet. Kris, Gran charged, was too spoiled since she was the baby of the family. She mentioned although she had her own notions about things that may be marginal, she was correct on this.

Before getting to a letter from my friend, Gloria, I was startled by Leigh as she scurried to the table. She grabbed her letters. "What's the rush?" I asked.

"Date."

"Do I know *him*?" I taunted, trailing her back to her room.

"Don't be smug. You're getting to be a little chastity promoter like Nora. Any day now the bridge of your nose will be covered with a splatter of freckles, and you'll be in the midst of sin paranoia."

"Why the snit?" I blustered. "I don't care if you're dating the prom queen."

"Frankly, I think we're in the midst of beauty queen overkill." She fanned through her letters. "I'm abandoning the apartment for the evening. Belle is visiting Sanchez and I'm not in the mood for the old goose."

"You're in a gruesome mood. Your *date* ought to be thrilled."

"I'm supposed to run a tour Saturday with a batch of freshmen archeology students. Infant pothunters. I'll need to speak baby talk."

"You'll certainly need to modify your language," I agreed. "Academia frowns on telling kids to examine the fucking pre-Columbian pottery."

"My luck, one of the little shits will trip over a sarcophagus and revolutionize the antiquities program. That's bitching."

"I'm sure you weren't born with a copy of Heizer in your cradle."

"I was the fucking bookmark, Benjamin." She glared at me. "I suppose you have a date with the bean."

"Eduardo." I headed for the door with my grimace. "You don't like Mexicans, Americans, virgins, Aztecs, freshmen, and you don't even like poor, old Belle."

"Poor Belle is as tall and brash as Sanchez is short and whiny."

"Leigh, Sanchez can't help being under five-foot," I defended. "She's cute."

"It might be her pituitary glands went out on her. At least," she stabbed, "it wasn't her sex glands. But we don't know that about her." She targeted my eyes with her mocking stare. "Maybe neither of you has action-packed sex glands."

"Leigh, you're upset because you'll be tomb-hopping with all those inferior frosh neophytes. And we know you're an underscored bigot. So I'm going to overlook your commentary on my sex glands."

"Glad you're rooming with the Portland Princess," she chided. "It will give you a chance to learn all about pricks and prickettes. Nora could write the heterosexual handbook on misinformation. She originally thought you could get pregnant from French kissing. But then, the fact you can't is probably news to you. And if you're wondering what French kissing means, look up your pal Robot and ask. And Kelly, don't rent out my room while I'm gone. And if you and goober guy use my bed, change the flipping sheets."

* * * * *

NORA WAS ENVELOPED in a maudlin state. Michel had not called her; Eduardo had called me. Eduardo invited me to dinner. Nora was miffed she was not going to be doubling with us.

While she sulked, I met Belle Esquivel. Belle was Edith Sanchez's dearest friend. Belle was nearly six-foot tall. At least the steepness about her frame made her seem very tall. Even without her Red Cross, laced shoes, she was tall. She commented she had reached seventy-five and was going for a hundred. Her once-elegant clothing draped her thin body. The suit hung as if it were still on its hanger. Belle's gesturing was extravagant. Her exaggerated expression would freeze mid-sentence for dramatic effect. There was an over-statement about her silver-violet hair. I was captivated by the two women and their blend. It seemed a farcical, slapstick, and theatrical exchange between them. They were right up my alley.

Although I needed to get ready for my date with Eduardo, I was persuaded to have tea with Belle and Edith. Belle had brought a well-worn book with her. I had mistaken it for a Bible. It was, however, Emmett Reid Blake's *Birds of Mexico*. I politely inquired about it.

"Edith, Mrs. Sanchez, and I are both avid birdwatchers. We were bird watching at Montebello Lakes when we met Señor Victor Sanchez and my dear, departed husband, Señor Sebastian Esquivel. The tropical bird species were divine. But that was many years ago. Now the wild game reserves are dreadful. *Dreadful*." Belle's comportment showed her commanding authority. With saucer eyes penetrating, and her avalanching voice deeply resonant, she emphasized with repetition. Husky voice, husky stance, and I somehow suspected there was also a husky heart.

Tea was delivered. Indeed, as Leigh predicted, the bone china was wheeled out. So were the sugary cakes Leigh had warned me about. I declined the cakes, stating I had a dinner engagement. As they were revealing bird customs, my mind drifted to James' *The Bostonians*. Good old Miss Birdseye, I thought as I attempted to keep my connection with the conversation. Doing high tea in the parlor made me realize, not only was I in a strange country, in a different time zone, and among people of a different culture than my own, I was also aching for home.

Back where music was flashy and trashy, television was minced melodrama, and TV dinners were tacky tasting—home. Back where it didn't make any more sense than this.

* * * * *

WHILE SHOWERING, I thought about my tribe. My moistened eyes bolted shut before I allowed myself to become too homesick. As I toweled my hair, I entered our bedroom where Nora was still pouting. "I really like Belle," I declared in an attempt to take her mind off a dateless evening.

"Ask Eduardo if he knows why Michel hasn't called for two days."

"Sure." I slipped into my dress. "You know you could always join us."

"I want to be with my own *novio*," Nora moped. "Even Leigh is gone. She's probably out with those wild women who smoke pot and curse."

"Does Leigh smoke dope?" I grilled.

"Sure. Lots of kids down here have smoked. I tried it but shouldn't have," she self-chastised.

"I haven't," I confessed. "There weren't any big drug rings in the small town Kansas library stacks. And that's where I spent my formative years." There were so many things I hadn't done with my life—more than I had done. "I also didn't spend time in the backseats of cars."

"I haven't spent much time in backseats," she confided. "And thank gosh, I haven't been caught yet. If you get my drift."

I hadn't even been chased, much less caught.

* * * * *

I SCRUTINIZED THE oblong contour of Eduardo's handsome face. There were captivating sparkles being issued from his dark eyes. His neatly brushed waves of ebony hair shone. His stride was with a robust vigor. There was a glow from his smile.

After a sumptuous dinner, we danced in the lofty Belvedere Room high atop the Hilton Hotel. We perplexed one another with phrases difficult to translate.

He told me he had three brothers, and I told him of my one sister, Kris. He was curious to know if my sister and I resembled each other. No, I answered. Nor were we similar. Kris possessed a whimsical personality. She was inspiring. I got by as best I could. She was always connected. I never felt accepted, nor did I feel validated. Kris, I explained, has always been adroit at life. My life was a tangle at best. Kris was an exuberant, affectionate child. I was hermetic and abstract. Kris never dropped a stitch.

Eduardo and I danced to a romantic song. I felt his hand slide across my back. He pressed my shoulder blades. "Angel wings."

I caressed his back. "Are your shoulder blades also angel wings?"

"If you want them to be. Kelly, my favorite philosopher is Jean-Paul Sartre. If I have imagined you, I am lucky."

I had only read *The Age of Reason* and excerpts from *Being and Nothingness,* which didn't make me an authority. Although Sartre's work is profound, it didn't leave me with the overwhelming urge to read everything he'd written.

Certain authors had inspired me to read all their books. Woolf, O'Neill, West, Kerouac, Welty, Lawrence, Stein, Twain, Hellman, Synge, Colette, Faulkner, Steinbeck,

McCullers, Sandburg, Thoreau, Williams, Salinger, Nin, Tennyson, Brittain, Renault, Hemingway, Alcott, Rand, Chaucer, Shakespeare, and naturally, Whitman, were among the authors I hungered to read in totality. I had been content to be surface nourished when it came to Sartre.

I admired Eduardo's grasp of existentialism's heartbeat. He was also intrigued with Spinoza, Jaspers, and Descartes. I was not on firm ground, but promised myself I'd find out more about them all. Spinoza loved harmony and wrote a treatise on rainbows, and those things were not going to allow me entrance to any great conversation. And I had no idea Kant was more academic than Schopenhauer. It made it seem as though almost everyone was more academic than I was.

We sat, sipping drinks, when Eduardo asked what I thought of a supreme being. He wanted a rundown on my relationship with God—with a capital G. I wondered why we all gravitate toward the unknown. "God," I spoke cautiously, "may or may not be. But if I were a supreme being, a great director of the universe, I wouldn't sacrifice my own creation to this death business. It would be like destroying a novel you'd finished writing. Or burning a painting you'd painted. No, I wouldn't have humanity born only to kill them off. And I wouldn't make my people play this good, slash, evil, teeter-totter game. I wouldn't hold heaven over their heads. Or threaten them with hell."

Laughing at my sacrilegious stance, Eduardo quoted Pascal. "In *Pensees,* it states the existence of God is incomprehensible because of our limited logic."

"He also said, 'By thought I comprehend the world,'" I countered with a chuckle.

"But I'm with Heathcliff in *Wuthering Heights.* When Katherine is dying, he asks what we know about heaven and hell. We know nothing of life." I always found more wisdom in literature than in philosophy—a fact I would keep to myself.

Our eyes chained. I realized I admired his fervor as well as his mind. He then squeezed my hand and questioned, "What does your name mean?"

I chuckled. "It might mean harlot. There was this goddess called Kele and she was known for her loose morals."

"She was a *puta*?" He said the Spanish word for whore. "I think this cannot be. You are making fun, no?"

"Oscar Wilde said in the preface to *The Picture of Dorian Gray*, books aren't moral or immoral. Only well written or badly written. It may well be the same with my name. It's yours to interpret."

With great charm, he whispered, "Shakespeare says, 'come kiss me sweet and twenty.'" Eduardo gently kissed my lips.

There was silence when we parted. Our eyes locked. The waiter with a sorrel, shredded-wheat looking beard asked if we needed anything more. *Nada mas*, I answered. Nothing more. We were fine with my limited logic, my lascivious name, and our puppy-love gazes at one another.

* * * * *

"STILL GOAL-TENDING YOUR virtue, cupcake?"

"Kelly, what did Eduardo say about Michel?"

"Wait a minute, you two," I said as I brushed them both aside. "Let me get my shoes off." Nora and Leigh were in the midst of a midnight conference when I entered the bedroom. I threw my handbag on the desk while skipping out of my heels. "Okay, Leigh, my virtue remains. Nora, Eduardo hasn't talked with Michel since we doubled. He thinks Michel is busy."

I eased out of my waistless sheath and in my slip, sat on the bed's edge. There were two empty cerveza bottles on the floor and a couple more beer bottles on the bookshelf.

"Grab a beer, Benjamin," Leigh encouraged. "Maybe if you're loaded, you'll tell us the truth."

"I thought you two might be rolling some dope to smoke," I said with a cross-examining tone. "Where do you get the junk?"

"Nora spilled her guts, I guess," Leigh sighed as her eyes narrowed. She scanned Nora's guilty face. "She sure did. Well, I can get some good Columbian shit from a friend. Want some?"

"Why not," I agreed. "I'll try it. But where?"

"Behind the fucking barn, Benj."

"Nobody cares," Nora decoded.

Leigh's grin was open wide enough to mail a letter in. "Once Sanchez came in and smelled the smoke. I told her it was bug bomb for her plants." Leigh chuckled. "Now, when I light up, she carries her entire greenhouse into my room. Place looks like a botanical garden." Leigh took another swig of beer. "This summer when I was in Colorado Springs, I saw a film called *The Day of the Triffids,* and I thought of Sanchez's plants." Sucking in a breath, Leigh continued, "It's about a meteorite shower that left most earthlings blind. It sets down a spray of seeds that grows faster than a fart. These things produce man-eating plants." Leigh looked directly at Nora, mocking, "Get my drift, Nora?"

"We get your *filthy* drift. So what happened?"

"These fuckers, the Triffids, keep eating people." Leigh sputtered for Nora's benefit. "Like a homosexual orgy...."

With disgust, Nora stormed, "Darn! She's getting drunker and drunker." Standing, she brushed down her robe. "I'm going to the bathroom and when I get back, I'm going to sleep. If Kelly wants to hear any more of your foul language and sick innuendo, then you can both go to Leigh's room."

Leigh leaned over after Nora exited. "Wanna come to my room to hear more foul language and sick innuendo?"

"Not even when it's coherent. Thanks anyway."

"What's your favorite flick?"

"Maybe *Lord of the Flies*. Allegorical. Look, I heard the toilet flush. That was your notice." I grabbed her elbow, as I filled my other hand with empty bottles. I escorted her through the hall to her room.

She crumpled down onto the bed while I pitched the empties. She then questioned, "That's really your favorite flick?"

"Certainly one of them. What of it?" I confronted.

She growled. "Maybe you're not such a pamby-ass, after all."

FOUR

FROM THE CORNUCOPIA of knowledge-tumbled wisdom, culture, and enlightenment. My satchel was open wide to the cascading education before me. I wanted as much elusive, sublime stuff as possible. The evolution of humanity seemed to require such of each generation.

Gran had always instructed her children and grandchildren to get all the education we could. During her own eighth grade of schooling, her father insisted she stop. They needed her to help with chores. Education was a frontier luxury. Even for a boy—especially for a girl.

Gran's French stepmother interceded, allowing Gran to finish out the year. Her stepmother had taught Gran some of her language and a love of literature. Gran had never forgotten her desire for schooling. She'd given each of her children the opportunity to study. My mother had been sent to nurse's training. And my mother had appreciated Gran's efforts on her behalf. She knew Gran had cried into her stepmother's apron for the right to learn. Gran's story had become my exchequer.

Gran had also wanted me to stick with her people. Her poets. And they were, naturally, magnificent. Browning, Tennyson, Twain, Poe, Dickens, Frost, and Emerson. I was to leave Tennessee Williams, Lawrence, Ionesco, Cummings, and Kerouac alone. Any writer who wrote mumbo-jumbo was out of it. In Gran's estimation, they never belonged in it. Not there with the Brontes, Milton, and Shakespeare. With Gran's empirical knowledge of human achievement, she didn't want my head in Mount Olympus, nor did she want me hanging out with beatniks. She wouldn't have me wasting my time on *false* literature. And it comprised of books not on her recommended reading list. She issued the imprimatur. I was to abide by it. Gran's mind was an attic of unexpected treasure. So I was not to stray.

One struggles with the cumbersome snarls of a past. But so much of the past gets us through.

I kept Gran's story near each time I sat in a classroom. As learning unfolded, I listened intently for both of us. I cherished and appreciated the privilege of education. So it was in the creative writing lab. My ears were tuned in as I hooked up with Professor Calvin Thurston's lecture. Absorbed, I was angry when a little sycophant in the front row continued to ask irrelevant questions followed by syrupy praise for Thurston. Thurston was obviously embarrassed by her.

Calvin Thurston was a neat, compartmentalized man. He was there to translate those Edenic-based words that must have been designed for me. He would break apart solipsistic matrices and allow my mind seduction by the belles-lettres. He was there to challenge me with Goethe, Keats, and Milton.

In spite of the little chatterbox, Thurston continued his lecture on the scope and influence of the Elizabethan age. As the front row student again interrupted Thurston, the student behind me, in his mid-twenties, poked my shoulder. He whispered, "If she opens her mouth again, I'll choke her. I wanted to alert you in case you have a weak stomach."

"Keep it down," I censured with a glare back at him. His rust thatch of thick hair, mustache, and short beard were disheveled. Slender, athletic, he stood about six-two. Penetrating blue eyes squinted from his frown. Long, light lashes snapped with my message. His rugged face, with a

Roman nose, rumpled. Those intense eyes seemed strangely familiar. Even his slow, pigeon-toed plod was recognized.

After class, he followed me. His amble quickened to catch me. "I'm Carlos Picazo from New Mexico."

"You disturbed me during class," I lashed.

"Are you always so capricious and ill-mannered?" he asked with the sliver of a smile.

My equipoise faltered. "You don't look Spanish."

"I'm a mixture. I like the sound of Carlos better than Carl."

"I do, too. I'm Kelly Benjamin."

"I've never seen you before. I've been here nearly three years. You'll like Calvin Thurston's class. I'm a journalism major, but I try to take all his classes." There was an affable awkwardness about him. "What's your major?"

"Creative writing. I worked as an intern reporter last summer."

"Why would you go from a profession to writing make-believe junk?"

My eyes flared. "Who wants to write about crime and corruption? I don't want to end up cynical. After seeing a dismembered, elderly couple after a street gang had finished with them, I decided not to be a journalist. I'd become bitter in no time at all."

"I'm not bitter. Maybe that's why they allowed me entry to Thurston's class. They screen most journalists out. Need the room for you artsy folk."

"Hope the poetic soul rubs off on you. You're a jerk."

"I may need survival training if I'm going to date you."

"I wouldn't touch you with the other end of someone else's barge pole," I huffed.

"Before you come completely off the spool, I'll apologize. Sorry if I offended you. Anyway, you'll like Thurston's class.

He used to be a publisher in New York. He's written books and plays. He's considered to be one of the foremost authorities on the Virgin of Guadalupe. Wrote a play about it. Knew Tom Wolfe, Twain… Wrote a Twain biography. Lived next to him when Thurston was a boy. Hemingway. Steinbeck. Knew all the greats."

"Company doesn't come much more interesting than that." My blood pressure percolated thinking about it. I would make a terrific apostle for Thurston.

"There's a Jazz Palabra tonight. If you'd like to go, I'll take you. Not as a date," he quickly issued. "I've got a rich man's taste, but poor man's pockets."

"Fine. Not as a date," I repeated.

"My last class ends at five. How about we meet at the library and go on from there?" When I nodded my affirmation, he grinned. "Ciao, Kelly Benjamin."

"Ciao, Carlos." I leaned back against the tree as he cantered down the walkway. Leigh's approach interrupted my thoughts. With a staccato-like, quick shove of her sun-bleached hair, she eased her body onto the bench. "What's new?" I asked.

"Cupcake, do I have an opportunity for you. Weekend after next, let's go to the beach."

"I'm not going to any shark's cove with you."

Grinning, she scoffed. "I could open doors for you that you never knew existed. You have tendencies."

"*You* have a screw loose. Come on, Leigh, let's not read anything into the fact I'm not some fluttering little princess. I was a tomboy, but I've grown into a woman."

"The beginning of any good Sapphic saga. You're simply on the *Good Ship Benjamin* right now. One day you'll hear the voice of a goddess."

"I'll bet." After a moment's pause, I smashed back.

"Leigh, this weekend I'm going to Taxco with Eduardo. The trip will take care of my cupcake status. And your silly accusation."

"You're going with that *greaser*?"

When her bigotry roared, I usually rolled my eyes, for correcting her intolerant comments did no good at all. "And I've got a date tonight with another guy. Carlos Picazo."

"Can't you get a date with an Anglo?"

"I wish I understood your prejudice."

"I wish I understood why you'll go on a weekend trip with the chili prick and not me. It's a statement of intolerance. Plus, I'm really robbed of my confidence over this."

"If you dislike Mexicans, why are you here?" I challenged. My eyes narrowed. "Well?"

"My studies brought me here. Doesn't matter. People are shits wherever you go. It's the one constant in life. If you go to Taxco, it will only be a big disappointment. Virgin sacrifices usually are. Anyway, he's probably hung like a gerbil."

"Nora's got your number. You are terrible. A true female Alceste."

"If you're going to quote *Misanthrope*, please get my favorite speech in there. 'A friend of all mankind is no friend of mine.' I love that line." She chuckled, then continued chiseling away, "Well, what about the trip to the beach? After all, you're the little Kansas cupcake who wants adventure."

"Leigh, you are joking about all this, aren't you?"

"You want to expand your experiences. I'm not a triffid, so glue yourself back together. Get the goddamn antiseptic look off your face. I'm not a rapist."

"I'll bet." I munched my final, "I'll bet."

"Here's the bus, you going back?"

"Think I'll spend the afternoon in the library. I said I'd meet Carlos there later. Tell Nora I've got a date tonight."

"About the beach?"

"Leigh, not anytime soon."

"Come on, Kelly. I'm only offering you a free outing." There was so much sincerity in her plea, I almost laughed. "I'm a wonderful date."

"Then you won't have any trouble finding someone else to make the trip with you." If she was waiting for me to tell her to help herself, she was in for the wait of her life.

* * * * *

DRIZZLING TROPICAL RAINS, all misty and smoky, appeared each mid-afternoon through the week. There were great curtains of rain followed by floating steam. I gazed out of the university's library window. The tones of green on the mountainside were intensified by the showers. I didn't mind the weather or anything else about his lofty land of perpetual spring. In fact, I loved the graceful waves of falling rain.

Closing my notebook, I glanced at my wristwatch. Carlos was expected anytime. We would grab a bite of dinner, and then attend the Jazz Palabra. With the time until he arrived, I planned to study and write letters home to all my friends. They hadn't understood my sprint across the border. I couldn't tell them geography was the cure for my heartache. My heart had been split down the center. I couldn't tell them about my two slices of the internal drama.

When Carlos arrived, it was a rescue from thoughts of home. His easy chatter and charisma calmed me. We discussed his theory of women. To him, they were either Madonna or Prima donna. Where had he learned that, I asked.

He became somber. "My older brother. He's an advisor stationed in the Republic of Vietnam since last year. I'm always concerned about what's happening there."

"Having troops there couldn't be a good sign," I inserted.

"It isn't. Remember last May, when the Buddhists were celebrating, and nine people were killed? That's when the monks began their gasoline suicides. Hey, Kel, Diem is a sly bastard and Ngo Dinh Nhu is smoking opium. Madame Nhu says when the holy men put on their 'barbecue show,' she claps her hands. It's going to get bad over there. Be glad if you don't have brothers."

"I don't, but I've got friends, and my darling cousin, Rod. He's draft bait. Rod's much more at home with a dipstick in his hands than a rifle. He's crazy about his hotrod."

"Hope he's got fallen arches."

"Are your arches drooping?" I quizzed.

"Nothing about me droops," he answered with a grin. "I'll join the Peace Corps. Hey, let's get some *quesadillas*. There's a place called the *Café-Restaurant Tocaba* where they serve great tortilla tostadas."

"*Quesadillas*?"

"Tortilla is filled with beef or chicken, cheese, pumpkin seeds, and seasoning. Sort of a turnover. They fry it. Down here, it's called a Mexican hamburger. It's terrific."

Words were streamers throughout our trip to the café and a scrumptious dinner. We were both anxious to get to the Palabra. Actors and dancers worked from texts of Cummings, Keruac, Linsay, and Crane. Carlos told me there would be a Spanish version of O'Hara's *La Muerte de Lady Day*.

I'd always loved the songs of Billie Holiday. By the evening's end, I realized Carlos and I shared so many similarities when it came to the arts. We supplemented one another and it felt great. We traded information, expression and seemed to nearly always be on the same side. Carlos also sensed the hookup. After the performance, he walked me back to the apartment.

"Kel, I had a great time. Most women pressure a guy after one date. It's like they can't wait to get your retirement pay."

I laughed. "Not me. I save my plans and my passion for writing." I looked up at a cone of light from the night lamp, then at the sky. "Ah, stars! The blinking backbone of night."

"Eloquently stated. Garbage, sentimental, mawkish trash. Rubbish! Simpering sentiment—but eloquently stated," he teased.

A smile curved across my face. "Right. You're such a ribald, gauche sonofabitch."

"That's more like it." He grinned back, and then kissed my forehead.

FIVE

MIDWEEK HAD ALWAYS issued its own disclaimer. Part begun; part done. I rolled over, waking softly. Then I remembered my great sexual defeat. It was my twentieth birthday. I was still a virgin. Depending upon perspective, it was a tragic, pathetic, admission. My glands were atrophying.

Light rays filtered in, setting my stage. I gazed into the crepuscular morning mirror. "The rotting corpse of sexuality!" I muttered at my image. Attractive, with a willowy figure. Bright, passionate, and loving. But not sensuous enough, I conceded. I was not a hot number. How could I have made it through my teens with virtue intact? Something was amiss.

I was cool to the touch. Snow Whitish. Did men consider me to be *out of service*? Eduardo was always the perfect gentleman. Carlos was a pal. And back in Kansas, when my classmates had boyfriends who went at it like motorized plungers, I was anchored to my typewriter. Friends were double-booked with bonking appointments. My tombstone would read: Here lies Kelly Benjamin—she couldn't screw to save her soul. I was certain I would become a sideshow on any cemetery tour.

Now I wondered had I clocked too many miles. Maybe it didn't even work. Maybe I'd botched my potty training and life without sex was my destiny. Saintly living, sexually speaking, and if the crown of thorns fits, wear it. I'm sure my mother had intended to raise a perpetual virgin.

Dressing quickly, I had slipped into a green printed cotton skirt and matching blouse. I gathered my sweater on the desk's top where it had covered a chestnut-colored package. Wrapped packages are dangling question marks. But I'd carried this mystery in my suitcase, vowing to open it on my birthday. But first, I decided, I would take a morning walk. Snoring Nora would be awake by the time I returned. Then I could feel festive enough to open my birthday gifts.

Mexico City's streets had also awakened.

The honeycomb of colonies representing different nationality always intrigued me. I passed by the Angel of Independence. They would probably erect a statue of me in Kansas City. Legs clamped shut. I would be the statue of eternal purity. I was thankful the magnificent angel had not perished in the 1957 earthquake. It had been pieced back together after tumbling from its little angel perch. It was a beloved landmark. Statuary of the Chaste.

Perhaps, I speculated, it was why I so loved D.F. The statue-lined streets were juxtaposing huge trees and palms. Fountains sprayed, decorative pavilions were filled with flowers, and handsome buildings interspersed the lower arabesque structures of yesteryear.

I also adored the city's pitch. Voices clattered, traffic rumbled, and horns clamored. Smells of belching exhaust fumes merged with carnations, freshly worked leather, and the fruit and flower stands.

All the sights, smells, and emotions seemed more intense than anywhere I had ever been. I wondered if this city was to provide me with my lesson of sexuality, for the festive Mexican spirit was one of the greatest passions I'd encountered. In their poverty, and in their opulence, the Mexican was passionate. In their pauperism, their plentitude, in their squalor and their luster, in their agony, in their rapture, in their blemishes, in their beauty, and in all the calibrations in between, the Mexican knew enthusiasm.

I passed by aproned women who stood in arched entrances, elfin children, dour vendors stacking tortillas, shoeshine boys reading comic books, and the neatly groomed aristocrats. All passionate.

And then there was me.

* * * * *

DECIDING A VISIT to Chapultepec Park would certainly take up enough time for my roommates to rise, I walked across the street. The park had become my writing shrine.

I'd only walked for a few moments when I realized I was being followed by a small boy. I would guess he was six or seven. His burgundy shirt was rumpled and torn, pant legs were rolled up at the bottoms, and his oversized shoes scuffed as he tramped behind me. Turning, I gazed into his coffee-colored eyes. His oval, coppery face frowned as he scrutinized me.

"Lady," he blurted, "you are North American, no?"

"I am," I grinned. "What's your name?"

"Juan. John." His dark eyes were frisking me. "Like John Fitz-herald Kennedy. Your president. You know John Fitz-herald Kennedy?"

"Yes."

"You are friends?"

"I don't know him personally."

"You say you know him," Juan stated his objection to my disclaimer.

"I meant I know of him."

"I see him in the motorcade. I run to him. He gives me this." Juan pointed to a small PT boat tie clasp. "I know him.

We are both John. You like him, no?"

"I do like him. I would have voted for him, but I wasn't twenty-one."

"Your fathers, they vote for him?"

"My mother and grandmother did. My father is a Republican."

"He is loco." Piqued, Juan turned and walked away.

As Juan's slight frame left my field of vision, I murmured under my breath, "I'll tell my father you asked about him."

On my return trip from the park, Juan was waiting. Our strides matched. This time he told me how he lived with an ailing grandfather. Some of the time. He was on the streets the rest of the time. He was seven. His father had died, and his mother had abandoned him for a better life. He had been an encumbrance.

His spirit remained remarkably content. Life, he told me, was free. He had no restrictions. We both knew a child needs some restraints, but I didn't dispute his philosophy. He needed it to get by.

When he asked if I knew Dorothy and Toto from Kansas, I told him I did not. He muzzled his sigh. He said it was too bad and I didn't seem to know anyone worthwhile. Before I could call after him, he was gone. But then, there wasn't anything left to say.

* * * * *

MY DAY HAD been truly planned. Jammed, as it happened. It was tradition, Señora Sanchez, Belle, and the girls always celebrated birthdays with a luncheon at the *Mauna Loa*.

Nora had finished showering when I arrived back at the apartment. I began opening the gifts my family had sent. Gran had sent Sandburg's *Honey and Salt* and *Harvest Poems*. Also, she'd given me a book that had belonged to her stepmother. Inside the copy of Whittier's *Poems*, there was a twenty-dollar bill. The book had been inscribed by my great-grandmother, Antoinette La Tremoille Kelly. She had given it to my grandmother along with the inscribed message of giving books and wisdom. *Je donnerai le livres—sagesse.* Tenderly, I caressed the book. My fingertips grazed the words. I smiled.

Then I opened my parent's gift. A raincoat and two blouses. Kris had wrapped her gift in the Sunday comics from the newspaper. It was a two-record album set I'd been searching for throughout Kansas City. She had found it. *The Bessie Smith Story.* I loved the mellow, growling, blues songs.

"Kelly," Nora chirped, "the blouses are darling." Wet cables of hair hung and her thick lashes batted dripping water. She wound the towel around her head. Examining my new fluffy, lemon-colored blouse, she added, "I love your mother's taste."

I opened the birthday card that had come via mail. "Took her two hours to find," I reported as I read Mom's letter. "My father's 'stomach disorder' has been aggravated." I tossed the card down. "Translation, he's drunk again."

Nora patted my shoulder. "Need to talk about it?"

"No. But thanks anyway." I put the album on the hi-fi. After the record had begun to play, I asked, "Do you like Bessie Smith?"

"Isn't it a little scratchy?"

"It's old. The reproduction wasn't good back then. Bessie Smith died in her early forties after she was turned away from a segregated hospital. They refused her medical attention because she was black."

"I've never heard of such a thing!" she said, examining the album cover. "By the way, Michel finally called. We're going out." She crossed her freckled arms in victory.

"I'm glad for you." With a husky sigh, I listened to a line from Bessie's 'Down Hearted Blues.'

"Gosh, this is really a sad album. Too bad your sister couldn't have come up with something a little more lively."

"I love it. So many singers, artists, and writers have had sad lives. Virginia Woolf filled her pockets with stones and drowned herself in the River Ouse."

"Was she a friend of yours?"

"She was a writer who died before I was born." I paused. "You don't know much about literature, huh? There's even a play with her name in the title."

"I wouldn't know about that. No one ever wants to talk about my field," she said with a pout.

"So tell me what you know about this Vietnam business?" I urged.

Her warm thalo-blue eyes began to glisten. "Well, we have too many commitments throughout the world to be intervening in the mess. Communist guerrillas are infiltrating the south," she ratted on the Commies. "It's a civil war and the Soviets are stirring trouble."

"Think we'll get involved?"

Her words were granite slabs falling on one another. "Not if we're smart. An Asian war would be terrible." As a postscript, Nora asked, "They let the Negro singer die?"

"They let her die."

"Oh, before I forget, Leigh said to give you birthday regards, but she can't make lunch. She's babysitting some blankety-blank freshmen."

"Blankety-blank," I repeated with a grin. "Rumor has it those are the worst kind. I'm going to revive myself with a nice warm shower."

"Kelly, what did you want to know about Vietnam for?"

"Probably nothing."

* * * * *

PRANCING FLAMINGOS WERE fluffed cotton candy. With their coral plumage and dark-edged wing feathers, the birds strutted their stuff. They were well aware they were the stars of the Mauna Loa. With sleekly combed feathers, cane legs, and J-shaped necks, they were magnificent.

My birthday luncheon could have had no more perfect atmosphere. The Polynesian motif and exotic delicacies of the South Seas took me into another land. With grass huts, over-sized stone gods, and a waterwheel, the grounds were exceptional. Enchanted, I diagrammed it in my mind. I would make a drawing of it in my next letter to Gran.

"Phoenicopteridea," Belle's voice resounded.

"Sort of a harsh sounding name for such a lovely bird," I uttered.

Sanchez laughed, covering her mouth with an ornate, silver-handled fan she'd been twirling. Tittering, she said, "It most assuredly is. And did you know flamingos breed in May and June? Isn't that something?"

"Yah," Erika seconded. "Et iz something. I am glad I am not ze flamingo." She squirmed in her high-backed wicker chair.

When a deep honk stuttered from one bird, Nora added, "Sounds like they aren't too thrilled about it either."

Edith gave Belle a sour side-glance. The conversation was not staying tame. I was enormously glad we had preplanned an escape route. Erika had suggested to Nora and me that we bow out early. So after the feast, we planned to hail separate cabs. Nora, Erika, and I rode in a cocodrilo, which was a green cab with a row of sharp alabaster teeth painted on both sides. A crocodile ride. Yellow cabs were called canarios, canaries, red cabs were cardinales or cardinals, and green and yellow were catorras or parrots.

It was decided an excursion to the Left Bank would be more entertaining than accompanying Edith and Belle home for chat and tea. On the Left Bank, we would find, Nora explained, the Plaza de la Corregidora. Also known as Santo Domingo Square. Corregidora was the patriot who sounded the alarm announcing revolutionary plans had been discovered. She was a true heroine, and I somehow knew Gran would have taken to her. Gran loves legends. In Gran's world, scoundrels need not apply.

As we strolled along the square, I studied Corregidora's face. The statue showed a dour bronze expression. She must have been hatching plots to undermine the Spaniards. Across the way, Nora pointed to the National School of Medicine. It had once been the Holy Office of the Inquisition. Heretics went up in flame. How holy can that solution be?

Today, there was a plaza with snorts of traffic and hissing bus doors. And Corregidora was still telling Spaniards to blow it through their beanies. I could hear the dialogue. Inquisitors were ordering her to go and sin no more. And she was winking her way into the history books.

After our stroll through history, we took a rattling canary cab back to our apartment. The cab whipped through pock-marked side streets in order to avoid a lava flow of main thoroughfare traffic.

I explained Carlos's theory of Madonnas and Prima donnas. Erika was fascinated, as one can well imagine. Nora was tolerating the conversation. "It goes like this," I lectured. "Madonnas state their conviction and must be talked off their cloud on high. It takes work for a guy to do some smooth maneuvering and plenty of genuflecting. Prima donnas flaunt by doing a snob routine. They must be ignored, according to

Carlos. A guy needs to carefully evaluate women. Then follow the formula. Interesting, huh?"

"Honestly!" Nora grumbled. The cab's bouncing made her skirt ride up. She tugged furiously at the hemline. "Men are terrible."

"Not if zhey are rich." Erika laughed. Her olive complexion beamed. "Then zhey are terribly rich."

"Erika, honestly!" Nora snapped.

"Yah." Erika's eyes twinkled in jest as she signaled her agreement. "Honestly."

* * * * *

"HAPPY *FUCKING* BIRTHDAY, you little tramp," Leigh greeted me.

I was seated at the bedroom vanity, applying lipstick. She plopped down on the bed. "Thanks. Too bad you missed lunch."

"Showing punk fossil hunters the folly of paleoanthropology can get on my nerves. And I see you're primping. Working to shed your virginity. Better tuck a rubber in your amulet."

I glared at her. "My purity is none of your business."

"You said your father's side of the family is Jewish. Well, maybe you're trying out to be the National Yiddish Poster Virgin."

"Leigh, you're a fairly well-educated person. Bright enough. I can't believe you say those things. Prejudice is so stupid. Besides, I don't know anything about my Jewish background. My father's father was a Jewish intellectual and his mother was English. So that hardly qualifies me as an authority. I'd like to have known, but no one talked about it. I know more about my Irish heritage from Gran's stories. So leave off with your comments."

"Whew. I mean, really, you are touchy about your Yiddish mix."

"I'm not touchy. I'm very proud of my Jewish ancestry."

"Looks like you're tarting up for a big night with horny Eduardo. Do give him my love," Leigh said as she stood. She walked toward the doorway. There she lingered. "And while you're at it, he would probably appreciate it if you would also give him your love," her sarcasm scratched.

After Leigh's laughter had ended in a muffled flutter through the hall, I closed my eyes. Maybe, I considered, I had no love to give. No poems; no passion. Maybe nothing. I don't know why her jokes always impacted me. I figured either she didn't have all her marbles or she was a promethean woman on a seduction campaign.

One thing I was certain of—*she* didn't light up my promenade.

* * * * *

YOUTH PROVIDES ITS own center stage.

There was no doubt about Eduardo's allure. Wearing a tailored navy suit with coin buttons, he looked dapper. He had escorted me to dinner at the *Muralto*, which was on the forty-first floor of the Latin American Tower. In addition to the spellbinding scene that showed Popocteptl and Ixtaccihuatl, Mexico City was a splendid view. Eduardo had ordered the Tournedo Muralto, the restaurant specialty, and we dined. After dining, we danced at the *La Jacaranda*.

It had been a wonderful birthday celebration. I wondered as he escorted me home if he realized how I felt about him. I was virgin by lack of opportunity. But he remained tender, kind, decent, intelligent, and handsome. Eduardo had been a perfect gentleman, and yet I knew he desired me.

He looked terribly disappointed when he told me the weekend in Taxco would need to be delayed a week because of a family event. Perhaps he was as apprehensive as I was. Or worse, maybe he no longer felt I was attractive. However, there was a glimmer. And our goodnight kiss was certainly passionate.

My intention was to sneak into my own passionless bed so I could make an emotional evaluation. But Erika was waiting for the first available set of ears. She asked if I felt as though I might be falling in love with Eduardo. In all honestly, I told her, I knew nothing of love's mechanisms. Proust stated when we're in love we're in an abnormal state.

I couldn't improve on his summation.

SIX

"KRIS," I BUBBLED when I heard my sister's voice on the phone.

"Happy birthday late. You were on a date last night," Kris said with a giggle. "I want details."

"His name is Eduardo. I wrote about him, but the mail takes so long down here. Thanks for the record set."

"I told the store manager my sis was being held captive in a foreign country. The record was the ransom."

"Stuck to the truth, huh?"

As I talked with each member of my family, I felt nourished. My mother cautioned me to be careful. *It only takes once.* I teased if I were going to do any messing around, I'd be sure to do it twice.

Then I talked with Gran. Her voice strained to become amplified. She was attempting to shout down to Mexico. "I told you to stay up here in Kansas where you belong," she yelled. "I been reading about subversion nowadays," she huffed. "And you're missing the Harvest Festival this year."

"Gran, it's Independence Day here. *El Grito.*"

"Not ours," she smoldered. "Paying homage to another country! Well, don't you be spending any of the twenty dollars I sent for such a thing."

"I won't," I vowed.

With foreboding, she added, "Kelly Anne, I don't know what's going to become of you." There was a moment's suspension. "We miss you, girl."

"I miss you too, Gran." My voice tightened. "And I love you."

"You get homesick, you come on back," she tendered her case with prairie grandiloquence. "I won't hold you going off from Kansas against you."

* * * * *

GRAN HAD TOLD me she was in a dither about Castro throwing in with the Communists. Could Mexico be far behind? She didn't trust anyone other than her fellow Americans. She hadn't met Juan.

On the way to the bus stop, Juan had followed me. He gave me flowers. Leigh inquired about him. I told her I thought he was adorable. Leigh glanced over at Nora. "We'll see how adorable she thinks the little scavenger is when he pinches her handbag."

"I'll hide my bag down my blouse."

"Might as well," Leigh charged, "you haven't got much else there."

"And since I'm not going to the beach with you, you'll never know about my breasts," I hammered back.

"Honestly! Leave Kelly's bosoms alone." Nora defended the slam to my boobs.

"Oh, goodness gracious," Leigh mewed. "You two are so damned precious!"

"If you would be nicer to Kelly and me…."

"Oh, Nora, you're so wiped upon," Leigh continued. "Listen, you two, Sanchez and Belle left early this morning on their mini-vacation, so don't forget to leave the birdseed and bread crumbs on the window ledge. Their trip to Cuernavaca is perfect timing. We'll have the place to ourselves after *El Grito*.

I'm getting some weed from my connection. Fix Sanchez's plants up with a little grass," Leigh chortled.

"I don't think I should indulge in marijuana," Nora uttered.

"Save yourself the guilt. Consider the benefit to the violets," Leigh said. "Nora, you know you go to a torture chamber every month when your period is late. Well, at least pot doesn't make you with child."

"Because you don't worry about getting pregnant, doesn't mean the rest of us don't."

"Every time you're late, you *know* you're pregnant," Leigh taunted. "I figure you're constipated."

"Leigh, you're sickening," Nora lashed. "Well, I'm off to my dental appointment. So I won't need to hear more of your infantile gibberish, Leigh James."

As Nora stormed away, Leigh donned an innocent expression. She then rebuked me. "Now, see what you've done, Kelly. You've upset her again."

* * * * *

"ACTUALLY," PROFESSOR CALVIN Thurston instructed, "King Arthur is really a sophisticated version of *Beowulf*."

"I hadn't considered that," I confessed as we walked toward the classroom.

"Are you going to *El Grito* tonight?"

"Yes. My roommates and I are going. I can't wait."

"Take notes on the celebration," Thurston advised. "Tom Wolfe traveled through the country taking the best notes imaginable. They converted into the magic of his brilliant novels. By the way, have you the poetry assignment written for workshop?" His eyeglasses slipped as he peered at me with probing, azure eyes.

"Yes. I love writing, but hate the criticism," I confided.

"Miss Benjamin, don't worry about raves and rebukes. Continue to acquire experience and skill. Those are major ingredients you'll need. Be a *toward* person. It's important in your development as a writer. Believe in yourself. One can rummage through each experience in life to find excellent material. Then one must sculpt life's pathos."

"Your works are so beautifully knitted together. Neatly weaved essays and biographies, as well as your plays. There was one of your plays I couldn't find at the college library, so I've only read two of them."

"You've read my work?" he inquired with amazement.

"Yes. Everything I could find with the exception of the one. *Bronze Lady.*"

"Ah, we're in luck. I happen to have a copy I'll loan you if you like?"

"I'd love to read it. What's it about?"

"About three acts," he joked. "Actually, it's a continuation of my second play." He rummaged through his briefcase. "Here is a copy."

"Thank you, sir," I spoke as he handed me the tattered playbook.

I didn't understand why this literary man, this published author, the renowned New York publisher and lettered scholar would turn back to me with a smile. And why, with a twinkle in his eyes, my mentor would say with all modesty, "I thank *you*, Miss Benjamin."

* * * * *

AWAITING THE RETURN and results of my first short story assignment was excruciating. When Professor Nathan Roberts slid my effort across the table, I released a hearty sigh. He was celebrated for being miserly with grades. He locked off his 'A' grades. He dispensed 'B+' in the place of giving an 'A'. Because his credentials as a writer and editor were so remarkable, this trait was never disputed.

In his late fifties, Roberts was slightly stooped in a scholarly way. Gray, saw-blade eyebrows feathered over his wire-rim glasses and his squint. With neatly buttoned sweater vests, Scottish plaid bow ties, and baggy trousers, Roberts dressed for comfort. No matter how he dressed, there was a distinct respectability known to academicians. His demeanor was staunch. His *dare to get an A* challenge was understood.

Roberts attached wondrously detailed commentary to each student submission. I wondered how my short story could have merited a B+, yet could have been torn to shreds by his red pencil. His reluctance to give an 'A' did not in any way restrict my desire to have one.

I would spend the rest of the morning diligently rewriting. Fleshing out those characters, intensifying the narrative, and polishing the living jazz out of it. My mission improved the story. I turned it back to Roberts immediately. He was impressed enough to read it without delay.

Grimly, he looked up. The papers were carefully placed on his desk before him. In his precise diction, he spoke, "Miss Benjamin, it is almost an 'A', so give it another attempt."

"What can I do to make it an 'A,'" I questioned.

"Begin again." He handed me the story.

Nodding, I neatly folded it before sticking it into my workbook. I then spoke with determination. "I'll rewrite it." I began to ask him if he'd ever given anyone an 'A' before but thought better of the idea. "Do you ever—ever get tired of rereading stories?"

"I tire of students who don't make a second, third, or fourth attempt. His back stiffened. His eyebrows pleated. "For a moment, I thought you were going to ask if I'd ever given an 'A' for a story."

My lips curved. "Well, sir?"

"No." He adjusted his eyeglasses. For a moment, I thought he might have smiled. However, I could have been mistaken.

On my way back to the bus stop, I calculated how I might well have blown it with Professor Roberts, but at least Thurston liked me enough to loan me his play.

Thurston had suggested we have tea on Monday afternoon because I wanted to discuss his play with him. We could converse in-depth about *Bronze Lady*.

This would be the Taxco weekend, but I hoped to return early enough Sunday night to read the play. It would make it even fresher in my mind for the discussion with Professor Thurston.

* * * * *

ON THE TRIP back to my apartment, Carlos had suggested we grab something to eat and then tromp through Alameda Central Park.

Carlos purchased a sack of guavas. He carefully carved a slice with his pocketknife and slipped it between my lips. "There is nothing like breaking guava with a friend."

"Are you sure you washed them good enough?"

"They're fine, Kelly. Been vetted. And we're now going directly over to a little oyster bar. Best little oyster bar in D.F. We can get a dozen oysters on the half shell. Twenty cents buys you all you can eat. And oysters are renowned for sexual potency. You'll need them for Taxco."

My scowl continued until we stood at the oyster bar. We fed one another slippery oysters. I wiped the juice from my chin. "Do these really help?"

"Sure. My libido is already storming."

"Nothing's happening with me," I reported

"Well, when the oysters kick in, remember, I'm second in line behind Eduardo," he teased to my dismay.

"You think this is a take-a-number thing?" I poked him in the ribs.

"Nope. Not at all." He flinched his way to a denial. "I mean, I could care about you in a serious way."

"I care about you, too," I echoed. "I'm not sure about this sex business."

"From your description of Eduardo, he sounds charming enough to talk a cat out of a dairy. So he should be able to adequately seduce you."

I glowered. "I'm seducing him. He has amazing willpower."

"Look, Kel, sex isn't complicated. It happens. Hell, it's nothing striped alley cats can't do."

"So, am I a Madonna or Prima donna?"

"Difficult to tell. I do know one thing. You have a hide and seek heart."

* * * * *

COGNITO ERO SUM.

Descartes had seen history's theatrics as a most enlightened interval of time. And life is dependent upon thought in order to be. No wonder we're a planet skidding on imbroglios.

I gazed into the glassy reflection of blue mosaic tiles at the fountain's base. Within that surface, I saw the Bellas Artes' gold dome and my friend Carlos.

"Come on, there's more of Alameda Central to see," he ordered, pulling me by the hand. "And we want to see it all in one brief afternoon."

Walking through the oblong park was a study of decorated lamps posts, fountains, and statuary. Alameda Centro's beginning was tranquil. It had once been an Aztec market. During the Inquisition, it became an execution ground. Burning and strangling heretics was Spanish protocol. Then in the late eighteenth century, it was converted into a fashionable promenade. Embroidered into time's tapestry with well-stitched elegance, it was again tranquil.

Carlos pivoted as he sauntered toward the Juarez Monument. I was looking at the colossal white marble. His hand waved in front of my face. "Kel, what's bothering you?"

"Taxco. My investment in passion bothers me. I don't want any snags in our friendship. You and me—we can still just be friends. It's as though we sing the same youth blues." I hesitated. "I'm not experienced in matters of love. What if I stall?"

"Being defrocked of virginity isn't the worst thing in the world." His laugh was mellow.

"You're in great jeopardy of being called *poetic*," I chided. "Eduardo is tender and gentle, but I'm not certain about it."

"The first time should be a good experience. That sets a trend. My dad is a college professor. I met my first at one of the faculty parties. She was a new member of the staff. I was a horny high school kid." Carlos gazed into the sky as his memory unzipped. "My innocence intrigued her. And my anatomy," he divulged with a grin. "She was one divine lady. When I told my parents I was going over to her apartment to help out, they never suspected how much *help* it was doing everyone. Anyway, the first time should be special. Take precautions," he admonished.

"It's a little frightening."

"Hey, you've got a supple young figure, Miss Benjamin. It

should be enjoyed and allowed enjoyment."

I grappled. "I'm probably the last remaining virgin of my class."

"Sex isn't the turnstile into adulthood. It's more a sharing by two."

"But we're still autonomous," I speculated. "Nothing changes that."

Nodding, he whispered, "Not even love, really."

I gave him a hug for telling me the truth.

We walked to the base of the monument. A toddler Indian girl began her ascent up one of the stairs. Carlos reached for her hand to steady the youngster. A few yards away, her mother giggled at the young American's attempt to assist her child. Carlos finally lifted her high into the air. She chirruped with delight. When she was safely on the ground, Carlos assured her mother one day they would construct a monument to the child. The Indian woman's eyes gleamed with agreement. All treatises with the gods make possibility real.

We then walked to the *Del Prado Hotel* to see Diego Rivera's mural in the lobby.

A Sunday Dream at Alameda Park was as magnificent as it was controversial. Rivera had infuriated the masses with his conspicuous placard that read: God doesn't exist.

"So what do you think?" Carlos pried.

"Great. My Gran would have a fit because Rivera was a communist. She gets tight-jawed thinking about Communists. But her family was a pioneer family. Building a country was a harsh struggle back then. Gran lost her mother. She loved her stepmother. Frontier life was hard on women. They paid a price."

Carlos squeezed my hand. "Hey, Kel, Taxco will be fine. And don't tell your Gran you visited a Rivera mural."

"I won't. It would certainly get her down."

Touring Kelly's Poem

* * * * *

I'D MADE PLANS to meet Nora and Leigh at the far corner of the six century old *Plaza de la Constitucion*. The three-sided square was beginning to fill up. Next to the Cathedral was the National Palace. On the third side was the municipal pawnshop. We planned to have a quick dinner before watching history in the making.

Between eleven p.m. and midnight, President Mateos would step out onto the balcony of the National Palace, ring the bell, and shout the traditional cry of independence. *El grito!*

Leigh complained, "Glad we found you before the natives overtake us. Smells like a dirty aquarium."

"I can't wait to see the president," I said, purposely ignoring her bitching.

"I can't wait until we eat," Nora grumbled. "I'm starving." As we walked in search of a nearby restaurant, Nora began her lecture. "*El Grito* was the famous cry of Father Miguel Hildalgo before he was murdered in 1811 by a firing squad. A decade later, Mexico overthrew Spain's rule."

"He was a goner before he knew he'd won," Leigh explained. "They displayed his head on a corner of some grain warehouse. What a shitter deal."

"Then Diaz, who ruled for thirty-five years, made the fiesta *Grito* a national holiday," Nora inserted, attempting to get history back into a proper alignment.

"Yeah," Leigh added, "the old fart did that on his eightieth birthday. Cost twenty million pesos and there were twenty carloads of champagne consumed. Spiked ole Diaz's prune juice."

We finally spotted the restaurant. In honor of the occasion, *mole* was ordered. *Mole poblana* was, as they translated, an ancient Indian dish of turkey cooked in a sauce of chili, almonds, and chocolate. *Mole de Guajolote* had a curry sauce of pumpkin seeds with sixteen varieties of spices. Moctezuma served it to Cortez.

Leigh passed a basket of warm tortillas. "These are soaked in limewater. That's probably why Indians have white teeth." After munching one, she asked, "Say, how's the plan to de-virginize coming?"

"I don't know why Kelly lets you get by with that kind of talk," Nora censured.

"Because I'm her ticket to new experiences." Leigh gloated, "I've got the grass connection."

"Is that really why you think I tolerate you?" I questioned.

"If it isn't the dope, it must be my body," Leigh bantered.

"Be still my heart." My words were edged. My eyes narrowed to a scowl. "What in your background has made you so indelicate?"

She shrugged.

Nora must have figured I was safe, for she went to the woman's restroom. "Watch what you say around her. I know you're kidding, but Nora's beginning to wonder."

"Relax." She smirked.

"Look, *asshole,* I'm telling you to leave off."

"You even cuss with too much emphasis. You're ludicrous. I mean, really. It's like your sentences are framing the word. Anyway, who the hell do you think you are? A sweepstakes jackpot?"

Shifting back in my chair, I glowered at her and tried again. "Asshole, I'm excited about my trip to Taxco with Eduardo, Nora, and Michel. How was that?"

"It could use some work."

* * * * *

EARLIER, CARLOS HAD laughed when I confided my roommates planned a dope-smoking festival after *El Grito*. He nearly ruined it by telling me the grass has medicinal properties along with having recreational uses. I figured mortality only meant dueling with a supreme being for life anyway, so his story went to the wilderness of lost admonitions. We do search out our magical remedies as our ancestors did, but I was determined to give this pot-fest a shot anyway.

Once we'd returned to the apartment, Nora and I gathered around Leigh.

She carefully took out the packet. With a clandestine smirk and agility, she poured the weed into a pocket of paper. Then she rolled. The slow wink of the match failed to ignite the reefer that was clamped between my lips.

"Shit! Benjamin, have you ever smoked before?"

"I'm not used to smoking," I defended.

"You're not used to anything." Leigh then instructed, "Let it fill your lungs. You're not inhaling, Kelly. You're too fucking precious for words. Suck the thing. Then hold it in."

Finally, I inhaled, and then sputtered. Wine was being poured by Nora. I was relieved when she handed me a glass. I took a quick gulp before passing the reefer to Nora. "Not bad," I commented.

Candles flickered as scented wax mingled with the sweet, stale odor of marijuana. I noticed my appetite was insatiable as I munched junk food. Smoke rolled, billowing across the room. After two glasses of wine and numerous puffs on weed, I felt as though I had been plunked into quicksand. I was also experiencing a deficit inside.

I went from the bedroom into the living room. Leigh assumed I had gone to round up more houseplants. But I hadn't.

I stared out the window at the gentle curvature of flowing city lights. Dusky shadows were etched against a lambent tint of the skyline. Lashes of darkness blinked back at the glow. Earth's contents were unobtrusive. With staccato street noises, I became somber. Streams of light flashed electric rainbows. Swerving from reality, I felt my mouth drying out again. I returned to the bedroom.

"What a super lid. Columbian, for fuck sakes," Leigh appraised the grass.

Nora's eyes were batting. "In the primitive past, Indians chewed coca leaves to get stoned. Right, Leigh?"

"Still do. Archeology records all the dirt on people," Leigh explained. "My field of endeavor certainly has romance. Ah, to deciphering the past!" She inhaled, drawing smoke with relish. "On a dig, I can sometimes tell a blade is going to touch something before I feel the pottery, bone, or stone."

"Ex-C-I-T-E-ment," I spelled. Giggling, I asked, "Did I get it right?"

Leigh rationed her emotions. "You poor, guileless creature."

I choked on the wine when I began laughing. "Not bad, as *digs* against your fellow roommate go," I hooted. I was becoming cheerful. Nora was becoming numb. And Leigh was so stoned, she was going into the dumpster altogether.

"Mayan codices were written by people like you, Benj. Most of what they lied about was destroyed by the Spanish conquerors. Like you, Nora. Keepers of heaven's truth. The lousy idiots destroyed history," she blamed. "The shits."

"Leigh," I grilled, "why do you enjoy issuing disclaimers on any good aspects of humanity?"

Leigh shrugged. "Don't take chances. Hell, the same humans who create can also destroy. There's this tribe of Tupian people who bred their women with war prisoners in order to raise the children for butchering. Cannibal husbandry. How's that for a terrific aspect of humanity?"

I whistled lamely. Leigh wasn't handing humanity any form of approbation. I wanted to delve into why she was so angry. "And Aztecs killed people for feast days. Solved the hunger problem and kept the sun in the sky. But what's it got to do with your perpetual rotten mood."

"Put that question to the jury," Leigh snapped. "I could spend all night recounting tales of horror this species has committed."

"I'd rather hear Erika's abortion story again," Nora moaned.

"Speaking of Erika," Leigh said as she began to laugh, "look at that cactus, and tell me it isn't a phallic symbol. It could be Erika's flora logo."

An hour later, we were still chuckling over the jokes that bounced from us. And I was amazed when Erika arrived and Leigh related the joke to her. Erika hooted, but then I figured she needed to be propped up anyway. She partook in a couple rounds of marijuana and wine, and it completely wiped her out. Her eyes seemed to hop as her speech slurred. After we had blown out the candles, Leigh eased Erika up. I got on her other side, and we accompanied her, mostly dragging her, to their bedroom.

Erika slumped onto the bed. Leigh tossed a coverlet over her. Erika stirred and then wound her arms around Leigh's neck. "Zank you for helping. You are not zo bad."

Leigh and I went into the hall. I queried, "Does she get sloshed often?"

Our glances roped. "I'm not sure if she whores because she drinks or she drinks because she whores." Leigh's eyelids lowered to a near closed position. "Maybe it doesn't really matter. It's all the old theory of prostitute economics."

"What theory?"

"I got it. You want it. Sale made."

"Was that another of your cruel comments?"

"No." Her pensive intermission concluded with a quick, flashing smile of insincerity. Then her eyes went sad.

I wondered why her sadness never really went away. "Leigh, I'm sorry you're so contemptuous of life. It must be painful for you."

"Yeah, bitching! Excruciating."

"I'd better get to bed."

"Nora will wonder what *we're* up to."

"And I don't want Nora wondering anything," I added. "But Nora isn't so bad. She's trying to find herself. Like we all are."

"Nora's not so bad, huh? Well, one thing I can say about Nora. She's one hell of a bird sitter. Taking care of tossing crumbs to those fucking birds. Nora is the all-time saint of feathered friends. That's for believers in saints."

"I'm not certain if I believe in saints and miracles or not. Maybe I'm too young to have seen any."

"I sure as hell don't. I don't believe in anything or anyone."

"So where do you believe we came from if a creator didn't design us?"

"A spaceship maybe. Aliens then fucked apes. We descended from there. How the hell do I know?"

"Leigh, that's the nicest thing I've ever heard you say about humanity."

"Yeah, well, maybe earth is an examining table of the gods. Maybe humanity is the specimen. We're down here being spun in our little-controlled environment. Spun. Maybe to see if our brains eventually fall out."

"Anyone hanging around you for long must feel as though

the brain will go on the next cycle. Do you think your brain will fall out and taint outer space?"

"Naw. I don't buy into supreme beings. But you've got the Blarney stone and the Wailing Wall."

"And what do you have?"

"Not a fucking thing."

SEVEN

MY MORATORIUM ON blushing was still in place. However, Taxco was ahead of me.

Leigh entered the bedroom as I finished packing my overnight case. "A lust princess if ever there was one," she bantered.

"Leigh, don't start," I warned with a frown.

"Don't bring home any bug or packages that go 'whaaa' in the night."

"Isn't there some megalithic monument you should be exploring?"

"Cupcake, I'm concerned for you."

"I'll take precautions. Now then, I'm too busy to talk."

She giggled. "You'll think busy." When Nora entered, walking briskly, Leigh whistled. "You two are impatient to get laid."

"Get out of here," Nora stormed.

Leigh stood, went to the door, and then turned. "You two little ingrates take my advice. Legs together."

Leigh then snickered her way down the hall. I gave a shrug. Nora began last minute packing. She huffed, "Was she upsetting you again?"

"Nothing can upset me this afternoon."

"Kelly, you don't need to rush into anything."

"Tell it to my glands. I'm already the world's oldest living virgin. You get past biblical times and I'm pretty much it."

We'd finished packing and rushed down to the street, towing our luggage. Nora had delivered her venereal disease speech, and her pregnancy speech, along with a low-impact guilt spiel.

I scurried to the curb where Eduardo and Michel awaited. Eduardo agilely placed our luggage in the trunk. Juan approached with a suspicious scowl and a flower. He handed me a carnation. Then he interrogated. I answered Eduardo was my *novio* and Nora was my chaperone. Eduardo dug into his pocket. He fished out change to give to Juan. He then promised to take care of me. Juan would have preferred a more grandmotherly chaperone. His enormous brown eyes accused. I thanked him for his flower as we pulled away.

Songs of laughter continued as the auto coiled its way up the mountain road toward Taxco. When silence happened, I glanced into the rearview mirror to see the lynx-eyed Michel and the starry-eyed Nora in a tangle. They were getting a head start.

The gradient, steeply rising road lifted against the sunset. Then there was Taxco. It hung upon a mountain's side. Taxco was a conglomerate of twisting cobblestone streets, stucco dwellings with red tile roofs, and charm. The Hotel Victoria was perched above the center of town. With colonial ambiance, The Victoria was festooned with exotic plants and flowers.

Nora's cheeks were the color of stewed tomatoes when I insisted I stay with Eduardo and she bunk with Michel. For the sake of her conscience, I convinced her it would be best.

Eduardo fumbled with his luggage. I was also feeling uncomfortable. After freshening up, the four of us trekked to an outdoor café for dinner. Eduardo suggested a drink named after a revolutionary general—Pancho Villa. It was loaded with booze and sliced fruit, and I hoped it would take the edge off everyone's inhibitions. Especially mine.

We devoured chicken tacos while sipping our drinks dry. Then we strolled, hand in hand, along the cobblestone paths. Eduardo and I were aware of our synchronized steps. I gazed away from his face, watching the streamers of light that fell across the mountain village. It was lovely. I felt excitement for I recognized adventure.

When we parted with Nora and Michel, Eduardo pressed his key into the door lock. After the familiar click, the door fanned open. My nerve was momentarily paralyzed. He must have sensed my withdrawal. Or perhaps it was panic. He led me to the terrace where his arms wrapped protectively around me.

"I know you are innocent," he began. "I wish only to hold you in my arms tonight. If only to be near you."

"Eduardo," I stammered, "I don't want to be *innocent* in matters of love. I want to make love."

"We can wait until we're married."

"Married?" I repeated as I bolted back. "I can't even think of marriage. I'm attracted to you. I admire you. I want you to be the first. But, Eduardo, I'm not ready for any major commitment."

We gave one another permission to share the event. As we loved, I continued to think there should be some other additive. Some particle seemed to be missing. Poetry described magic, and an ecstatic, explosive, sublime mystery.

In all his sweetness, his tenderness and torridness, with his affection and kindness, he could only partially detonate my womanhood. Some portion of love was incomplete. Some flame had not been ignited. Although I was not disappointed, for I wondered if I'd been too tense for a *firecracker* kind of orgasm, I'd hoped for more. We partook in a very surface, basic sexual instinct. After, his romance allowed a euphoric nesting. And I... I had accomplished sex.

Pale morning brought a tranquil moment. I ruminated about sex. It was tumultuous, insurgent, oscillatory, and complex. How could one know the definition of sex, much less of love? For love is learned in such small portions. It forms slowly. All the properties are fragile and fleeting.

As a profusion of light meandered across morning, I heard the discordant squawk of a bird. Eduardo's arms enfolded me. I studied his handsome face as he slept. His hair was feathered over his forehead. His long, thick eyelashes pulsated.

There was affection, I admitted. His tenderness had been therapeutic. It had opened my sensory vault. But it had not fully satiated my appetite for passion. I questioned if there might be something physically wrong with me. Then I went through the psychological checklist. Did I truly believe going the extra mile with love would blister my heart?

* * * * *

WHEN THE PROPELLER whine of the telephone rang, Nora was on the other end. She began taking inventory. I was glad Eduardo was in the bathroom. Yes, I answered, we had taken precautions. Yes, it was fine and dandy. Yes, we would meet for breakfast. I was relieved when her inquisition ended.

Nora questioned if I thought I would marry him now. Gads! I exclaimed. What's all this talk about the chains of matrimony? I told her there may be, as Francois de la Rochefoucauld put it, only one kind of love, but a thousand different copies of love. My raspy laugh joined with hers. She thought I was a stitch.

"Kelly, you're such a card!"

I wasn't going to confess I wasn't certain if I might be associated with the deck's queen of hearts, or more probably, the joker. Jokers elude love at any cost, I surmised.

* * * * *

AFTER A SPICY Eggs Ranchero breakfast had been consumed, Eduardo and Michel went to settle the bill. I chided, "Nora, are you writing a documentary on my sex habits?"

"You didn't answer my question."

"Nora, what can I say? Wacker comparison done by virgins aren't likely to be credible. He was nicely endowed. Now enough."

"Just so we don't get pregnant. Honestly, the rubber products down here are so cheaply made." Her lashes bobbed. She ruffled her bushy, mahogany hair. "Here come the guys. Remember every detail so you can tell me later."

"Impressions are singed against my memory. And I can't wait to relay them to you," I muttered with open sarcasm. That had temporarily snuffed the conversation. Eduardo's confident, aristocratic stride was weaving through the tables toward us. The top two buttons of his mint-colored shirt were undone.

The four of us walked to the street. Nora immediately cautioned, "Don't step in any donkey doo-doo."

"You mean burro crap," I said with a howl. "Your euphemisms are priceless, Nora. Now then, let's visit Taxco."

Our jocosity continued as we wandered through Plaza Borda. The Santa Prisca church dominated the square. Gazing up at the rose-colored, ornate church and its lace twin spires, I marveled at the workmanship. No wonder Taxco had been and was a rendezvous spot for assorted artists. It oozed inspiration.

I felt inspiration when we strolled past the rows of silver shops. Vendors waved at us. They dangled chords of sculptured bracelets and necklaces.

When we decided to take a break from shopping, we entered the Bar Paco balcony that overlooked the plaza. I was told Steinbeck had tipped a glass or two at Bar Paco. I wondered if he had viewed the *zocalo* with such amazement. Or if he'd sipped *cerveza* with such gusto? Or scribbled notes about the laced ironwork, hanging baskets of geraniums, and pastel homes. I did not know. Nor did I know if Katherine Anne Porter had felt such exhilaration when she scripted *Flowing Judas*. And how in love with Mexico had Lawrence been when he wrote *Plumed Serpents*.

These authors had written great works. And I had written a B+ story. I felt the shockwave of fear and self-doubt. Perhaps my talent trove was as vacant as my passion treasury was empty.

* * * * *

"RETURN OF THE cupcake. Did he nail you?" Leigh scoffingly asked when I entered the apartment.

"Leigh, I assure you my bakery credentials are validated. So you can stop with the *cupcake* shit." I pirouetted, before heading to my bedroom.

She naturally followed. "Where did you ditch Nora?"

"She's looking for her compact. She thinks it might be in the backseat of the car." I pitched a pile of clothing into a laundry sack. My eyes targeted hers. "Leigh, she probably isn't in the mood for you any more than I am. So why don't you go set your traps elsewhere."

"I mean, really, you are touchy." She sat on the bed. "How did it go?" she grilled.

I continued sorting my cosmetics. "Terrific. And how are you?"

"I noticed you've only got a couple tubes of lipstick. That means you still have a chance at becoming a dyke. You know the old saying, 'powder and paint make a girl what she ain't.'"

"Leave off, Leigh."

"Thanks for asking how my weekend went. Boring. Except when Sanchez caused a commotion after she got back. Erika's late on rent payment. She also claims someone stole her sheets."

"Sheets!" I stopped sorting to laugh. "What? Were you inducted into the Klu Klux Klan?"

"Don't be a pain in the ass." Leigh rested her chin in the palm of her hand. "Listen, you little twit, I found out more about the beach party. Acapulco delight."

"The one for you and the girls?"

"Mixed company, actually. Paul and a friend are renting a beach house. We can go along at no cost."

"We! Have you got an armadillo in your pocket?" I sighed. "I like Paul Dodd, but not enough to spend a weekend with him and his tart." Paul was in my manuscript class. About thirty and he was always clad in ascot with a double-breasted blazer. A true dandy. There was a whining drone to his lisping sentences. "I think not."

"Let me sweeten the deal. Not only will it be a class event, but there will be a famous American playwright in attendance."

I sat down opposite her. "The one down here with his movie?"

"Bull's-eye."

"I'll go. But you keep your hands to yourself. I'm not interested."

"You're a sexual simpleton. You're a sophistication fraud. Some adventuress."

My eyes narrowed to slats. "I said I'd go. But if I go, you better behave."

"Don't come unstitched. I'll be exemplary."

"I'll bet."

"Do all Kansans say 'I'll bet' or is it a Jewish thing."

"You probably did steal the sheets, goy."

"Now who's coming on with the prejudicial crap? And for your fucking information, your people might have worn yellow stars, but mine wore pink triangles." With a riveting scowl, she stood, walked to the door and turned. "Well?"

"I dislike all flavors of prejudice. I'm not wild about the fact bigots also carved away fragments of ancient Greece's most famous poetess—Sappho. So I do have some sensitivity to the subject."

She leaned against the door jamb. She began chuckling to herself. "I have this visual aid of you in Taxco. Kicking your panties high in the air and yelling 'yahoo' down the mountainside."

My return glance told her she was trespassing, but she hooted all the way down the hall anyway. Gran always maintained people could be turned around. The term 'hopeless' came to mind when considering Leigh.

EIGHT

GRAN WAS MY life's first legendary person. I met my second, Calvin Thurston, for tea at Sandborn's House of Tiles. Clearing his throat, he probed, "Do you like the House of Tiles?"

"I love it," I answered, glancing around the tearoom. The House of Tiles was named for its exterior blue and white tiles. It had been a landmark since the fifteen hundreds. Waitresses swirled past tables in their traditional long, colorful Mexican skirts and blouses. When one of them delivered tea, we exchanged smiles.

Thurston was obviously a regular, for the waitress greeted him with 'professor' when we entered.

"Sir, I wrote my grandmother about your having known Mark Twain. That really impressed her. Mom said she told all of my relatives and all the neighbors."

"As a youngster back in Redding, Connecticut, I had little true appreciation of the historic value of having Mr. Clemens as my neighbor. Later, all the commotion over him became more reasonable. We did recognize he was special. And is your grandmother also thrilled you wish to follow in his footsteps?"

I squeezed lemon over my teacup. "She's supportive of my education. But she believes writers have troubled lives. She would far rather I be happy than to be a writer. But my being happy seems to be contingent upon being a writer."

Thurston folded his hands. His thumbs tapped leisurely.

"Even Twain was besieged by trouble. So she's correct. Writers often experience unhappiness. It is a profession, or perhaps better said, an art, requiring a great deal of monetary uncertainty. But recall my telling you that you must try to be a *toward* person. Perhaps that's the best lesson a young writer can learn." He leaned back. "I once attended a party given in the Clemens's home. It was a publicity party for Helen Keller's book, *The World I Live In*. She was such a pretty young woman. As a child, I found it difficult to understand why she should be inflicted with such limitations. Of course, now I understand the true beauty of her spirit did not allow limitations. She is perhaps the best example of a *toward* person. And part of her miracle was crossing the path of another toward person. Miss Sullivan."

"In high school, I read *The World I Live In*. I never thought I'd ever meet anyone who knew her. I remember in the book she said she loved being around children."

"Indeed. It was something I sensed. Even as a small boy, I understood her joy of life." After a sip of tea, he continued. "She touched our mouths lightly with her fingertips to communicate. I shall never forget the feel of her fingers. There was a sensitivity of barely even touching, but gliding above the skin." He paused. "What area of writing is most interesting to you, Miss Benjamin?"

"Poetry."

When he finished his tea, I poured more. Stacking two lumps of sugar onto his spoon, Thurston dipped it slowly into the steaming tea. He whisked in circlets. "Poetry—Thomas Wolfe wanted to be a poet. Although he was known for his novels, I once told him much of his prose was actually fine poetry. That was the best compliment I could have given him."

"I've always believed poetry needs to quickly touch the reader's soul, so it needs to be better than prose."

Thurston smiled slightly. "In accordance with the theory of Santayana, there are two classes of poets. One is the musician who works with sound. The lyricist. The other is the psychologist who furnishes the illustration. Wolfe worked as well with sound as any poet I've ever read. Even Coleridge. And I consider him to be the finest."

"I would have liked to know Thomas Wolfe. Although I strongly detested his anti-Semitic rants."

"Unfortunately, he was a product of his time and place. If you read his work, you arrive at a fairly accurate insight of the man. Imperfect, certainly. His Southern charm was perhaps his most memorable attribute. Other than his work, of course. Although charm was inserted into his work. He would turn out reams. Perkins chopped out entire chapters. Wolfe could write twenty thousand words at one setting. Maxwell Perkins was the carver of Wolfe's novels. Max was at the center of the literary crowd. His aptitude for discovering authors was enormous. Aikens, Hemingway, Lardner, Fiztgerald, and Rawlings, to mention a few. It was an exceptional time in publishing." He smiled, adding, "But how I do love working with all of you. The young writers."

"I'm not certain I can be considered a writer yet."

"You must always consider yourself a writer. If not, consider yourself whatever else you wish to be."

From the background, I heard a voice. "Calvin." A man in his mid-thirties greeted Thurston. He was a debonair, well-dressed, manicured man with a congenial smile. His short, neatly-styled flattop gave him a suave appearance.

"Kirk Underwood," Thurston said as he stood. Then he introduced me. "I would like to introduce you to one of my most astute and talented students, Kelly Benjamin. And Miss Benjamin, this is Kirk Underwood." Thurston pointed to an empty chair at the table. "Please join us."

"I'd love it. I only have a few moments though." He smiled in my direction as he extended his hand.

With fledgling enthusiasm, I greeted him, "I've read your book."

Amused, he straightened his tie, and then laughed. "Book. In the singular?"

Embarrassed, I responded, "Yes. *Isle of Adventure.* I wasn't aware you'd written more than the best seller."

"You're not in the minority. My publisher would attest to that." He threw back his head and laughed with certain indignation. Smiling, he appeared to have forgiven a moment of irritation. His slightly crooked teeth were polished whiter than a fresh sheet of typing paper.

After a quick interchange, Kirk Underwood excused himself. He was late for a meeting across town. He wished me luck on my writing efforts. Before leaving, he suggested we get together for lunch—to discuss writing. I quickly agreed.

When he left, I commented, "Professor Thurston, you must know every published writer."

"That's no longer so," he admitted with a grin. "Kirk has the talent to become a major writer. And I hope it will be the case. But I fear it won't."

"Why?"

"Kirk now considers his work to be a business venture. With his book on the top-ten list and a motion picture deal, he's being seduced by fame and fortune. From a critical standpoint, his first work is far superior to his popular second novel. But his first didn't become a financial success. His second did. Now he's more concerned with lawyers, financial planners, and the prominent people, than with the integrity of his projects. I'm not talking behind his back. I've told him my feelings. And I don't mean to impeach, but rather prod him toward his best."

"It's sad to have talent and misuse it."

"Miss Benjamin, in Khayyam's *Rubaiyat* I found a wonderful statement, it read, 'Oh, if the world were but to re-create, that we might catch ere closed the Book of Fate and make the writer on a fairer leaf inscribe our names, or quite obliterate.'" He quoted from memory. "I've always had a tender spot in my heart for the rubais."

"Sir, thank you for sharing your wisdom. And your afternoon. I'm not certain you know how much it means to me. I'm grateful for your help."

"My assistance to students isn't without a price." Thurston dispatched his challenge to me—his expectation of me. "You must continue your search for that fairer leaf."

* * * * *

CENTURIES OLD, THE forest of Ahuehuetes was the sentinel that bordered our stroll down the path that leads to Chapultepec Castle. I had been amazed when Kirk Underwood called me, asking I join him for lunch. I accepted. When we met for lunch, he presented me with a copy of his first novel, *Lasting Sunset.*

We decided on a tour of the castle. I studied the crooked teeth that gave his boyish smile a sweetness. I realized I was being pursued by a man with a best-selling novel. His short hair caught the sunlight. His face was full. His eyes would flirt, then dim like a smoldering torch.

I touched the frayed bark of the tree. I commented, "Poor old Montezuma. And his nephew, Cuauhtemoc."

Kirk's grin lifted. "Yes. Cortez thought if he tortured Cuauhtemoc, the Aztec ruler would reveal a hidden cache of treasure. Cortez burned his feet to get him to talk. Cuauhtemoc was a pillar of stoicism. When asked how he was holding up as they torched his feet, Cuauhtemoc answered that he was enjoying his bath. Actually, Kelly, I used that line myself a few times after my first book was released."

"Most writers have a difficult time at first."

"Charred toes." His anger percolated. "Critics like to see to that. It's their vocation. Some of them have taken torches and traded them for ovens. They really believe in bathing us in fire."

"But you're a hit now."

"Yes. But what if I'd listened to the idiots when they told me to give up my writing career? I wouldn't be a hit." His arm slid around my shoulder. "Enough about them. I suppose you know the castle was originally used as a military college. When General Scott invaded, most of the cadets were killed. The remaining handful wrapped themselves in the Mexican flag and jumped from the ledge of the building to their death. They didn't buy surrender."

"Amazing the Mexicans will have anything to do with us Yankees."

"Everyone got a chunk of something from the Mexicans. Maximilian and Carlotta wanted the castle for their private residence, so it was renovated. Max ended up going before a firing squad. Carlotta went mad."

"Do you suppose it was the internal affairs or the interior design project that got her down?"

Kirk chuckled. "Maybe you should go into comedy writing. However, Thurston tells me you're really quite good with poetry."

"*He* said that?"

"Yes. When I called him for your telephone number, he did say that. He said, when someone in the class was playing bad critic with your work, you hung in there. You always maintained your artistic integrity. The inference I took from

Thurston's real message was I had not maintained mine," Kirk divulged with a sulk. "Did you see Gable and Monroe in *The Misfits*?"

"Yes."

"I saw that film right after my second book was released. It immediately met with resounding commercial success. When Gable said the line about roping a dream—it was how I felt about my own life." Kirk's words were peppered with dejection. "I'll let you in on a secret. I haven't written since I've become a success."

"I thought you said you were working on a novel when you were in Paris?"

"Writers are forced to always have a project. And one must write in Paris. Actually, I partied, took notes I've since lost and answered fan mail." His jaw band twitched.

"You'll write again when you're ready."

"There's a movie deal. That will keep me occupied. Those assholes are a brand new set of charlatans. I'll work on the screenplay. Hollywood will bleed me dry." He hesitated as our gaze tethered. "Writer's block is the larceny of a writer's soul."

"Maybe that's what makes the quixotic poet. That infidel blockage."

His craggy, pearly smile flashed at me. He recanted, "Sorry, I shouldn't complain. Right now, conservatives are attempting to ban *Fanny Hill*. They say its pornography. An upcoming ruling by the courts will be vital to us all. I don't condone hardcore filth, but it has the right to exist."

"I agree. I wouldn't want them burning author's feet or author's words."

Glancing at his wristwatch, he muttered, "Hell, it's getting late. I have some errands before I need to leave early this evening for California. I'd better get back so I'll have time to get packed. I'm planning on a return trip down here the first of the year. Maybe we can get together again. I've enjoyed this, Kelly Benjamin."

"Me, too. And I'd like to see you again."

"And I'd love to see *more* of you."

* * * * *

NORA HAD A touch of frostbite since Leigh blurted out that I was accompanying her to Acapulco. She had been lounging on her bed with a book in her hand when I entered. Her shoulders crammed against the pillow. I reminded her I'd spent time at Eduardo's apartment, had been seeing Carlos, and finished a lunch date with Kirk Underwood. My sexual orientation shouldn't be questioned, I argued.

"You'll need to alphabetize them."

"But Nora, it proves my heterosexuality. Besides, Carlos and I are friends. I just met Kirk, so what's the big deal?" I bellowed my case.

"When a woman of good breeding has too much male attention, it's base and vulgar."

"Nora, you've been with more than one man. I haven't. Only Eduardo." I glared into her haughty face. "And I do not consider myself base and vulgar. I'd be having a much better time if I were."

"Kelly, think about this Acapulco thing. Going with Leigh! You must know how that looks."

"I'm going so I can view the famous playwright." Quickly, I began thumbing through Kirk's book. I didn't read the words but pretended I was engrossed. That did no good at all.

"Huh! Probably as perverted as his plays," she wailed. "And Leigh has let it be known she wants to make it with you. I'd slap her face."

"That fear must keep her awake at nights."

"And you never even talk about Eduardo. About love-making."

"That's private." I wanted to wall out her inquiry. I didn't relish sharing intimate details. I didn't know why it was so personal with me. I also didn't know why I didn't relish the intimacy itself. "Let's stop with the base and vulgar chat."

"Who is base and vulgar?" Leigh quizzed as she entered the bedroom. She shot a glance in my direction. "Looking forward to the beach?"

"Honestly," Nora expelled a puff of breath that sounded like a detonation. "This conversation is turning to sewage."

Leigh guffawed. "Spoken like a true little fly speck, Nora. Are you upset I didn't invite you?"

"Kelly is going to see the playwright."

Leigh chided, "She's been salivating for days with anticipation of getting me in the sack." Leigh slowly licked her lips.

"Kelly is running around with all kinds of men." Nora launched right in. "And while we're at it, this Acapulco business is going to ruin Kelly's reputation."

"I thought all those guys you just referred to must have already done that." Leigh grinned.

"Being queer is far worse than being a whore," Nora indicted.

Leigh's spring-action stance confronted Nora. Her arms snapped in the air. "You're a phallic worshipping little bitch. You're off on Kelly's reputation. You! Nora! The one who is on constant loincloth search. Well, at least I'm selective." She was belching smoke. "Grow up, you little sophist."

"Why don't you take one of *your* friends to Acapulco?" Nora's eyes were darts.

"I am her friend," I defended, attempting to abate the onslaught.

"I'm referring to her *queer* friends."

Leigh's face was right up against Nora's face. Grumbling, Leigh's mouth twisted before she ranted, "I'm sick of your crap about my morals. You don't know a thing about me."

"And I'd rather not." Nora flung her textbook down. "So leave this bedroom immediately."

Leigh exited quietly.

I followed after her to her own bedroom. "Leigh, I had no idea my going to Acapulco would produce this reaction."

Leigh drooped onto the bed. I sat opposite her on Erika's bed. "If you think this is bad, wait until you return. So don't feel obligated."

"Nora isn't my keeper." I then admitted, "I never felt sorry for you before. Now I do. They really heat up over this gay business, don't they?"

"I don't need your fucking sympathy," Leigh hurled her words at me.

"It's because I never realized how weird people get about homosexuality. I remember when I was working on the newspaper back in K.C. They took us into a lesbian bar. There had been a crime there."

"Zoo time. Watch the freaks."

"Maybe," I confessed. "Leigh, I'll admit I was appalled by the mannish looking women. But you're different."

"But those women have as much right as I have, or for that matter, you have, to do as they please. I admire the butch expression of freedom."

"I agree. And before you ask, yes, the other reporters and I joked about them. I feel badly about that now. And I want you to believe I don't dislike you for being lesbian."

"You dislike me for being an anti-Semitic, goy bitch, right?"

"People shouldn't be judged, jailed, or killed because of

bigotry. You are prejudiced against the race and religion of others."

"You don't get it. I'm prejudiced against the stupidity that litters the earth. Take an expedition back through time. An archeological dig shows people sustained hatchet blows on their three-thousand-year-old skulls. What's changed? In the name of country, gods, etcetera. In the name of one difference or one belief or another, people harm and kill."

"And that's why you hate people?"

"Everyone is a fucker underneath. Some are in better disguises."

My spine tensed. "Maybe you're right."

"You can take the cupcake out of the bakery. Shut the door on your way out," she instructed.

I had barely entered the bedroom when Nora began, "You honestly think she won't try anything when you get to Acapulco?"

"Nora, she knows I'm not interested," I said as I twisted around on the desk chair. I reached for my textbook. "This room is way too small. Not enough room to swing a cat. I can't concentrate on reading if you're going to moan."

"Moan! I'm only pointing out the pitfalls. Your parents would be devastated if they knew."

"Nora, my mother thinks Sappho is a laundry detergent. Besides, they raised me to be tolerant. My father claims people give you enough reasons to hate them. You needn't hate their race, religion, or anything else if it doesn't intrude on you! My mom just believes in loving one another."

She cleared her throat, probably thinking of a comeback. "Well, I'm certainly not going to mention this Acapulco trip to Michel. He might think I'm involved in some sordid way."

"Heaven forbid."

"Can't you be serious, Kelly?" she grumbled. "I would die

if my boyfriend thought I'd go to Acapulco with a lesbian. I would never tell him."

"Good thinking, Nora." I felt a snag in the conversation.

"What about Eduardo?"

"Leigh didn't invite him," I teased.

"You know what I mean. What would you do if he found out?"

"He's going out of town on business. For all I know, he's breaking tacos with some little hot tamale. We aren't married."

"Kelly, I know you're a good person. Underneath, you are."

"Thanks, Nora." The surface tension evaporated with our smiles.

"I'm concerned about you." Her cinnamon freckles seemed to pop out under the bright lighting. "Be careful with that Leigh."

I couldn't help wondering why we need to demystify the abstracts of love and friendship. Isn't their *being* enough? It should be so simple. "Nora, I'm glad you're a protective friend. But really, don't be concerned." I paused. My eyes had shut a moment before I stood. "Since I have a date later with Carlos, I think I'll make a dash over to the bakery to pick up something for breakfast now. That will give me time to get home and freshen up."

"Carlos!" she lamented. "I thought you might be staying in. Just a minute, I'll get my shoes on and go with you."

"I need to be alone right now. But I'll bring you a surprise from the bakery."

Although it was a combination treat and turndown, it seemed to pacify her.

* * * * *

BRISKLY, I SCURRIED to catch up with Sanchez's new maid, Lupe. When I tapped her shoulder, she turned to greet me. She lifted her shopping basket. It was filled with a colorful patchwork of fruits and vegetables. She was obviously pleased with herself for her careful selections.

I explained I would enjoy tagging along with her so I could practice my Spanish. She said she needed to go to the bakery, and I was welcome to accompany her. That, I replied, was exactly where I was headed.

Since she'd taken the job two weeks ago, I'd wondered about the teenage girl. Her quick dark eyes flashed with precision; however, they gave up few clues about herself. Motions were restrained. She shyly executed her daily tasks with great care. Directly from Indian blood, there was nobility about her. She told me she was in her seventeenth year. Lupe's thin frame was energetic, but possibly at times almost heavily so. Her face was handsome in the traditional Indian form. A black shining braid hung down the middle of her back. Her white smile was set in a narrow, gaunt face. But her face was enriched with a sheen. Although friendly, there was an underlying broodiness about Lupe.

When I mentioned to Sanchez that Lupe looked too young to be working, she informed me city maids age faster than rural ones. City maids, she claimed with resolve, talked too much. Sanchez bragged about Lupe being a true prize. For she never cheated Sanchez, nor would she allow merchants to overcharge.

She was loyal and intelligent. Those were the special qualities in Lupe that fascinated me. She could weigh up people's intent. Her evaluation of them worked for making her job easier. She was proud, yet servile with the irascible, somehow sweet, Sanchez. She cheerfully followed Sanchez's instructions and never made fun of the elderly woman's idiosyncratic ranting. And still there was total dignity. And she was quiet.

Lupe spoke slowly for me. As I chewed my Spanish words, she patiently listened, then nodded approval or assistance. She didn't mind my gringo pronunciation. We passed by the flower stall. She pointed to the staffs of scarlet gladiolas and sheaves of white lilies. Dahlias were the national flower of Mexico, she announced. I believed the rose was the flower of the United States, but I wasn't certain. It was unthinkable for a country not to have one, she said. And she inferred a country needed a flower to survive.

Entering the bakery, I inhaled the tantalizing scent of warm bread. A lemon aroma hung. I ordered lemon pastry. Lupe ordered the sugary cakes for an evening birdwatcher's party. As she ordered the iced cakes, she wrinkled her nose. We shared a laugh.

Once back on the street, I opened the bag of pastry and offered her a sweet roll. Timidly, she reached and pulled out the citrus specialty. After we'd eaten our sweets, I suggested we have some fun.

I would carry all the packages, wear her maid's apron, and follow her. This, we both knew, would throw the locals for a loop and make a mockery of the ethnic traditions. At first, she declined, but soon, I'd talked her into the role reversal. As I donned her apron and was loaded down with packages, she giggled.

Then we walked, watching as the passersby glowered at us. By the time we were within a block of the apartment, we had doubled up laughing at the chilled looks. I leaned against the building to catch my breath. She insisted I give her back the apron, basket, and packages before entering the building. She didn't want to anger Sanchez.

She also didn't want to bring disrespect to her family. She

stayed nights with her aunt, Rosa. Rosa ran the newspaper stand at the corner. Her aunt might tell her parents if she were to get into trouble. Her parent's village would also be tainted by any form of bad conduct.

She enjoyed the city, she informed me but loved her village most. She would rather wear sandals than shoes. She was the eldest of seven. She missed her family, and that was evidenced by her withdrawn gaze as she talked of her parents. Her father worked the land, and her mother and the children weaved baskets to be sold at the market. Her father played guitar and she missed his music. Her mother had taught her religion and basketry.

When she told me about her village with such deep emotion, I mentioned it sounded lovely. She then issued an invitation to visit. She told me she always returned home on her day off, every Wednesday afternoon. She would load city goods and specialty foods to take to her family. And gifts for the children, she added.

I wasn't certain if it was the typical Mexican hospitality from which her gracious invitation was offered, or small talk. I, however, accepted her invitation with gratitude.

Assured by her smile as we went up the winding staircase, I nodded, telling her it would be my great pleasure. She told me her family would be pleased. For the entire small village would talk of the visit. *Norteamericanas* rarely ever visited her hometown.

It would be a fiesta, she declared.

* * * * *

CARLOS WAS A doll. I'd never seen him in a suit and tie, nor had I imagined it. We met another couple for cocktails at the luxurious Delmonicos. The other couple had been drinking all afternoon, and when they left, they mentioned going to a party. I was amazed they had the stamina to continue boozing.

Carlos and I were celebrating his sale of a feature story to the Associated Press. When he invited me, he said he wanted to blow half of the fifty dollars on an elaborate date. The rest would go toward next quarter's textbooks.

He was doing it up right. We ordered the filet mignon dinner and a good bottle of wine. After finishing the meal, Carlos waved his hand in a circular motion of writing in the air, which is a gesture to attract the waiter's attention for the bill.

When the bill, *la quenta*, arrived, Carlos went titan white. "Jumping Jez," he half hummed. "Those goofs didn't pay their bar tab. They put their booze on our bill."

"You're kidding," I sputtered. Glancing at the tab, I clamored, "How can any two people drink forty-seven dollars' worth of liquor and walk away?"

"They were drinking Parictins and had appetizers. And this place isn't cheap. But, hell, that's more than our dinner bill." He ruffled his hair frantically. "I've only got fifty-five bucks."

Digging through my handbag, I whispered, "I've got seven." I slipped the crumpled bills over to him.

Squinting, he motioned me near. "Pretend you're going to the powder room. When no one is looking, make a quick exit."

"Let me call my roommates. They can take up a collection. I'm not leaving you like this."

"Kel, they won't hold the table that long. Look, get out of here. There's a magazine shop about a block away. I'll meet you there." Reaching for his wallet, he gave the hint of a smile. "An adventurous game."

"Be careful," I whispered. I kissed his cheek, glanced up at the two muscular waiters across the room, and I headed for the exit.

I hated abandoning him. And I also hated being on the street alone at night. Lights blurred into watercolor abstracts. I felt chilled. Passing by the magazine racks in front, I then entered the shop. The shopkeeper was gruff. Proper women don't walk the streets alone at night.

Browsing, I glanced at him a couple of times. Several feline smiles later, he asked if he could help me. With a pious expression, I nodded negatively. Through the doorway, I could see the long, shadowy street. I moved along the aisle as I perused the magazine headlines.

After what seemed like an eternity, I began to panic. I dashed out into the street. Carlos was walking toward me.

"What happened?"

He took a deep breath before answering. "They have an American manager. He saw how the bar tab was made out. Knew I hadn't had that much to drink. He said I didn't look like a college kid out hustling a free meal. I left my watch for collateral. I promised to bring the money tomorrow."

"I was so worried."

He took my hand. "It'll be okay. I'll get the freeloading sonofabitch in the morning. He has piles of money, so I'm sure he didn't do it on purpose. It's so fucking absurd. I wanted it to be a perfect night for you."

"It is. You're not rotting in a Mexican jail."

"So what would you like to do now? Remembering we're broke."

"What's going on at your place?" I questioned.

"Wine, music. Well, maybe music." With a slowdown to his frolicsome, slightly pigeon-toed gait, he took me in his arms. "Hell, I've still got your seven bucks. We could stop on the way and pick up a bottle of wine. Your treat."

"My treat," I said squeezing his shoulders. "Gladly."

"I'd better warn you, my apartment is a small, three-room dump."

"Put a tablecloth over it and no one will notice."

"Kelly, you're the most derailed woman I know."

Hugging his neck, I retorted, "And you're my best friend, Carlos."

NINE

FRIDAY'S CLASSES WERE deliberately fraught with an educational steepness. After arriving back in my apartment, I realized part of my lack of concentration was that I had other things concerning me. Today was the day Leigh and I were leaving for Acapulco. Which was more than enough for me to consider, but I also was recalling last night's conversation with Eduardo. The relationship seemed doomed.

As I sat at the dining room table sorting mail, I realized it was the first skirmish Eduardo and I had experienced.

Yesterday afternoon I had believed love duplicates rainbows. Eduardo had prepared a special dinner for us. When I arrived at his stylish apartment, he had readied a huge pot of paella. The fragrance was absolutely wonderful. Seasoned with peppers, onions, and a blend of spices and herbs, the chicken, fish, shrimp, sausage, and rice specialty was wondrously delicious.

After dinner, we cuddled on the sofa, and he announced his plans to leave for the weekend had been canceled, and we could spend the weekend together. When I explained I had made other plans with a girlfriend, he sulked. I wanted to share the evening hours with him, but he continued with his morose pouting.

He inquired how he was to know if I was safely being cared for. I had no intention of telling him the details. But I attempted to assure him. Finally, I asked if it was because he didn't trust me. He admitted it was partially true. When I assured him if I were going to have an affair with someone other than him, I would have told him. Then I added our relationship isn't exclusive. He, however, told me since we first made love, he had pledged himself to me.

When I said I didn't wish to discuss it further, he stood, extended his hand, and told me he would take me home so I might have additional time to consider my love for him. On the walk home, I felt the snap of a hammer with each breath. Or perhaps it had only been my heartbeat.

* * * * *

LEIGH ENTERED WAVING a white sack lunch as if it were a truce flag. "Sorry I'm a few minutes late. I stopped to pick up some empanadas for lunch." She handed me one and watched. As I munched the folded pie, I nodded approval. "Good, you like them. Jose and Paul are picking us up in fifteen. Jose is a real lassie, but he's fun."

"Oh, please," I muttered. Swallowing another mouthful, I rolled my eyes. "Don't tell me he's more noticeable than Paul."

"He doesn't exactly ladle on perfume, but he's not what you'd call a filthy, macho beast. Hey, it's not a cast-iron deal. If you want to bail out, fine."

"I'm packed," I coolly reported.

After we'd finished eating, I suggested we wait for the guys down on the sidewalk. A quick getaway would do my nerves a world of good—in case Nora's class got out early. I didn't want Nora gawking at Paul and his Spanish paramour.

As soon as we'd lugged our suitcases down, I leaned against the stucco. "Leigh, before they get here, I want to clarify some things. Boundaries."

"Kelly, I'm not out to lay you. I'm not like a man with a gun handle to notch. I don't thrive on penis envy. I don't want to be a male. If I were a guy, I couldn't be a lesbian."

"Don't talk so loudly."

Leigh sighed. "I mean, really. I'm not here to lead you into butch behavior."

"At least don't use the pejorative slang *butch.*"

"I promise I'll behave."

I searched for hidden codes in her face. "I'll appreciate it, Leigh."

We stood in silence until we were rescued by Paul and his slim-hipped tart, Jose. Although at first far too effeminate for my tastes, Jose turned out to be charming. Throughout the five-plus-hour journey, I even enjoyed myself.

As we neared Acapulco, I got a rundown on the famed playground's past. Paul's drone was highlighting his tour with stage-like sarcasm. "After the Mexican War of Independence, Acapulco became a smuggler's haven and *beware* all people. Mothers ran for daughters; daughters ran for mothers."

"Sounds like Sanchez and Nora," Leigh kidded.

"God," Paul groaned, "I've got to pee. We'll be there in a few minutes. I'm not fertilizing the palms."

Out of the blue, Leigh chided, "The Mayan god of maize is named Yum Caax."

Giggling, Paul chastised her. "Stop that right now. Don't make me laugh or I'm going to whiz my twelve-dollar silk shorts."

Leigh chuckled. "Well, don't hold back. We don't want your ding-dong going septic."

"Jose certainly *does not*," Paul accentuated. "I believe septic extremities fall off? And that wouldn't be good."

I laughed but quickly inspected Leigh's face. She pointed out the magnificent blue curve of landlocked water of

Acapulco Bay. The glistening beach against the Pacific Ocean was magic. I whistled through my teeth. My eyes were on stilts. "Wish my family could see this," I commented.

"Glad they're not here while you're in my custody." She issued a quick and insincere *whoops*. "Only kidding, Kelly."

"Why don't you ever talk about your family?" I explored.

Leigh executed a quick change of subjects. "We're staying at one of the bungalows at the Club de Pesca. It's on the edge of the bay with a private beach. Great for moonlight walks." She read my staunch face as she continued. "Caressing night breezes with warm Pacific surf. Anyone with sex glands would get horny thinking about it." She shrugged. "Nora claims you aren't all that sexually stimulated."

"I am. I don't deliriously rave about it. And Nora's got some nerve discussing it with you."

"She loves confiding in me," Leigh flaunted her words.

"Well, she doesn't know what she's talking about. Gran always says you should give things a chance to work themselves out."

"Would that be a definite turndown? You really don't want my tutorial?"

"Burn the letters with fire into your soul. Underscore and capitalize the word—NO."

* * * * *

MY RESOLVE WAS ice-blue. When we entered the bungalow, I surveyed the living area. There were two small bedrooms with double beds. "Leigh, if you get smart or come anywhere near me, I'll punt kick you to Maui."

While we unpacked, she was on excellent behavior. We had made plans to dine at *Armando's* and then go to *La Perla* for drinks and to watch the divers. The guys wanted to go on a midnight cruise. Cruise, indeed, I had teased. But, I added I didn't want to be in Leigh's vicinity when she was cruising. I was glad they thought it was hilarious.

Armadndo's was a couple of blocks from the *zocalo*. There was a Naples-like beauty about the square. We were all famished and ordered the recommended spiny lobster. It was one of the most delicious meals I had ever eaten. Not your typical Kansas fare. Then, on schedule, we arrived at *La Perla*. We sipped chilled drinks as divers plunged from the cliff's edge into shallow inlets.

After the men had delivered us back to our bungalow, Leigh talked me into one more drink. So we went to the hotel's Turquoise Bar where we listened to music. Leigh was swelling down scotch and I was nursing a daiquiri.

Her speech was beginning to slur. She coaxed, "Let's go over to the *El Presidente*. They have the *Bar Dali* there. You'd like it."

"I couldn't carry you that far. Dali. I love his work."

"I love Frida Kahlo's work. She dabbled in lesbianism."

"Dabbled?"

"I could show you."

"Leigh, tell me about Frida."

She took another swallow. "You know she was married to Diego Rivera. Well, he had his women on the side. She did, too. Anyway, I think her work has a more human, universal appeal. There's more emotion."

"I've only seen a couple of pictures in magazines. One was a self-portrait and the other was blood and gore. Not that I'm an authority, but that doesn't seem terribly universal. However, I agree, her work is emotional."

"Her work is haunting. It cuts her heart out." Leigh looked across the bar. "Let's leave this joint."

"Back to the bungalow."

"Shit, you're no fun," she jabbered. "I could use another drink."

"People in hell could use ice water." As we stood, she tottered to the side. We then walked outside. "Let's walk down by the beach behind the bungalow. See if the fresh sea air can sober you up."

"You're a real shrew."

"You're inviting a huge hangover." We peeled off our shoes and socks. Walking in the damp sands was invigorating. The scotch bombs she'd been gulping down were making her loquacious. I figured I'd take advantage to pry. I wanted to know about her anger. After all, doubt is soft knowledge. I was rankled by mystery. "Leigh, why are you so angry?"

"Being pissed off suits me."

We continued walking past the rows of palapas. She leaned back against the stilt as wind blew through the palm thatch overhead. Behind that sound, the sea unleashed its soothing metronome of rolling and splashing. Stars were a million chandeliers hanging above. We both looked up. I then glanced back at her anguished face.

I uttered, "You always seem to be sad. You seem frightened to enjoy life."

"I belong to a goddess nation."

She walked toward the sea. My feet were sinking into the sand as I followed behind her. Wet foam bracelets of sea lifted to cover my ankles. Leigh stopped when the waters reached mid-shin. With her back toward me, I could see only her silhouette. "Leigh," I called to her.

"Leave me alone."

Surf slapped my legs. I tugged at her elbow. She swiveled around. Tears were welling in her eyes. "Please tell me what's wrong. You can trust me."

"No. I can't." Tears spilled over the rim of her eyes. "I

was close to someone once. Never again," she slurred.

"Who?"

"My older sister." She began walking away, kicking at the water as she went.

"I thought you were the oldest child." I followed.

"I am now." She attempted to muffle the sobbing sounds sticking in her throat. "Cindy died when we were kids." Her face contorted, her head hung. "She's dead."

"I'm so sorry, Leigh."

"Everyone's fucking sorry. *Sorry!*" With cynicism, she added, "The world is a fucking sorry place." Her spirit was still sorting memories of a childhood where it seemed her flesh had been torn apart to spill out her heart.

"Leigh, what happened?"

"She was a year older than I was. We were so close in age we were almost like twins. And she died." Leigh whirled around. "I told you to leave me alone." She swatted tears away. "I can't talk about it now."

"I'm sorry I pushed you."

"In the play, *The Children's Hour*, there was a line that made sense. The first time I read the play, I was a teen. I was coming out. Mrs. Mortar told Karen that it was different because she was young. And Karen said, not anymore."

Leigh's eyes told me her own youth ended a dozen years or so ago.

* * * * *

I HAD HOPED if Leigh had a Coke and cookies, she might not suffer a hangover. I put them in front of her. Then I headed for the shower. After I had finished, I insisted she take a long shower to sober her up.

When she came into the bedroom, I was on my side of the

bed clad in baby dolls. She announced she would sleep on the sofa.

It stunned us both when I spoke. "I thought you were going to open doors for me I never knew existed."

Our glance formed a chain. Mute for several moments and she then asked, "Kelly, what did you say?"

I felt the trap going down. "Leigh, you're correct. Maybe I should experience different kinds of love." My pulse rushed. "The conditions are we both agree there will be no emotional involvement. And you keep your mouth shut about it. So frost the cupcake."

Leigh's toga robe slid from her body. In the way of an ecdysiast, she had made her first payment on my seduction. Even in the moonlight, I could see her face was flushed. I slipped out of my baby dolls. With an extension of my arms, I felt her warmth when she sat next to me on the bed. She trembled as her damp body clumsily moved against mine. Her cheeks brushed against mine. Our lips came within an inch. When they were barely touching, we simultaneously began to giggle. Romance was snuffed. The arousal was doused. My head ebbed back against the pillow. Our laughter spewed for several moments.

"Leigh, I'm sorry," I sputtered. "It's just that our friendship has always been platonic."

"I've never brought anyone out before," she confessed. "My own first experience was with a girlfriend when we were in our early teens. We sort of brought one another out." Leigh sighed. "Maybe I was too nervous and drunk."

"Leigh, face it, our chemistry is way off."

"Maybe you do need a man. But at least you gave it a shot."

"I did because I do care about you. You're my friend so I trust you with this. I don't want Nora knowing about it. She thinks this escapade is my moral destruction. No use in confirming it."

"She also thinks I lay in the weeds for you. No use in confirming her suspicions. But at least you won't be going home pregnant. Wonder if her weekend offers the same reassurance."

"We'll know a week before her next period is due. She'll be running back and forth anticipating the signs of hierarchal forgiveness. I've told her prayer is not a great contraceptive. However, she seems to believe if rubbers aren't available, then she can talk her way out of an unwanted pregnancy."

Leigh joked, "The great sperm callback by some mythological entity."

There was an intermission before Leigh said, "Kelly, thanks for at least trying."

"Yes." We both escaped into our own internment camps of autonomy. It was a buffer zone in which our sanctuaried minds tried to put our souls back together. We were, assuredly, both attempting to seal off from the world that which disappointed us.

I would tiptoe around our secret. And hers. I pulled her into the hook of my arm. I whispered, "Leigh, try to get some sleep."

I cradled her—cushioning her. With a soft humming, I protected her with Gran's traditional lullaby. I pushed the straggles of her hair away from her forehead. The lullaby reminded me of home. Gran had wrapped each of her children and grandchildren into the protective fold of her arms and heart. As Leigh drifted off to sleep, I wondered how she had managed all these years with such overwhelming pain. I understood her world without warmth. We are impoverished without security. Without trust, warmth, or shelter, we are the wreckage.

A film of ocean fog rolled in, covering the beach. And for a moment, it seemed to cover my heart. My lullaby continued for an hour. And again, each time Leigh stirred. I reflected upon Gran's warmth and love.

For it was there where I was safe.

TEN

WE SUNNED, SWAM, and skirted talk of the previous evening. Leigh had become my friend, in spite of herself. I had joined her gang on the playground because of my acceptance of her. As well, I imagine, as my attempt at a conspiratorial fling into Sapphoville. Leigh understood I didn't feel at home with her. But she would not have understood my failure to visit. In attempting initiation rites, I'd declared it's a rascal's life for me. Important stuff happens when one is in their early twenties. Stumbling toward the interior is missing adequate training.

Throughout the day, there had been no references to the past night. With the exception of her complaint about a persisting a hangover, she was tight-lipped. By evening, that sorry malady had also diminished. We donned our long cocktail dresses, and we were off to the *El Presidente*'s grand hall. It was a party with all the frills and flourishes, including orchestra, exquisite tidbits, drinks, and pretty people.

Leigh had puffed her hair up into a pile on her head and looked stunning in a lime-colored gown. My gown was a floral printed frock nicely exposed what little cleavage I had. Paul and Jose were also decked out to the nines.

Leigh and Paul had decided to dance. Jose went to freshen up our drinks as I perused the room. I stretched each time an entourage entered hoping to see the playwright. Leaning against the wall, I closed my eyes for a moment. Dormancy invited my favorite fantasy. I projected the success of my first volume of poetry. I could visualize the cover design, jacket blurb, and author photo above a sparkling bio. My days were spent feverishly rushing from autograph party to publisher to hallowed corner with typewriter where I gently *gardened* my floral words. Yes, the first slim volume would be called *Journey*. By Kelly Benjamin. Better, Kelly Anne Benjamin— K. A. Benjamin. Dedicated to Gran. Dedicated with love to my grandmother, Gran. For the best old broad in the entire world, I dedicate this book to my Gran. Too wordy.

"Certainly," the well-modulated voice behind me softly spoke, "no one in your presence would discard you. So you must be alone, no?"

My eyelids lifted. She was a tall, aristocrat woman of I guessed thirty-five or so. She was distinguished, beautiful, and definitely beguiling as she smiled. Dark, sable-colored hair, with wisps of curls at the temple, was pulled back into a classic chignon. Her olive skin was flawless. It seemed moistened with the sheen of a lover or a temptress. She had recently been anointed as Sapphic goddess. Lush, full lips were sensual with a lifting smile. Her smile exposed perfect, sparkling teeth. Luminous ebony eyes reflected warmth, softness, and intelligence. The fragrance of her was enticing. Her royal blue, fashionably cut gown was elegant. A slit up the side stopped at a tasteful place. The gown featured a perfect figure.

"What?" I quizzed. My throat was dry.

"With my apology for being so forward. It isn't my way. My name is Doctora Cresida Valdez."

"I'm Kelly Benjamin. Cresida? As in *Toilus and Cressida?*"

"The same. Except the Spanish spelling uses only one 's' in it. And you are North American?"

"Yes. I'm from Kansas City." Suddenly, my mind was

blank. I wished for something urbane to appear. I simply asked, "You're a doctor?"

"Yes. I did my internship in your country. Boston. I am a psychiatrist. At this time, I have a select practice and teach at the university as well. I also do some lecturing and writing."

"Impressive. I'm only a student. I write. Poetry, mostly." I realized my sentences were chopping up on me. I felt frail. As if my mind was going quiet, I needed to garner all my energy to be in her company. She was mesmerizing.

"Perhaps you'll allow me to read your work." She was aware of her words and of her power.

"I'm…" My thoughts stumbled. "I'm not… I mean, I don't belong at this party. I came with a roommate."

"I see." There was a moment's pause. Then her throaty laugh questioned, "Did you tag along with your friend for any special reason?"

"I'm a writer. I enjoy exploring the world."

Amused, she neared me. Her gaze penetrated mine. "I would think you have lovely orgasms." Leaning, she lifted my chin. "You *do* have lovely orgasms, no?"

My lower lip bobbed for an answer. "I'm not experienced." I wouldn't tell her my only lover's lovemaking hadn't rung my soul loose from my body. And my experiment with the Sapphic world was abject buffoonery. My eyes must have told my secret, however.

"My suite at another hotel is lonely." She slowly removed her hand from my chin. "Would you care to accompany me to my suite for the evening?"

"I just arrived. And I'm with others." My weak protest was empty. "And I don't know anything about you."

"My darling, I know nothing of you either. But your eyes tell me all I need to know. However, you have your reasons for declining my invitation, so I shall honor them." She then walked away.

Jose had been perched across the room, waiting for her to leave. When he returned to my side, he handed me a drink. "You certainly don't waste time with the riffraff. What is it the doctora wanted?"

My heart had a funny palpitation of excitement. "I have no idea. Do you know her?"

"I know of her. She's lovely," he commented with a stray smile. "She's part of the *in* circle in Mexico. Co-authored and authored textbooks." Jose motioned me near and whispered, "Her brother is a dictator in Latin America. She's from a prominent family down there. She likes young, artistic women. Are you at all interested in her?"

"Of course not," I refuted.

"Of course not," he wisely repeated.

Each time I observed her across the room, I noticed her watching me. Then her consulting gaze would dissolve. Our glance collided. I realized I not only had a desire to be with her, but she had seen it in my eyes. Immediately, I set up a line of exoneration. She was a fascinating woman. She would make a great character for a book one day. And why shouldn't I find out what makes her tick? My heart was boxing with my ribcage as I approached her.

I spoke, partially whispering, "Certainly no one in your presence would discard you, so you must be alone."

Her half-smile eased into a full one of warmth. "I hope not to be alone now. And you've come to answer my question?"

"I wasn't trying to be rude. I wanted to meet the playwright. Or at least see him."

"He is in his suite. If you like, I shall call and we can meet with him."

"You know him?"

"Yes."

"I don't want to inconvenience him," I declined.

"Then we shall await his arrival."

"And would that inconvenience you?" I asked with a shy smile.

Taking my hand, she led me to the elevator. "We shall go to his suite. You wish to meet him and so you will."

When the elevator door opened, he was walking out. After a kiss on the doctora's cheek, brief introductions were made. His genteel southern style was reminiscent of a bashful boy. He seemed unaware of his fame. His wistful drawl did not correlate with his brash, strong heroes.

I was in awe. The doctora was well-aware of my amazement. She had introduced me to the world's greatest living playwright. And she did so by telling him I was a fellow author. He teased that a great writer should allow confidence to become his or her plinth. And, he warned, watch the booze. He hadn't watched it, he confessed. "I began drinking to drown my sorrows," he claimed. "But as the old story goes, my sorrows learned to swim." He was nudged by a handsome young man. "Be naughty, darling, Cres," he suggested with a wink in the doctor's direction. He was then rushed away to the party.

"Naughty," I whispered to the doctora.

She smiled. "It is a bit of a joke between us. I happen to believe love is a blissful station of living. For me, there is no sin involved with sex. It is only a dynamic of life. A lovely one."

"I agree. Life is too short of a dance to have guilt as one's partner."

"Kelly, would you now care to accompany me to my hotel and my suite for the night?"

"Yes, I would." I glanced back into the ballroom. "I've got to tell my roommate. And I'll need to return in the morning because we need to drive back to D.F. tomorrow."

"I also must return to Mexico City. You'll fly back with me tomorrow evening."

"Then I should get my things. Would it be possible to drop by the bungalow and pick up my luggage?"

"Certainly."

I got the bungalow key from Leigh and was pleased she refrained from comments. But those questions were crouched and would be awaiting me. I returned to the waiting doctora's side.

"I have a question," I queried with a frown. "Why did you select me? I'm not really Sapphic."

Her eyes closed for a moment. Then, slowly, they opened to display a hollow pain.

"I want you to accompany me and pretend you love me."

I was completely out of smartass remarks.

* * * * *

DOCTORA CRESIDA VALDEZ'S elocution and demeanor were a perfect match with the spacious limousine, the posh *Pierre Marques Hotel*, and her swank suite.

In luxury, we sat sipping drinks. "Fanny Calderon didn't mention you in her book, *Life in Mexico*," I quipped.

"Perhaps I am mentioned in books about the tenth muse."

"Sappho."

"Yes. Would you care for another drink?" she offered on her way to the portable bar. I was enthralled by the elegance of her glide. There was a reserved quality about her. Although her motion was effortless, it was assertive. She was agile with a lissome mellowness but always in total command of the situation.

"No thanks," I answered. I looked into the half drink I'd

been swirling.

She refreshed her drink. When she sat next to me, she asked, "And what is it you're thinking?"

"I'm wondering if I'll disappoint you."

"My darling, I shall not allow that to happen. You're a lovely young woman. Fragile, yet indomitable. I find those qualities attractive." She spoke with satin words as she lifted my hand. "I shall attempt to please you and that will give me pleasure. Please don't concern yourself with inexperience." Searching my eyes, she asked, "Do you enjoy bubble baths?"

"Very much." I averted her glance.

She extended her hand. We stood. I followed her through the spacious bedroom and into the bathroom. She filled an enormous marble tub and then sprinkled scented oils into the swirling waters.

With ceremony, we began disrobing. She assisted me with the unzipping of my gown. "I'm pretty sunburned after spending the afternoon in the sun. And I'm too thin."

With hinting coquetry, she said, "I enjoy youthful, trim women." When my gown fell, she added, "And you're not too thin. You're lovely."

From the cut of her evening gown, I had surmised her figure was magnificent. But it was more exceptional than I had imagined. We submerged into the silkiness of the water. When our skin touched, I felt a shiver of excitement.

I blew suds at her as she laughed and then flicked water at me. For whatever reason, I was not feeling promiscuous. Nor was I feeling as though I were falling from grace. While soaping my body with lather, her touches were feathery. There was nothing seductive until she was toweling me dry. Her hands moved the length of my body. She lifted my chin. Her fingers traced my lips. Slowly, we moved together into an embrace. Her open mouth glided from my neck to my lips. I felt her tongue as she neared my mouth. We hungrily kissed.

Before slipping beneath pale blue satin sheets, she placed a record on the high fidelity record player. The mechanical stylus searched the recording's groves. Guitar music filled the room with the sound of *Spanish Romance, Forbidden Games.*

In the crystal blue dimness, she pulled clips from her hair. Locks were released and fell to her shoulders. Her fingers fluffed the soft hair. I'd never seen a more alluring, beautiful face. She eased into bed. Her voluptuous body neared mine. Captivated, I felt cosseted by her touch. We were snug in an impassioned embrace.

She made love to me. And it was more complete than I'd ever hoped expression and emotion to be. It was a passion of reaching—of hers and of mine. I reached for her mind, her body, and her spirit. I reached for what was happening to me. I continued reaching until I could no longer reach but was reached.

I had then experienced seeing inside of my own womanhood.

* * * * *

I GASPED FOR air.

"You do have lovely orgasms. I knew you would."

I embraced her. "Yes," I murmured against her shoulder.

She handed me a delicate snifter of brandy. I sipped before returning it. On the exact place where my lips had been, she placed her lips.

Certainly, I had charged this episode to my *learning* account. But with this encounter, there was more to be considered. As I could never explain the delicacy of a summer rain, rose petals, and breaking dawn, I didn't understand this revelatory moment. I was attempting to go outside of myself to please this woman and to be pleased by her. We covered one another's souls with tenderness. There was an electrifying envelopment. I had released myself. My entirety had been directed, exhausting my emotional reservoir. With the fervor of white heat, and a sensitivity I always knew I had but never knew how to express, love had been made. Enraptured, I'd vanished.

She cradled me in her arms. My fortress had fallen. Tracing her lips with my fingers, I expressed, "I want you to know, for whatever inexplicable reason, I did mean it. I wasn't pretending. You wanted me to accompany you here to pretend to love you, but I meant it."

"You're so young. You can't know what love means."

A molten spear seared my breast with its stab. "Maybe I don't know all the definitive meanings and gestures of love. But I'm attempting to learn. And you can call this whatever you wish. It won't alter the fact I meant it."

I would have easily cleared a polygraph.

* * * * *

HIGH PALM TREES with spraying fans of green feathers were overhead. I gazed along the surf's hemline and thought about the sea's majesty. The doctora's fingertips tenderly spread tanning lotion across my back as we sunned on the beach.

"Do people call you Cresida or doctora?" I inquired when I turned over and glanced at her face.

"My friends call me Cres. My family calls me Cresida. And my patients and students call me Doctor Valdez."

"Did you learn English when you studied in Boston?"

"No. I was first sent to boarding school in England. There my language skills were honed." Her smile faded. "I'm probably old enough to be your mother."

"I'm twenty."

"And I'm forty, which is probably about the same age as your mother." When I failed to confirm my mother's age of forty-two, the doctora looked away. Then she examined a necklace Eduardo had given me for my birthday. "And this is from your parents?"

"No. It's from a man I date." I watched the lapping waves against the lyre-shaped shore. I braced for some display of jealousy. I was relieved when there was none. "May I call you Cres?"

"Of course. Kelly, I'm fond of you. Last night was special. You are special." She glanced away. "I believe there is a secret hidden within you. If you ever need to talk, please know you can trust me."

"No real secret," I denied. "Ask me anything."

"Why do you display such a sense of urgency? You're so young; however, you seem to want to rush life. This behavior usually manifests itself in people facing death. Or someone who has recently experienced a brush with death. So I question if you have a sense of mortality more profound than most people your age?"

"Maybe you can see through me," I issued with an uncomfortable, tight laugh.

"Might you share your secret with me?"

"It isn't a secret. Yes, I have had a near-death experience. Our greatest literature tells us for to know life, one must recognize death. I faced dying." I paused, recalling. "I went on a cross-country skiing trip with friends. It was during winter break. The last morning of our Colorado high country getaway, I decided to go out on the trail alone. I mistook one of the advanced paths for an intermediate trail."

"You were endangered?"

"Yes. I might have been killed, but wasn't." My reluctant

memory was prodded. My confidence had snapped when I confronted a menacing advanced slope. The toothed, dangerous inclines would require vying off at a precise moment, exacting a maneuver, or it would mean piling into the pines ahead. The moment requiring courage meant working my skis with perfection. I could have made it if I hadn't clutched up. I clipped a pine and then collided with a sturdy fir. Snow-chaffed, my body spun out of control. I toppled, bounding down the steepness. When I stopped, I was sprawled helplessly on the cold snowdrift.

I didn't know how much time had elapsed before regaining consciousness.

What I did recall was a throbbing head. It even hurt to blink the frost from my eyelashes. Wind oozed along the mountainside and my body shivered. I was tangled my spirit was lame. I'd gone for broke and then caved in when it mattered. This crush of my courage hurt as badly as my battered head and twisted knee. I had run for cover rather than believe myself capable of challenge. I'd hit the current-breaker at the wrong time.

My words were nearly lost as I told the Doctora, "I survived a rough tumble down a ski slope."

"And?"

"And now I'm living life in full throttle. Learning and living. Our door opens at birth and slams shut at death. Every breath is the in-between that counts. Every heartbeat is now."

Cres was observing me. "Is there more?"

I began applying lotion to her shoulders. Even in her conservative two-piece swimsuit, she was sensuous. I leaned nearer, whispering, "This is our now. And I'm having difficulty keeping my hands off you." The bombarding sun caused a squint. "Do you think we could go back to the room?"

When she tipped back her sunglasses, there was a smile

within her eyes. "Yes. And then this afternoon, we shall take a canoe ride through the lagoon to Puerto Marques Beach. From there, I shall hire a motor yacht to circle the bay and take us to La Roqueta Island. There is a comfortable place I would like to share with you. A lighthouse."

* * * * *

THE DOCTORA HAD promised me a wondrous weekend. She had more than delivered on her guarantee. In total command, she executed plans. Loftily, she walked through the airport with her assured mannerisms in full stride. Upon our arrival in Mexico City, we were met by her waiting chauffeur and limousine. When we pulled up to the curb on Atoyac, she asked if I would like for her chauffeur to carry my suitcase inside.

With a grin, I reported that my nosey roommate, Nora, would faint.

"Kelly, I've enjoyed our time." She glanced around as I exited the luxury auto. "Your humor and sensitivity are refreshing. May I call you?"

"I'd like that." I scribbled my phone number on the back of a register receipt. "Thank you for a wonderful weekend."

"I realize our encounter may have left you with some confusion. Please feel free to call me if you have the need to discuss it."

With suitcase in hand, I gave a parting wave. Then I trudged upstairs.

"Who is minding the rabbit hutch?" I asked Leigh as I entered her room.

"Nora is out with a new guy she met. Erika ran down for some food. Sanchez must be out of something Erika needs. Sanchez is at Belle's."

"What did Nora say when I wasn't with you?"

"You'da thought it was a press conference. I told her we didn't devour one another's twats."

"You never!" I sputtered.

"Well, actually, I mentioned you didn't grace me with your womanhood. Pleased her to no end."

"What about my not arriving back here with you?"

Leigh leaned back from her desk. "I told her you ran off with a guy you met on the beach." She leaned back over the piece of ivory on her desk. As she studied it, she disclosed, "I should get an acting award."

"Thanks for the cover. Think she bought it?"

"She bought it. So take the stone from around your neck and relax. It was a rubber stamp job. I said it. She wanted to believe it, and she did." Leigh pushed her eyeglasses back. "Now, let me work. I need to turn in a paper tomorrow."

"Why are you studying the scratching on the tusk?"

"Scrimshaw," she corrected. She peered over her glasses. "Now you can feed Nora any bullshit you want because I told her I didn't know the details. Nor did I want to know, I said with complete believability. She loved it. Figured I was spurned while you were off kicking the air with some prick at bliss station. Even as we speak, she's conjuring up visions of you on the beach meeting up with some guy who looks like he has a lance in his bathing trunks."

"I hope you weren't upset when I left."

Leigh snickered. It was her dirty laugh that might well have cleared the entire building. "You didn't break my heart. And are you kidding? I was a cheerleader when you took off on the arm of the doctora. Wanna tell me about it?"

"It may not have been heaven, but you could see the promise land from her bed." I added, "I'm glad I went. And glad I got to know about your life. We have a better understanding of one another now."

"The doctora is a stunner. But from what I've heard, she doesn't team up with anyone. She spends a few overwhelming weeks with someone. Then she goes on to another challenge."

"I got that feeling. I'm not sure she'll even call. I had a wonderful time, and I don't care if she's a romance bandit."

"Sure you do. But take the warning to heart. If she does call, depend on the fact that one day she'll go her own way. Don't play puppies with an old dog."

I chuckled. "That's no way to talk about a friend or an elegant woman like the doctora." I paused. "I know Cres isn't interested in teaming up with a mere student."

"Cres?"

"Cres. And I won't be heartbroken if she doesn't call."

She inquired, "But you do care?"

"If there hadn't been an attraction, I never would have gone with her."

"Love?"

"Oy vey!" I said dramatically. "I'm going to unpack and leave you to your work."

When I reached my room, I plunged onto my bed. I covered my eyes thinking about how we are emotionally edified. Every encounter is one of chance. Gran always says there's a chance of finding a pill in every pot of jam. Leigh had not admonished me to forget Cres. She only cautioned the doctora doesn't stay long. And I was already inwardly aware of that. And, in fact, resembled it.

* * * * *

NORA WAS A walking inquisitor with a face like a cold pickle. She wanted to be put in the picture. It was interrogation time at the hacienda. "Nora, everything was fine. I met a doctor and we came back together. Leigh was not a problem. I had a great time. I haven't picked up Leigh's trashy ways."

"Eduardo's been calling you."

"I know. He called a few minutes ago to ask if we could attend the Gran Premio auto races next weekend. Then the following weekend go to Mixquic. Michel will call you about the plans."

"Mixquic. The Day of the Dead celebration! Oh, Kelly, that's great. We can double-date two weekends in a row."

"Yes," I snorted. "Terrific."

"I want things to get back to normal."

"I'll bet."

"I wasn't at all concerned about you doing anything with Leigh."

"Nothing as mendacious as perversion, huh?"

"Oh, Kelly, honestly. You make everything sound awful."

"No, you make everything sound awful." I tore open a letter from Gran and began reading.

"What does your grandmother have to say?"

"She says to peg back my ears so I can take in the benefit of her wisdom. Kris is listening to way too much Beatles music for her own good."

"Beetle music? Like bugs?"

"Beatles. A Brit singing group," I explained. "Gran also says Queen Elizabeth should send Profumo to the tower. And Kennedy should keep Johnson out of his hair." I smiled at Nora's bemused frown. "Gran has her own notions about everything."

"So it would seem," Nora muttered.

ELEVEN

IT BEGAN INNOCENTLY enough on Tuesday evening.

I'd spent Monday night making up with Eduardo. Tuesday was set aside for studies. I had the bedroom to myself, so I began immediately. Erika rushed in, hastily plucked Spenser's *The Faerie Queen* from my hands, and insisted we go for a quick dinner. Unfortunately, she insisted on a little Austrian restaurant. She was homesick. And she was dying for Beef Esterhazy and Spanische Windtorte.

Wednesday morning, we were both dying from nausea. I sagged when I awoke. My pajamas were soaked with sweat, my tummy pitched, and my bowels gurgled. I bolted for the bathroom the moment my eyes opened. Nora diagnosed Montezuma's revenge. I believed it was food poisoning.

Whatever it was, Erika and I were suffering. Leigh offered to fix tea. Sanchez slept through most of the morning. She wasn't about to concern herself if turista wiped us out. But after Nora and Leigh left for school, she brought in a tray of violets. I planted my eyes on one withered little cerise face. I figured the wizened bloom was my horticultural soul mate.

Sanchez then decided to make an infirmary out of my room. Erika took Nora's bed. I could only imagine how a night with Leigh might go down with Nora. The room was cordoned off as a plague and pestilence vicinity so I wouldn't need to hear Nora's complaints about her proximity to a *lesbie*.

Erika moaned as if she were headed for a crackerjack

orgasm. "I zink zat I die now."

"You do that," I rebuked her lack of fight.

I loaded a spoon with Pepto that was held high by surface tension. Before I could take it, Lupe entered the bedroom. She pulled the spoon from my fingers. "No. *Pobrecita*. I fix *te de manzanella e pan tostada*."

She would fix herbal tea and toast. "*Me siento mal*," I whined to Lupe, gobbling sympathy for all I was worth.

Lupe returned from the kitchen with dried toast rusks and chamomile tea. It soothed my stomach. I felt a renewed lease on the day. Turning over, I covered my head with the blanket. I faded in and out of sleep until mid-afternoon. Dazed, I was dreaming when Leigh shook my shoulder to tell me Carlos and Juan were there to see me.

The prospect of looking into a mirror was too much for me to even brush my hair. Erika's olive skin was now avocado and I figured mine must be milk-carton white with a shade of lime. "I look like a sorry mashed potato," I greeted them.

"You do look a fright, Kel," Carlos confirmed. "Don't worry. You'll recover in no time at all. In fact, by tomorrow you'll be in great shape. I brought you today's lit notes." He handed me pages torn from his notebook.

Juan extended an armload of multicolored carnations. The fragrance burst out at me, making me gag. Erika dashed for the bathroom. Carlos wisely took the flowers to the kitchen under the pretext he was searching out a vase. He would instruct Lupe to deep-six them when Juan wasn't looking.

Juan gazed down at me with great compassion and pity. He sighed. "You are mostly pretty. But not so pretty today," he reviewed with a frown.

"Oh," I muttered

With hesitant Spanish at half speed, he reassured me, "But you can keep the flowers anyway."

Touring Kelly's Poem

* * * * *

ACTUALLY BECOMING ACCUSTOMED to the small apartment of Carlos had taken some time. It was a rat's nest and even smelled like a rodent's burial ground. I flung open a window immediately after entering. Including two small bedrooms, separated by hanging Singapore beads, a bath, living room, and kitchenette, it was cramped quarters. Each room was a turn-around-and-you're-there entry to the other rooms.

Slices of hardened clay left by his sculptor roommate were scattered everywhere. On the table, a splattered spill cloth was haphazardly draped. Pogo cartoons were tacked on the walls, and a Bobby Dylan ballad was playing on the Hi-Fi.

I had confessed to Carlos how my sexual core was difficult to reach with Eduardo. He mentioned it might be the tension Eduardo placed on the relationship. So it was suggested Carlos and I become afternoon lovers. At least for one afternoon. He changed the album to a more romantic issue. Beethoven's 'Pathetique Sonata' was playing. He had changed the sheets on his bed, and my carnal knave even wore shaving lotion.

I slipped out of my clothing. "I hate not having gobs of boobs," I grumbled.

"You're young. You'll fill out more," he remarked in a gesture of placation. "The important part of lovemaking is in the mind. I can't be turned on by a trivial woman, even if she has melon-sized breasts. And you're definitely not a trivial-minded woman."

As he disrobed, I studied his athletic body. His iridescent eyes sparkled. I ruffled his hair as his hands slid around my shoulders. He drew me near.

Playfully, I kissed his nose. "You can be my male

butterfly."

"Lao Tzu's wisdom is butterfly-ish. He says if you're not a competitor, no one can compete. I see you as an astonishing treasure of my life. I want to be that treasure for you. One day maybe we can travel to Europe together."

"I'd like to, Carlos." His kisses were soft. His love was gentle. I could only reach an orgasm when thinking of the doctora and her touch. I was sorry, but Carlos would understand, even though I couldn't say the words to him. I kissed his temple.

"You're a terrific lover," he said in a hushed tone. "I know you felt satisfaction. So are you still worried about being a diamond-hard woman?"

Glancing at the soiled wall, my eyelids closed. I heard the doctora's voice and could almost feel the wrapping of her embrace. I swallowed away my fear as I heard myself saying, "You're a wonderful friend, Carlos."

"We do have fun together. I'm even beginning to like your poetry."

* * * * *

THE GRAN PREMIO autos zoomed in front of us as they left behind the smell of oil and burning rubber. I was not enthralled with the circling Ferraris, Coopers, and Brabhams, but I was glad to be near Eduardo again. Being at his side was normal. And the doctora had not called. And in all probability would not. The term 'weekend fling' came to mind.

To keep from going wacky, I studied a newspaper I'd brought with me. As I flipped pages, my glance snagged on an outside column was a photo of Doctora Cresida Valdez. She would be a speaker at a conference in Berlin tomorrow. Her theme was the structure and dynamics of creativity. I quickly ripped the article and folded it away, along with a Kennedy blurb I planned to send Gran.

Spectators lined the fences. They would hoot and shriek as autos sped past. I was not in the least interested. And to boot, Nora was becoming sullen because Michel was ignoring her. I touched Eduardo's sleeve and felt his forearm beneath it. My hand slid down until I felt his wrist and his pulse.

Nora nudged me. "Michel's not paying one *darned* bit of attention to me," she fumed. "He hasn't said a word in over an hour." Nora's brooding over his dearth of attention had not fazed him.

"Men are intrigued by sporting events. It's biological."

"Eduardo has been attentive to you," she sputtered.

"Probably only because I was sick last week."

"Michel doesn't care about me. Only the stupid race."

Nora's needle was stuck in a groove. I motioned for Eduardo to follow me to get a soft drink.

"Are you ill?"

"No. I needed to talk with you alone. Nora is upset because Michel isn't paying attention to her."

"I shall talk with him. At times, perhaps, Nora is too demanding. Men do not like their women to complain as Nora does."

"Women don't like being ignored," I dueled.

"I shall tell him." He clutched my hand. "You are displeased with me also?"

"Not at all," I answered. I leaned up to kiss his cheek.

We joined Nora, who was enraged. "Michel is so infuriating. We had a date for later and now he says he can't go. I guess he's going to drive me home and pitch me from the car as he passes by the apartment."

"Screw him," I whispered. "Come with us," I invited. "We're going out for a quick bite to eat after the race."

"I was a fat and ugly child," she sobbed.

I comforted her. "Nora, I was a skinny, ugly brat. We all see ourselves as awful children. But now you're a lovely young woman. Don't let him push your buttons. Knockers up."

A slight smile wiggled its way through. She asked, "Is that one of your gran's sayings?"

"Knockers up?" I chuckled. "Naw. Gran would tell me to answer the door if I said it to her."

With the smoke and dust, I was reminded of a Leonardo da Vinci painting technique. *Spamato*, translating as smoke, seemed to be the day we were all having. The day had an inherently substandard feel to it. I was glad when I'd returned to the apartment to study.

* * * * *

LEIGH WARNED, IF I visited Lupe's village, I would probably never be seen again. With my pathetic Spanish, she claimed I might be telling some machete-packing Aztec to hump his mother.

But I had every intention of going. And I intended filling every cranny of my mind with the afternoon's events. I was intrigued by Lupe Lopez and her tales of family and village. Her ancestral bloodline was an exquisite dynasty. She had unfolded Aztec stories. I'd written down one of the old traditional songs:

We come only to sleep; we come only to dream
It is not true that we came to live on earth.
We are changed into the grass of springtime
Our hearts will grow green again
And they will open their petals
But our body is like the rose tree.

It puts forth flowers and then withers.

Climbing down from the bus, I watched Lupe come into vision. She greeted me, explaining the three older children were working. But she had brought the younger ones. Elena smiled at me. Her five-year-olds curiosity examined the landscape of my body. Pedro, three, with a dirt-stained face, beamed. Mango juice dripped wildly from his small mouth as he munched the fruit. Maria, eight, wiped his face as best she could, but rivulets of juice flowed faster than she was able to mop. The children's round faces were adorable. Their brown feet scampered, making dust clouds as they galloped. Lupe seemed to have a sweet and silent control over them.

My tote was filled with small gifts and candies for each member of the family. There was an excitement as we approached the village. About forty homes, some of raw adobe, others with stucco, were clustered together. A dirt street was only wide enough for one and a half cars. Paint crumbled from the courtyard's arched entryway. Men, with hair spurting from straw hats, were seated on stones as they squatted in doorways. The plaza was a circlet of homes and a cantina with two adjoining buildings. Four empty stands in the *cuadrilla*, I supposed were for market day. Goats, pigs, chickens, and children bolted, running freely.

Each time I spoke, there was a ripple of social laughter. Elena clutched her straw doll as she trailed after us. We passed one man who was sprawled out in a yard. He clutched his red clay cup as he snored. Lupe whispered, *"Borracho. Mezcal."* A drunk and his drink, I thought as I watched the old man's mud-spattered pant leg twitch.

When we reached the Lopez home, I found Señora Lopez to be a quiet woman in her mid-thirties. She greeted me with a humble nod. I clasped her hand as I told her the children were beautiful. When Señor Lopez entered the tiny, candle-lit home, she glistened with pride. The children rushed to him for hugs and to be lifted. They continued clamoring for his attention. Pedro was lifted onto his father's shoulders.

After introductions, the señor beckoned me to follow him. We went to the back of their home where Tomas was weaving. Smiling politely, the boy's hands continued to pull a wooden pick through the wool. Julio, eleven, three years younger than Tomas, was the apprentice. Rosa, sixteen, was the nearest in age to Lupe. She had Lupe's frolicsome gleam in her eyes. She was involved in basketry.

Lupe then took me to see the stone grotto. Around us were villagers busily turning earth with primitive tools. A teenage boy prodded a donkey that carried a load of pottery. In the plaza, a woman weighed peppers on a brass balance scale. Men were caviling, hands motioning wildly. The village plenipotentiary was shaking hands of Indians who were trudging back from their fields.

Lupe knelt before the grotto and her lips moved silently. She made the sign of the cross. The air was thick with belief. We then returned to the casa where I dispensed the gifts. The children played happily with their new toys.

Villagers were convening in the plaza for the fiesta. The fragrance of steamy tortillas and the rhythmic slapping of the corn cakes made me smile. There was a scent of spiced foods and pungent fruits. The feast was succulent. Cornmeal patties, simmering mole, tamales with corn husk wrapping enclosed chicken chunks, a clay bowl of *pozole* with pork, hominy, and chili, and many other dishes filled the tables.

As the fiesta continued, there were nods and gentle pats on my back. I tried as best I could to communicate. As soon as my plate was nearing emptiness, women refilled it with *chile rellenos, quesadillas*, and finally, flan.

When the meal ended, guitars were brought out and the singing began. Gourds were shaken, drums tapped, and voices gave their rendition of Rancheros. Hands clapped, and children squealed. Too soon, the afternoon and early evening slipped from my grasp. The Lopez family walked me to the bus. We parted with *abrazos*. Through the windows, I waved and thanked them again. "Gracias." My gratitude was for a day that would remain in my mind through a lifetime. I watched their images fade from sight. Theirs was a lesson I required. A fierce history had taught them we are casualties by virtue of the fact there is death. We are heroes by virtue of our ability to continue to live. Nothing more, nothing less.

And they will open their petals.

PART II—ALL THAT WE PLAYED WITH HERE

Gather together, against the coming of night,
All that we played with here,
Toys and fruits, the quill from the sea-bird's flight,
The small flute, hollow and clear.
The apple that was not eaten,
The grapes untasted—
Let them be put away.
They served for us. I would not have them wasted,
They lasted out our day.

—Sara Teasdale "In a Darkening Garden"
(The McMillan Company, 1933, *Strange Victory*)

TWELVE

Upon a marshy island in a high mountain plateau, a tribe of Aztecs had constructed a land known as Tenochtitlan. Over six-hundred years later, a network of tree-lined boulevards, historic plazas, and sprawling parks would serve as my treasured campus—my beloved playground. Mexico City was to instruct me with philosophic tillage, emotional harrowing, and the reaping of an education. Experience is always available—but it needs to be planted, hoed, weeded, and harvested. Memories might be replanted to create wisdom. And naturally, it is a sense of identity that would become my bumper crop.

Education, I was learning, was an endorsed illumination. It provided us with a recitation from all great past wisdoms. Until we are educated, I'd told Juan, our brains are simply raw material.

I was also becoming aware we are reviewed by love and by logic. The undercurrent of love must be kindness. As we converge slowly into tomorrow, our pounding nodule of a heart quickens. Passion is carved directly out of *love*.

An important lesson—there is valor within earthlings. And we are strung together, dependent upon one another. Stitched to philosophy, religion, race, and culture—we are all born of hope. Only the indexing is different.

Youth is in its own category. It falls under very involved subheadings. For youth is filled with missing particles, artificial contours, and of mistakes. Of course, mistakes are life's tuition. And we learn we shall find queues of other lost souls in equal error. And it is hope alone that knows no defeat.

About our mistakes, I mused. We compensate for them by being and becoming the best we can be and can become. If not, even mistakes are unproductive.

* * * * *

AROUND THE LASSO-EDGED curves, we drove toward Mixquic.

Nora and Michel had spent the entire trip in the backseat attempting to muffle their gasps and giggles. Eduardo's remoteness subsided only long enough for him to give me a guided lecture on the Day of the Dead ceremony.

Mexicans, he related, believe death leads on to a better place. Therefore, paying tribute to the jolly old souls in graveyards was a fitting honor. The celebration for was them and with them. More than that, he disclosed, it was an opportunity to become more comfortable with death.

I believed death to be a crouching mystery. To those in Mixquic, death was an opportunity for the rustic village to show off its festivities. We arrived to assist with the celebration. Although Eduardo was not in a celebratory mood, he was beginning to come around.

Makeshift, jerrybuilt stalls displayed an assortment of delicacies, drinks, and trinkets. Corner vendors offered their street meals that ranged from powdery pastry to crispy tacos. The trip had made us hungry, so we gobbled as we strolled. I passed on the *sombreroed* sugar skulls. They were decorated with names. But nothing even closely resembled *Kelly*. However, with great relish, we all ate *bunuelos* and washed them down with limeade.

"We'll die of dysentery still attached to the throne," Nora

speculated. "And since they don't practice embalming procedures down here, your remains remain."

"Terrific," I spewed. Then I tucked another bite into my mouth. "Even Electra finally covered Clytemnestra's body." I frowned. "Not that they pickled her and chased away the rats."

"They probably covered her with a *gran huipil,*" Nora joked.

"Is that a diaphragm," I asked.

"No, silly." Nora snickered. "They are pleated, lace head coverings for Indian women to wear with their Sunday dress. Legend tells of a capsized sailing ship having washed some elaborate European baby dresses ashore. The Mexican women thought they were headdresses."

"Did Leigh tell you that?" I suspiciously grilled.

"It's true. Even Leigh couldn't have made that story up." She paused. "Speaking of diaphragms," she whispered, glancing around to make certain the guys were well behind us. "I'm going to get fitted. Rubbers are too chancy. I'm late again."

"Nora, you're closing the barn door after the cows have hightailed it. Some doctors won't give them to single women. Carlos can help you. I'll ask him, and he'll be happy to take you to the doctor. He can pretend to be your husband. I'm sure he'd be happy to do it. He helped me out."

"Michel never would. I don't even know Carlos very well."

"He might want a trial run for the effort...."

"Oh, Kelly!" she bellowed.

"I'm kidding, Nora. He's a gentleman. And a dear friend." As the men approached us, I directed, "Well, let's flock around some graves and act related."

Eduardo took my hand in his. "You see, my Kelly, this is a fiesta."

"Not without the national drink," Michel challenged as he passed a *pulcheria*. The men ducked into a bar.

"*Pulque?*" I queried. My answer came when Eduardo handed me the miniature clay cup. I could tell it must be rank by the way Nora was grimacing when Michel handed her a cup.

"The drink of rural Indians," Eduardo stated.

Slimy, greenish booze had not been on my list to experience. However, to show my support, I took a gulp. I also downed an expletive that nearly forced its way out of my mouth.

"*Salud!*" said Michel, then chugged his drink.

"How much did you pay for this?" I asked.

"Fifteen *centavoes*."

"Including the cup?" Nora asked.

"We shall return the cups." Eduardo pointed out an old man with several pesos worth of *pulque* in him. "He was getting a refill when I was at the counter. He tells me he is the guest for next year's Day of the Dead. A few more pints and he might have been this year's guest of honor."

"Anyone could be tucked under the dirt by this time next year," I lamented. I glanced away, lifting my head to see as much of the sky as my vision would allow. I wanted to block away all parts of earth and view the heavens alone—in case the spirits were listening in on my confusion.

* * * * *

WE HAD CLIMBED the winding, chiseled rock stairway to an old stone church's steeple tower. And there, with Eduardo's arms around me, we gazed out of the open-aired window. As if seamed together for the moment, we traded warmth. I thought of the doctora. I wondered if she might be thinking of me.

Then my mind returned to Eduardo's world.

Below us were the milling villagers. They danced, moving rhythmically to the tolling bells, crisp trumpets, and guitars. There was the droning of human voices as the procession moved around the mounded graves. Those memorials were decorated with flowers, bells, and tall candles with dancing flames. The vigil was an all-night picnic. Food and jewel-toned bottles were being passed around.

"*Te amo*, Kelly," Eduardo murmured in my ear.

"I love you, too." There was an inert stillness inside, I conceded. I had been thinking of Cres. But I had only recalled her loveliness. Not the fact she had told me I was too young to know what love is. I wanted desperately to reinforce my feelings for Eduardo. It would make my life less complicated. Who doesn't want societal approval and acceptance? "I wish we were alone."

"You will have your wish later."

We left the church and drove to Xochimilco. The floating gardens were closing by the time we arrived. Most of the vendors were gone. Most of the flower-laden boats were docked and deserted. We did find a couple of eager oarsmen. They were willing to pole the gondolas along the canals. Nora and Michel took one of the flat-bottomed barges, and Eduardo and I another. We leaned back on a large serape he had brought from the car. I inhaled the fragrance of fresh carnations and roses that decorated the scow's arches.

By Eduardo's directive, we drifted in another direction from Nora and Michel. I soon heard the faintness of their voices disappear. A golden moon above volcanic mountains served as our romantic backdrop. The slosh of the pole in the swampy, bottle-green waters was the only sound. Our gondolier navigated the winding canals with the least amount of sway possible to ensure a large tip when the trip ended.

Continuing to a secluded area, I watched as the boat was secured with a knotted rope around a giant poplar. The oarsman jumped to the marshy land. After he was out of sight, Eduardo and I slid down onto the serape. The swaying waters underneath increased my passion. Thoughts of the afternoon boat ride in Acapulco with the doctora unleashed my passion. Our mouths enticed one another as our bodies twined.

"Is there something wrong?" he asked.

I moved away. "No," I lied.

An O-shaped moon splashed light across his face. I felt his warmth blanketing me. My eyes closed with the heavy clamp of weary lids. Sitting, I rubbed them. Sprays of light danced through lacy trees as night's mist had started to burn off. The silver haze was a gilded monochrome outlining landscape.

"Are you seasick?" he quizzed with a laugh in his throat.

"I think I'm worried Nora will be upset with us."

Eduardo called to the oarsman and we returned.

As I had imagined, Nora's eyes flashed. "Where have you two been?" she demanded with great indignation. "Well?"

"We got lost," I offered as we slipped into the car.

"Don't lie."

"Nora, we wanted time together. I wasn't aware I needed your permission."

"Kelly, don't patronize me. I was worried."

"Worried! Nora, what were you worried about? An armadillo might have kidnapped us?"

The men howled. Nora briefly smiled. But she continued. "Honestly, Kelly, you are impossible."

"Apparently not," I teased. "Come on, Nora. Cheer up. Nobody ever got pregnant from laughing."

I folded my arms when her simper became a chuckle. Simultaneous laughter converted to a roar. The old melted presbyter routine hadn't fooled anyone. Gran would have said,

'Seraph is as Seraph does.'

* * * * *

I SAT OVER an empty typewriter for the better part of an hour in contemplation.

Eduardo did not understand what I meant when I told him marriage cuts a person in half. He believed it makes two people whole. We were on the landing before I went inside the apartment when he again approached the subject of matrimony. He would have been everything a woman could want in a man. Then why, I questioned, was my spirit dismantling each time I thought of Cres?

Eduardo's jet-black eyes of night had lashed me when he left. He couldn't have known of my turmoil. I was logging the mileage known to broken hearts. I was traveling a path that might leave repair bills for my days of fast boulevards. Eduardo's somber, riveting gaze had expressed the forecast indicating we pay our traffic tickets with flesh. We pay for the hearts we mishandle with one muscle transplant at a time. One graft at a time.

As I studied, I concurred there was ambivalence. My usual succinct poetry had erected a divider.

Draping the cover over my typewriter, I sighed from weariness and the pain of uncertainty.

* * * * *

"YOU'VE GOT THE affability of a goddamn pissed gorilla," I indicted.

Leigh laughed. "Is that any way to greet me? I take it your visit down Poet's Row was shitty?"

"Eduardo is angry at me. Nora has been in a snit, and I'm

worried about my term paper. And you charge in here to confront me about the doctora."

"I asked if you had any good dreams about her lately." Leigh sprawled out on Nora's bed. She threw her book down. "And Nora isn't quite as cranky since she got her period this afternoon. I mean, *really*, I have enough to worry about without being concerned with Nora's needing to get her womb shoveled."

"I don't want to hear that talk," I objected with a scowl. "Nora is sensitive and you go for her. You violate people. Nora was an overweight child. She still carries the rejection. To make her feel better, I told her I was a beanpole brat."

"Some things never change," she chided. "You'll never be accused of having heaving bosoms. Now, speaking of deluxe bosoms, back to the doctora. Why haven't you called her? She gave you her number."

"She can call me. She's probably skirt-chasing. Dorothy Parker had it exact. 'A heart in half is chaste, archaic, but mine resembles a mosaic.' I'm not certain where I'm at with any of this. I was only an interlude for Cres. She won't call."

"As it happened, she did call while you were on your stroll earlier."

"Why didn't you tell me?" I snapped forward.

"Sisters stick together. I wanted to make certain you'd return the call." Leigh showed me the slip of paper. "I intercepted this." She swayed it through the air.

Grabbing for it, I glanced at the numbers. "Thanks."

"Think nothing of it. Always willing to help budding love. Archaic, mosaic. Most poets are frumps at heart."

"Leigh, I refuse to allow you to upset me."

"I'll bet she's something in bed. I even get excited watching her outrageously sexy walk. Whew! Is she all that sensual?"

"Yes."

Leigh rocked back against the wall. "Yes. Well, what was she like?" Her eyes were nailed to me.

"Use your imagination."

"I don't have one. Help me along."

"Cres and I made love. We took a bubble bath and then made love."

"A bubble bath! Holy shit, this is good. Tell me about it." When her request met with my stonewalled silence, she coaxed, "Come on, Kelly. I saved your goose on this message thing. You could have been in the soup with Nora and you know it."

"I saw how you jumped on the bubble bath material. Not another word."

Smirking, Leigh probed, "So when are you going to call?"

"As soon as Sanchez hangs up the phone. And I do appreciate you nabbing the message for me."

"*El placer es mio.* The pleasure is all mine, indeed."

"I'll bet. I'll bet," I repeated.

* * * * *

CHAINSAW SOUNDS CLATTERED from the sluggish school bus. I had noticed ostrich plumes of smoke belching from the exhaust pipe. I hoped the bus would reach the university. I also hoped my dark peach herringbone knit suit would not be smudged as I dueled for a seat on the bus. After grabbing an aisle seat, I brushed my suit jacket and adjusted the collar. I tightened the knot of my blouse's fluffy bow. I recalled picking out the outfit back in Kansas City. Dressed up, but not formal. I loved the blouse's marbling paisley colors of beige, apricot, and mahogany.

Glancing up, I watched Carlos leap onboard. As the bus

began to roll, he hop-scotched down the aisle to where I was seated. When he crouched, he commented, "You look wonderful. Did Eduardo finally call?"

"Nope. I have a luncheon date." I looked out the window as the bus coiled up the curlicue road. "Eduardo hasn't called. Mr. Machismo will fix my wagon. It's lunch with another friend." I wanted to loop the conversation back to safe ground. It required a hasty question. "You almost missed the bus. Oversleep?"

"Kel, I needed time to think some things over. I've made up my mind. I'm joining the Peace Corps. Why don't you come, too?"

"I'm finishing school first. Then I may consider it. You're nearly through with school, why not wait?"

His russet eyebrows dipped. "Kel, things out there need to be done now."

"I'll miss you."

"And I'll miss you. I'll finish the autumn quarter if my papers have been processed by then. They might give me an assignment right away. If it takes longer, I'll be here winter quarter."

I ruffled his mop of hair. "What made you decide this?"

Grimness shadowed his face. "Maybe it's a safe haven. It would keep me out of the draft. Things are likely to heat up. Kel, what do you think about Nam?"

"What about it?"

"Over the weekend, the South Vietnamese generals overthrew the government and killed President Ngo Dinh Diem and his brother. That's one of the reasons I decided on the Peace Corps early. I want to help people learn to live together, not die together. And, Kel, it's volatile there now. I'm not certain I could kill anyone. I'm definitely draft bait."

"I'm not sure I could kill either."

"I worry about my brother over there. The guy is tough and geared for battle. Hands like shovels and they make into atomic fists." His stare broke as if an avalanche of sadness was crushing him. He clamped his eyes. "I'm not the courageous type."

"Emerson says a hero is no braver than any ordinary man. Only braver for a few minutes. Carlos, you've got mettle, spirit. And courage when you need it. I do know that about you."

"You're not disappointed I'm not like my brother?"

"Of course not. Bet he can't write a news story."

Carlos smiled briefly. Still kneeling in the aisle, he leaned to kiss my knee. I cupped his cheeks with my hands. My lips drifted over his temple. "You'll do fine," I reassured him. I didn't want some conveyor-belt fate in the name of war to take Carlos from the world. He had conviction. And courage. And he had his own brand of confidence.

Confidence smears badly when stranded between reality and hope.

"We shouldn't be in Nam, Kel. It's never been peaceful. I'm sorry they're fighting, but no one has ever been able to exert their will over there. Conflict is part of their existence. Americans need to stand for something else. We can never win there. Even my brother admits that."

I felt a chill. "Maybe we won't send troops."

Carlos didn't answer for many moments. His head slumped. "*Maybe* is a sad word."

* * * * *

CRYSTAL SCONCES SPLATTERED wedges of dim light around the sleek *Rivoli* restaurant. The glimmer of mirrors, the velvet-backed salon chairs, and unabashed luxury was the order of the day. The doctora's eyes twinkled with her laugh when I filled her in on all the comedic events of my world. The house of Sanchez was perfect material.

For a moment, my sentence was lost. I wondered how I could have forgotten the doctora's extreme loveliness. But then, I hadn't really.

During one pause in the conversation, she smiled across the table at me. "I have thought of you often, Kelly." Lambent refractions from her dark eyes glistened as they targeted mine. "And you?"

"Often. I was reading a Sandburg poem and came across the line, 'it is all there in the fragments of Sappho,' and I thought of you."

Her smile was wispy, her voice lulling. "I'm glad you did." Her perfectly tailored ecru suit seemed to anticipate her equally perfectly tailored moves. Her hand neared mine. The touch was meant to appear accidental.

"I also thought about you when I saw a newspaper story about your European lecture."

She picked up the menu and unfolded it. "I have a very special fondness for you."

"Isn't that what people say about their pets? Fondness. I'm so *fond* of my poodle?"

A grin escaped. She lifted her glass. "To fondness." After a sip, her lips sensuously lingered on the rim of the glass. "Of course, I didn't mean fondness in that way. I was moved by all we shared while in Acapulco." Her expression converted to a mock pout. "One cannot always say the words one would like while in public. Or behave as one would wish."

I camouflaged a wink in her direction. As I did, her leg grazed mine. "One statement you made has never been out of my mind," I disclosed. "Do you really believe I'm too young to know what love is?"

Slanting back in her chair, she inquired, "Why do you ask? And more importantly, why has it concerned you?"

"Because," I stammered momentarily. "Because love is the one thing in life we should know about. Participate in with complete understanding." Her silence was prodding me on. She delved with her quietude. "Goethe believed a person doesn't learn to understand anything unless love is known."

"Perhaps that is a very relevant theory." She closed the menu. "I recommend the *Chichen-Itza*. It is chicken baked in a large banana leaf and smothered in herbs. A Yucatan specialty named after the Mayan ruins."

"It sounds excellent." I placed my menu on top of hers. With a teasing growl to my voice, I flirted. "You've never recommended anything that wasn't excellent."

The chicken was delectable. The meal's tangy spiciness was capped off with a desert Cres also recommended. Sachertorte, she explained, was a famous cake of Vienna. I joked my roommate was also a famous tart of Vienna.

"I have very much missed the way you cheer me, Kelly."

"I hope my cheer isn't all you've missed."

"I think not. As you know, I've returned from Europe, and this was the first opportunity in my schedule. My excuse for not calling isn't because I didn't wish to phone you. Only that I've been abroad."

My leprechaun grin bounced. "I thought you may have gone *after* a broad."

She expelled a throaty laugh. Then her hand slid over mine. "My darling, I have not even had time to go *after* the one young woman with whom I wish to share time. Until now."

"My life has also been hectic. A real circus."

"Circus." There was a quiescent pause before she continued. "As a child I loved the circus. The great masquerading."

"Would you care to run away and join a circus with me?" I invited.

"Do you believe we would meet the requirements to be in a circus?"

"We probably should brush up on our tumbling act."

* * * * *

ZONA ROSA, THE Pink Zone, was a section of Mexico City that stretched for a few square blocks. It was considered one of D.F.'s artistic neighborhoods. With exclusive, fashionable shops, it bustled with sidewalk cafes, boutiques, gift stores, luxury hotels, and upscale restaurants.

The doctora and I strolled, enjoying the sybaritic European ambiance. By the time we reached the feet of the bronze statue of Cuautemoc, I felt as if I were honing in on Docotra Cresida Valdez. She had told me only surface background material. But it was a starting point.

Cuautemoc's bronze reflected a valiant stance.

"There is no statue erected, nor street named for Cortez," Cres murmured.

"After what he did to the Aztecs, it isn't any wonder."

"Cortez was brutal. But he did give a less bloody religion to the native Mexicans. The practice of human sacrifice was eliminated. And Spanish became a unifying language. He instituted the first university on the new continent. And he built hospitals." With an impeditive tone, she uttered, "Politicians seldom please everyone. That has always been the nature of governing."

"Governing shouldn't include cruelty."

"I agree. But history often fails to see the full picture. For example, Dona Marina of Malintzin became Cortez's mistress. She was a multi-lingual beauty who interpreted most of the negotiation between Cortez and her people. Today Mexicans call traitors 'Malinchismos' after her. They perceive her as a person of betrayal. But had she not intervened, perhaps many more lives might have been lost."

"The conquest was vicious."

"Unfortunately, from peccadilloes to the most wicked offenses, the political crime most harsh is vendetta. And what law exists against misjudging those with the intent to make things better for their homeland, but without the capabilities of doing so?"

"We are all judged. Our work is. Writers have critics. The writer, Kirk Underwood, told me critics are murderers of creativity. Have you read his work?"

"I have heard of him but haven't read him." With eyes stationary, she surveyed my face. "Is he a friend or a lover?"

"Friend." My word blistered as my body tensed. "Cres, I hope you don't think I jump into bed with everyone I meet just because that was the case with you. It was the first time I've ever been impulsive."

"I apologize for my insinuation."

"Cres, I've never made love with another woman before you or since you. Two men. And I knew them both before making love with them. I cared for each of them. I shared love with a friend. We explored our feelings, and it only happened the one time. And probably won't happen again. The other is someone special. I've made love with him a few times only. That's a candid as I can be with you. I haven't been in a convent, but I'm not a tramp either."

"Of course not, Kelly. I think you're lovely and would have expected you to have been with men."

Tensions were tamped back down, but my heart stung. "I care very much for you, Cres. I won't lie to you. I don't even understand this. I went with you out of some compelling, magnetic desire. I find you beguiling. And you know I'm enamored with you. Why else would I be here now? How can you doubt me?"

"Perhaps I can't. That may be what frightens me." She deliberated. "Kelly, I have plans tomorrow evening. Could you possibly fit me in on Wednesday night?"

"I'd love to."

"I shall send my car by for you at six. We can dine at my home, and perhaps you would enjoy staying over. I have a pleasant morning garden."

"I'll bet," I said with a swagger in my heart. After which I felt glumness. "Cres, one question. If you thought I was a wanton, little hussy, where would the attraction have been for you?"

With an introspective glance at the sky, she qualified her words. "Kelly, had I believed that of you, I would never have pursued our affair. I also hope you don't believe me to be promiscuous."

"No."

Then she carved an emotional gash. "I also hope you understand my natural mistrust of youth," she impugned. "Any youth."

"Terrific," I lashed back with sarcasm. "How about if I buy you some bobby socks and 45s, then teach you to say 'groovy, babe.' I'll borrow my Gran's shawl and gulp down a Geritol cocktail. Would that do?"

Unable to contain a chuckle, she shook her head.

I knew the feeling.

THIRTEEN

BUSY TO THE bone on Wednesday late afternoon, I had no time for a meeting of my roommates. I had wanted to finish getting ready for my dinner date with Cres. I'd packed for overnight by placing a few things in a large handbag. I didn't want Nora becoming suspicious.

As in all plans having a few flaws, this one was simply falling apart before my eyes. Nora wanted to call an assemblage of the women to discuss Sanchez's upcoming birthday. I'd attempted to put it off, but she smelled a rat. So I succumbed.

Nora, Leigh, Lupe, and I were in attendance. We were seated around the dinner table with staunch faces. Nora had wanted to meet when Sanchez was out, but Erika hadn't arrived yet. As we waited, I found my mind taking me back to my lunch with the doctora. I was only remotely aware of my roommate's chatter.

The doctora and I had swapped stories of our past. Admittedly, no matter how I grilled her, she extracted more of my history from me than she had given up about hers. Words were slowly shunted from my heart. I told her of my joy and of my pain. My father's alcoholism had always been difficult to discuss, but I told Cres. My father had returned from World War II a far different man than the one who had married my mother. Lillian Hellman in *Toys in the Attic* states people change but forget to tell each other. The doctora understood.

From her, I learned she was fluent in all the romance languages and German. Her father was much older than her mother was, but she hadn't truly been raised by them. Cres had been left to nannies and governesses. She had attended boarding schools. Her family had provided advantage—the best education in the best universities. She was cultured in the arts and in society. However, she didn't consider herself to be a tribe person. She enjoyed swimming, tennis, and skiing.

She was epicurean and aware of it. She was stunning, and somewhat aware of it, too.

Somehow, when excavating her past, I felt she might well have asked her nannies and governesses to pretend they loved her.

"Let's get started," Leigh muttered. "I don't want to spend the night waiting for Erika."

"Kelly! Kelly," Nora interrupted my thoughts. "Are you listening? We'll take Sanchez to dinner on Sunday afternoon. Monday night, we'll throw the birthday party for her." Huddled, Leigh, Lupe, and I all nodded in acquiescence to Nora's plans. "About the cakes, Lupe can pick up her sweet ones."

"Some not so sweet," I directed as I handed Lupe the money.

"Now," Nora continued, "I'll get in touch with Belle. She can let the church and bird people know. What about the gift?"

"I agree. I'm for buying her a bird," I recommended. "She has an empty cage."

"But when her bird died last year, she said she didn't want to go through losing a pet again," Nora vetoed.

"So maybe this bird will outlast her," Leigh interjected.

Nora's eyelids quivered at Leigh's comments. "Stop that!" Nora glared. "Kelly may be onto something. Maybe she would like another bird. Let's consider it." Her eyes roped with mine.

She was going to ignore Leigh. "A parakeet or canary would be cheerful for her."

"How about a parrot. Mexicans love a good parrot joke," Leigh howled, then translated her humor for Lupe. Lupe grinned as her eyes dipped. Leigh then asked her if it wasn't true.

"*Si, es verdad,*" Lupe shyly reported.

"Will Erika like the bird idea?" I asked.

"Erika doesn't give a rat's ass one way or the other," Leigh said with a snort. "She'd probably suggest a crow."

"Can we get on with this," Nora grumbled.

"Nora," I conferred, "I think we should look for a parakeet or canary—whichever strikes our fancy. We could get the one with the most personality. We'll know it when we see it."

Leigh muffled a snicker. Nora glared as she declared, "We'll get the bird. I'm off to my room to get some studying done."

"You run along and study," Leigh said as her hands dismissively waved Nora to the hall. "And Kelly can get ready for her dinner date." Her eyebrows fluttered in my direction.

"What dinner date?" Nora wheeled around.

Leigh interjected, "The one coming for her at seven."

"Kelly, who are you going out with?" Nora insisted.

"You don't know my date."

Nora was caught on the edge of my words. "I don't know him?"

My jaw clamped. She stomped away, complaining to Lupe as they left.

"Mouth!" I said to Leigh.

"Nora is an emotional claim jumper. Sorry I let the medic out of the bag. I'll make up for it. Notice I said seven instead of six." Pulling off her glasses, she rubbed the bridge of her nose. "I'll take Nora to dinner tonight at five-thirty. I'll tell her if we're back by seven we can conveniently run into you and your date."

"And I'll make a clean getaway at six."

"A safe rendezvous if ever there was one." Leigh's shoulders lifted proudly. "Nice work, if I do say so myself. I'm stymied as to what the doctora sees in you, Benjamin. I mean, Nora can *only* get men, and you're only slightly better."

"Nora's adorable," I defended.

"She's a baton twirler from way back."

"I'll bet your mother stuck a baton in your fist before you even saw a rattle."

"Benj, she did! I used my baton to beat the shit out of some little snot who always gave me goofy looks. Then I tried tap-dancing."

"And?" I pried.

"*That* didn't work out either," Leigh confessed. "I'm not showbiz material.

"But then, my field of endeavor is not without spectacle. Shard farce and tomb burlesque. Yeah, Kelly, archeology is sort of its own extravaganza. The earth is stagecraft."

* * * * *

NESTLED IN THE *Jardines de Pedregal* barrio, the doctor's home was less than half an hour's drive. Rodolfo, her chauffeur, was a stocky, huskily-built man in his mid-fifties. Gruff voice, stern eyes beneath caterpillar eyebrows, graying sideburns puffing out from either side of his hat, and dark glasses reflected his stoicism. He was a brick, one could tell from his military gait.

I was expecting a silent ride as we slithered through the colonias and barrios. But he had given me a guided tour as he drove to the fashionable Jardine area. He explained the

Pedregal is located on ancient lava beds that had buried past civilizations.

Prompted by his loquacity, I delved for as much information about Cres as I could get. It was a tough interview, but I grilled for all I was worth. His answers were tentatively suspicious. He had been with the doctora for nearly thirty years. I wondered what a ten-year-old would need with a driver. He had been and was her bodyguard, he corrected. Questions lurched. Her brother had certainly not been in power for that long. He answered that it was not unusual for prominent families to employ guards in countries of unrest. And the doctor's father *had* been the presidente.

When I pursued the information, I quickly found that Rodolfo was also the doctora's guardian. He would shield her enigmatic mystic, as well as her body. He was her sentry when it came to nosey young women.

With this message, the grim, portly man switched channels. I told him my beloved, favorite cousin was named Rod. His lips twitched into a semi-smile. I wondered if he was aware of the sparks that flew between the doctora and me while riding together in the limousine's back seat. He must have been, I surmised.

After all, he was a licensed driver, and thus, was not blind.

* * * * *

WHEN THE WELL-POLISHED limousine pulled into a circular driveway, I viewed Cresida's home. An ultra-modern, sprawling home was exactingly landscaped with pockets of flowers, decoratively stacked lava, and arching lush trees. Full-length windows wrapped around the aproned center portion of the double-story home. Adjoining was a single story wing that spanned in another direction.

The steadfast Rodolfo opened the door for me. I was escorted into the entranceway where I was met by a middle-aged, plumpish maid. She introduced herself as Maria while leading me to a sunken living area. Cres was seated on a large, nearly oval couch. She placed the books she'd been reading on a correspondingly round glass-topped table.

She stood to welcome me with an *abrozo*. After Marie had exited, Cres embraced me with passion. "My darling, I've been anticipating your arrival."

"Me, too," I divulged. Gazing around the spacious, elegantly decorated room, I commented, "Your home is lovely." Through a large arch, I could see the dining area. A large clerestory window was the focal point. A glimmering chandelier hung over an exquisitely carved table set. Off to the side, a long mezzanine extended from a second level. In the living room, a circular fireplace was prominent. Paintings and tapestry decorated the walls. Topaz area rugs blended with the coral furnishings. Matching four-foot high piebald vases were sentinels at the arched entry. Each had an aigrette flowing from it. Beige plumes burst from pilasters on the walls. "The ostentation of a plutocrat never fails to dazzle me."

"As long as you find my home comfortable, it pleases me." She poured drinks from a narrow crystal decanter and handed me a square-shaped glass.

"Wherever you are, I'm comfortable." I lifted my glass and toasted, "It's good to be with you." I sipped the whiskey and Canada Dry. I marveled at her attention to detail. She had remembered what I'd ordered in Acapulco. The sign of pedigree, I thought as I scanned her home. She was more than merely affluent, I considered. Aristocracy showed in this home. And why not? This was the residence of a thoroughbred.

"It will be a short time before dinner is served. If you like, I can acquaint you with my home."

When we reached the bedroom, she turned to me. With a glint in her eyes, she asked if I approved of her room. "Very much so," I declared. The round, oversized bed was piled high with robin-egg blue satin spread and pillows. A magnificent sapphire blue canopy hung overhead. Sheer panels dropped down and had been tied at one edge. "Tempting," I teased.

"I had Maria put your bag in the adjoining bedroom. I attempt to maintain discretion. When it's time to retire, you can ready yourself in there. But I hope you'll be tempted enough to then join me in here."

"I'd love nothing more," I answered.

On our way back to the dining room, her hand slid away from mine. "I'll await the moment when we can again be near."

The luxury was captivating I had to admit. "Cres, I somehow thought your home would be more traditionally Spanish."

"My childhood was filled with darkness. Walls hid the sunshine. There were iron-clad windows and drafty, huge rooms." She paused, cracking back the door of her memory slightly. "It was difficult to decide if the gates and guards were for protection or if they were a form of prison. A small child doesn't understand such things."

"I like the bright, openness of your home. There is complete tranquility."

"I must credit my decorators. They also did my villa in Cuernavaca. It, however, is much more reflective of my spirit."

"Villa in Cuernavaca. Doesn't everyone have a villa?" I gently teased.

A hint of her smile appeared. "It is a most relaxing place. I work on papers and books there. I'm in hopes you'll visit me. It's a wonderful prod for creativity."

"Between you and your villa, I have no doubt but that my

creative juices would flow."

"We shall have a wonderful evening, my lovely American."

With a frisky grin, I whispered, "My roommate, Leigh, thinks that bubble baths and you are the things naughty dreams are made of."

She laughed. "We shall retire early so that we might share a bubble bath. If that meets with your approval?"

"My approval and desire." I gave her a frolicsome kiss on the cheek. I then hummed a few bars of "I'm Forever Blowing Bubbles." No wonder she thought I was entertaining.

* * * * *

THE DOCTORA WAS romance. I was making every attempt to gain entry into the emotional treasure of such romance.

After an extremely formal dinner of *salade panache au cesson, vichyssoise, caneton a l'orage, riz sauvage,* and *fonds d'artichauts,* I was too full to enjoy the *doigt de dame.* Pressing one of the finger cookies between her lips, I felt a shiver when she delicately bit.

We then assembled back on the circular couch for a cordial of Grand Marnier. I wanted her to fill out the questionnaire I was making up with each conversation. But I knew I would need to interrogate her repeatedly. "Have there been men in your life?"

"Yes." Her amused facial expression told me she would take my line of questions in good humor.

"But they weren't for you?"

"I prefer women. My heart is at home with Sapphics."

"Who was your first?"

She poured amber liqueur. "My first lover was an art teacher. I was in a French boarding school. I was a student nearing graduation. She was lovely and fancied me." With a mellow smile, her teeth glistened. "She taught me a great deal more about sensual appetites than art. Although I'm not artistic, I've always been drawn to those with an artistic nature."

"What happened to the affair with your teacher?" I delved.

Closing her eyelids, her lashes remained tightly clamped for many moments. "I returned to my homeland. Just as one day you'll return to yours."

"Maybe not. I haven't made plans that far in advance. Because your first lover was creative, is that why you're drawn to artistic people?"

"With all your questions," she chided, "you could become a psychiatrist."

"Writing is much less complex. I only need to write about people. Not rearrange them."

"It is one of the great misconceptions about my profession. We diagnose and direct. Only a person can change." With a wry smile, she added, "We are not sorcerers."

"You've cast a spell over me. Are you going to answer my question?"

"Perhaps I have selected creative people because of her. But I might have been attracted to her because it is my natural inclination to polarize toward the creative mind. Now then, my lovely, let us move to another topic."

"Such as bubble baths?"

Kissing my fingertips, she murmured, "I shall have our bath drawn at once."

Cres went to her bedroom, according to plan, and I returned to mine. I disrobed, brushed my teeth, and scattered cosmetics. I even ruffled the bedding to make it look as though I'd slept there. Some guise, I thought as I studied my face in the mirror. I did understand the doctor's rigorous prudence. I was not her student but was certainly young enough to be.

Absorbed by the promise of pleasure, I roguishly winked at my image. I waited for the knock on the door. And when a rap on my door happened, I took one more inspection in the mirror. Clad in a pale pink robe, I gave my curls a shake. That, I mused, must be the definitive look of horniness. I then gave a thumbs-up sign before moving to the door.

Three months ago, back in Kansas, I wouldn't even have recognized myself.

FOURTEEN

DOCTORA CRESIDA VALDEZ had wrapped her beautiful nude body in a fluffy crimson towel. I was amazed at rediscovering her loveliness each time we parted, even for moments. My hand slipped into hers as we walked with the lightness of bare feet to the bath.

Black and white, marble tiled flooring led us to a sunken, shell-formed, oyster-white tub. Overhead was a waxy fern that sprayed through the corner of the room. Sudsy blue water was garnished with a half dozen floating gardenias. The sweetness of blossoms lifted with soft steam. I mentioned the doctora must have a penchant for circles. Yes, she answered. A circle is the symbol of life. From the orbiting globe to the atom, all that comprises our existence seemed circular. Sometimes oval—but always a singular ring.

When my robe slid, the towel around her torso also fell. After entering the bath, we were magnetically drawn to one another. Braiding her body to mine, I felt the rush of water surround me. There was an urgency to touch her and to be touched. Our mouths locked in a passionate kiss. Our breasts pressed. I felt the rapid cadence of our heartbeats. The dexterity of her caresses still had the ability to unravel me. My head went into the water and bubbles snapped in my ears.

This bubble bath was much less innocent than the first had been. It was much more orgasmic. More fantasia than glissando, our nearing was electrifying. Satin waters swirled as we relished the rapture of our desire.

Exhausted, we stretched against the tub's edge. I batted dripping water from my eyes as I looked into her face. It was a face of beauty and of complexity. Her hands cupped my chin. She softly kissed my lips.

We continued lovemaking in bed. Then, while resting, I inspected the gathers in the batiste drapes that were drawn back around the bed. I caught a glimpse of the moon. I considered the myths of goddesses. Cresida was such a woman—the type of woman who inspires myth. She also created a mystery of warmth. "I adore you," I blurted.

"And I adore you, Kelly." She paused. "I find it surprising you're able to handle our affair without guilt. In view of the area and background from which you came, it's remarkable. You're truly uninhibited."

"I vowed never to blush while in Mexico. I don't have time for life's detractions such as guilt and remorse." With a playful tickle, I teased, "And, I wouldn't complain about my being uninhibited if I were you."

"Is there anything we do you find uncomfortable?"

"Leaving your arms in the morning will be uncomfortable." Closing our embrace as tightly as I could, I added, "You enhance my life."

"And you enrich mine. You make me feel contentment. I am much happier than I have been for a long time." Her voice drifted. "A very long time."

"Maybe I'll be able to share your love longer than other women have."

She scanned my face. "Of course, your friend must have mentioned to you that I don't develop lasting relationships. I plead guilty. Kelly, I have not lived with another woman because of my position as an educator and medic. But that is not to say I'm unable to form an involvement. I have, in the past, formed an involvement we shall discuss one day."

"Cres, I understand. And I understand your reticence to even consider a relationship with me. I don't consider myself to be a lover of women."

"I am a woman."

I smiled. "That is an *understatement*."

"You can't deny what happened between us," she challenged.

"I am not lesbian," I stressed defensive words that locked behind themselves. "I don't want to denounce Sapphism, but I'm not like you are. I want a normal life. That means men. Marriage, children, and family life."

"Normal," she repeated. The word had wounded her. Her eyes snapped shut as her head lowered. With great deliberation, she lamented, "Kelly, I'm aware of the limitations of my lifestyle. I understand societal norms and mores of 1963. The stigma involved. We both know I can never contend for your love in a legal or socially acceptable way. You've brought me great pleasure. I don't wish to hear all the reasons you could never accept my way." She looked at the wall. "I know them all by heart."

Reaching, I traced the curves of her shoulders. "I care about you."

She brushed my forehead gently with her lips. "I want your happiness. I want you to be a complete woman. Mostly, I wish for your self-recognition. Whatever that might be." Her lips were always warm and moist. She cradled me in tranquility. Moonbeam slivers showered her sullen face with empyrean light. I cuddled near the upper portion of her breasts. The flush of her bosoms stirred my desire.

"I don't think I could ever feel this way about another woman. In Antonine de Saint Exuprey's *The Little Prince,* it was a singular rose that most mattered."

"My flower is ephemeral and has only four thorns to defend herself against the world," the doctora quoted.

I cited the conclusion, "And I have left her on my planet all alone?" I smiled thinking how we had memorized the same excerpts from many works. "Cres, you are the only woman I have ever desired. That's what makes this so much more special."

She gathered me into her arms. After swamping my face with her downy lips, she sighed. "Perhaps, my darling, you are learning about love."

* * * * *

BEING BACK AT the university was a shock to my system. When afternoon classes ended, I quarantined myself in my bedroom to study. Concentration met resistance. My thoughts seemed always to spin back to Cresida. I recalled the morning, taking breakfast in the courtyard. The area was flanked by exotic trees with palmate shadowy designs, and a trellis that spanned the entire wing of the doctora's home. It offered a sense of privacy. Climbing, verdant vines wound their way across a stone wall. Behind the split-level, a pool and glass-enclosed sunroom were lined up next to a tennis court.

Mostly I reflected on the doctor's somber eyes when I explained I couldn't accompany her to Cuernavaca next weekend. It was to be Sanchez's birthday celebration.

I remained cloistered with my studies until Eduardo called, inviting me to dinner.

I accepted but immediately wished I hadn't.

"Glum looking," Leigh said as she entered the bedroom. She sorted the bundle of mail she was carrying and tossed a packet of my letters to me.

"Not glum, weary. I made a date for tonight but should

study." I ripped open a letter from Gran.

"What does the Kansas dowager say?"

"Gran says," I mumbled as I scrutinized my grandmother's handwriting, "she's glad I wrote a poem about Kansas. Now, I'm getting somewhere with this writing notion. She says John Kennedy has spunk. She's afraid I'm not taking proper care of myself. She doesn't want me coming back to Kansas thin as a cornstalk. My father has been seeing through his cups darkly. To translate her Irish, it means he's been drinking again."

"You can't win. I'd almost forgotten you've not only got Yiddish—you're filled to the brim with dumb Mick genes."

My glare hadn't impressed Leigh. I then opened the letter from Kris. "Kris says she got another John, George, Paul, and Ringo record. She's in quadruple love."

Pulling off her glasses, Leigh inquired dryly, "Did your parents make an effort to exclusively raise tarts?"

Snickering, I disputed her accusation. "Leigh, Kris is a kid. It's bad enough you plunder my sex life without going for my kid sister."

"Speaking of *plundering*, how was dinner with Doc?"

"Terrific. Great conversation. Avant-garde home. Served a seven-course gourmet dinner."

"Was that an Irish seven-course dinner of a six-pack and a potato?" she howled. "Couldn't resist it, Kelly. I don't like only making fun of your Jewish heritage. I like going for the Irish side, too."

"Are you finished?" I snapped. "As long as people like you are insensitive and crass, the world will never get along. And hatred isn't a joke, Leigh."

"Okay. So are you caught up in love with the doctora?"

"I do care about her."

"So what else?"

"Cres has excellent thighs."

"Jeez," she whistled through her teeth. "From you, that tidbit is a real shocker."

"She's a wonderful person. Intelligent, kind, and has a sense of humor."

"She'd need one to be attracted to you. Come on, Benj, give me more details like the thigh comment. I love a good sexual awaking tale."

"Ecstasy is the word that comes to mind." My eyebrows pitched up dramatically.

"That's it? Hey, Kelly, I have a joke for you," she vied for my attention as I opened another letter. "Old psychiatrists never die, they shrink away." She began a great gust of laughter. "Get it?" she sputtered.

"Leigh, go play with yourself."

"After your excellent thigh comment, it shouldn't be difficult."

Scanning my mother's letter, I bolted up. "Mom says Gran is sick. She had a cold and it may be going into pneumonia. The doctor wanted her in the hospital, but Gran refused to go." I swallowed. "Gran hates hospitals as much as I do."

Sharing my apprehension, Leigh placed her arm around my shoulder. "Hey, she'll be okay. She's a tough old girl. I can tell from her letters."

"Yes." My eyes misted. "*Mi abuela.*"

"And she must love you. She puts up with your running off and still sends you letters crammed with Kansas news. She'll fight it," Leigh commiserated. She gave my shoulder a squeeze. "And I'll bet she would laugh at my shrink jokes."

* * * * *

GLAD NOT TO have been forever banished from Eduardo's world, I vowed to enjoy his company for the evening.

However, when he announced we would be going to the *San Angel Inn* for dinner, I hesitated. I was not enthusiastic because of the proximity to the doctora's house. Certain parts of my life were to remain off-limits. Her area was reverential. I knew the restaurant was a regular dining spot for Cres. I had already accepted, so I could now only hope she would not be dining out. I realized she would never do anything to cast a negative light on me, but my fear was that it might hurt her to see me with Eduardo.

Although I suggested another restaurant, Eduardo was set on wanting me to see the colonial atmosphere. We entered the lush, peaceful courtyard leading to the Inn. When we were seated, I glanced around to make certain Cresida wasn't there. She was not, so I relaxed. I felt somewhat less vulnerable tucked into a corner. I had suggested it for intimacy. Hiding was an obvious benefit as well.

I watched Eduardo's eyes gleam when I extended a fork filled with avocado and ham mousse. As he nibbled, his hand covered mine.

"I've missed you, Kelly."

"I've missed you, too."

"I wish you could understand how intense my feelings for you are."

"Eduardo, I don't want to have skirmishes—to have words with you. I relish your company, but I don't want to rush things."

"I understand. You are less certain of your feelings for me than I am for you."

"It isn't that. I need time. And I wish I could be everything you want and need. And I can't be."

"I need only your love. I have, perhaps, rushed you. I apologize."

Throughout the evening, tensions eased. His eloquence

soothed me. His laugh pampered me. His touch ratified my heterosexuality. He didn't mention going to his apartment but returned me to mine. With a polite kiss, he reassured me he would take things more slowly. But he requested my indulgence in case he slipped. He was also a man and was attracted to me.

I was also attracted to him. But I was exploring how much of that was because he was a sweet, gentle man and how much was fear. I didn't want to use him as the remedy to negate my concern of being Sapphic. I didn't want to live within the essence of being a lesbian. And certainly did not wish to admit it might be the residence to which I belonged.

Youth believes in the simplicity of everything. Even address changes.

* * * * *

AUTOS EELED THROUGH streets and spun around glorietas. Wreaths were being placed at the base of El Angel. I gave a wave to Juan. He was busily matching centavos with another boy.

Nora was aware my feelings for Eduardo had been replenished. I had spent the lion's share of the weekend with him. I barely made it back for Sunday's birthday lunch for Sanchez. Nora had wanted to grill me, but her first opportunity was Monday afternoon on our way to the pet shop to purchase the señora's feathered gift. The evening was to be the señora's birthday party.

We were to meet Leigh, so I kept the pace brisk to cut down Nora's interrogation time. When we arrived, Nora muttered, "We'll get back to the conversation later. Put a little bookmark there. Leigh is waiting for us over in the reptile aisle."

"Why doesn't that surprise me?" I murmured.

We approached Leigh. Nora was chattering her plans. "We'll hide the bird in our room. I know Sanchez will provide a loving aviary."

"Plenty of selection," Leigh offered with a nod toward the wall of caged birds. She pointed to a canary grouping. "Let's listen in on their singing. We don't want any crabby birds around. The throaty one on the perch looks healthy."

Squinting into the cage, I commented, "It is nice and fluffy."

"Don't step anywhere!" Nora shrieked. "I've lost a contact lens."

We all dropped to our knees, crawled as delicately as smoke, and searched. When she found the small disk of glass, she picked it up with her fingertips. She took a small bottle of solution from her handbag and began to wash it."

"Clean it good," I bossed. "Don't want any parrot crap in your eye."

Leigh cackled. "Shit, the Mexicans would love that line. Let's pick a bird and get the hell out of here. People are gawking at us."

"I like the Harlequin parakeet," Nora debated. "But I also like the canary. Oh, let's get the canary. We'll need birdseed, too."

"How about a bell and mirror," I suggested. "We're flush. Erika kicked in this morning so we should have enough for both."

"Must have been a lucrative evening," Nora chastised.

"I like Erika," I defended.

"I'm amazed she hasn't picked up clap or some awful disease," Nora said with a huff. "Honestly, with all that action."

"Yeah, Nora," Leigh chided, "think about what we could

pick up off the toilet seat."

"Huh! God knows *what* queer women pass around," Nora indicted.

"Maybe yeast infection," Leigh bantered.

"*Honestly!*"

* * * * *

"DON'T LOOK NOW, you little Heb, but I think you've got an enemy of the people over there gulping down cheesecake," Leigh whispered to me at the birthday party. "Señor Hermann over there is a Nazi from way back, Fraulein Benjamin."

"Naw," I objected. I examined Sanchez's German party guest. Hermann's rotund, ellipsoid figure and spherical head were much more slapstick than S.S. With flush complexion, sponge-like skin, steel-gray hair, pudgy face, and well-ground teeth, Herman looked harmless.

"Where are these old gobblers putting all this chow?" Leigh muttered as she filled the pastry tray.

"Leigh, if you want to be miserable, fine. But let everyone else enjoy the party without your bigoted commentary." Her jokes usually got a grimace and a glance of disapproval. Now they were getting my glares and steaming ire.

"I have an idea," she divulged, "of how we can find out if Hermann is Nazi. I'll ask if anyone knows what S.S. stands for. If he yells 'Schutzstaffel,' run like hell, Benj."

"He's wearing a dilapidated felt fedora and those baggy britches," I commented. "If he is former Nazi, the military dress code has long ago worn off."

"I'm betting he *is* a Nazi Kraut."

"You're saying he's an old Nazi Kraut to make me react. So go on over and check him out," I prodded.

I was near enough to overhear each syllable of the

dialogue. When Hermann asked why she wanted to become an archeologist, Leigh confided to him she'd made the decision when seeing an old Jean Harlow film called *The Blonde Bombshell*.

"It was an eye-opener," Leigh remarked. "Harlow said, 'Here I go, out to work another day. What's a way out of this?' Well, I didn't want to feel that way. So I decided to go where my heart was. And what was your occupation before you retired?"

"Many jobs," he answered with what one may interpret as being said with purposeful obscurity. "Confucius says to choose a job you love, and you'll never have to work a day in your life. Archeology is a most interesting field of endeavor. I have always thought it fascinating."

"What other philosophers do you enjoy?" Leigh pried. She wasn't allowing him to slip the net.

"Many. I have had much time to read and reflect." Hermann was going along with her, pretending not to notice she was acting nuts. He politely asked, "Where are you from?"

"Colorado Springs, Colorado. And you?"

"Europe."

"What part?" she zeroed.

"I lived in Hungary for some time." He fidgeted.

As I approached with a tray of hors d'oeuvres, Leigh introduced me. She mentioned that Hermann was also interested in archeology.

"I'll bet," I mumbled. "And I'll bet you two have a great deal in common," I charged. That seemed to float over Leigh's head.

"Now then," Leigh prattled, turning back to Hermann. "I have a joke. In the archeology department, when we get tourista, we call it a *mummy* ache."

I had been nibbling a cookie, so I nearly choked laughing.

The joke wasn't great, but it was one I hadn't heard Leigh tell a hundred times. Nora strained from across the room to hear what she'd missed. Or if the language was acceptable. Leigh peeked back at her. "Hey, Nora," she yelled, "hold it down over there."

When Leigh made a return trip to her room, I followed. "You smoking grass?"

"Naw, enhancing the tea with a little rum." She extended the bottle she'd pulled from the well of her desk drawer. "Listen, I got a radiocarbon on Hermann. I tell you, he's off some Brazilian Nazi barge all right." Taking a huge gulp, she continued. "Having an old Nazi here really livens up the party."

"I figured you'd like an old Nazi. There is a commonality between you."

"You've got me all wrong. How many times do I have to tell you." She uncapped the rum for another spike in our tea. "I don't like Nazis. I don't like anyone. I mean, really. Particularly Nazi *men*."

"Have you ever liked anyone in your entire life?"

She slid the rum back into the drawer. "Nope. Not so much."

"Pathetic."

"Benj, you just haven't been let down enough. Someday you'll wise up."

Back in the hall, we ran into Nora, who was carrying the small bamboo cage. We followed behind her. There was a moment of doubt about the gift. I hoped Sanchez didn't really mean what she'd said about not wanting another pet. When we entered the living room, Sanchez gave a squeal of delight. We had, indeed, made a good selection. She fell in love with the little canary.

"I'll name it Victor, after my dear, departed husband," she

announced. "Yes, that is what he'll be called. Little Victor."

Belle ruffled her violet-tinted hair. She inspected Victor through tortoise-shell glasses. "How delightful. I'm sure your late husband, Victor, would have been most pleased. What a fine gift you young women selected. That is a sweet idea," her baritone's voice declared. "And it's a most lovely bird."

Nora whispered, "Who would have thought she'd name it Victor?" Blinking wildly, she answered her own question, "Certainly not me."

FIFTEEN

CALVIN THURSTON, THROUGH no fault of his own, had been neglecting me. Other students had crowded me out of my place on the bus next to him. They had clustered around him after class. In short, I was off to the side. Each time we began a conversation, we would be interfered with. And so he suggested we meet for tea.

Attentive to time, I entered the *Hotel Majestic* lobby with five minutes to spare. I felt relaxed when I heard the gurgling stone fountain and viewed the arches. The elevator ride up to the rooftop café gave me time to consider my thoughts. From the terrace table where I sat waiting, I examined the teeming traffic below. Tourists milled the Zocalo Plaza. Vendors and pickpockets mingled right after them.

A sip of warm tea was a welcome caffeine boost to my system. I was experiencing an afternoon sinker. Fatigue was my worthy adversary when studies and social calendar overwhelmed me. I would brawl for additional energy.

"Ah, glad you ordered, Miss Benjamin," Thurston spoke as I poured him a cup of tea. "I apologize for being detained."

"That's all right. I needed the time to relax and unwind. It's been a busy week."

"Which reminds me, I wish to invite you along to the Lady of Guadalupe festivities. Each year, I escort a group of my students."

"Yes. I'd love to attend," I quickly accepted.

"And how are your studies?"

"Still trying for an A in Short Story class," I declared. "I'm also adding to my series of poetry on Mexico. What do you think of the title *When All the World Was Mexico*?"

"That's a fine title. I would most certainly like to see it when it takes hold. By the way, you might want to read Shapiro's *The Bourgeois Poet*. Within the text, he asserts poets think universally through mutual creative currents. He also states poems are what ideas feel like."

"I'll read it. Gran gave me a copy of Sandburg's *Harvest Poems* and I thought of you. He says poetry is a phantom script telling how rainbows are made and why they go away. Great, huh?"

"Sandburg has been known to make even the most stoical of us weep." Pausing, he removed his glasses. "Are you still planning to return next year?"

I hesitated. "Depends on finances. If my money lasts past spring, I can return to the States to make enough money working the summer, then return."

"Perhaps a scholarship would assist you. I'll look into it. There should be no problems academically. Publishing would definitely help. If you'll take my recommendation and write a story about prairie life in Kansas. Perhaps the slant might be through the eyes of your beloved grandmother. She's given you a treasury of material. The story you told me about when she was a girl struggling to continue her education could be most insightfully written. I'll assist in any way I'm able. It would undoubtedly please your grandmother."

"It would. She believes Kansas is the heartland of the planet."

"Believe it through her. The story you wrote about Lupe's village would also be a saleable work. The Lopez family is not so different from the pioneers of the Plains. Their problems are relevant to them. I have written a play about a miracle. The true miracle of literature, as well as of life, is when we're transformed."

"I'm impatient for success," I confessed.

"Success may never come. But it surely will never come without diligence. Continue on to write honestly for those who will read your work, as well as for yourself. No matter how long the wait might be." He cleared his throat. "If we speak of success as seen by the world, we must get to this subject. You're aware Kirk Underwood's book has been number one for the past several weeks. He called, mentioning he'll be returning to Mexico for a two-day trip. He'll lecture at the university. He asked after you."

"Me?"

"Yes." Thurston tapped his spectacles against the table several times. His frown deepened. "His life is quite filled with literary circuits and travel. He's being seduced by the lavish acclaims, adulation, and wealth. Although it isn't any of my business, there is something I feel I must mention to you." His eyes riveted mine. "Kirk is married. I believe them to be separated, but I feel it incumbent upon me to make mention of it to you. I've come to think a great deal of you, young lady. I feel my sense of honor requires my making you aware of his marital status."

Attempting to hide my dazed expression, I uttered, "I wasn't aware of it. No, he didn't mention it." I inhaled. "I appreciate you telling me. We currently have no involvement, but I believe he was hoping for one."

"Kirk is charming with women. I felt a cautionary word to be appropriate." He stirred his tea. "You seem fond of the young man, Carlos Picazo."

"Yes, I am. We're friends. I date a man named Eduardo Rivera."

"Young Picazo seems a nice sort. I shall mention Guadalupe Day to him. And please feel free to invite your Mr. Rivera."

"Thank you. I've mentioned you to Eduardo."

"Is he also a writer?"

"No. An architect."

"I've always believed romance is better when not confused by two writers folding pages."

"I wonder what we would have had if Anne Hathaway had written."

"Perhaps an exercise in futility," he answered with a smile. "Or we might have had an even greater wealth of literature."

* * * * *

I ACCOMPANIED CARLOS to his apartment to study for our literature midterm test. We had sprawled out on his bed since the chairs were filled with books, papers, art supplies, and clothing. I had wrapped a blanket around me like a cocoon while he quizzed me.

Feeling comfort with Carlos and the Bard, I knew I would leap the Elizabethan hurdles with no problems. However, when Carlos quoted from Donne's 'The Relic,' I guessed it was Ben Jonson's work. "First, we loved well and faithfully, yet knew not what we loved, nor why. Differences of sex no more we knew, than our guardian angels do," he continued citing the poem. He then frowned and shrugged. "I say he's talking about homosexuals."

"Would that make a difference?"

"No difference. To each his own. I, personally, don't believe it is demonic behavior."

"Is that really how you view homosexuality?" I hoped he wasn't displaying his liberal armor.

"I'm not one. But they have the right to exist, sure."

"I agree." I sat up and stretched. "I'm glad I have a couple more days to study. Tomorrow, I'm skipping school."

"Why?"

"Kirk Underwood is flying in for a speaking engagement. He's been invited to be the guest at a famous author's lecture series. Anyway, he wanted to spend the afternoon playing tennis."

Carlos leaned back against the pillows. He pulled me toward him. "You said Thurston told you he was married," Carlos grumbled. He then kissed my forehead. "Kel, you're too bright to get involved in a mess. Aren't you?"

"We'll talk about publishing. I find it interesting."

"His pretentious shit impresses you?"

"Of course. I'm a writer."

"He wants in your pants."

"I'll hide behind my Kansas purity. Or ask him how Mrs. Underwood is doing."

"I don't trust the commercial fuck."

I chuckled. "But you'd trust me with someone who writes textbooks and medical papers. I could screw my brains out with an intellectual and you'd approve."

"I'm not your keeper. I don't like the guy. He's too slick. But it's your life. You're free to screw up if you want." He frowned. "Camus said free press can be good or bad, but without freedom, it can never be anything but bad. Same with love. You're free to get into all the trouble you want. By the way, *The New Mirror* folded."

"Times change. Another newspaper will crop up. Saturn will be launched. There are plenty of good things to be written about."

"Saturn. Hey, that launch only increases the danger of an ultimate war." Dejection filled his eyes. "Remember, it was the

U.S. dropping the big one first in WW II. Some warlike heritage."

"I don't see why scientists can't all work on saving lives, like my grandparents, the Benjamins, did. I hate the thought science created an ultimate killing machine. On the other hand, they create life-saving machines and medicines.

"Your grandparents were scientists?"

"Professors and research scientists. They both had died before I got to know them." I unwound from the blanket. "I've got to scram. Thurston gave me a list of books to read. Wisdom is a lonely pursuit."

"Don't confuse wisdom with knowledge. You have the knowledge telling you Underwood is a total turd. And you don't have the wisdom to scratch the date with him."

"I hate it when you're argumentative."

"Why don't you stay? I'll fix us dinner. You've been losing weight," he charged. "You're going to look like a flute."

"No, thanks. I've had your peanut butter and leftover sandwiches before."

"We can discuss literature."

Sitting on the edge of his bed, I huffed. "You always want to get into those boring, bloody revolutionary Russian novels. Rand's *We the Living* is about as much of that business as I can take."

"Can I walk you home?"

"You'd better stay and study." I crammed books into my tote bag as I slipped into my sandals. "Ciao."

"Watch out tomorrow. Remember, nice girls *don't* with slimy writers."

"I'll mention you send your love." I blew a kiss on my way out.

* * * * *

I WAS ABSORBED in Milton's *Il Penseroso* when Kirk's call came. He would be picking me up at noon. He boasted he could get into the tennis club and would have a court reserved for us. We could then return to his hotel, change for dinner, and then go on to his lecture. I quickly agreed. Cres had mentioned tennis was her favorite game, and she had her own court, so it wouldn't hurt to brush up on my game. Glad I'd brought my racket and tennis gear. I felt enthusiastic about the plan.

After changing into my outfit, I took a few practice swings as I surveyed the pleats on my tennis skirt. I hadn't played since summer months when I was in Kansas. I hoped my legs wouldn't convert to foam rubber out on the court.

Kirk was on time. The best-selling author of *Isle of Adventure* knocked on the door. With a quick, jaunty suavity, he entered the apartment. He was dapperly dressed for the game. He flashed his boyish ivory smile.

I studied the dashing, confident-to-cocky walk as we strolled to the MG roadster he'd rented. With urbane polish, he swung the door open for me. As the sports car swirled through traffic, he told me about his hectic schedule. Then he asked, "Have you heard about the outcome of the *Fannie Hill* decision?"

"No," I admitted.

"A three-judge court ruled it obscene. Buried the book." His eyes flamed. "They contend filth, even if it's wrapped in fine packaging, is still filth. Banned it." He unbuttoned the top button of his sports shirt. Silky ashen-blond chest hair protruded. "The witch hunt begins. Blacklists. We'll all buckle under or be banned."

"Not so fast," I debated. "There were heroes with the McCarthy fiasco. What about Lillian Hellman?"

"It was the kiss of death for all but a handful. She resisted, lost everything she owned. A farm she loved."

"Now maybe more will fight."

"Glad youth is optimistic," he said with a lashing sarcasm.

"Anyone with a number one book should have some optimism."

"*Isle* has been good to me," he changed subjects. "I bought a sailboat. Yacht, actually. Hope I can take you sailing one day. You do plan on spending the night with me tonight."

Ruffled at his assumption, I retreated a moment. I took a deep breath. Issuing my rejoinder, I spoke with clarity, "I take it you didn't bring your wife along on this trip. No, I don't plan on spending the night with you tonight."

"If you know I'm married, you also must know I've separated. It isn't any secret." There was a jitter in his voice. "So there's no reason for you to resist my charm. Well?"

"I'm not spending the night with you, Kirk. It isn't my style."

"Holding onto your virtue until the right bidder steps into your noose?"

"I'll spend the day with you, but the ground rules are we're friends. And my virtue is none of your damned business."

He pointed to the glove compartment. "There's a bottle in there I'm working on. Have yourself a slug, and then pass it to me."

Pulling out the half-emptied pint that was wrapped in a sack, I commented, "I'm not thirsty. And if I drank straight whiskey, I couldn't play tennis." I passed it to him.

Looping the auto into a parking lot, he glowered. He then drank from the bottle. His face went sour when he hit the brakes and the car was tucked into a space. With a final gulp, he pitched the empty bottle out. The shatter of glass rang in my ears. "Well," he said as he opened his door and pulled out his racket, "I hauled this racket with me so we could have a game. Ready to play?"

"Tennis. Yes."

* * * * *

MY GREGARIOUS MOOD had dwindled. Kirk had made a remarkably bad entrance when he insisted on a terrace table in the sun. He'd come to Mexico for a tan, and, *by God, he was getting one*. He also was on his second double shot on the rocks. He was becoming louder and more abusive to waiters. He sarcastically grunted orders each time the waiter approached. His intoxication was unpleasant for the staff and an embarrassment to me. He roared his displeasure with the fire of a basilisk. He complained about the Mexican *siesta* mentality.

Glancing around to see the stares of people sickened me. Then, I sucked in deeply. It was as if a concrete block had bashed my lungs. The doctora was two tables away. She was with a man I'd seen at the party in Acapulco. She turned to observe the ill-mannered, boisterous American. Our eyes met. I smiled tentatively. She acknowledged me with a nod. She swung her chair out, tilting it to watch in my direction.

Meanwhile, Kirk was carrying on about being subjected to poor treatment. Didn't they know who he was? His tirade continued. "I'm the number one author in the universe. But these illiterates couldn't possibly know that. We're supposed to have a court by now," he slurred. "Snails. They breed snails down here. They put sombreros on them."

"Kirk, I really don't feel like playing. Let's leave." I attempted to hush him. My mind was muzzling him, placing manacles on his limbs, putting him in leg irons, knotting the ends of a gag, snapping him into a straightjacket for safe keeping, leashing him to a tree, and placing him in a cage on the outskirts of Havana.

"We're playing. I carried the fucking racket on the plane, and I intend to use it." His surly reply was insistent. As the waiter passed by, Kirk grabbed his arm. "We've been waiting for nearly an hour. I'm Kirk Underwood. Doesn't that mean anything to you illiterates? My book is number one." His volume was increasing.

"Please, Kirk," I implored, "keep it down."

"Bring me another drink," he commanded the waiter.

"Sir, perhaps it would not be a good idea," the waiter began.

"I said bring me another drink. Now," he shouted. Lurching to his feet, he screamed, "You imbecile, get me another drink." As he began to grab for the waiter's white, starched lapel, my heart was pounding and I wanted to cry.

Cres was approaching the table. She extended her hand, taking Kirk off guard. "Miss Benjamin. And I recognize you, Mr. Underwood," she said as she reached for his fist. "My name is Doctora Cresida Valdez. I'm a friend of Miss Benjamin." Her words and smile had diffused his anger temporarily. "My partner and I now have a court. We would be most pleased if you would join us for a doubles match."

"We really should leave," I protested.

"We have time for a game," Kirk snapped.

Acquiescing, I walked slowly, following Cres to her table where she introduced Roberto, a fellow professor, to us. On our way to the court, I whispered to her, "Thank you, my aegis. I feel terrible having you see me with him." My head sagged.

"Perhaps the game will have a sobering effect." We walked to the court.

It was evident from the offset Cres was far superior on the

tennis court than I was. And even sloshed, Kirk was a more proficient player than Roberto. Kirk was throwing his anger into the game. Each time he would miss a ball, his masticating curses would spurt. Cres returned a lob, and then they went into a fierce backhand volley. Finally breaking, the ball whirled at me. I stretched as it flew by. A second bounce lifted a cloud of chalk at the line. When I reached the net, I leaned to tie my laces. Cres also leaned near me.

"Well, doctora, tennis is the secret of your firm body."

"And you are the other secret," she said with an enigmatical smile.

After she had delivered a second ace, Kirk shouted at me. "Kelly, why don't you return the ball? Are you blind?"

"I must be," I agreed. "I'm here with you, Kirk."

"Well, pull it the hell out and hit the ball."

Attempting humor, I replied, "I'm waiting for one with my name on it. I'm warming up."

With a sneer, he chaffed, "And when do you plan on being warm?"

His question had not only been obnoxious, but also loud enough for Cres to hear it. I knew from her riveting stare. "Kirk," I barked back, "this is a friendly game. Not Wimbledon. So stop with the criticism and your innuendos. I don't want to hear any more of that talk. Not now. Not ever."

Scowling, he served with such velocity I figured the cannoned ball was taking the brunt of his anger. Back at the net after Roberto had missed, Cres went to retrieve the ball. I met her there. She commented on his anger control problem, and his drunkenness.

"He may have his jockstrap snarled," I remarked.

She chuckled. "Please be careful," she warned. She backed toward the baseline. Our gaze strung us together.

Kirk and I had won the first set but lost the second. He

remained back at the net talking with Roberto while Cres and I rested on the bench a few moments. "I'll bet you're wondering what I'm doing with such an arrogant jerk."

She wiped her brow with a towel. "That is a bit of a mystery."

"To me, too. Cres, every time someone yells *love* I think of you."

"As I do you, darling." She motioned in a cautionary way the others were approaching. "Well, we are rested. All ready for a final set?"

"Ready," I replied.

Kirk's ice-blue eyes zeroed in on me. "You could give me some help out there."

"Kirk, next time you play, invite Rod Laver to be your partner."

I gripped my racket. My anger smoldered. By the time we were losing and nearing the end of the match, I had executed some fairly decent smashes. My attention to the game had not improved Kirk's sulking. "You've only got one more to miss," he spat.

I whirled around and walked toward him. I became confrontational. "Your behavior has not enhanced your image."

"Who the fuck cares what you think? You're a waste of time."

"I'm a waste of time because I have no intention of ever being bedded by you." I turned back around, smiling at Cres, who had heard the entire exchange. In play, the serve was headed toward me. I barely returned it. My racket fanned as it felt like a whip lashing the air. Cres saved the point with a rush to the net. The ball zoomed past Kirk. On that note, he pitched his racket at the post. Splintered as it snapped, the waffled strings plunked as it folded back. He stormed from the court.

"Kirk," I called after him. "Get back here and pick up this racket."

He rotated around with a stumble. "Pick the sonofabitch up yourself. I'll be waiting for you in the car."

"Would you prefer we see you home?" Roberto asked.

"No. Thanks anyway. I'll get him back to his hotel, and then take a cab home."

"Please," Cres cautioned, "don't allow him to drive."

"No." I flung the demolished racket into the trash receptacle. "Well," I commented, brushing my hands, "at least he won't be moaning about having to carry the racket back on the plane with him."

* * * * *

I STORMED TO the sports car. Leaning over the driver's seat door, I roused him. He slumped back. "Kirk, give me the keys and scoot over."

He mumbled, "You know Wolfe's book, *You Can't Go Home Again*? One part is about how we are hollow men." He quoted, "'Searching out our own obituary. We make up half of the other person's description.' Kelly, my wife wanted me to be a failure. That's the obit she wanted to write for me. But I didn't oblige her. Yes, we are hollow men."

Pulling the final poignant line from memory, I cited, "Do not be too sure."

"Was that Wolfe's or your feeling?"

"Both. Do you have a problem with that?"

"No." He slid down into the seat with a sulk.

"Fine, because I don't want to hear about your problems with your wife. I don't want to hear about your problems with censorship. They may be your problems, but I don't have problems. I have challenges. Now," my laconic rhetoric became a demand, "I'll take those keys. You shove your ass over."

Pulling them from his pocket, he threw them at me. He slid over to the passenger's seat. "Ever driven in Mexico City?"

"No." The engine popped like machine gun fire when I turned the ignition key.

With a pout, he quizzed, "Have you ever driven a sports car?"

"We do have roadsters in Kansas," I dryly answered. "So bolt your butt to that seat, sport."

SIXTEEN

FRIDAY NOON LUNCHEONS had become a Chapultepec Park tradition for Nora and me. We had a three-hour space between morning and afternoon classes so we would meet for a lakeside confab.

November 22, 1963, our lunch began no differently.

We met at the small outdoor torta hut perched beside the lake. I attributed Nora's calm to the waters below. With an excellent view of the castle, as well as the park and lake, it seemed so perfect for relaxing. Dwarfed boats left trails of goose bump waves. Children fed torta crusts to show off swans and ducks. Balloon vendors roamed.

"So," I inquired while stuffing avocado back inside my torta, "tell me about the new guy you met?"

"Sweet. Kelly, he has large button eyes and an adorable face. Like a teddy bear. And he's tall, muscular, and cuddly. I flipped over him the first time I looked in his eyes. He's considering pre-med."

"Pre-med?" My eyes widened. "I can't wait to hear how your Christian Science parents are going to take that news."

With a disparaging sigh, Nora continued. "Oh, Kelly. Gosh, they won't be angry. It isn't like I'm marrying him. Maybe I won't even mention that part of it."

I felt a bristle in the air as I saw two women behind the counter pointing at us. "I wonder what's up. They look upset."

"Maybe they're wondering where our chaperons are."

Nora twisted around. "They *are* acting strangely."

Nodding to one of the women as she kneaded a towel with her hands, I waved. She appeared shaken—distraught. Her return nod and wave was tentative. Then, as if our locked stares had magnetized, she moved to our table. "*Norteamericanas?*" she asked.

"*Si,*" we answered in concert. Instinctively, Nora and I glanced back at one another.

"*Que pasa?*" Perplexed, we stood.

The woman asked us to accompany her back to the kitchen area. As we moved into the cramped quarters, we saw two other women and an elderly man huddled around a radio. One woman turned toward us as her eyes spilled teardrops. I felt my skin ripple. My heart pounded as they turned up the volume.

The words were impossible. I checked Nora's face to register if my Spanish had been correct. I hoped my translation of the news was wrong. Nora was meringue white. Words were grenades going off in our souls.

The women chimed, "*Lo siento. Lo siento.*" They were sorry.

My mind felt to be short-circuiting in its attempt to comprehend the translation. I picked apart the message. President Kennedy had been shot. The bulletin said he was wounded while riding in a limousine motorcade in downtown Dallas. Others in the presidential delegation had also been wounded. The women's grief was now clear. Our president had been shot.

"Kennedy was gunned down by a sniper in Dallas," I repeated.

"*Muy critico,*" the old man confirmed.

"We'd better get back to campus," Nora ordered.

We thanked them as we began to leave. When we reached the edge of the platform, we were called back. We again entered the kitchen area. The radio announcer said, *"Presidente Nuevo de las Estados Unidos,* Lyndon B. Johnson." My mind went blank as words weaved together for the newscast. *Asesindo. Kennedy ha muerto.* Assassinated. Kennedy was dead.

We grappled with disbelief. Clutching one another, Nora and I were barely aware of the women patting our shoulders and mumbling prayers. My eyes pinched shut as tears gathered on my lashes. Our Yankee youth and arrogance had prepared us to be members of the most powerful and purportedly civilized country in the world. Promises peered out from our youth. We were no longer dancing in the cabaret of callowness. We were made to feel mortality on this day.

We hastened to the bus stop where bewildered students were exiting the bus. They couldn't understand the events. Nor could I. As they fanned by, they told us classes had been dismissed as soon as the embassy confirmed the death of our 35th president. The border of the United States of North America and Mexico were officially closed.

News reports were jumbled. Others had been wounded. Another member of the entourage may have been killed. In our attempts to extrapolate the facts, we found accurate news was slow in arriving.

There was one confirmation. We were cordoned off from our land.

We approached the newspaper stand where Rosa greeted us. *"Se ha enterado de la triste noticia de su muerte?"* she asked.

"Yes," I answered. We had indeed heard the sad news of the murder.

Rosa handed me the *Ultimas Noticias Excesior.* I opened my handbag to pay her. She shook her head. These first editions, she explained, were for her American customers. She would take no money.

We clustered among other students as they debarked the bus. One American student lifted his fist and began screaming at the radio.

No one said a thing. It almost appeared normal.

* * * * *

BY THE TIME we reached the sidewalk in front of the apartment, I had whirled around. "My god, I've got to find Juan."

"He'll be fine. He can fend for himself."

"Not on this one," I shouted over my shoulder as I began to run. I scurried back to the park to search for Juan. I wondered what I could say to him to comfort a boy who had lost his idol. Tragedy does not provide rehearsal time. I would offer my shoulder and I would cradle him. Juan saw his own dream in Kennedy.

And when Juan asked me why our beloved leader was slain, I wondered what my answer might be. Perhaps one line from the movie, *Rebel Without a Cause.* I might tell him that it's the age where nothing fits. I sped toward the park bench in Poet's Row.

* * * * *

WE TREMBLED AGAINST one another as I cushioned Juan's damp face on my shoulder. He had been waiting where I would find him. He told me he had to know the truth from a real American. He found truth in my tear-stained face. Truth, to my *gamin de la rue*, was answered. Our words were only fluttering imitations of sounds.

His eyes were bundled with tears. His sobs were deeply

profound. "Juan, he selected you to give his PT boat clip to—that means he knew you are special."

"But they shoot him."

"They can't kill his ideas. His legacy." I frisked my Spanish dictionary. "His *legado* is your *herencia*. Your inheritance."

Weeping, his anger suddenly burst through the pain. "I kill them."

Tenderly, I pressed his hair back from his forehead. I inspected his face. I wanted the return of his gentleness. And I knew I would need to ask for it. "We can't be angry and bitter. We can only go on."

"You no want me to kill bad men?"

"No. I want for you to grow into a fine young man. I don't want you lumbered by hate. I don't want that for you." I thought about Sarpedon, who the Fates had marked for death. How does one explain destiny—Kennedy's or Juan's. I couldn't explain it by myth, religion, or draw of the card. I would only be speaking from a position atop pins and needles. We are perishable. We are fragile. And our hearts become lost within one another when we care.

"God takes him. The mans who do this, I should kill them back."

"No, Juan. Study hard. I'll help you with your reading. Learning love and compassion is more important than hating." I swallowed as I recalled how Gran once said that without compassion, we are all goners. I didn't know the translation.

Juan held on to me for many minutes without a word. Then he looked away. I pulled another tissue from my handbag. Mopping his damp face was a feeble effort. It only made way for new tears. I had wanted to whisk Juan's pain away. And I couldn't.

My own was in the way.

Touring Kelly's Poem

* * * * *

WE CONTINUE TO strike poses in our own minds.

Trudging through sadness, I considered, was one of the loneliest parts of being alive. I left Juan in a tropical green path of poets. He was clutching his PT boat clip—his relic of hope.

When I left him, I'd told him I loved him and he was my favorite boy in the world. There were no words to heal the breakage of a child's heart. As I ambled across the park, I was made aware of the sensitivity of the Mexican. There were kind words. No more were the passes made by men. They were now paying respect. Certainly, my light coloring displayed my nationality. And certainly, my sorrow broadcast my origin.

A quote from *Much Ado about Nothing* seemed to ring through my mind. 'Everyone can master grief but he who has it.'

I hoped Gran was being comforted. I knew how much she loved the youthful president. I thought of my family. I realized as a foreigner, I now *had* to be away from my family until the border reopened.

This was my first glimpse into territorial boundaries. And it was the only time I considered myself a foreigner in Mexico.

* * * * *

EDUARDO WAS SEATED on the apartment landing's top step. One of his legs was pulled near his body, the other stretched over the lower couple of steps. His suit coat was thrown over his shoulders. His necktie loosened, his sleeves were rolled up. Standing, he moved down the steps. I walked into the envelope of his embrace.

Upon hearing the news, he had come directly from his

office. He suggested we go for refreshments. As evening approached, I needed to grab a sweater and to also freshen up and check for messages from home. Cres had called. While Eduardo and Nora visited with Sanchez, I dialed the doctora. She invited me to her villa for the weekend, but I declined. I would need to be with my fellow Americans. And I was certain Gran would be trying to call me. Cres extended her sympathies, and her final words, burdened with emotion, were that the mechanics of power are not without risk. And not without cost.

Attempting a return call to Carlos was fruitless; he was out. I went back to the living room when Leigh was arriving. They clustered around the table as she unfolded the latest edition of the newspaper.

After scanning the news, Eduardo suggested we go for a walk. He took me to a small churreria. He led me to a table in a remote corner of the quaint shop. We sipped sweet flavored hot chocolate. He slid the plate of steaming churros toward me. "You must eat," he encouraged.

I usually relished the doughnut-like pastry that is smothered in sugar and served hot. Not today. "I'm not hungry. This is like a bad nightmare."

"It is difficult to believe." His hand reached for mine. I felt the heat from it. He was emotionally bracing me and his kindness was genuine. For I could tell he hurt, too.

I shared each thought. "In a movie, *From Here to Eternity*, Monty Clift played a soldier named Pruitt. He said, 'because you love something, doesn't mean it's gotta love you back.' Kennedy wanted to protect freedom. Why would anyone want to kill him? Why would anyone not love him back?"

"Buddha says that if we saw the results of our evil deeds, we would turn away from them in disgust. But I believe some people enjoy evil. Sartre says we are our own choices."

Eduardo took off his tie, folded it, and tucked it into his pocket. "Perhaps evil is what our hearts regulate. Crime is what our minds must interpret, and then regulate. If that is so, then evil is from the interior. Crime is from the exterior," Eduardo reasoned.

"I'm glad you came to be with me."

"I do love you, Kelly."

I hesitated. "And in my own way, I love you. But please give me time."

He reached, caressing away a tear from my cheek. "You look so tired."

"I'll be fine. I have trouble considering mortality." Our silent communiqué told one another how lost a heart can sometimes feel. "Being with you helps." I clasped his hand near my lips, kissing his fingers. "There are so many stars up in our galaxy. All the vastness of the heavens." I paused. "If there is a supreme being, the Creator has a handful to contend with down here."

SEVENTEEN

"PRESIDENT KENNEDY CAMPAIGNED right up here in Kansas. In our little town," Gran declared. My family had finally reached me through the clotted telephone lines. Gran was going right to work on me. Her voice strained in an attempt to shout her message at me. "He was up here in Kansas," she bellowed. "Where you should be."

"Gran, Kennedy also visited here. The Kennedy newlyweds honeymooned in Acapulco. The Mexicans loved him," I protested.

"Humph."

"Gran, how's your cold?"

"I'm right as rain now. Back to the business at hand. President Kennedy only vacationed down there. He didn't go running off to college there."

"I miss you, Gran," I aimed for another corridor.

"Girl, there are people up here who love you. We have us a national crisis and you're packed off in that primitive country. Why, they even eat dogs down there."

Skirmishing, I twisted the telephone cord. She wouldn't have said such a thing about dogs unless she were terribly upset. Her message was, if they would see fit to eat Lassie, then how could her prized granddaughter be safe. "Gran, the Mexicans have been wonderful to me," I assured her. "And they don't eat dogs."

"I read it. And are you taking to lie for them? Or am I

telling a falsehood? Is that what we mean?" she stormed.

"No, Gran. I mean I've never heard of them eating dogs."

"There's a plenty you haven't heard about, Kelly Anne," she snapped. "If you're not careful, you'll be throwing in with those Mexicans for good. I dread the thought of you not coming back home. That would break my heart right in two." She hesitated, giving a pause to allow her lecture to sink in. "How are your chums down there doing?"

"Sad. But we're holding up."

"It's as bad as it can get up here. As your mother told you, we're all shocked. Now, Kelly Anne, here's what I have in mind. Since you're bent on writing, you get your pen a going. Remember the poems about Mr. Lincoln written by Walter Whitman?"

"Yes."

"That's what I have in mind. You write on our Jack Kennedy. For he surely does need some poems. In the Old Testament, Jeremiah says, 'written with a pen of iron and with the point of a diamond.' You get that Professor Thurston to help you out. He's top notch, as he writes about the Blessed Virgin Mary. Which you should also do."

"He's already written about her, Gran."

"Is that you acting your Jewish heritage?" she bristled.

"Gran, I'll write a poem for Kennedy and dedicate it to you."

"A step in the right direction, girl. I'm an old trout and I've clocked up many a year, but this is the nastiest piece of infamy I've seen." Her voice cracked. "Now, here's your sister to talk to you about how you're needed up here."

"I love you, Gran." There was a lump in my throat I had to swallow away when Kris came on the line. "Did Gran coerce you into pitching me to return to Kansas?"

"We do miss you, Kelly. We worry there might be fighting

down there. You know, because of the Cubans."

"Mexicans don't generally care for Cubans," I explained. "In fact, they tried to pin it on the Cubans right off the bat. One headline read Jackie Kennedy's first words were, 'Oh, no, the traitor Cubans killed my husband.'"

"After the Bay of Pigs, it isn't so farfetched," Kris retorted. "We do miss you. Gran thinks you're being indoctrinated into the Communist party. Mom thinks your morality is going down the drain. Dad is certain your education will suffer."

"And what do you think of my iniquitous degeneracy?"

"Since you're my only sibling, I naturally think you're the victim of a slur. I don't care if you're turning into an ignorant, tawdry, commy tramp."

* * * * *

SANCHEZ HAD CLEARLY had it. With frizzled hair doing an aerial routine, umbra rings around her eyes, and blood-red face, she knew how to mourn. She went to her bedroom to rest.

Nora, Leigh, and I continued to watch the small black and white television set Sanchez had borrowed from an elderly gent one flight up. We attached tin foil flags to the bent rabbit ears to tame the distorted picture. From TV, we learned a mouse-faced, thin-chinned Lee Harvey Oswald was the accused assassin.

Long after the TV had been shut off and the others had gone to bed, I sat at the dining room table. Books were surrounding me as if they were my fortress. But I had turned out the light.

"Why iz it zat you are in ze dark?" Erika quizzed as she turned on the light when she arrived.

"Just thinking. It's been a tragic time for Americans." I

paused, studying her face. Her makeup was marbled, her eyes filmy, and the chalk-white of her eyes was threaded with red. In her semi-drunk stupor, she would jabber incessantly. I braced for an onslaught.

"Vel, ven you die, you got no more the troubles. Kennedy has no more troubles." Erika took a swig of my cold tea. "Zat is right."

"Gran always says being struck off means your soul is going to be retrieved by an army of saints. And some bright, shining creator bedecked in a long robe. What do you think comes next?"

"I sink it iz like ze New Year's Eve party. No more memoryz." She frowned. "But maybe we getz ze new body."

"Death. You believe it is either a lost weekend or a new body?"

"Yah. And life iz when I goez to ze party."

With a wide yawn and a lethargic shrug, Erika went to bed. Lingering after her was the odor of perfume, stale liquor, and the smoke of a nightclub. I stacked my books and carried them to my bedroom.

There were such vastly differing beliefs about what comes next. Hopes, fears, speculations, and contemplations, and no one *knew*. Who are we and what is our relationship to one another? Why do we have such trouble with kindness? Why the struggle for power and fortune? I had no answers. Well, maybe one. Perhaps we are all strays with only an insatiable need to belong. And *belonging* changes within our minds and within the minds of others.

The crisis of November 22, 1963, was dropped right on our doorstep. It was the turning point for much more than our belief in fair play. It wrenched into another turn the moral development of our nation. Although it would stop the frame in our memories, it cut a swath far wider and deeper than we could know. It has never been the same.

* * * * *

SUNDAY MORNING, I sat alone at the apartment's dinner table. Eduardo had flown to Pueblo on business. Sanchez and Belle were at a Christian Science meeting. Erika was in Acapulco on a dirty weekend with a gentleman friend. And Nora was on a *pristine* weekend with her latest sweetheart.

Leigh was still asleep, and I was expecting Carlos. The three of us had decided to watch TV while the Kennedy news coverage was going on. It seemed as though brand new announcements were being released by the moment.

My ploy was to wake Leigh so we might talk. After fixing coffee, I entered her room with cup in hand. Books were sprayed around the floor. I stepped over them, along with the khaki, moss-tinted expedition bag, pick, trowel, and jacket. On her desk, an assortment of small brushes and an ice pick circled the carefully positioned jigsaw of potsherd.

Leigh's body was tucked tightly with the exception of one stray leg that hung from the blanket. Her disheveled hair was strung wildly across her forehead, and her brows were withered into a frown. I tapped her shoulder.

"I've made coffee for you."

Her dark eyes snapped open. "Aw, fuck." She rubbed her eyes, and then smacked the pillow. "What time is it?"

"Noon." I handed her the coffee.

After a sip, she rallied. "Shit! This is boiling."

"I wanted to wake you up. Hot coffee does the trick."

With a scowl, she asked, "What do you want?"

"A chat."

"In bed?" She forged a grin.

"Leigh, I'm not in the mood for humor. I'm feeling down

and out."

"And besides, I'm not your type. Come to think of it... when I first wake up, I'm not anyone's type. What's the doctora like when she wakes?"

"Wonderful. *And* she's cheerful."

"So she is a true beauty with no makeup?"

"Actually, she's more beautiful without makeup. She's soft," I reported.

"And?"

"Sometimes I can't control my base animal instincts and I ravage her."

"Whew!"

"Come on, Leigh, I need to talk about the great hereafter."

"Nora would love to know you've come running to the agnostic dyke for guidance and counsel. So spill it, kid."

"Funny how judgmental we become. If anyone would have told me..." my sentence faded. "Gran has a saying. All Indians walk in single file. At least the one I saw did. It's a statement about prejudice. Anyway, I'm thinking about this life and death thing."

"Shit. You poets are always expounding on death. You're enamored by it. You and the press are having a field day with this assassination. Everyone is going through some cathartic sorrow or another. Especially Vaughn Meader."

"Leigh! You always do that. When I begin communicating, you do that." I sat on the opposite bed. "You must think about death, too."

"It's my fucking life's work. I perform an autopsy on earth. Carve away the layers of centuries to study the remnants of death. So if it's the big D we're talking about, I think about it more than you do. Archeology is the stuff death is made of." With an additional helping of cynicism, she added, "Hey, we're all headed for box city. And you, being a poet, ought to fit in here in Mexico. They wear black for years after the death of a loved one. Black armlets like they're wearing now. As you've noticed, they've got the windows trimmed in black for Kennedy. They even want to get in on *our* mourning. That's how crazy they are about snuffing it."

"You make fun of Mexicans and their traditions. Even their kindnesses. I'll bet you even violate tombs to be malicious."

"Yep. You'll like this tidbit. In Egypt's burial chambers, scribes always get the best seat in the house."

"If you think mourning is so stupid, why are you still mourning your sister's death?"

Her face flushed rose. "Mind your own fucking business, Benjamin. I should never have told you about it."

"I want to be your friend."

"Then stop throwing my past at me." She hesitated, raking back her hair. "So how are things in the People's Republic of Kansas?"

Our mutual grins surprised us both. "Gran is upset about Johnson being president."

"I know I'll regret asking, but what exactly did she say?"

"She referred to him as an old ham bone."

* * * * *

"Hemingway believed the first and final thing you have to do in the world is to last it," Carlos recited. His sullen eyes were shorn of energy. He placed his worn safari bush jacket around the shoulder of the dining room chair, and then numbly collapsed into it. "We wanted more. This changes everything."

My arms circled his sagging shoulders. "Still plan on joining the Peace Corps?"

"Especially now." Carlos flinched. His quivering jaw

clamped. Tears spurt from his glum eyes. "Why him?" His frail question plummeted.

"Maybe the collective humanity we're in is some humanity ethical time warp and we're no longer guided by reason."

While Leigh and Carlos fiddled with the TV controls, I fixed a snack tray. By the time we were ready to watch, Sanchez, Belle, and Hermann had returned. I was pleased Carlos would meet him since I had told Carlos about our suspicions he was a Nazi.

Clustered, we peered at the small screen. We were experiencing group gloom. Kennedy's coffin was being transported on a horse-drawn caisson, led by a riderless horse. Carlos told us the reversed boots in the stirrup were the symbol of a slain soldier.

I motioned to Leigh to join me in the kitchen when I went to brew another pot of tea. While waiting for the water's gurgling boil, I inquired about the phone call she'd received. It was a British-accented woman. I hadn't recognized the voice.

Leigh expelled a deep sigh. Her eyes narrowed. "Her mother is English. Her name's Lindy. She was one of the student's I met on my last excursion. She's an undergrad. Her parents are divorced. She lives half time with her mother in London and the other half with her father in Georgia. Goes from speaking deep South to high Brit."

"If she's from the deep South, it doesn't surprise me you'd have a great deal in common," I indicted.

"Now who is being a little leftist judge?"

"Leigh, tell me you don't have anything in common with her?"

Grinning, Leigh remarked, "It probably would surprise you. Anyway, I wouldn't mind a little Southern comfort under the belt." She then roared. I was certain she'd told that joke numerous times before.

"This Lindy," I pried as I poured water into the teapot, "does she know you're interests are *interesting*?"

"I'm not sure. I do know we seem to be linking. I could be wrong. And she moved out of an apartment after living *with one of the girls* since the term began."

"Maybe she found out the girl was lesbian."

"I don't think so. I heard they were really tight and had even come down here together. They transferred from another college."

"Is that her real name? Lindy?"

"Yes. And she's one gorgeous kid. Always volunteers to assist me. She's a straight A student. I hope she doesn't turn out to be a straight student." She laughed. "Pretty good, huh? Straight student."

Giving the tea a final swirl, I watched the steam billow. We both looked up as Carlos entered the kitchen. His face was pale. Our glances strung together as he reported with disbelief, "Lee Harvey Oswald has been shot. Someone killed him."

Bewildered, I repeated, "Killed the assassin?"

His answer was barely audible. "Yes. It happened. The guy they think killed Kennedy. They were transferring him to another jail or something. It was being televised in the States. A murder on television." His voice strained.

Staggered by the news, we entered the living room. Both older women were wailing in low-pitched moans. Their tears gushed into lace-trimmed hankies. Hermann attempted to comfort them by saying there was way too much turmoil in politics.

My jaw tightened. As the frenzied reports detailed the murder, we were left with a fusillade of questions. Belle, with her voice down in her boots, condemned Oswald's killer, as well as Oswald. Sanchez agreed, but Hermann said it takes more compassion to forgive the guilty than to sympathize with the innocent.

I mumbled a bitter, "I'll bet," for it sounded as if it might be a Nazi excuse.

The melody of Howe's 'Battle Hymn of the Republic' streamed like a fireball through my thoughts. The Pledge of Allegiance was a flow of words that became some lost reveille. But I believed the large droplets raining from our eyes would turn to frost before they reached our hearts.

We would long recall the anguish. We would not let it be forgotten. Our nation's wound would long lament the hush from within.

It was the hush that nearly deafened us.

* * * * *

IT WAS TIME for our somber pilgrimage to honor our martyred president.

While John Fitzgerald Kennedy's coffin was taken by caisson to Saint Mathew's Cathedral for a funeral Mass, the American colony of Mexico City assembled at the Basilica of Guadalupe. Seats had been reserved for Americans.

As young John-John was saluting his father's flag-draped coffin, we were a country away saluting Kennedy in the only way we could. The final leg of our journey across Mexico City to the basilica was by streetcar. Nora, Leigh, Carlos, and I traversed the city in silence.

Arriving, there was still only minimal conversation. We made our way through the plaza, passing cocoa-skinned, wooden-faced merchants. We stopped for Nora, Leigh, and I to put mantillas on our heads. While we busily pinned down our lace head scarves, a Mexican handed Carlos a small American flag. Carlos fished his pocket for change, but the peddler moved away. He had wanted to give an American one of his flags today.

I was in awe when we entered the basilica. It was magnificent. Transfixed by the image above the altar, I wished my Gran could see this. At the atrium was the venerated, miraculous painting of the Virgin Mary. I recalled hearing that Kennedy had visited this place. He had worshiped the image of the Madonna. I reflected, wondering if he had prayed for guidance and peace or if he had prayed for a world without violence.

I bowed my head. My side-glance rested on Carlos' hands. He gripped the fabric of the small flag. After the reverential services, he handed the flag to me to keep in my handbag. He then told me I should take care of it for him until he returned from the Peace Corps. I told him I would be honored.

When Mass was finished, we filed out into the plaza as if we were weary warriors returning from a lost battle. Kennedy's charisma and vision had ended. The Mass had ended. But the memory of blazing candles, the aroma of incense, the Latin chanting, and the congregation of fellow Americans would remain.

None of us could grasp it. But we all knew we'd been transformed. The chill of reality caught us. The fragile thread that ties us to life's most precious aspirations had been weakened. Our leader was lost. The life of our youthful, vigorous president had been severed.

It not only had shattered Camelot, it had rearranged history. It had rearranged us. It was seared into our memories. It painted our justice system with the primary colors showing our deficit—our infamy. It displayed our inability to resolve a complexity that yielded only faded images on tattered canvas. Throughout the muddied investigation, a futile search would continue. Our frailty was to be exposed. It would also brush away our own beliefs of immortality, for a portion of our best hope had been destroyed.

No one lives forever. Youth of the 1960s, like all youth, believed otherwise. But this act intruded upon our security.

We shall miss him. We shall miss the part of *us* that was Camelot.

PART III—ALL LOVELY THINGS

Death devours all lovely things:
Lesbia with her sparrow
Shares the darkness,—presently
Every bed is narrow.

After all, my erstwhile dear,
My no longer cherished,
Need we say it was not love,
because it perished?

- Edna St. Vincent Millay "Passer Mortuus Est"
(Harper and Row, Publishers, Inc. *Second April*)

EIGHTEEN

NORMALLY, THANKSGIVING IS my favorite holiday.

My first American holiday in my beloved Mexico had been marked by assassination. Carlos was spending the four-day holiday basking in Acapulco. He needed the time away, and with a carload of students, he invaded the shores of Mexico's primo resort. Leigh was off on an expedition with a couple of professors and several other students. Eduardo was visiting his grandparents in Pueblo.

And Cres had invited me to spend Friday, Saturday, and Sunday with her in Cuernavaca. I accepted. She would leave earlier in the week, and I would arrive on Friday. It would be perfect. I'd be in D.F. for Thanksgiving so Nora wouldn't need to be stuck alone with no one on the holiday with her. The plan was Nora, Erika, and I would dine out together. Erika didn't give a hoot about the pilgrims but was happy to accompany Nora and me.

The three of us decided to dine at the *Chalet Suizo*. The Swiss Chalet would be serving turkey with all the trimmings for their American patrons. That would take care of Nora's concerns for the holidays. But it left me concocting a goofy alibi for the three days in Cuernavaca. Nora did not want to spend those days out of my sight, but I told her I was going to Acapulco with Carlos. He agreed to back my story. He was a willing co-conspirator. I vowed that Nora's bleating question-and-answer session would not rile, nor would it rattle me.

Her tirade began after the serving of pumpkin pie. Taking it in stride, deception seemed justified for all the carping I endured.

Cuernavaca promised the tranquility I needed. There would be a bloodletting of my words, forming what I hoped would pass for poetry. I could get my studies done. My ragtag alibi was filled with deceit, but it was for a worthy cause— three full days with my temptress and my typewriter.

* * * * *

BEING A CUERNAVACA castaway meant sending Nora out for a last minute pastry break. While she was at the bakery, I wrote a note telling her Carlos had decided to leave early. Then I walked three blocks in a direction opposite the bakery to where Rodolfo awaited. How I hated trickery. But I was discovering I was fairly competent at it.

My pulse quickened as we drove through Cuernavaca. Called the city of gardens, the atmosphere was one of relaxed elegance. Tempera-washed, coral-pink colonial homes were topped by tile roofs and surrounded by high fences. Lavish gardens, exotic birds, and promised tranquility were the semi-tropical city's mystery. I breathed in the balmy, sweet fragrance.

Cres had mentioned her retreat's decor was near to her self-description. With a colonial ambiance, the mission-white hacienda offered perfect seclusion. It was rococo luxury with colonnades of glazed tile arches and windows decorated with filigreed swirls of ornamental iron. It was magnificent.

Her villa was designed to offer sanctuary. It was surrounded by swaying palms and blazing floral colors. It was not only the doctora's hideaway, but it seemed it was her old friend. And it was a friend with whom her spirit mellowed.

Again, I was led to an adjoining bedroom. I was certain it hadn't fooled the villa's caretakers, Vincente and Isabel Garcia. Isabel, with a braid twisted around her head, had a round face that reflected her soft temperament. Vincente was jovial. His stocky form was slightly bent, but his steps were hurried and light.

I knew, while chatting with them in my stilted Spanish, they were appraising me. They were gracious, and I didn't mind their scrutiny. They only wanted the best for their employer. And they were willing to put anyone through a check gate.

After freshening up, I met Cresida on the terrace. The courtyard was spectacular. We reclined on pearl-white wicker chairs. I thanked Isabel for the luscious looking pina colada. I toasted, "*Amiga mia.*"

"And to you, my lovely one," she lifted her glass. Her hair flowed over her shoulders and her lashes gleamed as they caught the sun's rays. "I hope you'll enjoy being here. Vincente and Isabel are marvelous. I sent Isabel to France to be instructed in continental fare. She is a superb chef now. And Vincente oversees the garden with much love."

"They seem nice."

The conversation dwindled a moment before her eyes swayed away from mine. "I've missed you."

"With the tragedy, it's been hectic."

"And have you been in contact with Mr. Underwood?"

"Not since playing tennis. I took him back to his hotel, instructed the staff to get him to his room, and wake him in time for his lecture, and then I returned home. He called the next morning. I didn't even bother talking with him. No one needs to be mistreated." Considering my mother had been abused for most of her married life by an alcoholic, I saw the trap ahead. I didn't want to walk into the jaws of a bottle.

"He was not a gentleman."

"Cres, I felt so badly about that day. I appreciate your assistance. I hadn't wanted to be seen with him. I hadn't wanted to be with him."

Her hand grazed mine. "My darling, you've told me you see men. It isn't my intention to complicate your life. I'm grateful for your honesty."

"My feelings are complicated."

"The young man of whom you spoke, Eduardo—what do you tell him when you are with me?"

"Only that I'm away with a friend."

Her hand remained shrouding mine. "He has no idea?"

"I guard my pronouns."

Her full cinnamon lips curved. "There are parts of Europe where people are much more enlightened. But Latin men aren't accepting. Diego Rivera did overlook the dalliances of Frida. But he was sexually robust himself."

"That is another way of saying he was disloyal to her."

"Another way, however, it doesn't excuse his actions. For Frida considered his infidelity cruel."

"In my area, stepping out on your wife is the talk of the town."

"Yes." She glanced across the gardens. "The people in your area of the United States are not known to be the most approving about such matters. And certainly, they wouldn't approve of lesbianism. Your family would find it unacceptable, no?"

"My parents would definitely not approve. Not with a man before marriage and certainly, not with a woman." I sipped the refreshing pineapple and coconut flavored drink.

With a playful smirk, she spoke, "I am not only the wrong sex, I am also twice your age. I'm certainly not a suitor you would feel comfortable taking home with you."

"Probably not. But then I'm not in your social circles either. Anyway, I'm sure one day you'll toss me aside for some gorgeous nineteen-year-old."

"Only if you don't marry first."

"I'm not marrying. At least not for *many* years. I'm not even considering the future."

"One must not preclude planning a future of some type."

I realized she was probing. I turned her game. "What are your future plans?"

She smiled. "Continuing my practice, my teaching. And yours?"

"Writing volumes of erotic poetry based on our delicious adventures." I inspected her face. There was such passion, and I wanted to unbutton my emotions. "Cres, I love…."

When my sentence broke apart, she repeated the word for me. "Love?"

"I love being with you." I had retracted my original expression. My throat was parched; my feelings harnessed.

"I also love being with you," she cautiously responded.

Grinning at our mutually muzzled declarations, I chuckled aloud. "Well, doctora, I would say that must mean we both love one another's company."

Her eyelids lowered. "I would not refute that for an instant."

* * * * *

AFTER TWO DAYS filled to the brim with swimming, sunning, loving, and relaxing, I was in the soul of tranquility. I had been pampered, fed scrumptious delicacies, and revitalized with exercise. Sensual and otherwise. The sadness of last week had eased.

Each embrace renewed me. Each orgasm recharged me.

Cres and I shared love, laughter, and I was beginning to give over my heart. I wanted to write of my feelings for her. I wanted to shout them. I would settle on scribbling a few careful lines of poetry dedicating my love to this woman.

Crawling from the bed, careful not to wake Cres, I leaned and kissed her temple. I eased the Siamese silk bedspread around her shoulders. Robe-clad, I went out onto the terrace. I'd left my notebook on the terrace table. I strolled past the decorative stone arches, observing circlet shadows beneath my steps.

When I sat at the table, I took a few moments to go over 'The Lie' in my head. We would be returning to Mexico City tomorrow afternoon. I would be dropped off at Carlos' apartment. He would accompany me back to my apartment for Nora's benefit. The Lie would be solid and believable.

My thoughts turned sadly to leaving my goddess, Cresida. Even watching her soft breathing excited me. Our torrid, irrepressible love was splendor. I attempted to extract honesty. Could it be this was mere infatuation? Not at all likely. I wondered how this version of love could be so intense. Glancing down at my robe, thoughts trickled. Some portion of me wanted to be in her life for a very long time. Perhaps, I admitted, forever. I had been warned she doesn't have long relationships. Even if I were falling deeply in love with her, I was aware we are swept down the street of life by a broom of uncertainty.

I could be left behind at any given moment.

But I was unable to turn away, even from this love of total dubiety. I could not deny my love for her. It was beyond sexual desire. Yes, when she brushed her hair back with a flip of her hand, there was desire. Yes, when she laughed, I was enamored. And when she bent, exposing her cleavage, my glance would anchor to her with lust. That tethering glance would send us into seclusion. When she placed a gardenia in my hand, the one she had brushed over my body, there was a raw yearning. Even when we played chess, and her chessmen vacuumed mine from the board, I wanted her. I was captivated. Her fingertips gently caressed my body as no others ever had. I feared I might never again feel like this. Her lips nibbled tenderly, her eyes glimmered for my affection, and although sensuous, all these were more than tools of wanton satisfaction.

The streamers attached to my heart became fireworks. When she spoke English, the preciseness enticed me. When she spoke French, she lured me. And when she spoke Spanish, she tantalized me. Lust placed aside—there was some magnetic, emblazoned emotion that made our souls harmonious. I cared deeply though she had never expressed the depth of her emotions to me, and probably never would. When I met that truth, I knew I wasn't merely beguiled by her. It wasn't simple infatuation. This I recognized.

"My darling," Cres whispered into my ear as her hands glided over my back. "You are writing by moonlight. Romantic thoughts? Or are you unable to sleep?"

"Both," I said, twisting round and encircling her hips with my arms. I pulled her to me. "I would rather be doing something else by moonlight." Our glances went steamy.

"Yes?"

"Yes. Let's go skinning-dipping."

"Swim nude in the pool?" Her eyebrows arched.

"As lethal as it might sound, I promise I have my lifeguard badge. Everyone in the house is sleeping. They can't see the shallow end of the pool anyway." I slipped out of my robe and raced to the pool.

She followed slowly at first, and then caught up with me as we neared the pool's edge. I unfastened the belt of her robe. As it slid past her shoulders, I leaned up to kiss her. We embraced tightly.

Moonlight was overhead and tussocks of grass spurting from between stones were beneath our feet. The scent of her perfume, the alluvial soil, and spicy aroma of sleeping flowers mingled. Moonbeams projected lacy shapes of leaves against the metallic reflections on the indigo pool.

As I held her near, I felt her grasping me to her. "Cuernavaca is ours."

"Only ours?"

"I have never before brought a lover here."

"Cuernavaca is ours," I confirmed.

We dove into the pool. Splashing, thrashing, we swam two laps before she caught my arm when we turned at the pool's shallow end. Floating toward her, I began blanketing her body with kisses. We leaned against the pool's lip. I began twisting with sensory palpitations. There was the occasional flutter of waves as we drew deep breaths and twirled underwater. Her amative caresses enticed me. I relished the luscious delicacy of her. With each tantalizing touch of pleasure, my body was prodded onward. I quivered when I felt a sheet of water flowing over me. Immersed in an amative baptism of love, my senses were being devoured.

Our bodies magnetized. I felt my exhausted limbs bounce against the bottom of the pool. With a burst of energy, I exploded through the water. Again, I felt the detonation of the lambent flame that was her body's warmth. Our legs braided, flesh wrapping flesh. Rekindled, we ignited again and again.

There was no denying my ravenous craving for her. I could not explain the way she could secure me to her. And within the limb wrap, my heart was hers. She could lift me to unknown corners of excitement. She could soothe me, making my heart sedate and gentle.

The waters often swamped us, but our spirits were

buoyantly seeking euphoria. Bluish fluorescent patches of light rocked on the pool's surface. Beams against wetted tiles became mango-colored crystals. And we embraced. There was the calm of a post-orgasmic pause. Tucked against her, I wanted never to forget the moment.

We climbed from the pool, shaking our hair, and laughing. She turned to me, and I looked into the face of love. "What would you say," I murmured, "if I told you I love you?"

She inspected my face. "What is it you would want me to say?" Her eyes became moist. She blinked fiercely.

"I would want you to say you believe I've explored my emotions. I know what I'm saying. You know I haven't experienced all the permutations of love, but I have searched my heart for my feelings. I wouldn't want you to say I'm too young to know what love is."

Easing from my embrace, she turned, gazing up at the moon. "Then say the words, I shall not respond by telling you you're too young."

I walked around her, confronting her. Face to face. "Why did you move away from me?"

"I'm uncertain." Her lips moved slightly after her words were spoken.

"I think you *are* certain. We both are. And I think you love me, too."

"Yes." Then she repeated, this time, not looking away, "Yes."

* * * * *

"NO DOILIES IN your life," I teased Carlos. I had to nearly batter the door down to awaken him. I glanced around the daylight drabness of his room. The gauzily draped window coverings were faded. I pushed a stack of papers and books from his bed and sat. "Aren't you going to dress so we can go back to my apartment together?"

"Oh, yeah. The Lie. Sorry. I was hammered when I got home. Needed to sleep." He had used his blanket as a shawl around his nude body when answering the door. It dropped from his athletic body. He had only his socks on. "I'm the door prize," he muttered.

Looking the other way, my eyes diverted toward a lamp on the bedstand. It was cochineal-colored, chipped, and under a gaudy magenta shade. "Open a window. It is absolutely rank in here," I directed. "And get dressed. There's only so much a woman can resist," I teased.

Turning, I watched as he pulled up his trousers. My glance meandered. Light rays were trajectories through the drapes, spilling untamed designs. Clothes were piled into bundles. He rummaged for a crumpled shirt. He smiled as he put on a tie that had been a lasso on the dresser over his head. A dousing of aftershave combined with the odor of Tom's paints, turpentine, clay, and mustiness.

"When's your maid due back in?"

"Tuesday. She's in for a treat this week," he answered with a hearty laugh. His eyes did a panorama of the room. "You don't like slumming it?"

I smiled as he wrinkled his sunburned nose. "I didn't come for a cocktail party. The Lie," I acknowledged. "I've got to get home, study, and write letters. *Tengo que escribirle a mis padres.*"

"Some Mexicans speak what they call Juarez English. Well, Kel, you speak Brownville Spanish."

"That bad?"

"Worse. But keep practicing." He took a swig of warm beer that had been sitting on the window's ledge. "Did you have a good time this weekend?"

"Yes. Carlos, you're my best friend down here, but I can't tell you more for now."

"That's cool. It's enough, Kel."

* * * * *

WE LOOKED LIKE tourists as we trudged back to my apartment. Carlos was swinging my suitcase, and I hauled my overnight case. "I'm not grilling you," he began, "so feel free to shake your head. Was your weekend worth The Lie?"

"Yes. I'm rested and invigorated. How was Acapulco?"

"In Plutarch's *Conjugal Precepts*, he states when the candles are out, all women are fair. My roommate might agree, but not me. I tell you, it was slim pickings. Everyone was paired up. Except me and a few bar women. I'm sure they were hoof-and-mouth carriers." Carlos switched the suitcase to his other hand so he could grab my free hand. "Who wants a lifetime of scratchy balls for a weekend romp?"

"You didn't get laid?"

"Nope," he said with a groan. "See that old guy over there?" Carlos pointed to a decrepit beggar with a strong resemblance to Le Sorcier de Trois Freres. "The one with the Briggs and Stratton haircut. Well, feature him with a long, scraggly wig. It was a lonely time of it. But the sun and beach were outstanding."

Rounding the corner, we sighted Sanchez. Her arms were loaded down with groceries, and her shopping satchel was blooming full. She held the grocery sack so tightly she could barely peer over the rim of the sack. Carlos manipulated the bundles from her arms.

"Thank you, dear boy," she said. Her voice fawned over him. "You're so kind. I do miss Lupe when she takes the day off."

"Have the others returned yet?" I inquired as I took the satchel from her grasp. "I'll carry this."

"Thank you, dear. Erika is in. Nora is out with her young man—Gabriel. Leigh stayed over with a fellow student named Linda."

"Could it have been Lindy?" I pried.

"Why, yes. That was It—Lindy." She scouted out Carlos. "She stayed with a woman. I did ask. I don't like my girlies staying with men."

Carlos declared, "I assure you, Kelly and I slept in separate quarters."

"Yes. Very separate," I verified. After Carlos had delivered the packages to the kitchen, I walked him back to the landing. "Thanks. I'm glad we ran into Sanchez. It validates The Lie." On my tiptoes, I reached, kissing his beard. "I appreciate your covering, my male butterfly."

"Did you know female butterflies are larger and live longer than males?" He would often play the game of accelerating information.

"Did you know that male butterflies wear perfume? Pheromones?" I asked.

"I didn't know you knew about butterflies." He then challenged. "Did you know females usually only mate once?" He knew he had me when I didn't respond. He had won the block building of facts no one cared about. He queried, "And did you know they have coiled tongues?"

Sheepishly, I swallowed before spinning around to enter the apartment. "Ciao, Carlos."

"No more butterfly facts?"

"Not after the last one."

"Kelly?" his voice strained while he calculated. "Who *were* you with?"

"Ciao," I repeated. With one skip, I was inside and had

shut the door. My eyes were sealed as my head pressed against the door. I was transparent with Carlos, and I knew it. I couldn't have lied to him, even if I had wanted to try. Secrets are some sort of gap between truths.

NINETEEN

CHATTING IN A muffled conference, Leigh and Paul were seated at a corner table in the student center. Collaborating as they leaned on their elbows, they sipped soft drinks. I took an empty chair and confronted Leigh. "You were with Lindy last night."

Smirking, she crossed her arms. "Yep, I mean really, I *am* in love."

My glance vaulted back to Paul. He trilled, "A budding romance, me thinks."

"This morning Sanchez told Nora," I gossiped. "Nora whispered to me that she bet you were with one of those *queer* women."

Cackling loudly, Paul slapped the tabletop. "Is this Nora person always so bitchy?"

"I live in a fucking coven," Leigh remarked. "Nora goes for public hangings when it comes to gays. But Nora is the all-time sperm collector, so she shouldn't talk."

Paul choked on his Coke as he giggled several stanzas. "Well, Lindy is a lovely young woman. A true find," he added with well-lubricated drama.

"Find? You make her sound like a fossil or a silver chalice." I issued a wry expression.

"What Paul means is she's an absolute doll. Doesn't resemble a Pithecanthropus Erectus," Leigh divulged with a laugh. "Or any other erectus." She leaned and confided, "She should be here in a few minutes."

"I'll wait." I glanced down at my watch. "No matter how long it takes. I've got to see your true find."

"Well," Paul droned, "I've got to scoot." He adjusted his ascot, grabbed his briefcase, and flounced away.

"How's the fabulous frock?" Leigh inquired.

"Frock?"

"Brit word for doctor."

"Oh. Cresida is fine. You ought to see her villa."

"From what I hear, she's flush. If I had her bucks and she had my feathers, we'd both be tickled."

"Does Lindy relate to your humor?"

"First time we met, she asked, 'Whoever are you?' in her Brit bitch accent."

"So fill me in."

"We'd been doing clandestine flirting through the trip. Leaning against one another. She pushed the hair out of my eyes when I worked, and I would push her cap back for her. We got back to D.F., and I offered to assist her with her project. You know, tidy her field notes. When we got to her apartment, she asked if I would like to stay over. The score was on the board."

"And?"

"It was wonderful," she gloated. "Those European boarding schools must crank 'em out. Whew!"

"I'll bet," I said with a grin.

"Now, talk to me about the frock."

I revealed, "She's a love tech." Leigh's face became a burlesque question mark. "Can't you be serious a minute?"

"Okay." She sat up stiffly. "So spill it. I can't hold this pose forever."

"I told her I love her."

"You said *love*?" Leigh lurched forward. "I told you about

her. She's skittish. A heartbreaker. And that might frighten her off."

"I don't think so."

"Think! Shit, you poets are all on Froggy's magic carpet ride. And the Kansas wind has blown your gray cells to Oz. Kelly, what makes you think you're any different from the ballerina or the other artists? If she calls again, tell her it was all a drastic mistake."

"She implied she feels the same way."

"Concerning the doc, brace yourself for the worst, Benjamin." Leigh glanced over her shoulder. "There's Lindy, by the door."

Pivoting, I clamored, "Leigh, you never mentioned she's colored."

"Don't you love it? I can insult the pea-soupers and sharecroppers all at one time. After all, unlike a true bigot, I don't dislike Negroes any more than I do Limeys."

Examining the attractive, soft bronze woman, I first noticed her flashing, deep ebony eyes. They housed intelligence. She was long-limbed with the body of an athlete.

Her carriage was that of a model. Her neck was long, Audrey Hepburn long, and her clothing was European with elegant lines. Her hair was stylishly formed into a lamb-like, short Afro. Her complexion was lovely and her smile exquisite. "What does she see in you?"

"I'm her goddess." Leigh's eyebrows shot up. "That's right. She not only thinks I hung the moon but created the galaxy."

"What a shocker. She actually goes for you."

"Yep."

"She's magnificent. I guess you'd call her mulatto."

"You'd call her mulatto," Leigh corrected. "I call her my favorite little darky. But if I were you, I wouldn't call her that.

Stick with mulatto, Brit, or Leigh's woman."

"You're a complete bigot. An intolerant racist. It's all most of us can do to converse with you. Why would she give you the time of day?"

"Because I adore her. And she also gives me the time of night. And the time of my life."

Reaching over, I gave Leigh's arm a squeeze. "I'm happy for you. Even the most lowlife, insensitive person still deserves love."

"Trying to tell me I hit the jackpot, Benj?"

* * * * *

ADMITTING TO MYSELF that Leigh might be right about Cresida, I found it an excruciating week. Although the doctora had mentioned her week was packed, I'd expected at least a telephone call. As the days dwindled to the weekend, I became increasingly depressed.

I hadn't expected to hear from Eduardo, but he called to invite me along to a fencing match in Puebla. He asked me to spend Saturday with him, and I agreed. Because I had worked diligently on my studies the entire week, I felt I owed myself a reprieve. The hidden agenda was to keep myself from fretting over the fact I worried about being dumped by Cres.

Eduardo arrived early, and the drive was pleasant. We carefully avoided pushing one another's buttons. When we arrived at the gym, I spied Michel, who had finished his pools in the tournament earlier. To my distress, Michel was with a French woman named Renee. She spoke no English and in fact, acted as though the thought of it was abhorrent to her. I hadn't practiced my French for a while, so I welcomed the opportunity to chat with her.

Her frenetic French was as energetic as she was. Because

of my friendship with Nora, I'd hoped I wouldn't like Renee. But I did. Attractive, but in a way one wonders how she could be—she was also *perky*. Like, maybe, she had a glucose IV drip going off somewhere. Her diminutive, wiry frame was never still. Her nose was slightly too small for her face, and her eyes were too large. They were coal-dark and thickly lashed. Her smile became a small rosebud. Her narrow chin gave her a doll-like appearance. Jet black hair was short and combed, pixie-style, toward her milky face. Everything about her seemed out of balance, and but she was adorable.

Eduardo had changed into his fencing uniform. During his match, I saw him in a new dimension. With controlled lunges, agility, and grace, the execution of his moves was poetical. After winning the competition, he suggested we see the city.

Puebla, the Rome of Mexico, was lovely. We toured the cathedral and the Hidden Convent of Santa Monica. The convent, he explained, had a racy past. In 1660, it was used as a residence of colonial wives whose husbands were abroad. Then, later, it was an institution to reform prostitutes. After that, what else? It was a young girl's college. Finally, before becoming a museum, it was a convent. The gutsy little nuns defied the edict that would attempt to stomp out Mexico's conventual establishments. With elaborate trap doors, secret passageways and the balls of Huns, those nuns escaped detection. If walls could blab, I thought.

Eduardo sensed my reticence to stay over with him. I had praised his sallies and parries with the sword but had not encouraged his amorous feelings. That had not escaped his detection. The drapery of night lowered, and we drove back to D.F. with amiable conversation. We were both convinced a friendship would be salvaged if we allowed no confrontation.

I entered the darkened apartment. When I tucked myself into bed, I seemed lonely. Dangling ribbons of thought waved over me. Eduardo had finally accepted my words about taking it slowly. He had not smothered me. He had not expected me to climb onto the pyre with him. He had no questions; I gave up no answers. That got us home without an argument—which, I surmised, was either a beginning or an ending.

Uncertain if I felt alone because Eduardo stepped away or because Cresida hadn't called, I unsuccessfully attempted sleep. Ibsen says the strongest person is one who stands alone. Eduardo and I had spent the day standing alone, even when near.

I may disappear on the sword of loneliness, I meditated, but one phone call from the doctora could revive me.

* * * * *

THERE WAS DEFINITELY a slight reverse spin on my life. Chaos proves to breed difficulty, I mused. I would throw myself deeper into my studies. Academics allowed no time for invading concerns about life's decisions.

I was being ignored by someone I was falling in love with. The affair was thick with taboos. A lesbian relationship with a woman twice my age was not an enormous societal laurel. I'd made a fine, socially acceptable man the consolation prize. And in the process was doing great injury to my heart. Cresida might never again call.

When she did, I was in the very center of victory. She explained she had called twice before but hadn't left a message. She didn't want to arouse suspicion by leaving her name. She suggested we meet for lunch. I quickly accepted.

When I returned to my books, Nora, the grand inquisitor, wanted to talk. She had news. Her mother would be arriving to spend Christmas in Mexico. Gab, her new flame, was wonderful. Midway through her flight of enchantment, sexually speaking, I grumbled that I was hungry. We decided to go out for chile rellenos so she could give me the details on a full tummy. She detailed the affair with each step of the way to the café.

We slid into the booth, and I gave up hopes of a quiet dinner. Nora had not wound down. "What are you planning for Christmas?" she delved.

"I'm not certain. Maybe I'll go back to Kansas. Leigh is going on a dig."

"With that colored girl?"

"Lindy. Leigh told me they might even move in together after next quarter."

"Honestly!" Nora blustered.

"I like Lindy. She's good for Leigh."

"Kelly, Leigh has been acting nice to get you on her side."

"I'm not an apologist for her lesbian cause, but she has a perfect right to live however she wants. So let's switch topics. Tell me more about Gab."

"Kelly, I miss doubling with you like we used to. I'll check and see if Gab has any available friends."

"Nora, I'm too busy…" I began to dispute.

"We used to have such fun. What's the matter? Don't you like me anymore? What did I do wrong?"

"Nothing. Fine." It wouldn't hurt me to double with her. And not doubling with her was killing her. As expressed on her woefully contorted, pitiful face, Nora missed our togetherness. "Yes, Nora, we'll make plans."

"Oh, Kelly, you don't know how happy that makes me. It will be like old times."

She knew she had successfully blindsided me. And she reveled in it. I took a bite, feeling a spicy heat of the rellenos. "So hot it makes your eyes water and your skin shutter," I commented with a barking cough.

"When we get back, I'll call Gab. Ask him to find someone suitable for you."

"Fine," I agreed. But not with any degree of true sincerity. The legitimacy of adolescence often seems stuck on the apathetic. I squinted down at the meal that was hot enough to melt bedrock. With a throaty anthem of resignation, I acquiesced. "Nora, we can do whatever you'd like. Please feel free to make the plans." She would anyway. It went without saying.

TWENTY

YEARS TICK OFF in everyday increments. Bookmarkers are placed on special dates. For me, December 12, 1963, was a day that would leave a permanent imprint. I was to witness the holiday set aside for the Patroness of Mexico. And I was to see it through the vision and wisdom of Professor Calvin Thurston.

I was aware of the legend of the miracle of Guadalupe. Back in 1531, a pious Indian named Juan Diego had seen the vision of a dark-skinned Virgin of Guadalupe. She had instructed Juan to gather roses from the barren, frosty slope. He obediently gathered roses, bundle them in his tunic, then returned to present them to a dubious bishop. Per instructions of the lady, Diego reported. When Juan opened his tunic, the roses tumbled to the feet of the cleric. Stamped inside the cloak remained an imprinted image of the Virgin. And so the Lourdes of Mexico was built. The cloak was displayed behind a thick plate of glass with a grandiose gold frame that was placed on the cathedral's main altar.

Each year, Thurston conducted a pilgrimage. He had disclosed the conversion of faith that he had years before. When he lived in New York, he'd visited Mexico several times. He'd thought the Guadalupe Basilica a waste of tourist time. Finally, he did visit. He told how he had ignored the Madonna on so many occasions and how she had turned his life upside down. He converted to Catholicism and moved to Mexico City. He had written extensively of the miracle of

Guadalupe, as well as his internal miracle.

I'd invited Eduardo. We followed behind Thurston and the others. Eduardo was much less captivated by the tour than I was. For me, the love and magic Thurston wove together as he led us through the legend was enthralling.

When we entered the Chapel of the Little Well on the basilica grounds, I spotted Carlos standing alone. While Eduardo and the group examined the waters that were believed to have miraculous healing power, I moved near Carlos. Under the guise of pretending to borrow Carols' area map, we exchanged greetings. He had been scrutinized by Eduardo, and all three of us were aware of that.

"Getting up to any tricks at this soiree?" Carlos questioned.

"None. Eduardo is in his lukewarm mode. I should be so lucky as to reside in that state of enchantment right now."

"Lover's inferno?"

"Something like that." My answer was as honest as I could forfeit.

"Well, keep kissing those frogs, Kel. There are a few princes left."

"I wouldn't trust most men if I had eyes in the back of my head," I teased.

Carlos gazed at the flushing waters. "Thurston provides a great excursion. After we're through here, you'll wonder where the Creator ends and man begins."

"I've got to scram. Eduardo is glaring at me."

"Hasn't he found the art of fun? He looks uptight."

"See you later, Carlos."

Eduardo took my hand, in a show of possessiveness, I assumed. Pride of ownership, perhaps. But I smiled as I gave his hand a squeeze. We walked silently toward the basilica.

Once inside, I could feel the spiritual energy of the

pilgrims. Snippets of prayer faded in and out, as we passed by the faithful. Energy rushed through my tense body.

"And now," Thurston spoke reverently, in a hushed manner, "we shall gather to show respect to the miracle I know most about." We streamed past the sacred relic. A multitude of gifts, flowers, and tokens had been presented to the Virgin. My eyes tethered with the cloak's image. The face of the Virgin was one of warmth and kindness. Certainly, I reasoned, the gentle people could be represented by no finer image of kindly benevolence. Unadorned, there was a resplendent calm expression on the lady's face.

Then one of the other students leaned near, cautioning, "Watch your handbag. This is a pickpocket's holiday."

* * * * *

BACK OUT ON the square a carnival atmosphere was flourishing. There was celebration aside reverence. Peddlers, entertainers, and pious Indians milled. Aquiline-nosed dancers were bedizened with feather-fringed costumes. Sombreroed mariachis strummed guitars.

I was mesmerized by the roping streams of torches held high by pilgrims. They snaked their way up the winding mountain's side. Burning torches flickered, releasing long clouds of smoke. The air was thick.

Lines of Indians crawled through the plaza on scuffed and lacerated knees. Most of them had edged their way for over four miles from the Zocalo as an act of faith. Garments and squares of rugs were thrown in their path to ease their pain. By the time they reached the plaza, the chunks of material were blood-stained.

Thurston murmured, "They bring gifts. Their veneration and belief allow them to endure pain."

"Surely, a supreme being wouldn't want suffering?" I countered. There was sadness when considering the anguished strain on their faces.

"Their suffering is also their joy," Thurston replied with benevolence.

"Joy?" I repeated.

He understood my skepticism. For it probably once belonged to him. "Miss Benjamin, belief is never a rudderless, drifting of one's soul. Often, it is only through our suffering that we come to know and accept real joy. And therein lies the miracle that counts."

* * * * *

WE WERE FATIGUED by the time we reached the apartment. Eduardo suggested we talk in the small courtyard garden behind the building. We sat on a wrought-iron loveseat. My head rested against his shoulder. Looking up at the pin-point stars, I sighed. "This is relaxing."

"Yes. Kelly, if only we could always be together like this. If only we could be near one another for all times."

"Eduardo, I realize our relationship isn't perfect. But I'm attempting to understand myself. You're finished with school. Settled in a profession you love. I'm still learning and exploring."

"I do not require a date be set. If we could only plan a future together, I would be happy."

"I can't promise anything."

"You know I would never allow harm to come to you. I would always provide and care for you and our family. I would be a devoted husband and father," he vowed.

"I realize that. But I'm not settled down yet."

"The man you spoke with. The tall, reddish-haired man

wearing the tan corduroy suit—do you care for him?"

"We're friends. He recently joined the Peace Corps. Eduardo, it isn't a person keeping me from making a commitment. I'm not ready to make plans for the future."

Grimly, he grilled, "Then what is it? Me?"

"No. It isn't you. It's me. Right now, I'm simply unable to give you the kind of love you seem to require." I closed my eyes and then suddenly buried my face against his chest. "I know you're a good man. And in my own way, I love you for your goodness. Maybe I'll never be able to give you enough love. That's one of my concerns."

"Perhaps," he said as he stood, "I should not expect love to be there."

I reached for his arm. I felt his coat sleeve pass through my fingertips as he walked away. "Eduardo," I called.

The gate clicked harshly as it shut after him. I shivered as I made my way up the winding stairway. I pulled the edges of my sweater nearer for warmth. I whispered to my loneliness, "*Ayer noche hizo mucho frio.*" And will be much colder, I predicted.

* * * * *

"*Is fait beua temps?*" I issued a weather report when the doctora reached for my hand. We gave one another a friendly fleece-soft kiss. Her chic, honey-colored outfit went wonderfully with her coloring.

"Of course," she elaborated, "the weather, as well as the day, is wonderful when you're in it." We walked inside *The Ambassadeurs*. "And what has been happening with you, my lovely American?"

"I've been looking forward to seeing you again," I answered. We were seated in the posh, fashionable dining room. "I attended the Guadalupe festivities."

"And you enjoyed it?"

"I did enjoy it a great deal, yes."

Flipping back the menu, she asked, "You attended with the young man, no?"

"Yes." I quickly commented, "Everything looks delicious. What do you recommend?"

"They specialize in French cuisine. The crab mousse is excellent, as is the steamed Patzcuraro. I would also recommend the baked Alaska."

"Would you mind ordering for me," I suggested. "Your French is better than mine is."

After she'd ordered white fish, mousse, and wine, we discussed the evening at Guadalupe. I told her of my enormous respect for Thurston. I explained what he'd said about faith.

"Yes. I am also Catholic," she replied. Smiling, she added, "And I see that amazes you. I was raised traditionally Latin and that means I was raised in the church."

"I was raised Catholic, too. I know the church doesn't accept Sapphics."

"Ah, yes. How to reconcile one's faith while living a life that seems outside the church? For me, faith is a tool. It is a soul salve that is slightly reassuring. For me, it can never be a total reassurance, nor can I offer total belief."

"Maybe that's where I am. I can't seem to grasp a way to make the two conform. The church isn't accepting."

"The church is judgmental, of course." She took a sip of wine. The pause was meditative. "The Bible has many harsh statements I find contrary to my beliefs. However, there are censures that lag behind the commonly acceptable practices of today. For instance, it was believed wrong for a male to wear short hair. Today we find that ludicrous. Knowledge has expanded our awareness that homosexuality is an inclination in most animal species. Animals are not given free choice to elect to sin. One must deduce that if the sexual disposition was created by a supreme being, it must be acceptable. Perhaps I am rationalizing, but that is my belief. There are many more divergent areas within religion. For me, it is more a station of comfort within the church. Like a peaceful beach. It is my tradition, so there are many things that have been indoctrinated."

I smiled. "I understand."

"Are you agnostic?"

"I'm not sure what I am. I'm not even certain if it matters to me. Being brought up Catholic makes it difficult, but I've never been in tune with a male god."

"Perhaps that is why I often refer to the supremacy as a creator. I perceive the creator to be a spirit rather than a defined gender. Yes, it is a power that is unique and within us all."

"Maybe that's also near what I believe."

"And have you plans for the weekend?"

"I've got to work on my term paper. I'm doing research on the Globe Theatre."

"I shall be leaving for Cuernavaca in the morning. Perhaps you'd care to join me? There would be ample time for your studies. I've also got a paper to write."

"Dueling typewriters," I joked. "Yes. I'd love Cuernavaca."

"We can return early Monday morning if that meets with your approval." She leaned toward me allowing her hand to graze my arm. "I would embrace you if we were alone."

Brushing her fingers with my own, I whispered, "Can you feel my heart caressing yours?"

"I can."

"There was a passage from Saint John of the Cross.

Cantico Espiritual. I was reading it and thought of you. I quoted, 'Rejoice, my love, with me and in your beauty see us both reflected.' That's how I feel about you, Cres."

When steaming platters were served us, she smiled. Her glance then slowly lifted to meet mine. "I *do* feel the caress of your heart. So often, I do."

* * * * *

I WAS PERUSING my mother's letter when Leigh entered the apartment. She sat across from me at the dining room table. "Guess I'm going back to Kansas for Christmas vacation," I announced.

"You sound overjoyed."

My glumness was evident. "It's a long trip."

"So?"

"My father has ruined every holiday I can remember."

"Then why go back? I'm not fucking with all that crap. My family can survive without me being miserable in Colorado Springs."

"I'm *sure* they'll miss your sparkling personality, Leigh."

"I won't miss their nuttiness. So are you on some masochistic revival?"

"My mother misses me. And I miss her. And Kris and Gran." I took a sip of tea. "I wish they could be here with me."

"Here with you! But let's not fill Mexico with any more nutty people. So, speaking of goofy American expatriates, where's everyone?"

"Sanchez is marketing. Nora is leaving for the day with Gab at ten. They're going to spend the weekend in Guadalajara. Hope he's on time. I'm off to Cuernavaca at noon."

"Wish I was spending the weekend with Lindy. Hell, you

wish from one end and shit from the other."

"Why can't you two be together?"

"She's studying for finals and so am I. We can't get anything studied when we're together, I'll admit it." Leigh unwadded the bakery sack she'd pitched on the table. "Try an apple turnover."

I dipped my hand in, pulling out a gooey pastry. "You'll have the place to yourself. Erika is off to Acapulco. Rent is due, she said. Belle and Edith are going bird-watching with the Nazi. Too bad you can't have Lindy come over for a little 'alone' time."

"She's so damned disciplined. She won't even phone me until she's completed her studying. She gets it from her father."

"Stereotypically, aren't the Brits discipline nuts?"

"Her father doesn't tap dance, Benj."

"I didn't mean it that way. Or maybe I did and wish I didn't."

"Her father is the disciplinarian. He was a track star. So was Lindy." Leigh bit into the pastry. "These are so flipping delicious. I haven't eaten all morning. Anyway, Lindy was a sprinter."

"Funny. First time I saw her, I thought she looked like an athlete. You said she *was* a sprinter."

"She was training for the Olympics, like her father. Then she had a serious injury that ended her career. Says she knows she can't be a runner again, but she wants to be the best in her occupation. I like that quality in her."

"Speaking of professions, I have a question your field of study might answer. It's about the past. Gran says they eat dogs down here. True or not?"

"As it happens, Benj, old Granny is right. Hell, of the four types of dogs originally indigenous to the area, two are extinct.

The Spaniards saw Indians chomping on dogs. So they began taking them on their ships for food on the long trip back to Spain. Those fucking Spaniards were hard on Indians and dogs."

"Sirius was Orion's dog. After Orion's eyes had been put out, Sirius might have led him around. Hence, Sirius was the first seeing-eye dog."

"Why do you do that? We were getting into some solidly researched facts and you come up with that legendry bullshit." She tore apart the crispy pocket of her apple turnover. "I think you do it to annoy me. Speaking of annoyances, what's this about Nora fixing you up with a friend of Gab's?"

"Just to please Nora, I'm having coffee with him."

"A coffee date doesn't give you much time to castrate him," her sarcasm lashed. "By the way, Mrs. Lawrence is arriving soon. Nora informed me I was to be polite and to watch my language around her mom. But I'll leave before her mother arrives. I'll bet they're a matched set."

Folding my mother's letter back up, I began tucking it into the envelope. A small packet fell out. Examining it as I dumped the small mustard-colored pills into my palm, I shook my head. "Mom sent meds for upset stomach."

"Does she think you'll come down with malaria?" Leigh snickered.

"She's a R.N. I guess she wants to cover all the bases. She believes you can't be too careful when it comes to health."

"I'm amazed she let you come to Mexico. Did she suggest Sweden?"

I laughed. "Nope. She wasn't happy about my decision, but she recognized my desire to come down here. She doesn't want me out of her sight. I guess most moms are like that. What did your mother say when you decided to go to college out of the country?"

"It was cheaper down here. And she knew I wanted to go to grad school, so coming to Mexico was a good financial choice. My mother is a card player. She's our lady of canasta. When she caught me kissing my first sweetheart at fifteen, she called me aside. Told me I should develop more interests. Like parlor games. There's nothing like a board game to keep you outta another woman's panties."

"My mother would never believe the things I've gotten up to down here."

"Radclyffe Hall wrote one of the first coming-out books. It was a best seller. *The Well of Loneliness*. Read it?"

"No. Sounds like a fun read."

"Seriously, it's some kind of literary classic. I'm amazed you haven't heard of it in your tromp through the land of make-believe. I have a copy on loan somewhere in Mexico. I'll see if I can find it. If not, read it when you go back to the States over Christmas vacation."

"I'll make that my first stop, Leigh. Run to the library in a small town where everyone knows everyone and order the blockbuster lesbian how-to book. Not that they probably have ever heard of it."

"You act like such a solid heterosexual. And we both know the truth."

"The truth is that I love one woman. Not all women."

"Well, I don't *love all of them,* either. They won't let me," Leigh chuckled.

I inhaled deeply, sighing as I released a breath. I took another quick bite of pastry. Leigh's stare over the rim of her eyeglasses was brutal. My own self-denial was smacking me around, and I didn't need Leigh's exploratory as well. I argued, "Most women probably look at other women like that at least once in their life."

"Not Nora. But be honest, aren't women a special treat?"

"The doctora can certainly tune my body. So to answer your question, yes."

"It's more than a passing affection, Benjamin. Be honest."

My lips moved slowly. Then I declared, "Yes, I do love her. And it's beginning to feel like much more than a trivial fling."

"So stop the deception, Benj. Stop running for cover. Don't you know, in days-gone-by, we would both have been burned alive at a stake?"

TWENTY-ONE

As CHRISTMAS APPROACHED, the days were rolling by so rapidly, I didn't have time to realize they'd passed. One of Gran's old sayings was true. I was rushing around practically running up my backside. But I wanted to be ready for my holiday trip with my family.

Spending nights frantically studying and weekends with Cres, took every spare moment. I had mentioned to Cresida I needed to go to one of the markets to get gifts reflective of Mexican culture to take to my family. She suggested a shopping spree at the market in Cuernavaca on Saturday morning. We could then go into quarantine at her villa for studies and relaxation. It would solve my problem about gift purchases. I quickly agreed. By Saturday morning, I'd made a list of possible gifts.

Rodolfo delivered us to the heart of the market, and then parked the car. Cresida and I walked through narrow streets, glancing at the wares. Rodolfo caught up, following behind as if he were some great monolithic spirit guarding us.

We mingled with tourists and natives as we moved past the stalls surrounding the main plaza. From the salubrious scent of fresh fruits and vegetables to the cloyingly fragrant aromas of flowers and candy, the air was thick with unusual scents. We passed by a vendor hawking fresh fruits that were piled high. Then a man carrying a tray of lush cream custard ambled near us, and I inhaled nectar fumes. Another roaming peddler had an armload of roses. I purchased a bright solar yellow one, and then presented it to Cres.

"Thank you for the lovely rose." Her smile was my reward.

"Thank you for bringing me, Cres."

I inspected the filament passageway that was lined with stalls. Shaded by canvas awnings, the small cubicles were alive with color. I stopped to browse at a stack of shawls, rebozos of hand-loomed wool, and other embroidered goods. I selected a peacock-blue shawl for my Gran. "She loves blue. Have you got your family's gifts?" I inquired.

"Yes. My parents live in Spain. My father is in his eighties and is in poor health. I've come to know them better since becoming an adult. Earlier studies consumed my time. My adulthood was spent building my practice." She glanced away. "My father was in the government and had very little time for family."

"I like knowing about your life."

"You seem close to your family."

"Yes. Very close to my sister. Maybe our sibling bond is because my father is an alcoholic."

Just as I had sensed, she didn't wish to talk about her family, she backed away from questions about my father's alcoholism. She expressed a generic comment. "Unfortunately, most families are problematic in one way or another."

We traipsed ahead, browsing at baskets, onyx, the straw woven merchandise, pottery, and lacquered goods. I purchased some black Coyotepec pottery. I selected half a dozen designs of angels in long skirts that concealed bell clappers. I was captivated by their mercurial gleam. "My aunts will love these," I commented.

Passing by a small gem shop, Cresida directed, "Come, you must see the stones I most love." When we entered, she led me past counters filled with turquoise, lapis lazuli, and chalcedony, to a tray of geodes. The oval stones had been split in half. Their interior wall was a stage of crystals. Lifting the two halves, she pressed them together. They fit identically and had once been one. She purchased the two halves. As she slipped one half into my grasp, she whispered, "For you, my love."

Gazing at the stone she'd placed in the cup of my hand, I said, "Thank you. It's lovely."

"It's for my favorite person." She slipped her half into her purse. "Now we share a part of the earth that had been formed as one."

"The geode is your favorite because they're round. It's your globe theory of the worlds and the atoms, right?"

"Correct." She touched the crystals inside my geode. "These are millions of years old. I love the thought we each have a portion of a stone belonging to one another."

"I'll treasure my half."

"As I shall mine," she echoed.

When we walked out onto the street, I glanced over at her. She had given something of herself, I contemplated. It was something personal and symbolic. I was so emotionally moved that it frightened me. I didn't want love's tyranny to harm me. I didn't want my heart to be life's soft underbelly. I didn't plan to be vulnerable, and I was becoming exactly that.

As we strolled, the conversation seesawed. I had purchased Kris and Rod rings. I had filled my shopping bag with gifts. By noon, the shopping had been completed. I wanted only to be alone with Cresida. We were both rather somber. I attributed it to the fact we had each realized the enormity of our feelings.

"What is it you wish to do now, my lovely?" she questioned.

"I wish to return to your villa," I added, "and gobble you up."

When my language and candor would shock her, she would begin with a delicate grin. Soon her throaty laugh emerged. She asked, "You have completed your shopping?"

"Absolutely. I want a wonderful weekend with you."

"And then?"

"Then?"

"What is it you want beyond that? From life?"

"I have no long-term plans. No permanent goals in life. With the exception of writing, I haven't really planned. I'd like to remain here in Mexico. But it all depends. Nothing is permanent."

"There are times when you speak of the future as if it were your enemy." Her eyes probed. "I understand you are reticence to speak of *our* future. But not of *your* future." Wearily, she spoke, "For now, perhaps we can pretend all the differences aren't there."

"Can't we accept how things are without pretending? Cres, I'm not seeing anyone else. Not sharing love, I mean. I'm trying desperately to understand this." My eyes closed a moment as my hand automatically covered them. "I hadn't expected to feel this way about you."

"I apologize if it seems I'm pressing you, Kelly. I have no expectations of you. Please believe that I was only attempting to assist you in working through your emotions." As she adjusted her sunglasses, she walked ahead of me. I wanted to kiss her moist lips, just as I wanted to quell her questions, as well as my own. "Are you coming, my darling?"

"Yes." I had evaded both of our questions, temporarily.

She turned. "Forgive me for upsetting you."

I issued a hopeless smile of resignation. "Doctora, as my Gran would say, you'd need to shoot a nun in the back to get into my bad books and upset me."

Her laugh was reassuring. She mouthed the words 'I love you.' My heart fell back into place.

* * * * *

MY GLIMPSE SWAYED to familiar faces. The Lopez family had brought weaved mats and baskets to market. "Cres, I see friends."

I took her hand and led her toward them. Both parents and three of the children were in attendance. I gave them abrazos and introduced them to the doctora. With measured conviviality, she shook their hands and asked about their basket weaving. Although there was a reserved stiffness about Cresida at first, her rigidity soon toppled. She sensed how fond I was of the Lopez family. And accordingly, she became more gracious as we conversed. She purchased several baskets, saying they would make perfect gifts for colleagues who collected basketry.

My immediate concern was that Lupe might mention the meeting to Nora. Certainly, the family would tell Lupe, and she would have no reason not to mention it. I would intervene, requesting that Lupe not tell Nora or the others. I would explain that the doctora was a professor. I rationalized with a mental grin—Cresida had taught me a bundle. That could not be disputed. Lupe could be trusted not to break a confidence, nor would she pry into my reason. Gran would call her a true-blue person. And so would I.

After returning to the car, Cres inquired, "Lupe is your maid?"

"Sanchez's maid, actually. She's my friend. I was invited to her village to meet her family." I knew that Cres was fond of her own loyal staff, and they were devoted to her. I figured she understood. Rodolfo, her sentinel, would give up his life for her in a blink. "Do you have any Indian friends?" I queried.

"Not any. And do you have many Indian friends?"

"Not nearly enough," I asserted. "Not nearly enough."

* * * * *

SINCE MY REPORTER internship in Kansas City, I had not witnessed the excessive gore before us.

A crowd looped around the head-on auto collision. Eyes were seamed to the disaster. Immediately, the doctora instructed Rodolfo to pull over and to bring her black bag. She rummaged through her purse and then extracted a medic's ID clip and attached it to her collar.

We moved rapidly toward the accident. There were no police or other medics. An elderly couple had been taken from their auto, and they were at the side of the road. Those in the other car had not yet been pulled from the wreckage. I could see a man and woman, and I could hear the cries of children. The couple's car was crumpled, and the family's auto seemed nearly mashed.

Cres began issuing directives to the men who were assisting. She cautioned them on lifting procedures. Promptly, she examined the elderly man. She took a tourniquet from her bag and circled his upper arm. She applied pressure to stop the massive bleeding from his lower arm. Motioning to Rodolfo, she delegated him to oversee the tourniquet compressing.

After dispatching the workers, she requested sheets and blankets be brought from nearby homes. When we knelt beside the woman, I asked, "What can I do?"

"When the blankets arrive, cover each victim." She looked down at the woman, brushing her hand over the crescent wound on the woman's head. "She's going into shock." Cres applied gauze and tape to the gash.

I felt a chill when looking into the woman's glassy eyes. I wanted to comfort her; however, I wasn't certain enough of my Spanish. I patted her shoulder as I told her they were bringing her a blanket.

I followed the doctora around the other vehicle. A man in his mid-twenties was being lifted from the auto. Blood strung down his mutilated face and gushed from his limbs. Expeditiously, Cresida eased down. She pressed the bend at his elbow. "Kelly, quickly apply pressure until we get a tourniquet."

As my thumb dug into the pressure point, the blood flow slowed. Cres ripped a sheet, then fashioned a tourniquet. She abruptly stood, rushing to a small child being lowered to the ground. With celerity and gentleness, the doctor examined his lacerations. She moved immediately to a shrieking toddler with a crushed leg. The small girl clutched Cres.

I turned my sentry task over to a bystander. I had used a small branch to serve as the tourniquet's handle. I hastened to Cresida to assist with the thrashing child. I watched as the doctora wrapped her leg. Her touch was tender. I witnessed the maternal side of Cresida. She assumed her role as dedicated medic with the same grace and concern as when she probed the mind.

The family's mother was finally freed from the wreckage. When she was placed on the ground, Cres adroitly began applying bandages and tape. The woman's skin was clammy. The doctora reassured her help was on its way. Blood splattering on her legs smeared as her skirt hiked up when she knelt. She leaned to hear the woman's groans. "Kelly," the doctora called me. Her eyes darted back to the car. "Hold the mother. Her infant is in the car. I must get her."

"I'll do it." Without looking back, I rushed to the

smoldering car. The front end was smashed and smoking. The seats had been jammed against the dash. I looked down at the floor. Locked beneath the tangle of steel and cushions was the fringe of a pink blanket. I pressed into the cavity under the dash. I squirmed, squeezing, as I extended my arm inward through the debris.

Suddenly, I felt a tiny arm. My heart drained. The thought of pulling a dead infant from the car paralyzed me for a moment. On the chance the child lived, I struggled. Finally, I felt a slight movement. But some portion of the garment was in the vise of tangled steel. The child was pinned tightly. My hand felt the fabric. I continued probing. When my fingers grazed her chest, I felt the pulsating heartbeat—shallow, but there. I carefully began tugging an inch at a time.

Soon, I'd unwrapped the baby from the confines of her blanket. Slowly, I extracted her. Her squeal in my ear made something inside my soul pray. I clutched her tightly as I turned from the wreckage of the car. I began to make my way around to the doctora. Within seconds, there was a blast that rocked the ground beneath me. Dazed, I realized I'd been thrown to the street, yet protectively clutched the child. Gaseous fumes were nauseating me.

Clearing my eyes, I saw the baby's wrinkled face. She couldn't have been over a few weeks old, I guessed. My eyes were transfixed on the child. She was fine. I looked back up. Flames were shooting into the air. Cres rounded the auto and saw me as I began to stand. Her face was strained. Her eyes watered, and then closed.

Instantaneously, I understood how near I'd come to being killed. And I saw the same fear in the doctora's expression.

I issued a smile. "She's fine. Minor cuts only, I think."

Cres nodded. "And you?"

"Amazingly, not a scratch." There was a lift of fear in my

voice. "I'm fine."

She steadied me. "Are you certain?"

"Absolutely. Let's tell the mother her child is alive." I handed the infant down for her mother to see. A woman helper took the child to wrap her in a blanket.

With blinking lights and sirens, two ambulances and police arrived. Cresida was reporting injuries. After the first ambulance had begun its evacuation, she returned to my side.

"Kelly, I shall go with the ambulance to assist. Do you think you should have someone look at you?"

"I'm fine. You can examine me later."

A rapid flicker snapped in her eyes. "Yes. I'll have Rodolfo take you back to the villa."

"Are you okay?" I took a strip of sheeting and wiped the smear of blood from her forehead."

"Yes. I was terrified when I thought you might be inside the automobile. That you might have—might have perished."

The second ambulance was being loaded. I pointed to it and said, "I hope they are all okay."

She looked at me apologetically. "I must go with them. My profession requires I assist. You were not required by profession, yet you assisted." We walked to the ambulance together. She nodded to the attendant.

"I'm a professional human being. We're supposed to help one another. Besides, my mother is a nurse. She believes in making people better if we can." I touched her arm.

"And I wanted to impress you," I teased.

"And so you did." Her glance anchored mine. "And so you did, my darling." She climbed into the ambulance. I watched as it careened away.

Rodolfo's arm was extended toward the limousine. The excursion had been excruciating for us all. We had reached the villa's gates before either of us uttered a word. I then commented, "The doctora is a wonderful woman."

He nodded. "She has always wanted to be a healer."

"When she was a child?" I grilled.

"Yes." With warm remembrances, he shared, "She would care for injured animals."

"She has no pets now though."

"No. Not since those many years ago, when they were all lost."

"Lost?"

"There was a coup. Her country was in great unrest. The family fled the palace. When the rebellion was put down, we returned. Her pets had been butchered by the traitors. The insurgent soldiers accused the family of being bloodthirsty. Cruelty breeds only more cruelty. But a small girl should not have lost her beloved pets in that manner."

He had, for the first time, told me more than I'd asked. He was aware I had fallen in love with the doctora.

* * * * *

F. SCOTT FITZGERALD said that if you'd show him a hero, he'd write a tragedy. That crossed my mind as I lowered my body into the bath water. Perhaps I had been on a pilgrimage to Cresida. I knew she was a kind person and dedicated to healing. Now, having seen her in such a horrendous emergency, I was emotionally dropping to my knees. My veneration of her nobility was not without justification. Today had validated my love of her.

Before entering the bath, I had tried to wash as much blood from my skin as I could. I'd removed my high school class ring and examined my fingers, hands, and arms. I had correctly reported my condition to the doctora. Not even a scratch. My gaze then rested on my ring. Why was I uninjured when there was so much carnage?

Suddenly, memories of the wreck flashed back at me. Those sobs, the gushing blood, raw punctures, and the grizzle of it all prowled my mind. My eyes twitched spasmodically as I attempted to focus on the rushing bathwaters. Behind the water was bright tile. I became lost in the reflective bits of light.

I ached for the people and their pain. Cresida had bound their gashes, blanketed them, and whispered assurances. From tacking down scarlet, pendulous flesh, to gently touching their cheeks, she comforted. Her patrol over those mangled bodies deepened my respect for her and my love for her. She had brought order to the scene with assurance and dedication.

I ached for her also. I thought of her losing her pets. She'd never mentioned her childhood love of animals. I covered my face with the washcloth and sobbed into it. I knew it would be easier to deny my feelings if I had no reason to cherish her.

Soaking until the waters cooled, I then reached for a towel. As I stood, I looked back down at the soap residue mixed with soot and dirt. It was clinging to the tub's edge. Round, miniature volcanoes were where soap bubbles had exploded. I thought of the bubble and its brevity. Fleeting life. I had narrowly escaped death a second time in my life. I wondered if the third time was a charm.

The bubble was circular. And then there was the geode.

* * * * *

ISABEL ANNOUNCED THE doctora had arrived. She would be bathing. I rushed to Cresida's bedroom. The door was shut. I knocked, asking if I could enter.

"Of course," she called to me. Cres was seated on the edge of her bed. She wore only her slip. Her fingers held the yellow rose I'd given her. Its long stem bowed in front of her. Her legs were blood-stained, her eyes brimming with teardrops. She blinked them onto her long lashes. "The young father died. With the head injuries, it was best he did not survive. I believe, barring complications, the others will all survive."

I went to her adjoining bath to wet a towel. When I returned, I knelt, washing the dried blood that streaked her legs. Tenderly, I then wiped them dry. She eased slowly onto the floor beside me and into my embrace. Her head fell against my shoulder. As if deteriorating in my arms, her castellated heart let down the drawbridge. She wept. Then, as if covering her weakness, she retreated by pulling away.

"I shall now bathe."

"May I rub your neck and scrub your back?"

"No. I must be alone."

I stood, offering my hand down to help her to her feet. I turned to leave. I suddenly stopped. "Cres, as long as I care about you the way I do, there's no way you can ever be alone again."

Her gaze held an enormity of emotion. As she issued a lifting smile, she said, "Perhaps it would be nice to have my back scrubbed."

When she entered the bath, she placed the rose in the soap tray. I sat on the tub's edge, massaging her back. Kneading, my fingers wreathed her neck. I inhaled the ambrosial fragrance of bath oil and the lime tree that was outside the window. I leaned to kiss her neck. "What you did today was wonderful."

"My credentials are for healing the mind. I'm ill-equipped to patch the body." She closed her eyes as I rinsed her back. Giving the water a swirl, she mused, "Of course, I have been trained to heal the body. But a general practitioner would have been more comfortable with accident victims."

"I thought you were brilliant. You took command."

Looking away, she disclosed, "My profession is my Lambarene. I am glad this infrequently happens . Today was the worst emergency. Before, when I was the only medic at events, it was illness. Illnesses and other accidents were mild. There has been the need to administer procedures to restore breathing and circulation at events. Yet nothing on this scale—nothing like this."

"It was the worst accident I've ever seen. You amazed me."

"I'm sorry the young man died. I've seen death before, but I had hoped he would survive." Her eyelids closed a moment. "He fought to live. They all did."

"You did everything you possibly could for him. For them all."

"I was so frightened when I thought you might have been in the auto explosion. Kelly, you took a terrible risk."

"Not so big," I laughed. "The supreme being hasn't sent a hit man for me yet. A few bruises, but not a scratch."

"Perhaps this is an example of why I believe in guardian angels."

"My guardian angel should have combat pay today."

Chuckling, she shook her head. "What does your mother do when you misbehave?"

"Shall I clean up my language or make it Kansas City verbatim."

"Well?"

"My mom pisses and moans when I act up." My hands reached to touch her face. I leaned toward her kiss. "But you aren't my mother. You're my lover."

The kiss was warm and erotic. I felt its surge.

"Kelly, promise you'll not take chances."

"When death is ready for me, I'll do my best to elude it. How's that for a useless pledge," I teased. Pushing back a strand of her hair, I commented, "You are so beautiful."

"My face must be strained. I think not beautiful at this moment."

"It's more beautiful now than ever before."

As if trapped in her own enigma, she looked away. "Please accept that this is not a statement of conceit, but many people tell me I am beautiful when we first meet. Perhaps it is their intent to flatter me. You have waited until now."

My roguish smile emerged. "I assumed you were already aware of your loveliness. But I did notice when we first met. "Now, my emotions are deeper. I see more beauty than your mirror image. You're like the geode. Mysterious, well-formed, and intriguing on the outside. But inside, you are crystal and splendor."

Pulverized by my statement that she was analogous to the geode, she took my dripping hand and kissed my fingertips. "I truly do adore you, Kelly."

There were no additional words. For my breath had escaped into the caves of my lungs. It felt as though there might be a beach ball lodged in my windpipe. I was consumed and admitted it. When she stood, water droplets steamed in runnels. I threw a towel around her flawless body.

I handed her the rose for the second time that day. It had been a day that was a century ago.

TWENTY-TWO

"YOUR BLIND DATE was miserable! Ricardo was a dud!" Nora screeched her repetition of my response to her question. How could that be since she had choreographed the details? Nora had been stationed at the dining room table waiting for me to arrive so I could give her a report. She folded her arms and grilled, "I don't understand! Gab told me he was perfect for you."

Before plunging into the story, I poured tea. I slowly sat. With a lingering sip, I sighed. "Nora, after ten minutes of sitting beside him in a booth, I felt the trap going down. We ordered coffee, and by the time it arrived, he was doing an octopus imitation. He sees himself as a playboy. I saw him as a jerk."

"He must have a bad impression of easy American women."

"He didn't get that impression from me. He didn't get anything from me," I assured her. "I was an ice princess. I was totally in control of my emotions. Besides, nothing gives him the excuse to walk around with his dick hanging out." Her face flushed like a neon sign. I rapidly added, "And don't bother telling me how I'm beginning to sound like Leigh."

"Well, your language is like hers. It's unbecoming for a lady to say."

"I was a lady on the mini-date, Nora."

"Maybe he would be better on a date if we doubled. We

could go dancing."

"I'd rather dance with a three-legged Clydesdale. And I see no reason for a group date because he can't control his urges."

"Honestly, Kelly. American women aren't respected."

"Nora, I've had sex with two men in twenty years. I may not qualify for sainthood, but I don't think I'm ready for admittance in a pushover palace."

"I know we aren't harlots. But golly, I want to be a lady. Maybe I'm nervous with Mom arriving Friday. I don't know what Leigh's going to be like."

"Gone. She's leaving on her dig. She did threaten to put up lyrics from a Christmas carol."

"What would that matter?"

"She was going to plaster the phrase, 'Make the Yuletide Gay,' on her door."

Nora gulped. "Well, she won't. I'd never speak to her again."

"Don't promise her that or she might reconsider and do it."

Nora glared at me. "Kelly, you don't mind bunking with Erika when Mom's here?" Nora slid off her flats as she began unbuttoning her magenta shirtwaist. By the time we reached the bedroom, she'd practically shrugged her way out of the dress.

"No problem. I'm leaving Saturday morning. I'll ride up as far as San Antonio with Carlos and Tom. Then I'll take the bus to Kansas City from there. And I won't even be here Friday afternoon. I'm going to the Toluca market with Carlos."

"Will you have dinner with Mom and me on Friday?"

"I'd love to, but I'm going to a party at Eduardo's. He called."

"I'm so happy for you," she gushed as she gave me a sisterly hug. "Maybe now the two of you can work out your differences."

"I told him I was only willing to be his friend."

"You're ruining your chances with him."

My teeth clamped. "I hope he understands."

When the door slammed, I heard Leigh's familiar tripping plod. She tossed mail on my desk. "Nora, you didn't get any mail," she announced. "However, Kelly, you have a terrific mail call. Two letters from Kansas. Do let me know how sorghum and pork bellies are doing." After getting no reaction from me, Leigh turned to Nora. "Nora, I heard the blind date you set up for poor Kelly turned to absolute shit on a stick."

"Gab told me Ricardo was nice," Nora defended with a squint.

"Kelly told me he was a creep with a dildo attached."

Before Nora had a chance to yell, I interjected, "Nora, I said no such thing. I said he was fresh. And he kept calling me *chula*."

"That means cutie," Nora translated.

"Nora, I'm aware of the meaning. I don't want men calling me cutie."

Pouting, Nora, announced, "Well, I've got to study. I have three finals in the morning."

Leigh laughed. "I'll get the United Nations on the phone to let them know how you're suffering for your education. Ennobled by tribulation, you're destined to become an ambassador."

With a glare, Nora loaded her books into a stack. "Why don't the two of you go to Leigh's room if you want to have a chat?"

"Good idea, Nora," Leigh said. Motioning to me, she added, "Kelly, Nora can't take more than ten minutes with me."

"Not many can," I replied dryly.

We tightly clamped Leigh's bedroom door behinds us. "Benj, Nora's really crazy about you. That must be because you're not a representative lesbian."

"So what do you want?" My voice had a decided edge.

Leigh swung around, putting her feet up on the desk chair. "Sanchez hates it when I sit like this. Tells me it's hard on the chairs. So tell me about the frock."

"As I recited the events, I did so with relish. I had expected Leigh to love a story that lionized a member of her colony. But halfway through, I sensed her withdrawal. "Well, what do you think about the doctora and the accident? Everyone was amazed by her."

With an exasperated sigh, Leigh kicked the chair. "I think that people watched the extravaganza. She was being a performer."

"Leigh!"

"People are shits. They were watching other people's pain and loving the spectacle. Standing room only. They were getting their jollies."

"Call me a shit if you want, but you have no right to call her one. People were helping. And Cres was saving lives."

"Before you become a total disciple, find out what she's really about."

"What are you saying? Come on, you started this," I fumed. "So spill it."

"Kelly, she plays games with people. She entices them to fall in love with her. Then she dumps them. That's her little ego sport. The hunt, and then she drops her prey. She's a love angler. Gets the hook in good and deep, and then leaves her lovers behind at the edge of the lake to be eaten by ants. You're a past-time. A hobby. Until now, I haven't worried. I figured it was a game to you, too. But I have warned you."

I scowled. "You don't know what you're talking about," I

barked.

"Maybe *you* don't know her. I don't suppose she mentioned to you that she keeps detailed records on her affairs. You're all specimens. That's why she picks creative people. She documents them. She writes them up in her medical treatise. She also probably hadn't told you about her little ballerina lover who tried to overdose when the frock dumped her. So don't give me that high and mighty bullshit about how she saves lives."

"You've heard some vicious gossip. She never would harm anyone," I protested. "And she wouldn't make a study out of me."

"Take it easy," Leigh backed off. "I'm telling you this because I don't want you hurt." Leigh's tone changed. "I don't want you thinking she walks on water."

"I don't believe anything you said."

"Even when truth encroaches, you're oblivious to it. You've had too fucking much poetry for your own good."

With great deliberation, I went to the doorway and turned. "Leigh, maybe neither of us knows what is for my own good. But let's assume I know a little more about me than you do. If you value our friendship, don't *ever* say another derogatory word about her."

* * * * *

TO MY WAY of thinking, life is chiaroscuro. We are in between arcane light and hushed shadows. We are trapped in the mystery of a planet being pitched through time and space. We may be emblems of our past, but we are dependents of our future. We do the best we can. We attempt to swerve from the soft shoulders of gloom. We don't want to be weighed down by darkness. Nor topple. We want to elude heaven's stopwatch.

We want to know eternal sunlight. That's what I wanted, and that's what seemed impossible.

Naturally, I also wanted Leigh to be wrong in her accusations against Cresida. Just as I wanted Eduardo's stony face to soften. He explained to me that he was in the neighborhood, so he stopped by to tell me what time he would pick me up for the Christmas party.

We went to a nearby wine bar. Our conversation began over a bottle of the bar's best. He wore a light blue sports jacket with dark trousers and shirt. He tugged at the collar with anxiety. Fumbling for words, his speech was minimal. We were careful of one another for we both knew how quickly our conversation could snarl.

Holding high our goblets, we toasted the evening. We promised to be more pliable and understanding. Then we discussed his family's *pasoda* on Friday evening.

He said his mother wished to meet me. I watched legs of wine glide down from the goblet's lip. I felt the accompaniment of a hint of guilt. I had been with a woman, and that was certainly considered a sin in Mexico. It would not be approved of by my own mother, much less Eduardo's mother.

I wondered why I was making life difficult for myself by caring for the doctora.

But somehow—I wasn't certain why—it felt right. And even as fine as Eduardo was, he didn't seem correct for me. Maybe if I tried, I considered. I took another quick sip and then reached for his hand.

"I've missed seeing you, Eduardo. I wish things were different."

"They can become different. I'll wait for you to care about me."

"Eduardo, I'm too uncertain. My emotions don't seem

stable. I don't want to lead you along. Misrepresent my feelings. I'm not in love with you."

"It's difficult because I'm in love with you. I don't want to lose you."

Those words echoed in my head. I should feel the same, I chastised myself. Our walk back to my apartment was quiet. Our steps seemed less heavy than before. We dodged the slouching autos, as well as those that raced the streets. I felt the squeeze as his fingers gripped mine.

Why was I turning from respectability and the security of a good man? It wasn't that I'd needed time to finish my education. I had the feeling he would wait.

When we reached the doorway, he told me he would pick me up at seven on Friday. We had a final goodnight kiss that warmed me but did not flare my passion. And then we parted.

I had no desire to become a ready-made victim of matrimony—as my mother had done. Alcoholics furnish their descendants with irrational doubt. I didn't feel worthy of either Eduardo or Cresida. My reticence to be tied down was understandable. I had always fought off belonging. I had never wanted to be a victim.

I'd rather be a sonneteer.

* * * * *

ALTHOUGH IT WASN'T so, I felt to be dead-center between Horace, the Egyptian god of order, and Seth, the god of chaos. Final tests always made me feel that way.

Late in the afternoon, I headed back to the creative writing building. I made it in time to catch Professor Roberts. Placing a deck of exams into his oversized, mahogany-colored leather case, he glanced up at me. "Miss Benjamin, how are you this afternoon?"

"Fine, sir. And you?"

"Examination time is difficult for professors. We, however, are not graded. At any rate, I suspect you're here to pick up your rewrites," he asked in his monotone voice. Opening his top drawer, he took out a stack of my stories. "They are all greatly improved. Once again, I have given you a B+ on each, with the exception of one."

"Which one didn't I get the B+ on?" My heart dipped.

"The one titled, '*Mere Pioneer*,' about your grandmother's French pioneer stepmother." He fanned my stories out on the desk.

"Gran thought the world of her stepmother," I remarked. My heart was now buried.

"You have earned an A- on that one. I enjoyed it enormously."

"An A!" I exclaimed.

"An A-," he corrected with his sanguinary inflection.

"Yes, an A-."

"Well, does that satisfy you?"

My eyes retreated to the story momentarily. "Sir, I'm grateful that I have the A-, but I'll continue to work on it until it's a good, solid A."

"But you very nearly have a solid A now," he declared with disbelief.

"I want a good, clean A. So I'll continue working on it."

"Good luck, Miss Benjamin," he issued his challenge. "By the way, you've received a good, clean A on your examination."

My smile bobbled its way to a fixed position. "Great!" I hugged my stories to my breasts. "An A on my test and story!"

"An A- on you story," he again corrected as he removed his glasses. He then smiled. This time I was certain that he had.

* * * * *

As Carlos and I roved the Toluca Municipal Market, I harped on his roommate's state of constant alcohol consumption. "Keep the goof sober when he drives. Or I'll take the bus," I warned him. "And no marijuana. I don't want to spend the holidays in the hospital or in jail. Or worse."

"Kel, I told you, I'll drive if Tom is in the cups." Carlos looked like a pack mule when he threw the sack of last minute gifts over his shoulder.

I marveled at the markets color and motion throughout the gigantic iron barn of a building. An over-spill of canvas-shaded stalls sprawled out for several square blocks. The market housed everything. There were gifts, food, and clothing. Even crates of live chickens were stacked boob high filled with chickens clucking for their freedom. A toothless merchant was beneath a hat that could have doubled for a pool umbrella. He gave one of the crates a kick to quiet the hens.

I browsed, examining lacquered carved figurines. I mumbled, "I hate going back up to the land of deep-freeze. This sun energizes me."

Carlos didn't answer. He was listening to the reverberating barter that had progressed to a shouting match. The market's sounds were unique. Just as were the sounds of crunching Chicklet gum or the crackling-whoosh of a candle's wick being snuffed. The market produced an amalgamation of distinct noises.

"I think I've got everything on my list now."

"Good. Let's scram out of here. Go to a nearby cantina. Disinfect the food we ate with a brew," he suggested.

"No sense in tempting turista any more than we have," I agreed.

We ambled toward the cantina. Carlos stopped at a flower

stall. He purchased an armload of roses and carnations. With a slight bow, he presented them to me. "For you, my lady."

I kissed the side of his mouth. "You don't strike me as a flowers kind of guy. That was really sweet of you." I rubbed lipstick from his beard.

"I didn't do it for romance. It was a way to show out-of-context absurdity."

"Cut along the dotted lines," I whispered as I delivered another kiss to his fuzzy chin. "I really got some bargains today."

"Down here, it's *caveat emptor*. I wouldn't buy condoms at the market," he said as we entered the cantina.

"The women of the world thank you for that." I placed the bale of flowers on top of the table. Lowering my weary body to the chair, I expelled a sigh. "Whew. This place smells like a mastodon's breath. I can see why most women don't come in here." I knew the patrons were staring because I was not only a woman, but an American woman. Their disapproving gawks didn't bother me. As the gruff barman placed bottles in front of us, I issued a quick smile.

"And to make matters worse, you're drinking a beer." Carlos pinched the tent-shaped wedge of lime over the *Carta Blanca's* glass lip. Juice trickled down the rim's neck and into his beer. His index finger hammer-tapped the lime into the bottle. "I can't wait to get on the road, Kel. I'll love the Peace Corps. It should feed my hunger for excitement."

"Good. I don't want your spirit taming out. You're the last of the great crazy men. Promise you'll never change?"

"You've got my word." His brow snagged into a frown. He lifted his glance until his eyes stabilized, chaining with mine. "Sooner or later, everyone needs to sit across from themselves."

I took another sip of beer, dousing my thirst. "To our self-confrontation. To our dreams," I toasted. We clanked bottles. "Please always remember, Carlos, no matter where you are, my love will be with you."

"You too, Kelly."

I reached to caress his fingers. "I'll miss you though."

"I'll miss you. Come with me."

"Maybe one day I'll join up. I need to stay on the rail with my education."

"Speaking of learning experiences, are you ready to meet Eduardo's family tonight?"

"As ready as I'll ever be." After which, I planned, I would return to the apartment to sleep for a few hours. I would meet with Cresida for breakfast. She had suggested, since we hadn't seen one another that week, we should assemble at the Continental Hilton's coffee shop. She would be meeting colleagues for a morning colloquium and had hoped I might have time to meet with her. I assured her, I would make time.

I would have a chance to ask her about Leigh's charges. I hadn't planned to ask in Leigh's words. I would ask more gently than if the doctora left lovers as carrion rotting on the banks after her sex excursions. "Carlos, could you pick me up at the Continental Hilton in the morning. I'm having breakfast with a friend."

"Sure. But I warn you if I run into Anita Ekberg and Sophia Loren, and they want to ride back to the U.S.A. with me, there won't be room for you."

"Carlos, aren't they a little old for you?"

Laughing, he quizzed, "What do you have against older women?"

"Absolutely nothing." I closed my eyes. Taking a gulp of beer, I considered the current situation. With less volume, I repeated, "Trust me, absolutely nothing."

Touring Kelly's Poem

* * * * *

EDUARDO'S CAR PROPELLED through city traffic. I viewed the glisten of the Christmas season. Bedecked with glitter, sparkle, and spangles, the glossy passageways were streamers of light. We neared the *colonie porieriate*, a metropolis of Frenchified mansions. I surveyed the intricately carved cornice atop rows of aristocratic homes. Gleaming white plaster cloaked the outside of his parent's home. It was a lavish blend of nineteenth-century porfiriate style and baroque. My thoughts whirled to my family's frame home. It was done in early track suburbia fashion.

I pondered about which society was the best fit for me. Both of the people I dated belonged to completely different social strata. They were obviously of the aristocratic herd, and I was purely middle-class.

Eduardo rounded the car to help with my exit. I lifted my long, ruby-colored formal dress as I walked beside him. I was glad the clothing was inexpensive in D.F., and I had found a bargain that not only fit but also looked superb. Eduardo looked debonair in his white dinner jacket, black bow tie, and matching cummerbund. It had definitely been tailored by an expensive designer.

Taking his hand, I experienced trepidation. This was where I should want to be. He was the one I should want to be with. Societal propriety dictated those *should* rule. Before entering, I whispered to Eduardo, "Thank you for sharing your family with me."

Feliz Navidad, his family warmly greeted me. His portly mother gave me an *abrazo*. His distinguished father extended his hand. Eduardo had acquired his glinting ebony eyes from his mother. Her ink-black hair was parted in the center and pulled back into a stylish bun. From his father, Eduardo had inherited his tall, agile, lean frame. His father was charming. Neat waves of graying hair were clipped similarly to Eduardo's hair style. Eduardo would probably look exactly like this man in two and a half decades, I considered.

Señora Rivera, had a lovely round face and spoke with a cheerful, melodic voice. She was short, but her proud carriage made her appear taller. Señora Rivera had a refined attractiveness. Both of Eduardo's parents were gracious, and obviously well-loved by everyone at the party.

Eduardo led me through their home, down the steps into an elegant courtyard. Clustering friends, family, and neighbors had gathered. The group was festive, including youngsters and proud grandparents.

Eduardo's seventy-year-old grandfather scrutinized me as we were introduced. We then discussed Mexico for nearly ten minutes. After which, Eduardo expressed a desire to mill around so I might meet his brothers. His grandfather then whispered something to Eduardo.

"What was that all about?" I inquired with a smile.

"My grandfather has always told his children and grandchildren, if they married an American, they would have his permission. But if they married Mexican, they would have his blessing. He told me that if I married you, he would give his permission and blessing. He said you have a great love for our country."

"But I only talked with him for a few minutes."

"Yes," Eduardo said with a laugh, "but he could tell your heart is now Mexican."

"True. But let's not tell my Gran."

By the shank of the evening, I realized I was made to feel at home. Then, to my amazement, his mother asked me to join her. She took my hand and led me up an elaborate staircase. We went into what must have been Eduardo's childhood bedroom. On the dresser was a photo of the child, Eduardo, at eight-years-old. He was clad in a soccer uniform.

His mother told me he had broken his ribs after the photo was taken. I hadn't understood the word 'ribs' and so she poked my ribs. Together we giggled as I repeated the word, *costilla.* She then questioned how many children I wanted. I explained I love children but would trust the number to the future. She misinterpreted my meaning and said that I was correct. The Lord would grant as many as he wished.

After returning to the party, I crossed the courtyard. I approached Eduardo. Teasing him about his sexy little legs in soccer shorts, I also mentioned his ribs had healed nicely. Then I told him I liked his mother. He divulged he had told his mother of his love for me. I told him she had questioned me about family size. He solemnly replied that she knew he wished to marry me.

Although I was glad to be back in his arms, dancing to the velvet sounds of guitars, I didn't want to give him false hope. I wanted him to know I cared about him but was very confused. Although I had vocalized my apprehension, he had not listened carefully. Or I had not adequately explained myself.

We danced, laughed, and sampled various delicacies throughout the evening. I could feel the love that flourished in his home. When we said our goodbyes to the family, I realized how truly lucky he was to be so loved and so secure.

My thoughts vaulted to the painful holidays in Kansas. Our pasts were a million years removed. He wanted to share my future. However, could I replicate the harmonious family love he was used to having—and he deserved? I wondered if I could even comprehend it—much less duplicate it.

I saw myself as a universal carpetbagger. I no longer wanted to belong in Kansas. And I was uncertain I could ever completely dwell in a foreign place. Or perhaps my heart was that foreign habitation. Could I comfortably lodge within another social arena, I questioned. The exposure of one's heart is difficult to view, no matter if one is doing it from the outside or the inside.

TWENTY-THREE

BEFORE TRAVELING, THERE is a sense of abandoning and of abandonment with which to contend.

Seated in a corner booth at the Continental coffee shop, I nodded and smiled when the doctora arrived. She was dressed in a tailored, midnight blue suit with small white rhombus checks. She looked lovely. After we'd ordered breakfast, our talk seemed to go in ringlets. We didn't want to acknowledge our parting. Finally, I spoke of it. "I'll be thinking of you as I wend my way back to Kansas."

Stirring her coffee, her face grew somber. "I shall miss you, my lovely American. I'll be hoping your Christmas festivities are wonderful."

"I'll be trying to survive it. But it will be good to see everyone again."

"And last evening, it went satisfactorily?"

"Eduardo's parents are charming. I enjoyed the party. My difficulty seems to be making Eduardo understand my feelings for him. I told him how I love and respect him as a person, but that I'm not in love with him. I have no intention of dropping everything to marry him. The world is immense. I don't want to stop my studies. Anyway, he doesn't really seem to listen. I don't want to hurt him because I do care about him."

"Is there anything I can do?"

"No. Thanks though."

"And what is it you'll do while on vacation?"

"I plan on writing. That always makes things more tolerable. Enter some fable where things are safe."

Pensively, she gazed away. "I sense reluctance about your trip home."

"My father is difficult." I then asked, "And you mentioned you're going to Acapulco with friends."

"I shall fly in and out, only to be spending two days there. My patient load around the holidays is full."

"I can imagine. My father's drinking usually accelerates around the holidays. Gran says he's bitten by the jubilee grape. Anyway, I'm glad you'll be with friends."

"I shall be staying at the beach home of an American friend named Joy. She's seeing a model. They will both be there. I've known them for many years and we often spend holidays together. In fact, had you stayed, I would have invited you to accompany me. That is if you wouldn't have made plans with your young man."

"I would like to have met your friends."

"I've been selfish in keeping you to myself. But then, I have not been introduced to your friends."

"With the exception of Leigh, it might be difficult. And Leigh is seldom on good behavior. She has an insulting personality. She even gives everyone names. She calls me cupcake. Or did. Now it's Benj."

Amused, the doctora asked, "Has she a name for me?"

"Yes. She calls you *the frock*. Last week I asked her what she wanted for her birthday, which is next month. She said she wanted two weeks in bed with her girlfriend, Lindy, and the frock." I smirked. "Claimed it would make her Bartholin's glands spin themselves right off."

Cresida laughed. "She would want me *and* the young woman she loves?"

"She's all talk." I paused, putting the toast down. "I'd like for you to meet Lindy. And Leigh is fine in small doses." Hesitating, I took a deep breath. Then sluggishly, I muttered, "Leigh said something that I wanted to talk with you about. Things she's heard about you." I bit my lower lip.

Cresida's eyes had swerved before her glance snapped back to me. "You have questions to ask of me?"

"Yes." The air bristled. I stalled. "I don't know where to begin. I'm sure there's been a mistake."

Sternly, she enunciated, "Allow me to assist you. I've been accused of having a cold, impervious nature. In matters of love, my brutal, savage heart is legendary. But it's untrue, Kelly. I am the first to admit that I have not always been an innocent bystander. Yes, I have regrets. But I am not cold. Is that what you wish to know?"

"She told me about a ballerina."

"Eight years ago, I was having an affair with a young woman. We had been seeing one another for over a year. She attempted suicide. Everyone assumed I was responsible.

"And I *was* responsible for having miscalculated her emotional problems. Of all people, I should have recognized her disturbed condition. I interpreted her actions as an attempt at emotional extortion. She wanted for us to live together. I refused. I take any threat of suicide seriously. She had, however, threatened her family and other friends multiple times. I ignored her threat but made every attempt to assist her. It was clearly the most costly mistake I have ever made." Her eyes clouded. "I never played with her emotions. I was honest with her. As I have been with you. Kelly, it's important to me that you believe my words." She paused. "I would not have harmed her. And I shall never harm you."

"I believe you." I reached to touch her hand. "Is the dancer okay, now?"

"She was not discovered in time. Although she carefully

set up a plan to be found, her friends had been called so many times with false threats, they assumed this was another. The wait was too long. They saved only her life. The overdose cause irreparable brain damage. She was institutionalized and will be for the remainder of her life. I had visited her nearly every day for a year after, but then her family took her back to France."

"I'm so sorry."

Cres glanced down. "I shall live with the scars of that tragedy for the rest of my life. The heartless rumor persists. Many say I caused her to attempt suicide. In reality, no one causes another person to take his or her life. But I am guilty of not doing more to prevent it. I had been trained and should have intervened earlier. Therein lays the regret and remorse I shall always know. And accept. Kelly, perhaps I should have told you. But even now, it is difficult for me to speak about. She was lovely and I cared deeply for her."

"Were you in love with her?"

"No," she whispered almost apologetically. "And I told her that I was not. It was the reason I wished not to live with her. When she insisted, I decided it was unfair to her to stay together. That is when I attempted to separate from her." She rubbed her temple, and then added, "There were additional circumstances in her background that made her fragile. She had not been candid when I asked about her past. I felt she might have been abused. But she denied incest. Her suicide note confirmed she had indeed been abused for years by a much older brother. I tried to help her, but I couldn't save her."

"Cres, I'm so sorry I asked about it. I didn't want to hurt you."

"It's best you know. Do you have other questions?"

"Leigh also said you do studies on your lovers."

"That's another ridiculous allegation. I make notations,

nothing more than journal notations, about my life. Just as you write descriptions in your journal, I make notations in mine. I certainly don't recruit lovers to do behavioral studies. I confess I find artistic people more mentally stimulating. Is that why you think I'm interested in you?"

"I would hope not."

"When I first approached you in Acapulco, I didn't have a clue what your interests might be. For all I knew, you might have been a nun."

We both laughed a moment and then I asked, "Why did you approach me?"

"Because the one thing I recognized in you was that you were a good person. And from your eyes, I saw qualities that interested me. You seemed intelligent, aware, and energetic."

"Could you tell you also interested me?"

"Not at all. I thought you were insulted."

"I must not have been," I remarked. She turned her hand palm upward and clutched my fingers. "I can't even imagine anyone being insulted by you, doc."

"Kelly, my only promise to you is that I shall never do anything I feel might harm you in any way. Have I ever given any indication I could hurt you."

"No."

"And I never shall purposely do anything that might harm you." She looked at her watch. "Our time is dwindling. Kelly, I would like to call you on Christmas, but I imagine it might be difficult to explain to your family."

"I could call you," I schemed.

"I'll give you Joy's number. Please call collect." She wrote the number on the back of her card.

I scribbled my number on a page from a small notebook. "I doubt if you'll need to call, but in case of emergency."

"Will you be okay?"

"I'll be fine. Other than, I'll be missing you. But I'll be thinking of you," I vowed.

"Perhaps it would be arrogant of me to ask that you return to me. So I shall ask that you return to Mexico."

"Cres," I murmured as our eyes warmed, "I'll be returning to you both."

* * * * *

CARLOS HAD SEEN my final *abrazo* with the doctora. Of that, I was certain. I crossed the lobby to meet him. He greeted me with a quick hug. He took my enormous, bright-colored wicker basket. I'd purchased it to carry gifts I was bringing to family and friends.

The car was right outside, he muttered. *Thank heavens*, he commented about heaviness of the basket. He also asked if I had my passport, and *who* was that knockout, beautiful woman. Which woman? Oh, yes, the stunner I had embraced and shared farewells with—that woman. A friend, I replied. He wet his lips and offered his friendship anytime to a woman like that. I cautioned myself to leave it alone. I deflected his comment in an area where neutrality was not possible.

As my cousin Rod always said, no sweat. We were on our way up through the interior of Mexico where we would then enter my homeland. I was pensive about the return. Vertiginous thoughts matched the snaking Pan American Highway. Pearl-gray mist burned off the landscape as Tom's old Chevy grunted and groaned in its struggle with the inclines.

Tom Gilmore's propensity for a carefree artist's life gave our excursion a rudderless sensation. As the odometer clicked, ticking off miles, I considered being reunited with my family and friends. My *no blush* year was designed to prowl my own meaning. I had wanted to explore the world, life, and love, and mostly myself. This intermission seemed to puncture my search. It put me back in a strange setting. I had eluded death twice in the past year.

Risk. I questioned why I had roved away from my patch of home. My answer was simple. Home was even less safe than a jagged mountain or a smoldering auto that was ready to burst into flames.

Home had never felt safe. In returning, I would find only the security of Kris, my mother, and grandmother. But to share their time, I would need to be reinstated in the painful world that included my father's drinking. Throughout my memory, the family had been discordant. We orbited his self-hatred.

As we traveled, I said goodbye to Mexico City. The gradient steepness between Jacala and Tamazunchale was an extraordinary elevator ride. Lush, conical peaks lifted us, and then plunged us down into the twisting valleys. Lowering from the Sierra Madre to a tropical canyon was spectacular. Finally, I leaned into the crook of Carlos's arm and dozed off. When we neared Cuidad Victoria, he nudged me. He didn't want me to miss the dense, thickly brushed forests. Groves of mango, banana, and avocado trees were profusely growing.

Our trip up the charcoal highway ended for the day when we checked into a small hotel. Since we were all on student's budgets, we decided to bunk together. Carlos and I would take the bed, and Tom had a sleeping bag.

Tom went out to the car to bring in his bag. Carlos opened the drapes. We hooked our gaze on a silver, lantern-bright moon. "Nice," I lulled. "I'll miss Mexico."

"And I'll miss you," Carlos disclosed.

"I'll miss you, too."

"Even this room isn't half bad."

"Amazing, since Tom checked it out. Tom—who lives in a bedroom garbage pail." Tom, with his light-white hair, his pale-blanched coloring, was not too fussy about his cleanliness. "And he's remained somewhat sober. At least until this afternoon."

That had all changed when we hit the first cantina and he drank lunch. After a couple of ecru drinks, Tom went the color of mutton. He was about my height and walked on the balls of his feet when he was sober. When he'd had his share of booze, it weighed him down. Carlos finished driving throughout the afternoon into evening. He forecasted that he would be stuck with all the driving from then on.

"I know he won't be in any shape for driving."

"I can help," I offered.

"Last trip I took with him, I did all the driving after the first day. I was sure he'd be the same on this one. But he promised."

"Drinkers don't take promises seriously. As long as he isn't driving or puking on me, I don't care," I commented with a sigh. "He wants to waste his life, not much anyone can do about it."

"Maybe do exactly what we're doing. Be there to try to keep him out of trouble."

My jaw clamped tightly. "Right." I had no idea why people like Tom and my father felt it was their right to hoist responsibility to others. "Right."

"On the trip down, he kept asking if we were there yet."

Yawning, I sat on the bed and kicked off my shoes. "And?"

"I kept telling him we weren't there yet. We were wherever we were. But he never knew where he was. He's got a definite problem."

"Carlos, when you get your Peace Corps assignment, you'll be careful, won't you?"

"Sure, Kel." He frowned. "I won't be going into battle."

"Be careful all the same. You're not a map kind of guy. You could get lost. Take my advice and keep a compass handy."

"A compass." He was amused.

"I don't want you getting lost." I tickled his ribs.

With a pause, he inquired, "That gorgeous woman... is she a teacher?"

"Why yes, she is," I answered. I was getting good at tainted conversation. "Very much so." My response was no lie. Waltzing on spider webs, I considered, but truth is wisdom unto itself.

* * * * *

THE PANORAMA OF luscious orange orchards was magnificent. We were on the outskirts of Monterrey. Tom suggested a tour of the Cuauhtemoc Brewery. Naturally, there was the *draw* of free brew at the end of the tour. Tom didn't need an enticement for bargain suds. We went to placate him. It was his car.

After, we stopped for lunch. Seeing a full platter of food might have a sobering effect on Tom, we had hoped. It did not. He continued to order beer and got totally sloshed. With sarcasm, I mentioned to Carlos how an afternoon of Tom's drunken ramblings would make a punishment cell out of the auto.

Carlos and I would take turns driving, so I hoped Tom would pass out in the backseat. Thankfully, he did sleep most of the drive over flat plains and the arid desert between Monterrey and Laredo.

We arrived late in San Antonio. My sleep was restless, and I was anxious about returning home. Booze was my father's recipe for holiday disaster. I looked forward to the reunion with my family and friends but with trepidation about my father's drinking.

Morning in a strange motel room began with its dimness and drabness. I groaned as I recognized the spongy, squishy feeling of my monthly uterine flush. After a warm sudsy shower, I felt better. My freshly shampooed hair dripped and strands clung tenaciously to my neck. I dried, shot up with a Tampax rocket, and was ready to face the world. I hadn't had sex with Eduardo for the past month, so my period was no great relief. Again, it was only my three days a month of inconvenience.

Starving, I urged Carlos to wake up. He stirred as I continued to bounce on the bed. After dressing, packing the car, and waking Tom, we went to breakfast at a small coffee shop. We toasted our coffee, dunked tortillas into egg yolks, and said 'ole!' with each breakage of the yolks.

I hated the thought of going our separate ways. Traveling with Carlos was fun. And I didn't relish being alone at the bus stop. Carlos put me on the bus headed for Oklahoma City, en route to K.C. I would arrive in Kansas City about six in the morning on the day of Christmas Eve.

We'd made arrangements for our return trip. Carlos would call if they had trouble along the road. I had also asked if he would have a journalist buddy do some checking on Leigh's story.

My gut told me there was more to it than she'd divulged. Carlos had mentioned he had an ink-slinger pal living in Denver and could easily find out about what happened to her twelve-year-old sister, Cindy. Check the obits, news stories, and so on. I gave him the data, and he assured me it wouldn't be difficult to run the story down. It would only be a matter of checking reports of a dozen years ago.

I felt badly about snooping, but I hated a mystery. And I wanted to better understand Leigh. I felt what happened then was a key to why she's so angry now. Angry, bigoted, and arrogant—she'd become.

That was on my mind as the bus crossed the plains of Texas and Oklahoma. And as it did, I was also becoming more despondent about going home.

When the bus rested, we were given half an hour to gulp down food at a small truck stop. I knew I was in the U.S. when a cowboy called me *baby doll* and offered to drive me to K.C. An offer I could and did refuse. The jukebox was blasting Jimmy Gilmore's 'Sugar Shack.'

Back on the bus, the teenager sitting across the aisle turned on his transistor. Two or three songs played, and I didn't recognize them. The top-ten list had changed in such a short time. But so had I.

A crisp evening was beginning when I arrived in Oklahoma City. I called my family.

Feeling warmth from my mother's excited voice, I heard the words, "Kelly, when will you get here?"

"I'll arrive at six in the morning, Mom. I'm still in Oklahoma City. But that's so early, so take your time. I can hang out at the depot."

"Honey, of course we'll be there when you arrive. We've been so worried you wouldn't get here for Christmas."

"I'll be there. I can't wait to see you."

"How do you like Oklahoma City?" Mom joked. It was clear she didn't want to hang up the telephone.

Grinning, I answered, "I won't be staying. I can't wait to see you. There's so much to tell you about." And, I thought, so much not to tell. For my life had become a new version. And I was willingly dragged behind the changes that were becoming me.

"You watch out for characters," she admonished. All perverts, rapists, and low-lifers were lumped into my mother's catch-all word—characters. "Kelly, your Gran said to tell you there are more characters in other areas of the country than in Kansas. So beware."

With a smile big enough to swallow, I replied, "Tell her I'll be careful until I reach the state line. And tell her I love her."

TWENTY-FOUR

WHILE THE BUS neared Kansas City, I slipped my flats back on my tired feet, pushed back my hair, and applied a little powder and lipstick. From the words of Shapiro's *Travelogue for Exiles*, a message was divulged. 'The earth is taken; this is not your home,' I mentally quoted.

Familiar landmarks were blinking by. They contributed to the rippling, mock goose-flesh. The reflection of a dun-hued city glinted back from window panes. The bus lumbered on, voyaging through a corridor of town where I had worked as an intern reporter.

Debarking the bus was an excruciatingly slow process. I finally spotted Kris weaving her way toward me. "Kelly," she squealed as we clutched one another. "A petunia in an onion patch. Let's talk characters!"

"You made it over here so quickly," I teased. "I thought you might be the tour conductor."

Mom grabbed me, her clutch warm. She pushed back my hair and gave me a kiss. "You've lost weight, and you didn't have any excess to spare. Look at those bags under your eyes," she assessed.

"I've been on the bus all night. No wonder I look ropey," I defended.

She cupped my chin with her hands as she continued evaluating my condition. "No, you need more than rest. You need some good Kansas cooking."

It would do no good to dispute her diagnosis. I studied my mother's attractiveness. For being nearly forty-two and despite all that my father had put her through, she had not lost her sparkle. Her seal-brown hair gleamed and flashing blue eyes shimmered. Her loving, wide smile, almond complexion, and gentle nature had not changed. Kris was mother's carbon copy. She had Mom's coloring and features, as well as her good nature.

Kris snickered. "Kelly, what she means by Kansas cooking is that you'll need to begin with a couple dozen cinnamon rolls stuffed down you." Kris had trimmed her hair to about the same neck length as our mother's and from the back, I considered, they could be twins.

"I'll definitely go for some cinnamon rolls. And home cooking."

Observing my father as he crossed the sidewalk, I recognized the signs. He had been drinking, for there was the beginning of a glazed, wild look forming in his eyes. A paltry shadowing of his beige-cream skin told me he'd probably been hitting the bottle heavily for some time. His thin face flushed when he saw me. Pitch-forking his sandy, gray waves of hair, his fingers bypassed his receding hairline.

"Hi, Dad," I muttered.

"How was your trip?" he inquired.

"I hated to leave the tranquility. The trip was fine. During the first part, I counted cactus, and the second part, I counted tumbleweeds."

"Should have brought a tumbleweed back with you. We could have decorated it up as a Hanukkah bush," he kidded. His glassy eyes blinked.

I turned back to my mother. "How's Gran?"

"Her cough certainly frightened us," Mom reported. "But fine now. She said she can't wait to clap eyes on you. You do look exhausted."

While my father hoisted my suitcase and basket into the trunk, I whispered to Kris, "Up to his old tricks again, I see."

"We aren't supposed to notice. I hate it. He's nice when he doesn't drink," Kris excused.

As our parents rounded the car to get in, I murmured to Kris, "If he were so *fucking* nice, he wouldn't drink like a madman."

Kris sat back. Her eyes snapped open wider than a full moon. "What did you say?"

"You heard what I said." I knew she would be shocked at my newly acquired language. I wouldn't bother explaining that next to my roommate, Leigh, my speech was Saint Modesty the Chaste.

Kris giggled. "I heard you. I didn't believe it."

"What was that, dear?" Mom questioned.

"I was telling Kris how a person never forgets our Kansas state motto. *Ad astra per aspera.*"

To the stars through difficulties, I quoted.

* * * * *

FOCUSING THE VIEWFINDER on Gran, I snapped the new instant Polaroid camera. Carefully, I peeled away the olive-black strip. I then watched for Gran's image to appear. Kris quickly made several swipes across the print with a preservative roller bar. I fanned it dry and then showed it to Gran. She was looking lovely, I thought. She wore a lavender dress. Her silver hair was fluffed out. I had mentioned she didn't look to be in her mid-eighties. She informed me when people get gussied up, they look younger.

The gathering of family and friends was a post-midnight Mass celebration. I was again in the bosom of my people. We had all attended Mass after which we would return home for the traditional festivities.

I thought about driving back to the house after Mass. I studied the gray-green frame home. It was fenced by waist-high hedges. Helmet-shaped junipers reflected the light flakes of granulated frost. Early morning had also dusted the driveway with a rime coverlet. I thought about the chilling winds. I had arrived back into the cold storage of winter. And my body was not acclimatized. Nor was my soul.

But inside, it was at least warm in my Christmas-tidings home. I was a wren, bouncing from branch to branch between relatives and friends. The gift exchange earlier had been wonderful for I was happy I was able to bring each of them a gift from Mexico. It was sharing a part of my new country with them. Souvenirs of salmon pinks, fuchsias, peacock blues, and the citrus colors of lemon and lime brightened the season. It also made me lonely for Mexico. I wondered how my new friends and lovers were doing.

My mother took great pride in decorating for Christmas. Although it was a home of disharmony and deceit, it was cloaked in reds, greens, whites, and silvers. The name on the marquee was mine, but I didn't belong, I thought. Not now. Maybe never.

Mom always tried to make things as happy as possible. She was ready to throw herself on a sword each time my father would sneak out to the tool shed for a belt of booze. She was impaled upon a church and societal bond. She needed camouflage to protect him. He needed one more drink, and then another.

Everyone foraged on multitudes of excellent food. Then the company dispersed. Gran had gone to bed earlier. I went in to kiss her temple. Her eyes opened, so I sat on the bed. "Gran, I feel as though I'm abandoning all of you in this muddle."

"Nothing you can do here, girl."

The night's dimness made us both more somber. "I wish Mom would leave him."

"Our faith says if she divorces him, she can never remarry. I don't think your mother wants to spend the rest of her life alone. She believes he'll change. She's got a good heart in her. He works on her sympathy. Well, my time is nearing."

"Don't say that, Gran. I need you."

"You keep on reading. When I'm gone, I want you to have all my books. Promise you'll keep on with your studies."

"You have my word."

"Something else." She took her antique gold pocket watch from her nightstand drawer. "I want you to have this. It's your inheritance. Along with the books."

"Gran, don't you want to keep your watch?"

"Might get lost in the shuffle. You take it." She pressed it into the envelope of my hand.

"Thanks, Gran." I studied the engravings on each side of the delicate timepiece. On one side was a cottage. On the other was her initial, which was also mine—K. My grandfather had given his *Kate* the watch as a wedding gift.

As a child, I recalled playing with it while seated on her lap. I would open the spring clasp, stare at the white dial face, and watch the lacy gold hands moving. They were so fragile they reminded me of golden threads that swirled time away. Memories flooded of Sundays when Gran would always dress up and wear her timepiece like a lavaliere. It would dangle over her apron top when she cooked dinner. Her after-Mass specialty was a steaming pot of beef, carrot, turnip, and potato stew, accompanied by Irish soda bread. I loved her pudding with honey cream sauce dripping over it.

Tears filled my eyes. I pressed the watch to my breast. She had made me guardian of her most precious possession. My moist face eased against hers.

"Kelly Anne, our bodies are like that watch. Ticking time is our life. I've had a good long time." She smiled as she wiped my tears. "Anyways, I believe heaven is a candy factory. I've never been able to get my hands on enough sweets since I got this darned diabetes. So when I trade this old sack of bones in for wings, I'm going to eat every fluff of cotton candy I can get my hands on."

I smiled. "And candy bars."

"I'll have them all. Wheelbarrows filled to the brim." She paused. Her eyes became stern. "I'm sorry I light into you on this Mexico business. And about you wanting to be a writer. Well, you be a good one."

"You don't mind that I want to become a writer?"

"I been thinking some on that. Some of my best friends are books. I can't read as much as I used to though. My eyesight is going to the dogs. Well, you be that writer. And don't be one of those soft-soap authors. Steer clear of meanness of the heart. Don't do tattling, and you stand up for how you believe. You better go on and do it, as you've had it in your head for nearly all of your days. What matters most is that you keep you a good heart."

I kissed her cheek, drew the afghan up around her shoulders, and smiled. "One day, I'll write an A+ story about you. Thanks, Gran. I love you."

Switching off the light made me feel a hollowness—an aloneness. I went into my room. Clutching her watch near to me, I wept. If Gran said heaven is a candy factory, I believe it must be. A supreme being could do worse than being a confectioner.

* * * * *

TAKING NOTES WHILE Gran reminisced was an afternoon treat. She called her life a nearly completed portfolio. Certainly, she had witnessed and lived history. She had finished telling a story of frontier life. She related childhood memories. When she was young, wandering bands of starving Indians would make their way through the land in search of food. She could recall seeing the frightened faces of weary Indians peeping through the windows. Her mother told her not to be fearful. They had been displaced. They only wanted food. She would place a gunny sack of potatoes and grain on the porch. The Indians would take the small bounty and be on their way.

"Your stepmother was a courageous woman," I commented.

"She was that. I remember the first time I clapped eyes on her. She'd come all the way from France to marry my father. She got us kids in the bargain." Gran smiled as she reminisced. "I recollect their wedding day. My, but she was dressed all elegant in a prim, white blouse with delicate lace on the bodice. Pearl buttons climbing up the center of the neckline. And a dark skirt of billowing taffeta. She walked with the most graceful carriage I'd ever seen. Her hair was waved and styled. She was the most refined woman you could imagine."

I rapidly filled the pages of my notebook. "Your father was in love with her."

"He was. You know, Kelly Anne, you are no blood relation of my stepmother, but you have so many of her ways. The way she picked up from her country and came off to this strange country. She fell in love and stayed until her dying day."

"Your father must have been a good man or she wouldn't have stayed," I offered.

"Yes. Your great-grandfather was a fine man." The burly, gentleman from Ireland, Gran reported, was hardworking, husky, and had a penchant for singing Celtic songs. "My daddy could sing a lullaby that would have us sleeping in no time," she boasted proudly. "He was a good man. Wasn't easy settling the land." Blinking away tears, she concluded, "Anyways, I seen plenty of changes in my day. I'm about to pack it in." With a chuckle, she added, "And if you live this long, girl, you won't be any better looking than I am." She leaned back against her chair. "You remember where you belong. This country cost us a price. Pioneer women died in childbirth, families starved, and men died in battle to forge this country of ours. It's still costing. You keep hold of your patriotism."

"I'm going to, Gran."

"I worry about you, Kelly Anne. There're Communists down there," she blustered.

"Up here, too."

Rebuking my statement with a squint, she declared, "Not *here* in Kansas." She had won her case. She would need a nap. "Well, I'm getting worn out by all this jawing. You ought to have your notebook filled to the brim by now."

"You'd better get a little snooze."

With notebook in hand, I was closing her bedroom door when Rod arrived. "Gran needs to rest," I whispered to him. I ushered him down the hall. "Rod, could you take me somewhere?" I asked my favorite male cousin.

"Sure, Kelly. I want you to see how terrific my car is. Mags like mountains. Polished up so great you need to put your sunglasses on. That chrome will blind you."

On the way to his car, I explained, "I need to get away awhile. And I want to make a call."

"Why can't you make it at the house?" He replaced his glasses with sunglasses. He then pulled his shirt collar up. With his tight denims, slackened loafers, and yellow shirt, I teased that he was becoming a *hood*. He gave his dark hair a flip back, pressing it into a ducktail. "Well, why can't you call from your place?"

"I want a private conversation." We strolled to his candy-apple red Ford. Flame decals and pin striping decorated the car's fenders and sides. "Looking terrific!" I exclaimed. When I crawled inside, I gave the white stuffed dice that hung from the stem of the rearview mirror a tap. "I need privacy. I'll even spring for a soft drink and burger."

"Okay. So if you're not going to tell me who you're calling, can you tell me why you're writing down Gran's tales? Are you making a book on her?"

"I wanted to get her stories recorded. She's been telling us about pioneer days since we were little." I paused. "It's important. And sure, I'd like to write a story about it."

"She misses you."

"I miss her, too."

His mellow voice asked, "Then why go back to Mexico?"

"I can't explain. I really love it there."

"I don't care if I never leave America."

"Rod, your mom is concerned that you'll drop out of college. I'm frightened for you, too. This friend of mine has a brother in the military. He's in Vietnam. Claims things are getting worse there. I don't want you to be drafted. Conscripted into some stupid war. So please, stay in school." I gave his shoulder a playful shove. "I've always been protective of you. I had to nurse you through the croup."

"We were only a year old when we had whooping cough, Kelly. I don't think you can take the credit. Besides, you were a few months older than I was and everyone swore you gave it to me in the first place."

"They lied. At any rate, please don't let them draft you."

"No sweat," he evangelized. As Rod pulled into a parking

lot, his muffler popped. "Nice touch, huh?"

"Nice touch," I repeated. I made my way to the phone booth and swung the door securely shut. I clasped the phone tightly. I quickly called Cresida. We traded greetings, briefed one another on our Christmases, and told one another how much we missed being together. She would be going to a faculty party on New Year's Eve. I would be attending a party with my friends. My bus would be leaving the following morning. So I would make the Eve party an early one. Cres suggested we dine together first thing when I arrived back in D.F.

I returned to Rod's car. My heart vessels swarmed with a pounding. My thoughts of Cres remained a drumroll. "Want to drop me off in Mexico City?" I kidded.

"Not me. I'm a homegrown boy." His prized car ambled at a slow promenading pace back across town and into my driveway. "See you later, Kelly."

"Please remember," I lectured, "what I said about staying in school."

"If I get drafted, I'll go over there and give it my best shot. I'm an American. We don't take crap off anybody." Then, with a mellow grin, he added, "I don't want any dumb shits coming over here and taking my car."

I gave his neck a squeeze as I hugged him. "Let's both promise to survive." I kissed his cheek, and then got out of his car. I watched his body sink back into the auto's low seat. He revved up the engine. Slowly, he rolled his car back down the driveway. The car crept to the corner stop sign where I heard the musical horn. Its pipe-flute melody played, "I'm a Yankee Doodle Dandy."

And off Rod went. With a dilatory motion, I pulled my jacket collar around my neck as I trudged to the house. Trailing was the melodious warble, 'a real live nephew of my Uncle

Sam.' It continued until I heard the sound of the storm door buckle closed behind me.

* * * * *

LOUISE BOGAN WROTE that women have no wilderness in them. They wait when they should journey. But I dispute that. My great-step-grandmother made her journey. I believe women have always journeyed for the betterment of their families. But I certainly agree with most of Bogan's other words. In *A Poet's Alphabet*, she states, "Poetry is often generations in advance of the thought of its time." Valid as far as I was concerned. I vowed to work on a few poems I'd scribbled while riding the bus home.

Snuggling down under protective bed covers, I thought about how solitary my childhood seemed. I never felt comfortable having friends over to visit. That might be the reason for my fated hibernation with books. As now, my father had made holidays horrible. This year Christmas dinner was in shambles. He nearly had Kris in tears when he snarled. Gran could barely eat.

We walked on eggshells to keep him from drinking. There was nothing that could have kept him from his bottle. And after he drank, we feared for our safety. He had beaten my mother, hospitalizing her once. He made our home a pressure cooker.

Studying the shadows against the wall, I resigned myself to six more days. Unhappiness can't be concealed, even if it is well-isolated. It didn't surprise me when my mother entered my bedroom to question why I'd gone to bed so early.

"I'm catching up on my sleep," I disclaimed my anger as best I could.

She sat on the edge of my bed, tenderly reaching to brush

hair back from my forehead. "I worry about you being so far away."

"I'm safe there." My eyes darted back to their fixed spot on the ceiling. "Mom, we've been endangered by that maniac out there. His drinking has always held us in peril. Even now, he's building up to rip-roaring drunk. We all know it. I hate it here."

She shut her eyes. "He's struggling, too. He isn't always like this," she excused. "He has some good qualities. His favorite movie is *It's A Wonderful Life*."

"Welcome to Bedford Falls," I unleashed my sarcasm.

"Kelly, he's your father." She took my hand. "He's troubled. He was despondent after the war. But when his parents died, he became devastated. You know the Catholic Church won't dissolve a marriage. And, Kelly, he wasn't like this when I married him."

"Then he isn't the man you married. The church, in its infinite wisdom, should recognize that if he's changed, it's emotional bigamy."

"I realize it's been difficult for you and Kris. I've prayed..."

"I don't want to hear about prayer." I was on the doorstep of crying. "Mom, I love you. I see you're trapped. Every time he gets loaded, he beats you. Or hauls out his guns. Brandishes his weapons and terrorizes us all. No one should be subjected to this kind of life."

"I can't expect you to understand. I married in sickness and in health. He's sick. I'm trying to help him."

"That's bullshit. He's a pathetic, self-indulgent, middle-aged man. Sick people have cancer and heart disease. He's a weak, brutal, gutless, spoiled man. He's been coddled all his life."

"I wish I could get through to you." As if the

communication lines were down, she stood. "Kelly, I love you. He loves you, too."

When she left, silence remained. I questioned the apparatus of love. Burrowing deeper under the covers, I realized I wished I was back in the wretched motel room in San Antonio, hiding under those covers, wishing I was home in Kansas. Battling back tears, I couldn't imagine where I truly belonged. I did know I missed Mexico.

But perhaps I hadn't even been to where I belong.

TWENTY-FIVE

"HOW LONG DOES it take to feed one mid-sized dog?" I questioned Kris. We watched our pinto-designed, mixed-breed dog playing with his food.

"Prince is working his paws to the bone even as we speak. Look at those kibbles. We're talking bland. No wonder he hates the stuff. Eat up, Prince," she instructed. She pushed his bowl toward him. He ate a mouthful of kibbles, wagged his tail, and then began roaming the backyard.

"Your little speech reinforced his decision to ignore his meal. Now he's revolting."

"Revolting. Like his food," Kris sputtered. Her familiar laugh rose.

I joined in. "You haven't changed. Prince hasn't changed either. Let's go shopping, Kris."

"He's overweight. The vet told us to put his food down for exactly fifteen minutes. Then pick the bowl back up."

"Sounds screwy to me. Why don't you give him smaller portions? He could eat an entire grain elevator's contents in only ten minutes if he sets his mind to it."

"He'll do it. Prince, get back here and eat that garbage right now."

"You're about as strict as marmalade."

She flashed her frolicsome smile before tattling, "He's a scavenger."

I suggested, "Let's tackle him, then pour that crap down

his throat." Continuing with our comedic palaver, we tried to flag him down. "Back to the starting line, Prince."

Kris finally hoisted herself onto the picnic table. She crossed her arms. "Tell me about Eduardo."

"He's a nice guy. Adorable."

"Do you go all the way with him?" she giggled her question.

"Kris! I'm too busy studying. I love living down there," I attempted to derail the conversation.

"I wish you were home. Even if it is cold up here."

"I'm like a goldfish. I require sun or I could lose my color," I prattled. "And the creative writing department is tops."

"I don't see why you want to be a writer anyway."

Rotating like a whippet, I defended, "Because. And I'm going to write. No matter what."

"Cool down." Kris turned on her charisma. "I didn't mean you shouldn't. It's that most writers and artists are so nutsy acting. And they make zero money. I don't see you as a beatnik. But then," she appraised, "you're not exactly secretarial material either."

"Thank you for recognizing that much anyway." I frowned, then leaned down to scratch Prince's muzzle.

"Hey, I remembered a joke I wanted to tell you."

"Shoot."

Kris took a deep breath. "Okay. These men were walking down the street. They pass this woman and one man said to the other, 'Isn't that Matilda?' 'No,' answered the other man. They walked on, passing another woman. The first guy asks, 'Isn't that Hortense?' The other guy answered," Kris broke, gasping for breath as her chaining giggle exploded. "He says, 'No, she's cool as a cucumber.'" Kris brayed as she held her sides laughing. She repeated through chops of laughter, "He said,

'No, she's cool as a cucumber.'"

Amused more at Kris than her story, I chortled my response, "Great. One of my roommates will love it. She delights in raffish jokes. One of my roommates won't love it. She doesn't delight in any jokes at all."

"What about your third roommate?"

"I won't mention it to her. Professional courtesy," I added.

* * * * *

MY INSOMNIA WAS worse than ever. Nightmares were occurring more frequently. Before going to bed, I'd fidgeted with a weekly news magazine. I perused the ghost roll call for 1963. The year's casualty list of writers included Frost, William Carlos Williams, Roethke, Sylvia Plath, Cocteau, Odets, and Huxley.

My eyes latched shut wondering which among us could fill those shoes. Then I read a list of *crowd* deaths. It had not been a good year for the masses either. A collapsed dam in Italy, a windstorm in Bangladesh, and hurricanes in Cuba and Haiti had polished off thousands. What a burial ground the planet is, I mused. The years wipe us away.

My addendum was sadder yet. Now, we possess the capability to take all life from earth in one blast. This year had also provided a military showdown within a stone's throw of our border. Cuba's missile crisis might have been devastating.

Strain exacerbated my insomnia. I longed to return to Mexico. The climate there, I told myself, was conducive to my sleep—and to me. My father and I had taken care to side-step one another. We were like a couple of starving sharks in a wading pool.

I had always feared his violence when he drank. I thought about how maybe the mastery of life is forgetting fear. But fear can be a healthy indicator to protect us. My shoulders bolted back into a steel girder as my anger incensed me. I had no control over any of it. Even if I could escape, truly escape, Kris, Gran, and my mother were captives. He could harm them—kill them.

Home had never been a safe place. Nor had it been a sacred place. My parent's shouting battles were never sane, nor safe.

Marimbas sounded much safer.

* * * * *

DAYS WERE FILLED, but none too busy to see that my father's alcoholism was getting out of hand. He was now more sloshed than not. Confrontation is often well-sealed before detonation. No doubt, my father was braced for a skirmish that would one day take place. Both of us imagined it would be in the distant future. There were stored-up words that would one day rage. My hostilities had smoldered for years. A splenetic hatred burned my insides.

So when our confrontation erupted, prematurely, we were not ready.

I had packed my bag before leaving for the New Year's Eve party. I would be meeting friends, taking a nostalgic wade through yesterday, and sojourning the past. And relishing it all.

After that pleasurable evening, I returned home. It would be my final night there before leaving for Mexico in the morning. I entered a dark house and realized that I would be glad to leave. How contrary to what family love should be. Kris had jumped at an invitation to a slumber party. She'd escaped. My mother and Gran had gone to bed. They had escaped. For as many years as I could remember, our family was escaping, or worse, not escaping, my father's drinking.

From the kitchen, I saw a light glowing in the outside workshop. That meant my father was alone—and drinking. It suddenly occurred to me this could well be the last time I would see my father. It would be the last chance I would have to confront him. For, if anything happened to Gran, I would simply tell my mother and Kris to come to Mexico City if they wished to visit me. I would stay put south of the border. Forever.

He would not be taking me to the station in the morning since Kris and her friends had volunteered. And Gran was my only reason for ever returning. She had given me her watch. Old people do that when they're ready to die. And I had already narrowly escaped death twice. Maybe I would be the first one to reach last gulp gulch.

If this were the final time to talk with my father, I didn't want words left unsaid.

There was an urgency to tell my father exactly how I felt. I'd traveled hundreds of miles to visit, and he'd ruined another holiday.

Throwing a jacket around my shoulders, I rushed out into the frosty evening. He had played havoc with my childhood. On this chilled New Year's Eve, there would be a showdown. My quick knock went unanswered. Ordinarily, there was no right-of-passage in my home. Privacy was the one securing position. Barricades were respected. So when I gave the door a shove, my father looked shocked. I had broken into his corridor. My invasion was vital and crucial.

With amazement, he muttered, "You. What do you want?" His head slumped back down over a small, tattered, ebony-colored suitcase. Stray hair and vacant eyes told me of his condition. His face was drawn. Unshaven, facial stubble made his face appear even gaunter. His liquid eyes were menacing when his head lifted again. I considered how dapper and handsome he was when sober. His carriage was tall and his clothing meticulous. When drinking, he was only my mother's love away from the gutter.

I sat on the chair opposite his. Between us was the workshop's table. "We need to talk," I announced.

"You've barely talked with me since you've been here," he slurred.

"I despise your drinking. I deplore what it does to the family."

"So why are you talking now?"

"Because it's important that I tell you how I feel." He was silent. I monitored his face. "I see you're browsing your old war photos again. You won't talk about the war, but you come out here and grieve your stinking war. That war was a generation ago. We're on the edge of a brand new war. And you're still entrenched in World War II."

"You don't know about the war."

"You think I don't. You've got a wife who loves you enough to stick by you. She still wants a future with you. And you're out here going over the past. Stuck in the past. It isn't fair to any of us." Words suddenly overflowed. "I wish to hell you would talk about the war so we can find some justification for the war you've made your family live with."

He opened the suitcase a crack, and then took out a handful of photos. He shuffled them. He looked at several pictures of bombed out structures in Europe. As if he had been dealt a bad hand of cards, he then threw them down on the table. "This is my war."

Glancing quickly at the photos, I shrugged. "I've seen them before. War is terrible. We all acknowledge that."

He reached down into a tackle box that was on the floor. Pulling out a new bottle of whiskey, he uncapped it. Before he could take his first swig, I reached and took it from his hand.

He was certain I was going to pitch it on the floor. I didn't. I took a large gulp. I followed that with a chug of the foul smelling booze. Calmly, I handed it back to him. I registered his amazement. He hadn't expected that.

Continuing to inspect the war-torn lands of France and Germany, I finally spoke. "You came back from overseas alive. You came back in one piece. You returned to a wife and infant daughter. The war ended, but you're still fighting it."

"You've never been to war." His hand smoothed his hair. The unbuttoned shirt sleeve of his wool Pendleton swayed as he talked. "My war. Hell, it was your war, too. Hitler had an oven for us all. You're part Jewish."

Attempting to measure his intoxication, I knew no matter how plastered he was, I needed to confront him and express my hurt for we had never before talked like this. His fluid, sardonic eyes blinked. His sip became a gulp of whiskey. I wanted to tell him of my embezzled childhood. I wanted to scream how his intoxication was my Nemean Lion. It had robbed my family of love. He betrayed each of us when he crawled into his bottle. He put alcohol first—his family second. I wanted to show him my pain. There was the pain of fear, the pain of being embarrassed by him. And there was the guilt. As a small child, I wondered what I had done wrong to make my daddy drink. As if trying to combat an ache, I could never do enough or be good enough. Thoughts ricocheted.

"I'm thankful Hitler was defeated. I'm proud that you served. But that was then. It's over. Time to get over it." I sucked air, before continuing. "So while your semi-lucid and not being too much of a sonofabitch, let's have the first real conversation we've ever had."

"I could never talk with you. I always held out more hope for Kris. She's not so surly." He took another swallow of whiskey.

Again, I picked up the bottle and drank. "Well," I refuted his charges, "I was a happy baby until you came back from your goddamn war. Then I saw surly in action."

Combatively, he seethed, "War would make you surly, too."

"I've seen and lived through domestic war. Mine wasn't a two-year war with a hero's welcome home and a medal or two on my chest. Mine has been a twenty-year war. The war of your past didn't belong exclusively to you. You manacled us to it right along with you. So finish the fucking war. Get on with it." My language and militant stance were shocking to us both. "The fact the war was hell is not news."

"You don't know." The hanging light bulb cast a shadowy light against his face. He took another guzzle and then handed me the bottle. "You can't know."

"I need to know. I'll probably never see you again. I'm not coming back unless Gran needs me. So tell me why you're doing this postmortem on the war. One day it might be too late for any of it. You might not be able to retrieve the rest of your family. You're losing me, and you could lose them, too. One day soon, Kris will be leaving. And even Mom might finally get a belly full of your bullshit."

He sneered. "You have your whole life ahead of you."

"Our lives are only as good as today. And we may never have another time to talk like this." Recalling that my mother mentioned how his real downfall came after the death of his parents, which was right after the war ended, I affixed a bayonet and plunged. "Do you think your parents would be proud of you?"

He slapped workshop table. "You don't know. It wasn't only the war. But it changed everything." His eyes were emblazoned with hatred. "I always loved you all too much to tell you the truth."

"What truth?"

"No one knows but me."

"Tell me."

"No." His glazed eyes were watering. "It would mean you'd carry the burden. The pain." There was a lameness in his voice.

"I'm already carrying the pain you caused by ruining my childhood."

He shook his head violently. "I can't do that to you."

"Maybe I'm stronger than you are. Tell me."

"You want to be strong?" his gnashing slur challenged. "Well, we'll see how strong you are." Spitting through his teeth, he fired, "No one is ever to know. No one. Not your mother. Not Kris."

"You have my word, I'll never tell them."

"You'd better be strong for this secret." He angrily looked away. His jaw clamped for many moments. "Your grandparents, my parents, were scientists." His fist clenched tightly, pressing against the tabletop. During the war, they were in Nevada."

My mind felt webbed. "So?"

"After my father died, I found his journal." He opened the suitcase back up and dug to the bottom. Pulling out a thin date journal, he held it in front of me. It was loosely bound with flimsy stitching. "He was in Los Alamos."

"Grandfather Benjamin was a professor and Grandmother was a medical research scientist."

"My father was a physicist. He knew chemical bonding. He was needed by the government because of his knowledge of the theory of atomic structure."

Bulldozed, I leaned back. I shivered. "God."

"He helped to build the bomb." Sensing my astonishment, he pitched the journal to me. "Your inheritance. The secret," he snarled. His face was basted in shame and hatred. "I loved my father. I believed in his peace-loving nature. He never once yelled at me when I was a boy." Tears formed in his eyes.

I thumbed through the book. It was unfathomable. Minute scrawls and symbols were jotted into the margins. I could only decipher a few words and phrases. Fissionable plutonium. Dr. Bucher. Dr. Oppenheimer. I scanned the nearly illegible handwriting, sifting for each word. Critical mass. Cyclotron. Circuitry for little boy. I leafed through the book. Toward the last half of the journal, the date of July 16, 1945 was circled. Gadget tested. Flash. Billowing boletus mushroom—thicker stemmed column.

My grandfather had recorded his life and the life of my grandmother. Notations were made in the workbook. The end of the month, there was one page with the words, 'She was diagnosed with cancer today. Our lives are over. I shall not live without her.'

I had been told my grandmother had died of cancer and my grandfather had died within months of his wife. No reason was ever given, nor was one talked about.

Quickly, I flipped pages to another circled date. August 6, 1945. It was also blank with the exception of the words 'nine seconds.' December 31, 1945 was the final page. I quickly read it. My grandfather wrote that the war had taken fourteen million military lives. Americans killed or missing tallied 322,000. Total U.S. casualties were 1,200,000. Murdered. An estimated quarter of a million Japanese civilians murdered— the atomic bombs.

My grandfather also did ghost roll-calls.

I handed the diary back to my father. He swatted it. "Take it. You said you're leaving for good. I don't blame you. But now you have my side of your inheritance. Your task of exoneration begins." Our eyes roped together. "All the excuses you're thinking about now, you'll be thinking about for the rest of your life."

Standing, I leaned across the table to hug him. Probably for the first time in my life. I then tucked the journal into my coat. It was snuggled against my side, digging into my ribs. I made my way back to the house on that blustering New Year's Eve.

My father told me I would search for some misappropriated, generational atonement. Entering my bedroom, I buried the journal in my suitcase, under my other belongings. Well-hidden, and still, I could feel it there. I didn't need to view it to know of its existence.

Preposterous, I mumbled to the empty room. The blinds were pulled tightly, but lines of light were sneaking through. I wanted to coax out my deepest tear but couldn't locate it that night. But I could also feel the tear was dug in deeply. It was there to stay.

I went away from that evening, for the first time in my life, angrier at a situation than with a person.

BOOK TWO: AS MEXICO AS A JOURNEY'S END

PART IV—HELP US TO BRING DARKNESS INTO THE LIGHT

Violence, destruction, receive our homage.
Help us to bring darkness into the light,
To lift out the pain, the anger,
Where it can be seen for what it is -
The balance-wheel for our vulnerable,
aching love.
Put the wild hunger where it belongs,
Within the act of creation,
Crude power that forges a balance
between love and hate.
— May Sarton
"The Invocation to Kali"
(Mustard Seed, New Poems,
W. W. Norton & Company, Inc. 1971)

TWENTY-SIX

AND MY *JORNADA* continued.

There is a grueling cavity that lurks behind secrets. When the truth bubbles to the surface, we climb out of our scorched trenches. We meet the truth. Its residue can spike even the bloodiest heart.

Time passes rapidly. The road ensures that much. There was a heart tug when I left my family. I kissed Gran, my raconteur of the frontier, as she slept. I was held in the thicket of my mother's arms. I squeezed Kris tightly, wanting to take her away to safety with me.

And I recalled the memory of seeing my father's head buried in the crook of his arm. He rested on his pantheon of photos. He had been the secret keeper.

I had entered his foxhole.

* * * * *

BUS FUMES BELCHED strands of smoke. The blond sunshine of San Antonio was giving way to umbra shades of evening. I spotted Carlos with his long, loping stride.

Disheveled, in crumpled gray corduroy slacks, a cable-knit sweater, suede desert boots, and a grin, he approached.

My own face crinkled into a smile as I embraced him with a limpet's hold. Carlos explained we would be staying the night in San Antonio. Tom was too shellacked to drive, and

Carlos had driven all day. We had a TexMex meal and then checked into a crusty, weathered motel. The day on the road had taken its toll. After showering, we collapsed on the bed to give rundowns on our vacations.

Finally, Carlos approached my misery. "Something's wrong? What's wrong, Kel?"

"Nothing." I leaned back against the pillow.

"Come on. Don't try to snow the snowman. I'm not a dumb *pendejo*. What's troubling you?"

"Kansas is an emotional place for me."

"Your father was hitting the bottle?"

"Yes. And maybe I realized I no longer belong there. I've changed. Maybe I never really ever belonged there. I was merely imprisoned there."

"So you've returned from the land of the missionary position. I'd hate Kansas, too."

"I don't hate Kansas. Only the circumstances."

"What else is bugging you?"

"Everything is complex." I explored his face. "I'm glad to be returning to Mexico."

"I'll bet Eduardo will be happy to see you."

"Maybe that needs to finally change as well. I've got to make him understand we can only be friends."

"Speaking of friends, that reminds me. I almost forgot. My buddy is going to check on Leigh's sister. He'll let us know."

"Thank him for his trouble, but I'm not sure I want to know now. Some things are better left unknown."

"I want to know everything."

"Honesty by divulging everything, sometimes it changes us and those around us."

"Meaning?" he delved.

My eyes closed as if that would redirect the conversation. I then answered, "Meaning the truth can be a form of distortion.

It can change feelings."

"Truth couldn't change my feelings about you. You're my friend."

"Want to test the truth, Carlos?"

"Sure." He pulled the cover around him and sat up slightly. "There's nothing you could tell me that would impact our friendship."

"I'm having an affair with a woman."

"Leigh?"

"No. The woman you saw me with when you picked me up at the Continental."

He peered into my face, recognizing truth. "Well, she is *muy guapa*."

"Yes. Maybe we are all androgynous in spirit. I'm not sure. It's very confusing."

"How did it happen?"

"I met her at the party in Acapulco. She's a doctor. Brilliant, lovely, aristocratic, and fine. She's a polyglot and a polymath and I'm a Pollyanna. It's damned overwhelming."

"Saves on condoms," he said with a laugh. He then kissed my temple. "It still doesn't change our friendship. And what the hell? If it enriches you, why not? A guy tried to pick me up once. I pretended I didn't know what he wanted and then got the hell out of there. Women are different though. More appealing. Guess I'm surprised, but not shocked." His smile teetered. "Well, maybe a little shocked."

"I'm shocked myself. Over the holiday, I watched a flick called *Susan Lenox*. Garbo and Gable. Well, he tells Garbo that she'll end up in the gutter. She answers, fine, but that she'll make it a worthwhile gutter."

"Kel, going to bed with a classy woman is hardly the gutter. So you've got a diversified sex appetite. Erotic and robust energies. And this *doctora* doesn't lack appeal. *Muy guapa*. And a pundit to boot." He kissed the nape of my neck, before whispering, "No. It doesn't change my feelings for you. You'll probably always be my very best friend."

His arms girded me with warmth and protection. Our wrapped bodies tucked into the curl of kittens. We slept.

* * * * *

WE SLEPT INTO the brightness of an Aztec-yellow morning. While packing, I studied the cadmic beams against my pinstripe baseball jersey. I would be taking my favorite jersey and cutoffs back to Mexico with me. To wear around the apartment—certainly not to appear on the street in casual garb like that. Not permissible, I considered.

When Carlos entered, I handed him his Christmas gift. It was a small leather notebook with his name gilded on the lower corner. Inside the small journal, I had tucked a card where I'd written a note: Fill 'er up!

He grinned and then said, "I'll think about us when I write my memoirs." Pulling a package from his bag, he handed it to me. "From New Mexico."

Inside was a beautiful silver ring with a turquoise stone. I slipped it on my finger. "It's lovely. And it fits perfectly."

"Kel, it has healing powers."

Suddenly somber, I asked, "Carlos, what am I going to do without you?"

"Kel, I'll miss you, too. You really are my best friend. I've never had a woman best friend before. I'm ashamed to say it, but women have always been lovers or barely noticed. When I get out of the Peace Corps, why don't we meet up to travel Europe together?"

"It's a date. We'll swashbuckle our way across the continent."

"By the way, I stopped by next door. Tom is hung over." Carlos slipped into his loafers, shook his head, and then commented, "I knew the goofy turd was going to go back to the car and get that quart. He is one wasted shit." Carlos lifted our suitcases. We headed for the car.

"So the driving is up to us. Terrific." Tom, with his saw-toothed hair fringing his forehead, his bruise-purple eyelids, and pale skin exited from his room. He looked terrible.

"Fellating a bottle again," Carlos accused.

My words were sad. "If he isn't careful, he's going to end his slide on his ass."

Carlos squinted. "Tom, you're getting to be a real bad bet."

"I'm not a fucking altar boy," Tom muttered as he crawled into the backseat.

"You're torturing yourself," Carlos chastised as we got into the car. I peered around. Tom's eyes were already clamped shut. "He'll be okay. Kel, we aren't all cut from the same cloth. I don't think he means to be such a turd."

We had driven most of the morning when Tom finally woke. He had been in the middle of a cornball joke when his smirk froze. His cheeks billowed. He motioned for Carlos to pull over. Carlos stopped the car on the crusty edge of the road. It was barely in time. Tom flung is body out and vomited his toenails. Before he again passed out, he told us about a professor named Leary who was experimenting with a substance called LSD 25. Leary had spent time in Cuernavaca where he became interested in certain varieties of mushrooms. They achieved the same psychedelic response as a drug synthesized by a Swiss biochemist.

Carlos grumbled that Tom would be chomping down mushrooms and would probably poison himself. He's doing that now, I charged. And then we left it alone. I refrained from lectures that I knew would do no good. My own *high* was my only concern. And my high was Mexico. Land of serenades and sangria. Of parasol-shaded trees, fiestas, and a rainbow of color. My high, I considered as we charged through clusters of villages, was this incredible land.

By the time we reached Ciudad Victoria, we had needed a rest. We decided to pack it in for the evening. Tom drank his meal in the room. Carlos and I went out for rellenos and cornhusk-wrapped tamales smothered in a delicious salsa.

"Great spices," I said between steaming forkfuls.

"Mexico is teaching you about spice."

"Yes," I agreed. "I'm definitely learning about spice."

"And sugar," he teased.

"Sugar with *spice*."

* * * * *

NIGHTMARES HAD BEEN nudged away with dreams of returning to Mexico City. When I entered the apartment, I felt I'd been safely delivered to a part of life that was home. Leigh heard me unpacking my suitcase. She made a dash for my bedroom.

"Sorghum is up. Pork bellies, down," I announced.

"We wanted to stage a pageant for your return. But as you can see, all your loyal subjects have high-tailed it out of here." Leigh perched on a chair and drew her legs up as she rested her head on her knees. "Sanchez and Nora left to take Mrs. Lawrence to the airport."

"How's Lindy?"

"We had a wonderful time on the dig. The only skirmish we had was about my language. She's given me replacement words to use."

"Replacement words?"

"Instead of saying *fuck*, I now say *farkle*. Farkle face. It loses in the translation, but I know what I really mean. *Shit* has now become *sugar*. Regardless, it's saving the relationship."

"Lindy is a wonderful influence on you."

"In plenty of ways, Benj. She's made it possible for my masturbation holiday."

With a tornadic sigh, I muttered, "That aside, you're lucky to have her."

"I see Kansas is still a training ground for virtue."

"Leigh, farkle off."

"Hey, come on, Benj. You know you missed me."

I rummaged through my bag to retrieve a gift. "Something for your spring field trip to the Yucatan." I handed her a water canteen. She had hinted she could use a new one.

"Perfect." She exited a few moments, returning with a set of records featuring Mexican music. "Here. Bean music doesn't light my fire, so don't play it too loudly."

"I'm impressed. You remembered I mentioned wanting this."

"I'm not a totally farkled-up bitch."

"Isn't the word *bitch* an infraction?"

"Benjamin, Colette called boring people 'undesirable.' At times, you can be truly undesirable. So how's that for improving my slur campaign?"

"Your language might be better, after all. By the way," I divulged, "I told Carlos about Cres. He thinks she's sexy."

"Farkle! Benj, you should never tell men about loving women. You're flipping mouth must run on batteries the way you blab."

With a sly smile, I murmured, "If my mouth ran on batteries, he would have called me sexy, too."

* * * * *

EDUARDO CALLED, ASKING to stop by. We'd planned to exchange gifts after Christmas. When he arrived, I greeted him warmly, feeling optimistic about an evening with no problems.

He surprised me with a rare, antique copy of Shakespeare's plays in Spanish. The covers were leather with wooden strip bindings. Words were printed on rich textured paper. The corners had become yellowed. The hand-painted illustration was bright and lovely. Turning pages, I spotted the play *Trolius and Cressida*. Quickly, I shut the book, and then gave Eduardo a hug.

He was also thrilled with my gift to him. I'd purchased a silver draftsman's pencil with his name inscribed. He graciously thanked me and promised to use it when designing future landmark buildings.

We decided to go for some *café de olle*. The sweet, spicy fragrance of molasses and cinnamon greeted us as we entered the small café. It reminded me I'd returned to the land of aroma, color, texture, and passion.

"I missed you," he whispered across the table.

"You, too."

After being served, I sipped the lovely coffee. "Delicious."

"And your trip, it was good?"

"Fine. The bus ride seemed long."

"You were alone?"

I took a deep breath. "On the bus, yes. I drove part way with other students."

Persisting, he grilled, "The bearded man was there?"

"Yes. He and his roommate."

"And the sleeping arrangements?"

"Eduardo, I'm not going to lie to you about Carlos. He's my best friend, and we did not make love."

"But did you sleep in separate rooms?"

"I answered your real question. Our sleeping arrangements

had nothing to do with sex. But Carlos, Tom, and I shared a room. The reason was purely a matter of economics, and I didn't relish staying alone in a seedy motel room."

His jaw clamped tightly. "You didn't make love with him?"

"No."

There was doubt in his eyes, as well as his voice. "How is it a man can stay with you and not wish to be lovers?"

"Because we're friends."

"You have been lovers with him?"

"Eduardo, I have no intention of continuing this Q&A session. On the trip, we were not romantically involved. That's my answer. Take it or leave it. I'm not making inquiries into your past sexual encounters. And you have no right to ask about mine."

"But since I have met you, I have not looked at another woman."

"Fine. Now, let's continue to have a lovely evening without this interrogation."

"Kelly, do you not understand that I have fallen in love with you? I wish to marry you." His fingers drummed the table's top.

"And do you not understand that doesn't give you ownership rights to my past?"

Standing, he reached into his pocket, pulled out change, and threw money on the table. "I do not accept your answer."

"Eduardo, I love you in so many ways, but maybe I can't give you the kind of love you need. I've told you I'm not certain about my life. I've told you, I'm too young to settle down. Or even consider it. I want to continue my education. I want to write."

"And I want to share my life with you."

"I've explained my feelings as best I can."

"But not to my satisfaction." There was irritation in his voice.

"That's too damned bad. Because I won't allow you or anyone else to complicate my life. Perhaps you should look for another woman. One you can control. To your satisfaction. I stood, grabbing my handbag. I added, "This won't work, Eduardo, I'm sorry."

"Kelly," he called after me.

"I'll see myself back to the apartment."

He pulled my arm. "I love you." He handed me the book I'd left on the table.

I pleaded, "How can I make you understand? I love you in my way, but it isn't enough." I investigated the pain in his face. "I need my freedom. I'm not going to live my life through a man. I'm not going to be made to answer to another for being myself. I don't want to live through your desires and your satisfaction. I've continued to think maybe in time we would work. But probably not to your satisfaction. Because it wouldn't be my satisfaction, Eduardo."

The two block walk home was a longer journey than the one I'd taken from Kansas.

* * * * *

WHILE CRAWLING INTO bed, I noticed Nora had returned. She'd opened the bottle of perfume I'd left wrapped and waiting on her bed. On my nightstand was a gift from her. I unwrapped it as quietly as I could, but her eyes pried open.

"Thanks a million for the perfume, Kelly. I was about out, and you can't get that brand down here. Gab loves it."

Turning the light on, I opened her gift. It was a copy of Elinor Wylie's *Collected Poems*. "This is wonderful, Nora." I was amazed she'd know I loved poetry written by women. And especially Wylie. "Really terrific!"

"I don't know anything at all about poetry, but I heard you talking about Marianne Moore and Elinor Wylie. They were out of the Moore collections."

"I love it." With a reverential hug, I smiled. "It's perfect." Placing the book on the nightstand, I knew I'd relish reading and rereading the collection.

"I think the poetess is still alive."

I knew of Wylie's untimely death when she was in her mid-forties back in 1928. I sat up in bed. "What would make you think she's still alive?"

"Must be," she answered. "The book was on sale."

"Well, there you are then," I concluded. The truth was, Wylie lives on through her words as I philosophized as I touched the spine of the volume. Nora believed the writer was alive because the book was on clearance. Nora may not have known poets, but she certainly had a grasp of the economics of poetry.

* * * * *

"I THINK THIS 'farkle' business is a riot!" I bleated as Nora and I walked to the bus stop. "Cleaning her foul mouth will help. Sanchez loved her pedestal compote dish that Mom sent down for her," I relayed. "She told me my mother is a superior woman. And she also said your mother is superior. I'm not sure what our mothers are superior to, but they are, in Edith's estimation, superior."

Nora chuckled. "Mom is a Christian Scientist, and that's definitely an advantage in being superior in Edith's eyes. Anyway, Juan also thought you were superior for bringing him a K.C. Royals baseball cap."

"Look what he gave me." I dangled the silver charm

bracelet. The charm attached was a tiny silver pencil. "He said he thinks of me when he sees a pencil. Maybe I'm too skinny."

"No. He thinks of you because you're always writing. And you've been teaching him English."

"With such a tough exterior, he's a marshmallow inside," I commented. "Wonder where he found the little pencil."

"Probably stole it."

"As Carlos always says, the belief down here is that the price of a stolen item is cheap. But I hope Juan didn't lift the bracelet."

A crowd of teens crossed the street, heading our way. They whistled to get our attention. Nora nudged me. "I hope Juan doesn't grow up to be one of those corner thugs."

"Not to worry," I assured her. "He has an *amisotos* smile."

As we approached the bus, I heard one of the teens shout at us. "Jankee, go home!"

I stepped back away from the door of the bus. I roared back at him, "I am home!" They looked puzzled, so I repeated my extemporaneous allegiance. "I am home." The look on their faces told me that no translation was required.

* * * * *

"I CAN'T TELL you how great it is to be back on campus," I declared as Leigh caught up with me. We walked to the student center terrace where I eased back into a deck chair.

Leigh plunged in an opposite chair. "Got Ancient Mesoamerica and Nahua Philosophy classes. Nora told me to tell you she got that Geopolitics course she wanted. She aggravates me. She asked where you were, so I told her I didn't know. Said we weren't joined at the hips. She gasped and took off. I figured you were getting signed up for all your artsy-fartsy classes."

"Where's Lindy?"

"She'll be here soon for a 'cupper.' Blends her tea like a chemist." Pointing to my charm bracelet, Leigh gave a jingle to her own. "Juan gave me one, too. My charm is a little nude woman. Think the kid knows I love women?"

With a jocular scowl, I mumbled, "I got a pencil."

"I should get one of those for that old swish, Paul," Leigh howled. "He suggested I get you a lesbian starter kit for Christmas."

"Paul comes up with some diamond lines. Told me he spent the holiday reading Moby Dick." Paul, with his epicene walk and natty attire, didn't give a rat's ass who knew he was gay. I liked that.

"He's been a good friend. Come to think of it, you've even been nice to me lately. Why don't you come on the Yucatan excursion during spring break?"

"I'd love to, but I'm not an archeology student."

"Look," she schemed, "you told me once you took a photojournalism class. And that you took photos when you worked at the newspaper. We could get them to issue you a camera and you could take field photos."

"I'd like to, but money's running out. I'm only down here because it's cheaper than in Kansas. If my scholarship comes through by next spring, maybe I could."

"Just my luck. You're invited and can't go because of lack of funds. And Nora isn't invited because of lack of *funs*," she giggled at her joke.

"Not bad for someone who gets excited about a class in Nahua Philosophy."

"Benjamin, that's the nicest thing you've ever said about me."

"It is, isn't it? Furthermore, it's most probably the nicest thing anyone has ever said about you."

* * * * *

WITH WILD ABANDON, I had joked that I had to *doctora* up the truth concerning my whereabouts. Each time Nora's net would drop, I would sprint, but facing Nora's sonorous quiz was getting to be like kicking a snake in the snoot. For that reason, each time I made a getaway, I felt victorious.

Arriving safely at the doctora's home, Maria ushered me through to the living room. She told me that the doctora was on the telephone but would join me in a few moments. She took my overnight bag to the guestroom. A ritualistic deception that fooled no one, I surmised. But I had been experiencing the acceptance of both Maria and Rodolfo. I brought them American Christmas gifts, and they seemed pleased.

"My darling," Cres murmured when she took me in her arms. Her embrace encircled me, making me feel safe. There was passion in each of our greetings, and it was so different from Eduardo's. There was no rough edge to anticipate with Cresida. Only her softness, I considered as her lips brushed my cheek. I inhaled the honeyed bouquet. "I have missed you, my sweet American."

"You look terrific!" I blurted. She was stunning in a flamingo-colored satin cocktail dress. She enticed another kiss when she touched my chin.

As soon as we were settled, I opened my handbag and presented her with a gift.

I'd noted earlier that she only used fountain pens, so I purchased the most elegant one I could find. Her name was inscribed on the side.

"It's lovely. So thoughtful," she mused. "Now," she instructed, "please close your eyes and give me your hand."

As directed, I extended my arm. I felt the glide of metal

across my wrist. "A bracelet?" I guessed.

"You may open your eyes."

She had secured a watch on my wrist. A gold timepiece, diamond encased, blinked up at me. "It's lovely. Thank you," I stammered.

"Is there something wrong?"

"No. It's that the two most important people in my life gave me timepieces. My grandmother gave me her pocket watch. And now you give me this beautiful watch!"

"Perhaps it is symbolic. We each want your time to be wondrously happy. And for you to think of us often." She caressed my fingertips. "I was concerned you might not wish to see me when you returned."

"Why wouldn't I want to see you?"

"I thought perhaps our last conversation may have made you reconsider."

"No. In fact, I've told someone I love and trust about us. My friend said that if it enhances my life, it couldn't be wrong. I believe that, too."

During dinner, I expressed the depth of my feelings for her. We shared laughter. She had not inquired about my sleeping arrangements, nor had she challenged my morals.

I told her the happy parts of my trip home. She laughed about Kris feeding the dog. When our conversation turned to her family, I realized that her abstruse quiet was an authoritative stall. I questioned if she had heard from her brother. Her answer was that he was well. That while they loved one another, it was difficult to be a close family. Rapid, sharp, and hammer-like, she hit the word-nails. He is a dictator, she told me. Bing, bing, bing, and the nail is in. No addendums.

The doctora was a punctilious hostess, a bemused audience, a wry elitist, and often, she was incommunicado. She had once told me we all pay for our father's sins. As if impounded by the past, she could lower the curtain on any conversation that delved too near her pain.

I could now relate to that.

I was realist enough to know and accept that the doctora had given her name, address, phone number, and her love. Most of the rest remained cordoned off. She was clandestine, and yet, did not bask in her charade. As for clues, there were few. Someone else had decorated her home. Her classic selection of clothing was the work of some New York, Paris, or Rome, designer. A modiste's interpretation of her was the best I could glean from her clothing. I remembered I had once asked a friend what to wear to a party. My friend answered I should wear shoes and cover my privates.

So who was the doctora? She was elegant. She was controlled by aristocratic pride. She was intense—passionate. She was intelligent, generous, and kind. She was in command; she was delicate. She was proper. Conversely, she allowed her deep, throaty laugh to surface when I delighted her with a bawdy story.

What I felt about her would fill books. What I knew about her could be said in a brief short story. She wanted to patch humanity's feeble mind. She lived quietly, with reserve. She was affectionate, bewitching, and possessed tranquility. She was benevolent, entertaining, and lovely. Until she elected to add the flavor, I would accept, and relish, her vanilla.

She wore shoes and covered her privates.

* * * * *

I WOKE IN the middle of the night. I was in her arms and felt her stir. The euphoric evening had been so passionate, so tender, I was filled with some sensual song that began deeply within. Her falling hair, the tuck of our bodies in a downy snuggle, had been the final awareness before I slept.

I watched her sleep. I was astounded by how comfortable I'd become within the wrap of her love. Shelby said a poet's food is love and fame. I was feasting on at least half of my daily requirement. Fame could not even be considered at this time.

Deep down, I knew Leigh might be correct about her detachable love.

When she shifted, I studied the graphite shadows that fell across her loveliness. With slow deliberation, her eyes opened. She cradled me. She whispered, "You are awake. Are you unwell?"

"I'm fine. I can't sleep. I'm sorry if I woke you," I responded.

She brushed my breasts with her gentle touch. Leaning, she kissed my neck. "And would additional love assist your sleep?" she asked while playfully biting my neck.

Tenderly, I pulled her above me. My arms enfolded her body; my nails drifted down the length of her back. I welcomed her love. My words unveiled my desire. "It certainly couldn't hurt."

TWENTY-SEVEN

ADVENTURE IS THE grist for life's mill. Leigh had mentioned Eduardo and I would keep trying until we got it *completely* wrong. Nora stated I was tossing Eduardo's love away—and was using both hands to do it. Carlos predicted disaster.

The inside whispering was like a terrier on its most miserable day. A muffled shriek was also buried deeply for I continued to censor my own decisions. I somehow understood societal acceptance meant belting out the song of heterosexuality. The lyrics of my own anthem left me bewitched, bedraggled, and bewildered. This, I acknowledged, was a plenty sad portfolio. My intentions were good. But often, as I conspired toward acceptability, I felt the resonance of the blues at its most fabricated, lonely, and somber moments.

When there is no melody within a soul, how is one to compose poetry? Where there are silent lyrics, how is one to be a poet?

Eduardo called early in the week, suggesting a truce—pleading his cause. We should begin again, as I requested—friends. He asked if I cared to accompany him on a tour of the Pyramids of Teotihuacan. I was careful in setting down the conditions for the outing. It was to remain a congenial day where I was not to be strapped into a dunking chair. A day without conflict was planned. I had expressed the idea of our becoming friends again would be agreeable. He accepted there would be no romantic skirmishes.

When he arrived, Nora pointed out how handsome he was in his sand-colored, boat-neck sweater. He also wore his smile without it seeming to be a prop. But when we arrived at the historical ruins, I became suspicious as he directed our tour. However, he remained subdued. We chatted about unimportant events. Each word was carefully placed. As we walked, he had not even reached for my hand.

I gazed across the ruins. Time had encroached upon this major city of a lost era. The Temple of Quetzalcatl, with its chiseled stone carvings, was a mystery. There were images of serpents, leering rain gods, and powerful designs. Tombs were chock-full of past kings, priests, and assorted big shots of their time.

When we walked down the Avenue of the Dead, Eduardo automatically reached to take my hand. By the time we were at the Pyramid of the Sun, he had released his grasp and slipped his hands securely into his pockets. Our peripatetic stroll continued sans touch. We climbed the Pyramid of the Moon. As we approached the narrower steps toward the top, I reached for his outstretched arm. On our descent, the latch our arms had formed was released.

All the stone monuments were the color of raw lamb's wool. Eduardo explained how at one time the pyramids had been smoothly stuccoed and brightly painted. The shell was cast away like a skin by the centuries. The ancient city had been abandoned. It had been left to wither, die, and rot.

We rested on the rubble-crusted top of a pyramid. I felt Eduardo's arm on my shoulder. It was no longer a passionate encircling—simply protective. Each time I looked into his lukewarm eyes, I felt as if a Toltec priest was slashing my heart with an obsidian knife. I was playing the part of a sacrificial victim. I wasn't certain why.

Cresida hadn't called throughout the week, and I hoped

her feelings for me hadn't eroded. Every interval without a call made me skeptical about the relationship. I questioned if this was the end of it. Even if it were a love that was unacceptable and socially off limits, I could never be convinced it was meaningless. Of course, I realized the inappropriateness of being with her. I also had been warned her love was temporary—by her choice. But I could not deny my love for her. Adding to the struggle was Eduardo. He would make a wonderful husband and father. For someone other than me. There was no explanation. Merely my emotional quandary. Eduardo's glances strayed from mine.

A forest of silvery clouds formed imaginary legions of ancient people. They milled above the ruins below. It had been their home. They no longer were alive and their city had been demolished centuries ago, emptied out so the tourist could visit.

Eduardo continued telling me tales of the city. His stilted voice made Teotihuacan sound idyllic. To me, this was a place of unrealized dreams.

"Eduardo, you seem distant today. Are you upset?"

His lockjaw ended. "I am confused by your actions. Last night I had dinner with a woman. It was nice to feel as though I am important to her. I no longer feel that way when we spend time together. And I no longer feel as though I can make you happy."

"You could have canceled today's outing."

With a lift of his head, he replied, "I wanted to talk with you face to face."

"I see. Do I know the woman who makes you feel important?"

"Yes. Michel and Renee have stopped seeing one another. I took her to dinner last night to console her. You told me you wish to see others."

"Yes. I need time to explore my feelings." I was at a loss as to what to say. "I can't expect you to wait."

"Women in my country do not explore." His voice was suddenly combative.

I thrashed back, "What we're talking about is the fact that the man is encouraged to be experienced. The woman should be in cold-storage until marriage."

His words were pain-studded. "The marriage vow in Mexico is *Si accepto*. It is accepting love. Not only sharing love."

I stood and then walked slowly to the sacrificial loft. Virgins were being carved apart and offered to the gods. *Si accepto*. And here comes a feathered sun goddess, looking exactly like Renee. She was ready with her blade. She would pluck my core and toss my bloody heart down the steps. Blood droplets would fertilize the crops and the frigging sun would stay in the sky. My mind screamed and my anger accelerated.

"Eduardo, I'm glad she makes you happy. I wish you both the best."

He looked at me with disbelief. "You could make me happy, but you choose not to try."

"I only hope we can salvage a friendship."

The remains of a once powerful nation were before me. The human heart is no trivial thing. Life is no trial run—it is once and for all. Cres made me happy. I elected to make her happy. I would await her call.

* * * * *

"HONESTLY!" NORA SQUEALED as she rounded the corner into our bedroom. "Kelly, you'll never guess who called."

"Michel," I dryly deduced.

"Yes. Did Eduardo tell you Michel wanted to call?"

"Not exactly. Last weekend, Eduardo had told me he's now dating someone new. Well, maybe not so *new*."

"Gosh, I'm sorry," she consoled me. She sat next to me on the bed. Her arm circled my shoulders. "What do you mean not *new*? Is she someone from his past?"

"I've met her before. The woman he's seeing had been dating Michel."

Nora jumped up like a flame in the wind. "Why didn't you tell me?"

"There wasn't any need to bring it up."

Her eyes were nearly bulging from her face. "Going from one man to his best friend is terrible. She must be a tramp."

"No. She seemed nice."

"Huh!" she huffed. "Well, I'm glad she didn't get her claws in Michel. I really am in love with him."

"I thought you might be." Wanting to change the conversation, for her and for me, I asked, "So what are we going to do for Leigh's birthday?"

"I don't suppose she'll want to renew her Klan membership this year." Nora's laugh became a sputter.

"Hey, that was an imaginative statement. Have you changed your diet recently?" I teased. Maybe she got a new comedy script writer.

* * * * *

MEXICO REFLECTED ITS wisdom when certifying a special day for pets. The Day of the Animal is a giant annual pet blessing held every year on the seventeenth of January. Dogs, cats, chickens, pigs, goats, burros, and other species were taken to a churchyard to be consecrated. Juan insisted we take Victor. Lupe had a word with Sanchez. Lupe's spin on it was that since Victor is Mexican, if he failed to attend, who could tell his fate?

Carlos agreed to accompany us. Juan carried Victor's cage with great ceremony until his arms tired. For a few blocks, I hauled it. Finally, I shoved the cage toward Carlos. "You hold this shitty bird for a while," I ordered. "It's your turn." I clasped Juan's hand. Leaning down, I cautioned, "You watch for *rateros*. They might swipe your baseball cap."

"Kel, I can't believe we're going on this pet pilgrimage," Carlos said with a sigh.

"Well, we are." We rounded the corner. When I saw the zoo, I knew this must be the place. In attendance were hundreds of parrots, canaries, and parakeets for which Victor could chirp. Silky-haired cats hissed. Bridled, roped, and leashed pets were decked out in bright ribbons, and even adorned with flowers. The priest milled, and holy water rained on pets and people.

"We could start a petting zoo," Carlos commented.

"Yes. Who would have guessed all these animals would need to be sprinkled with their annual spiritual vaccinations." I shook my head, as I rolled my eyes. "How much sin can a caged bird commit?"

"What dastardly deeds have Victor's names on them?" Carlos asked with great drama. This flourish always ticked Juan.

I offered, "We don't want Victor surrendering to demonic forces."

"*Es hora de helado, no?*" Juan questioned if it was time for the ice cream I'd promised him.

Nodding, Carlos confirmed that it was. "You bet, pal. There's a place down the street where we can grab an ice cream cone for you. Then we can go next door and get a beer for Kel and me."

My frown queried his selection of bars. "Another dive?"

"Not a black velvet painting in the place," he pledged with a grin. "My little *chulita*."

"Don't call me that in front of Juan."

"Is okay," Juan reported. "My friends, they call you *chulita*."

"Well, tell them not to," I censured.

"They wait to grow up for you. *El ejercico hace al maestro*," Juan declared.

Carlos translated after seeing my frown. "Practice makes perfect."

My lips curved. "Please don't let me forget Victor and leave him in the dive," I instructed. "He's just been blessed."

* * * * *

"So WE ENDED up in a bar toasting a recently anointed canary named Victor," I spoke in a soft voice to the doctora. She had been laughing since I began telling her about my week of direct hits. I glanced around the *Teatro de Bellas Artes*. She'd called yesterday, telling me that she had tickets to the theatre and was inviting me to join her. Of course, I wanted to be with my enchantress. She also told me we would be meeting with two of her friends. I was anxious to meet the people in her life and hopeful to make a good impression on them.

When her chuckle ended, she said, "I am better entertained by your escapades than I shall be by the performance."

I was grateful we'd arrived half an hour early. It gave us time to catch up on one another's week. "Well, the canary deal was the highlight of the week. That reminds me, my kid sister, Kris, made up a poem while we tried to get our dog to eat. It goes like this, 'Prince, eat those kibbles down, bark that bark. Or I'll kick your tail back onto the ark.' Not bad for someone who claims not to like rhyme."

Laughing, Cres asked, "Your sister doesn't like poetry. However it is your life. You are different, no?"

"We certainly are different in our appreciation of poetry. It isn't because she hates poetry. She's very bright and loves reading. But she says most poems are too abstract. Kris likes going out and having fun with her friends. She is the social butterfly. She never misses high school sporting events. I never attended one—during either high school or college. I never really enjoyed the high school dating quandary. It was terrible for me. Pawing in backseats was not my idea of a good time. I worked at the local newspaper after school and summers. And what little time I had left over was spent with a circle of friends in the arts. Our little enclave of writers, sculptors, painters, musicians, and actors was tight. As far as romance was concerned, it was a humble beginning. Remember how bad dates were with horny guys?"

"My darling, I was not allowed to be alone with a young man until arriving at the university to do my pre-med. Your question reminds me that we are not only from different cultures, but also different generations."

"Is that terrible?"

"Not at all. We share experience. I find that refreshing."

"Me, too. I've never sat in box seats before," I remarked. Looking around, I examined the red tufted chairs. "Kris used to call these fancy seats *pincushion* chairs."

"I think your sister has a creative mind, like yours."

"Yes, more creative really. So maybe we are similar. Anyway, this is my first time in box seats."

"My friend, Joy Nixon, insists on box seats. She and her lover, Brenda, are also always late." Cresida glanced down at her watch.

When Joy and Brenda arrived, I was in for a jolt. I'd expected scholarly, well-mannered women. Cres had told me the women were fellow Americans. Joy was an heiress and Brenda was a model. That was as much as I knew.

Joy Nixon made a stagy entrance. Auburn hair coiled in bunches around an extremely thin, brightly painted face. She flashed a huge, toothy smile every sixty seconds. It reminded me of a blinking neon sign. Blazing emerald green eyes batted between eyelash netting. Mauve nails, nearly claw length, matched glistening mauve lipstick. Her multicolored sarong wrapped a thin, coltish body. She was near the doctora's age.

Her debutante, clamp-jawed whine greeted us. "Cresida, it's been *too* very long!"

Brenda Warner, Joy's date, was in her late twenties, I guessed. She was stunning. She wore a gown cut so low that a person could have fallen into her cleavage. Next to Brenda's ultra-exposing gown, my own lemon-colored dress with a jewel neckline made me feel as though I might be ordained into a convent at any moment. Between Brenda's flawless body poured into her revealing gown, and Joy's chain-stitched giggles, the women created a total spectacle. My mother would have thought they were circus performers.

Joy winked at Cres. "Cresida, you do have superb taste in women." To me, as she crushed my hand with her vice-lock handshake, she murmured, "And you are tasty. When Cresida tires of you, you come on over to Joy anytime."

My hand reeled in. A cool shade drew downward. I swallowed my rancor.

After several moments of bristling air, Joy and Brenda went to the women's room. Cresida encouraged me to overlook Joy's shortcomings. My objection was recalcitrant. "I am not a pass-around playmate for your little lesbian cartel," I said with a grinding anger. I folded my arms to a clamped position.

"*Ma chere petite*, I have never given her that impression. Nor have I ever been with anyone she's been with. We don't have the same tastes in women. Please, it would mean a great deal to me if you would forget her vulgar comments to you. She meant nothing by them. She insults people without even knowing that she's done so."

"Then I suggest you set the record straight. I'm no one's protégé. I'm not even a member of your Sapphic retinue. And I'm not a one-night arrangement. I hope you value me more than that."

"Kelly, my darling, you mean more than anyone has ever meant to me. I hope you believe my words."

"The way she treated me was inexcusable."

"I couldn't agree more. Darling, try to understand that human beings come from many different backgrounds. Her upbringing was without love, and she is now very confused about life. Her immense fortune has assisted in ruining her soul."

"My family dug potatoes while her family ate vichyssoise. I don't believe background is an excuse for being a horse's hindquarters."

Her warm smile returned. "I agree. Although operant conditioning has been her downfall, she has free will to change, and perhaps one day she will. But, for this evening, please attempt to be pleasant to her. I think you'll find she is a most interesting character."

"Are you angry that my temper showed?"

"No. Not at all. You're a spirited young woman. I've been exposed to another dimension of you. So has Joy."

"I'll attempt to show her my charming side now. For you. But, Cres, if not for you, I wouldn't give her five seconds of my time. I could never share a life raft with her."

Amused, she questioned, "And you'll be pleasant?"

"No more 'off with her head' glares. I promise."

I was well-behaved, keeping my distance, until

intermission. I had made my way to the lavatory. While washing my hands, I felt an arm circle my waist. Looking into the mirror, I saw Joy's skeletal, tempera-washed face. Turning, my eyes burned. "I don't like being touched without my permission," I stated brusquely.

"Kelly," her voice shivered. "I want to apologize for insulting you."

"I accept your apology. But remember, I am *with* Cresida."

"Not many people stand up to me." She opened her small, glittering purse to remove a business card. She slipped it in my hand.

I glanced down at the card. Her name, address, and telephone number were on one side. Turning the card, her key was glued to the paper. Incredulously, I inquired, "What is this supposed to mean?" My lips curved at the sheer audaciousness.

She winked. "It means that," she accentuated her words, "you're welcome at my penthouse anytime. My bed *is* your bed." She gave a flip to her curls.

I handed her card back to her. I explained, "I'm not interested. When I am with the doctora, I don't want anyone coming on to me. Out of respect to her and to me. I don't welcome your attention. I don't want you touching me or approaching me in an unacceptable manner. Is that clear?"

"As you like. I'll wait."

"You're correct. You will wait."

When I returned to Cresida's side, I nudged her. "They're taking a cigarette break now. My Gran would say that Joy is not all-together. She tried to slip me her penthouse key."

Cres shook her head. "And did you take it?"

"She probably has three deadbolts on the sucker." I took the doctora's hand in mine and whispered my postscript. "Of course, I didn't take her key. Need you ask?"

* * * * *

"HELLO, DEAR GIRL." Paul punched his intonation. "What are you doing sitting here alone in the creative writing department's dreary and empty classroom?"

"Waiting for my favorite iconoclast," I spoofed. "Carlo is meeting me here. I figured I'd crack my books while I waited."

"I just saw Leigh. God, I don't know why that girl insists on calling me the old belle of the hall," he said with a giggle.

"Leigh and her raffish ways. And she claims you call her the lost dyke of Lesbos. I'm enjoying her outrageous word substitutes. Farkle this and farkle that. Saying *sugar* for shit! I get a glucose high every time she's around."

"Leigh and Lindy got intimate over the holidays. They made the yuletide gay," he hooted. Leaning back against the table, he quizzed, "And have you been seeing Doctora Valdez?"

"Yes. I see her whenever she has time. Leigh said you told her about Cresida and the ballerina."

"It's all hearsay. According to legend, the young woman fell helplessly and hopelessly in love with the doctora. She wanted to make it permanent by moving in with the doc. Cresida would have none of it. For professional reasons of propriety, she declined. The dancer attempted suicide. She's comatose." With a dramatic sigh, Paul looked at the ceiling before continuing. "She was a complete veggie from the moment they found her. But from what I heard, the girl was unbalanced from day one. She'd set it up to have the suicide rigged so someone would find her before she died. But there was a glitch, and her plan backfired."

"What I don't understand is why the doctora wouldn't have recognized the fact that she was unstable?"

"One would think she should have. But the young woman seemed fine to everyone at first. However, rumor also has it that doc's methodology includes intimate studies done on her young artist honeys."

"I've also heard that. I don't believe she does any sinister research," I disclaimed.

Leaning toward me, he ratted, "There is so much positively *trashy* information out and about." With a quick glance at his watch, he rapidly stood. With a quick, spurting sweep toward the door, he gave a wave and then wailed, "I really must be going. Ciao."

There was no time for evaluating. Carlos charged in, scooping up my books. "Let's get out of here," he ordered. "We can catch the rocket back if we dash. Grab some *rellenos. Chile en nogadas.* Chopped walnuts. You'll love it. It's cheap."

"If I'm going to get through next quarter, cheap is all that's in the budget. As Gran would say, I've got to be tight as a cabbage with my brass."

"At least you have your woman friend for the fancy feedbag."

"That's not how I view my relationship with her," I objected.

"Guess that couldn't be your motive or you wouldn't be wasting time going Dutch with me." Carlos stopped when we reached the bus stop. His frown indicated a problem.

"Well?"

"Kel, I got a letter from my buddy. He did an exhaustive probe on the Colorado Springs obits. He came away with nothing on Leigh's sister dying. There were no death records for any kid with the surname of James."

My head snapped back. I questioned dumbfounded, "What?"

"Nothing. Could the sister have had another name? Or could they have lived somewhere else?"

"No. No remarriage or anything. And the family always lived in Colorado Springs." My speech was remote. "Rats! Why would Leigh have told me that?" Curiosity lurched. Questions were lighting up the board.

"Would you like him to continue investigating."

Although the query had triggered doubt in her story, I backed away. "Nah. When she's ready to confide in me, she will. Time will flush this one out."

* * * * *

MY SLUGGISH, CUMBROUS steps plodded back to the apartment. I'd spent an hour at the laundry. My clothing was neatly folded in my duffle bag. I'd wanted to read while waiting for my duds to swirl their way clean. I had taken my Grandfather Benjamin's diary. I had invaded secrets. I deciphered his minute, slender strokes, but not without effort.

He had referred to Nostradamus, to the Enola Gay, to *Aesop's Fables,* and to his infant granddaughter. Tucked inside was a photo of my grandparents. I was only days old and in his arms. His dark, glowing, gypsy eyes beamed, yet his lids were drawn downward with concern.

He had written about me. He had written of his grandiose love of his wife and son. And of his successes in his work. He told of my father's love of carousels. My grandfather had drafted thoughts that explored his world. He wrote, 'Ripples don't end at the shoreline, as I once suspected. Nor do they begin in the center of a windstorm, as I had once imagined. The beauty of life strays from my heart when I consider our burden.' Continuing to patrol his beliefs, he added, 'Love cannot dilute the animosity in humanity's heart. My people are yet dying through atrocity. Through malice. We are being asked to turn back the waves of the sea and to capture the winds.'

I entered the apartment, wondering how my grandfather had seen himself. Perhaps he only wanted to tame the waves and harness the squalls.

Nora met me at the entryway. She sputtered, "Eduardo called. He confided in me. Said maybe he hadn't given you enough time to select between Carlos and him. I mentioned we were having a three-day weekend coming up. He's going to ask you to go to Veracruz with him this weekend." She gleefully spouted information. "And he truly wants you to get back together."

"He caused the split. I can only offer friendship."

"Well, don't tell him that. Carlos is leaving anyway."

"Carlos isn't the problem." I eased onto the bed. "I have missed seeing Eduardo. If only he wouldn't rush things. He got so serious so quickly."

"Kelly, he knows that now. Oh, Kelly, it's a second chance for you both. He promised to give you time."

"Time is the only test of time."

How lethal that truism was. The things of earth are a private matter. It is between each living entity and the planet we ride. The blend of spiritual and secular is simply an excavation of the synthetic. For we truly are each ostracized by way of not *being* the other person. Thought is a weird intoxicant. The term *hermetic* heart came to mind.

TWENTY-EIGHT

MY STUDIES SEEMED to sputter. Cresida had not called. For all I knew, she may never call again. I never really knew if our last goodbye was our *final* goodbye. It was all precious and all perishable.

Deciding to wear a new dress for my reunion with Eduardo, I hoped it would reflect my stockade attitude. With ivory pleated bodice and royal blue skirt, the outfit was perfect for traveling.

Eduardo mentioned I looked lovely. I was only going for *okay*. We'd planned to fly to Veracruz where he would meet with clients on Friday morning. The meeting consisted of delivering plans and a short consultation. That would give me study time. We then had the entire afternoon and evening. Early Saturday, the plan was to fly to Oaxaco. There he had another appointment. Again, we would have the afternoon and evening, plus the better part of Sunday to ourselves. We were to fly back to Mexico City late Sunday evening.

Eduardo had taken great pains to make this a perfect Valentine's weekend. Mend, not massacre, we both agreed. During the hour and a half flight, we had made every effort to keep things comfortable. No bullying allowed. We were contending for one another's understanding. Trading off points-of-view with the ambiance of consideration was our promise. And it was being maintained.

I realized he was also contending for my heart. But he

wanted more. He wanted the beat that went with my heart. He wanted my entire body, soul, brain, spirit, creativity, and every morsel of breath and thought. He wanted to be my nourishment, food, oxygen, sunshine, lord, and master.

I wanted to be in Cuernavaca.

I was beginning to acknowledge my self-deception. But I would attempt one final banquet at the trough of heterosexuality. Then, I wondered, how long would the struggle be until I accepted myself. A week? A year or two? A decade? Forever or *never*?

Maybe the rest of my entire farkling life would consist of subterfuge.

* * * * *

AFTER PICKING UP a rental car, we drove to the Hotel Villa del Mar. It offered the flowering passion of colorful gardens, a private beach, and our lover's bungalow. Through the evening, we were serenaded with the vibrato of an energetic mariachi band.

Hand in hand, we strolled through the arcades. We ate at an outdoor café. The calypso sound of the marimba band was playing my loneliness. We breathed the sea air, ate fresh crab sold by vendors, and could have been mistaken for a pair of young lovers.

My thoughts were of Cresida. Although she had finally called, plans with Eduardo had been made. She sounded genuinely sad when I told her I was going away for the weekend. But she wished me a happy journey. She said when I returned, we could spend time together. Her caseload was finally beginning to ease.

Meanwhile, Eduardo was attentive, polite, and proper. Our love pact continued when we entered the bungalow. I kicked off my shoes the moment I sat on the bed. He sat and his arms embraced me gently.

"You are tense, no?" he inquired.

"Eduardo, it's been a long day and I'm tired."

"I understand. You must rest. Tomorrow we shall see the city."

Lifting his hand, I examined his fingers. Neatly manicured, tender, they had adroitly created dwellings. And the attached man was kind, decent, and I was terrible to him. "Yes. Tomorrow maybe I'll feel more like myself."

I wondered if I would still be redefining myself in the morning. Without a heart, a human being is a cadaver. Not being romantic was casting aspersions against his manhood. I could not fortify him with sex and it seemed tantamount to castration. Once intimacy had been shared, the bell won't un-ring. And chimes seemed out of the question.

* * * * *

THROUGHOUT THE SLEEPLESS night, I attempted to understand what was wrong with me. After Eduardo had left for his meeting, I trod the beige sands of an ocean I'd never seen before. I looked out across the beach, the waves, and thought about the complications of life. And how strange my life had become since this journey began.

Memorizing those Atlantic waters, I hoped to one day write about the first view I had of them. Just as Illiers was a tiny village model of Proust's Combray, perhaps this section of the great ocean would serve as my representative of the Atlantic.

When Eduardo returned, we planned the day. We ambled through bustling docks, rode open-sided streetcars, and drank aromatic coffee. We drove to Boc del Rio, ten miles out of

Veracruz, then wandered isolated beaches. Rocking, weaving white caps rolled to the bay sands.

We were settled on a blanket. Eduardo's arm wound around my shoulder. We both recognized we were skirting problems with our silence.

I knew I couldn't settle for the gloss of romance without the substance of love. I could no longer look into his eyes and say the words he required. Things were simply no longer as they had been. His moist lips covered mine with strategic eroticism. I leaned away. I could no longer even attempt to renovate our romance. Although I would always feel affection for him, I could never be his. For if I were to be his, I could no longer be *mine*.

He feigned acceptance. However, it was obvious he had not accepted my lack of romance. I could always read his heart by seeing the contents of his eyes. His eyes snapped at me.

Our friendship was now a one-legged walk on ice.

* * * * *

IF LOVE EXISTS, I considered, it should be resilient.

My humor continued to catch him off guard and things remained congenial. We sauntered through Oaxaca's zocalo. We basked in the sunshine while seated on ornate white park benches under leafy shade trees. I leaned my head on his shoulder as we watched the bandstand, porticos, strolling people, and the enormous calabash trees that circled the plaza.

Eduardo had continued to apologize for his abbreviated affair with Renee. He had misinterpreted my coolness as attributable to that. He was being considerate by not pressing me for intimacy. However, by morning, he was aware that it had all changed. He suggested we venture out to see the ruins of Monte Alban.

That should have been a tip-off. We were never at our best when visiting tombs.

Sunday morning found us each introspective. I'd brought along the huge cameo-toned orchid Eduardo had placed on my pillow the night before. I'd thanked him and given him a sisterly kiss. It had not been the reward he wanted. He was becoming increasingly somber.

We arrived at the partially excavated ruins of Monte Alban by midmorning. Eduardo explained how the ruins had been pillaged by tomb robbers. Centuries before it had been a center of advanced astronomy. The acropolis was named Osemotepec, Tiger Hill. But the Spaniards renamed it because of the blossoms of the casahuate trees. They were fleecy white against the hillside.

We wandered the meadow-like terrain. Eduardo stopped, and then bent to point out a patch of wild verbena. "It is called *mala mujer*," he commented. "It is a poisonous weed."

Laughing, I translated, "Bad woman?"

"Yes. It was used on women who were unfaithful. Rubbed on them."

"I'll bet!" I continued chuckling. "They don't have any bad man plants?"

"If there would be, you would wish to rub it on me, no?"

Our eyes had strung together for several moments before I answered, "No. I would never want to purposely be the cause of your pain. I realize that now."

"I am anguished and saddened by the thought that my being with Renee hurt you."

"Please don't apologize for that again. It really isn't important. We don't belong to one another."

"I feel we do."

"We don't."

We climbed the primitive platforms to examine ancient

writings. "The workshop of the gods," I commented when we passed a terrace where rituals had once been performed. Now it was only a flattened hilltop.

"In ancient times twenty thousand lives were sacrificed for the dedication of a new temple," Eduardo disclosed.

"Some sacrifice."

"Is our love to be sacrificed because of my foolishness?"

Turning, my eyes dimmed. "No. Eduardo, it isn't because of Renee." I wanted to leave the world of stony beauty and brutality behind us. I observed the hanging pewter clouds above. My eyes lowered. I saw the patches of *mala mujer*. The weeds spread their mantas on the ground, unaware of having been woman's punishment. "Eduardo, I require my independence."

"If a woman in Mexico is independent, she is often a *puta*." His lips were tightly drawn.

"Because a woman doesn't want to be dependent on a man, she becomes a *puta*?"

The tradition was to rub a little *mala mujer* on her gynie and place her on display. "I don't want to be tied down with emotional stakes through my flesh. That's not my idea of marital bliss."

"You have no intention of marrying?"

"Not now. Maybe never."

"Women who do not marry and produce a family become lonely."

I sighed. "That is absolute baloney."

"Kelly, when the man Carlos is gone, we will again be together. It will be better. He has made you change."

"Carlos is not the problem. Eduardo, when he leaves, I won't feel different. Carlos is my friend. I want you to be my friend."

"Not your lover? Not your husband?"

"No. It's more complicated. I have feelings for someone else."

His eyes overloaded with tears. He stomped away to the car. I tried to match his strides. When he opened the car door for me, our eyes collided. I flinched. "We are leaving to return home," he angrily said.

With a sudden burst of emotion, my flurry of words tumbled. "Eduardo, I'm trying to explore life. I've attempted to explain this to you." My pain-embossed words poured. "Before life leaves me, I've got to feel it as having been. I don't expect to atone for living. You want my remorse because I've shared love. But I refuse to be apologetic in order to buy your friendship. If we can't be friends, how can we expect to share a relationship? It seems we can't share friendship, and I'd hoped that we could."

"You are sleeping with others and ignoring that I love you."

"If I slept with everyone in Mexico, it's my business." I slammed the door. "Find yourself a woman to clamp in a chastity belt. Have your family."

"Because of Renee, you think I do not know the virtue of fidelity."

"I don't really care how lily white you are. I've had it with recrimination. I'm not about to be the last of the red hot sacrificial lambs. *Mala mujer* is not a part of my life. And neither of us needs to have our purity reconstructed. What you did was understandable. I don't have a problem with you sharing love with Renee or anyone else."

"Because you no longer love me."

"That isn't true. I don't love you the way you require."

A holiday that was embellished with love had ended in disharmony. Just as Monte Alban had decomposed in a wink of the world's time, our love appeared to corrode within minutes.

As we drove away, I saw the orchid I had carried had fallen beside a patch of *mala mujer*.

Warm tears were streamlets gushing from my eyes. The hush made me wonder if circumstances might have changed our love. My eyelids burned as if a thousand flashbulbs were detonated at the same time.

We flew out of Oaxaca. I recalled that D. H. Lawrence had written *The Plumed Serpent* there. I wanted to tell Eduardo, but he hadn't even looked at me since we boarded the airplane.

So he wouldn't get to know.

* * * * *

NORA GRIPPED MY hand and wailed, "Honestly! You two are either in love or in hate. Kelly, he's a wonderful man."

Standing, I walked to the other side of our bedroom. I wanted to distance myself from her hovering consolation. I tossed a couple crumpled pieces of paper in the wastebasket to mask my escape. "Nora, he doesn't want me sinning with anyone other than him. He'll be the one to apportion guilt and forgiveness. He wants obsequious devotion. I don't wish to live like that." I plopped on the chair and my elbows spiked the desk's top. "I'm released on my own recognizance."

"Can't you be serious?" she carped.

"You want serious?" I lurched as I spoke. "He wants a possession. A person he can control. Spank when she's naughty. I'm not that person."

"I could fix you up with Gab."

"That has a roommate-incest feel to it. Please allow cupid to aim a blowgun at my heart randomly." I rubbed my eyes. "Leigh claims love is all hormonal anyway."

"She would," Nora grumbled as she exited the room. She would be a wonderful date for Michel if she didn't cheer up, I thought. Her last line was something to do with my being as bad as Leigh is.

She didn't understand I wasn't aching from love's loss. I waited a few minutes and then went out to the dining room where Erika and Sanchez were seated. "A letter from your grandmother, dear," Sanchez said with a hasty point to the stack of mail on the buffet.

Opening it, I discovered Gran had tucked a five-dollar bill inside. For Valentine's candy, she'd written. Gran also said she misses me. I knew the feeling for I missed her round the clock. "My Gran is diabetic so she thrives on giving others chocolate or the money to purchase some."

"Isn't she the sweetest woman," Sanchez gushed. Then, as if on cue, she began badgering Erika. "I would have more money for sweets if my food didn't disappear. Erika, the tea is mine. You've no right to it."

"Ze tea. Ze cheeze." Erika's hands flagged. "I borrow ze teabag thiz morning. Zhat is all. I get you more tea when I go out."

"Erika, why don't you borrow my tea?" I suggested.

"You getz ze American kind. I like European."

"I'll get European next time," I promised.

"Sank you."

"Now that's settled," I said, working for a ceasefire.

"Yah."

"What about my cheese?" Sanchez grumbled.

"I'll get cheese for Erika to borrow, too," I offered. I'll get whatever it takes to keep the peace around here. Señora, if Erika vows to borrow only from my shelf, will it make it better?"

"What about the rent? It's late again."

"I getz you ze rent."

"Very well. We won't mention it again." Sanchez began

nibbling on a piece of toast. Then she frowned. "Erika, we can have harmony if you'll stay away from what's mine." With that, Sanchez picked up her plate and shuffled off to the kitchen.

Erika nudged me. "Monster."

"Monster?" I repeated. "She's a little cantankerous, but she's not a monster."

"No. I tellz you to get monster cheeze. I like ze monster cheeze."

"Muenster," I repeated under my breath.

TWENTY-NINE

I WAS BACK in the custody of Cuernavaca. Smiling across the terrace table was Cresida. I had finished telling her about Erika and the cheese when I thought how lovely she looked when she laughed. I wanted to hold her. I blurted, "You are the most lovely woman alive."

She blushed. "I believe you are."

"I can't tell you how I've anticipated this weekend. I need the relaxation." I sipped the piña colada.

"You have been busy?"

"Yes. Last weekend was terrible. Eduardo and I have parted for good."

"I see."

"I'm tired of his male ego. Men are so demanding. It's their way or the highway. He wouldn't accept my friendship, and that's all I'm any longer willing to offer."

"The male identity is linked to their sexuality. They approach love with the end product of sex on their mind. Women approach love from the beginning, with no shortcuts. The male sexuality is focused. Women have many more varied zones of eroticism."

I grinned. "You've visited all my zones." I took another sip, and then asked, "Why do you think the sexes are so far apart on such an important aspect of life?"

"It is only a theory, but there is the Freudian ideology stating that man hurries the lovemaking because of a castration complex. Freud contends that man fears his genitals might be severed for punishment of invading the woman. Perhaps that is why the male is rushed."

"If men were afraid of getting damaged, why do they insist on bonking every woman they meet?"

"Freud believed that although the male seeks love for gratification, there is a threat of castration by the female genitals. It is called vagina dentate. Translated, toothed vagina." She was amused that I was finding the pronouncement hilarious. "Kelly, I have never feared your bite, so I have no need to hurry."

"I may be a nibbler, but never a biter," I whispered with eyebrows bobbing playfully.

She began to speak as Maria approached. The doctora was being called to the telephone. She promised to return as quickly as she could. I finished my drink, watching Vincente busily working in the garden. I decided to practice my Spanish with him. As I approached, I saw he was having difficulty steadying the bush that was being transplanted. Immediately, I got down on my hands and knees to assist in setting it right. He had waved me away at first, but I automatically packed dirt from the opposite side. I remembered so many summer days helping my mother in the garden. I was flooded with warm thoughts. After the plant was firmly in the ground, I was still holding a small gardening shovel. I began to tenderly turn some of the soil near one of the rose bushes.

"Kelly, what is it you're doing?"

I looked up as Cresida neared me. She lowered down to my level. I answered, "Cres, I'm helping."

"You must not get dirty."

"I enjoy gardening."

She scolded, "Whatever will Vincente think?"

"Why would it matter? He likes me."

Curtly she replied, "You are not my household staff. You are my guest."

"I enjoy working with my hands. After all, my heritage is Kansas farmland."

"If we all assumed the reasoning of progeny, we should all still be cave persons. You are a beautiful, intelligent young woman. You must be refined and have no need to do menial work."

"Cres," I began and then stopped. She was truly irritated, and I was bewildered. "I've always loved gardening. My mother's joy is working in her yard. The feel of earth, just now, allowed me to feel near my mother."

"Please call your mother if you wish. But never again do this. The staff will lose respect for you. As well as for me." She stood, then walked rapidly back to the terrace.

My eyes began to mist. The shovel slipped from my hand. Then I became angered. I stormed to the table. Holding out my hands, I asked, "Is it a sin to have dirty hands?"

"Wash them, darling, and please don't let it happen again."

"Don't attempt to control me. You aren't my parent. And," I leaned over the table, "don't ever tell me that I'll lose someone's respect because I'm willing to get dirty. Or because I might need to work for a living in some menial job."

"Living here is different than in the United States of America." There was an edge to her voice. "There are stations."

"Cres, let me clue you in on stations. You've made love to an errand copy girl and an ex-carhop. The summer before I started high school, I worked at an A&W Root Beer drive-in. When school began, I was a copy girl at the local newspaper. Menial jobs. I served people hamburgers and fries. I took pride in earning my own money. Had I not saved for college, I probably wouldn't be here now. I'm proud to be middle-class. I'm not an heiress. And after seeing your buddy, Joy, I'm damned glad I'm not."

"Not everyone with wealth is like Joy."

"I'll admit money comes in handy. I may be returning back to Kansas early to take a mundane job. But I'd rather have my work ethic than to be a snooty bitch like your pal."

"Do you resent wealth?"

"Do you resent my not having wealth?"

"Of course not. Darling, I've worked hard for what I've acquired. Yes, I concede that I've had advantages. But that does not preclude the fact I have also worked diligently." She paused, and then quizzed, "What did you mean about returning to Kansas early?"

"Maybe that's the part of wealth I would enjoy. The freedom from worry over what comes next. I'm sure things will turn out and I won't need to leave. So let's not talk about it."

"I apologize for being upset with you. Kelly, I can't expect you to understand social stations in the lower Americas."

"I'm sorry for my mercurial outbursts, but Cres, if we're going to spend time together, please attempt to understand that I don't want to change. I *want* to respect all work as being something to be proud of. I don't want my thoughts rearranged. It is who I am, and I'm skirmishing to locate myself in so many areas. But the one thing I know is that I respect a person's heart *first*. A person's mind next. And maybe near the last on the rung is what a person does for a living. The living itself is more important. So if I want to roll around in the damned mud, I don't expect anyone to attempt to *change* my thoughts of integrity about working. Anyone whose esteem is based solely on their title and wealth is a sad commentary."

She was studying my face as if my words might have been significant. "Kelly…"

"I want you to love the person I am. And I proudly have the heart of a gardener." Glancing down at my grimy hands, I commented, "I'll wash my hands for you."

As I walked by her, Cresida lifted my hand. She turned it over, and then kissed my palm. "I shall attempt to be more understanding, accepting, of your feelings. Is there anything else bothering you?"

"Why?"

"Since your return from the Christmas holiday, you've been tense."

I tenderly squeezed her fingers with sensual pulsation. "I know a remedy for tension."

After a warm, soothing bath, and mutual backrubs, we adjourned to the bedroom.

I had mentioned my studies were caught up, but I could use the practice with my Spanish. We had been conversing exclusively in Spanish with the doctora correcting my grammatical errors.

When we crawled into bed, she said we would continue practicing language. I closed my eyes and groaned. "*Nada mas*. Not now." I pulled her into my arms. The satin sheets caressed our nude bodies. "No more studies now."

"This study, my lovely, you will enjoy." She touched the tip of my nose with her index finger. She then kissed it softly and murmured, "*Nariz*." Her lips made a path to my closed eyelids. She pressed tenderly and whispered, "*Ojo*." Lifting her hand with a seductive sweep, she traced my eyebrows. "*Ceja.*" She coiled strands of hair around her fingers and noted, "*Pelo*. Beautiful hair." Her silky caresses skimmed my body as her lesson continued. Her savory mouth lingered, and her tongue traced my lips, exploring my mouth. Excitement built. When she nipped my shoulder, my hand caressed her chin, encouraging her lesson. She kissed my hand, and then licked my wrist. She declared, "*Muñeca.*" Then she blew where her tongue had drawn a circle. She cupped my cheeks. "*Mejilla.*"

I moaned when I felt the feathery brush of her hair trailing my body. A shiver grew inside me. Lifting me, her hands tracked my spine. Her nails swept my backbone with an erotic spurring snag. Soft, moist lips orbed my ribcage. Her tongue flicked playfully at my nipples. Embracing my hips, she canvassed my *cadera.* She grasped my leg as her fingers streamed the full length of my thigh. Kissing my calf, feet, and toes, she tickled them briefly, gently. Repositioning her body near mine, she pressed her ear to my heart. "*Mi corazón.*" Her finger tapped gently. "*Latido del corazón.*"

"*Si.*" My legs tangled with hers. I felt the glow of her ardor. Her fleecy caresses were electrifying my every muscle. A glistening stirred deeply within. As she made love, there was an explosive tremble—then a flurry attacking my nerve endings. There was the rushing invasion of ecstasy that rises with the cadence of love.

Time became a whirling spindle. Breath became a ruffling sound of passion as it was happening. The throb of the heart, the thirst of the skin, the peeling away of one's self, the winnowing emotion, and then suddenly there was that libidinal detonation. There was a coddling of sensation. There was a bursting storm of pleasure. There was a free-fall gratification. It captured and seized senses. And for that brevity, there was an enslaving of one's soul. There was understanding oblivion of everything except that moment. It meant a trading of one's vulnerabilities. A cyclonic stillness became an implosive orgasm. The self-surrender found identity regressing. The opened gate that becomes post-orgasmic release was a touch of love deeper than we'd known exists. I could doubt much about the world of truth, but I could never doubt this.

Gazing at Cresida, with the light configurations against her polished form, I could see light crystals. I savored her warmth. Her magnetism had penetrated my heart—it was piercing my soul. If she were Sapphic, however, could it be wrong?

I craved her. I began with a jovial whisper as I kissed her nose. "*Nariz.*" Soon, I was experiencing her delectable elegance. In my urgency, I forgot to name names. But her Spanish was flawless.

When we had exhausted one another, I wound my arms around her. I lifted above, and then dipped to kiss her lips with tenderness. Then the kiss warmed, even seared. "I do love you, Cres. More than you know."

"Kelly, we must talk." She sat across from me. I watched her eyes as they became concerned. The depth of love was reflected in her question. "What did you mean about returning to the States to work?"

"If my scholarship doesn't come through, I'll need to return. I'm unable to work here because my visa doesn't permit it, or I would flip tacos," I teased.

"Would you allow me to assist you?"

"No. No, of course not," I rapidly replied. "I can do it on my own. At any rate, Professor Thurston is certain the scholarship will go through. It's taking longer. Not to worry," I said with a smile. "I'm a phoenix propelling out of the ashes of poverty. I'll survive. And I don't need anyone's help. Now, let's cuddle without a frown."

"And if you were to need help, would you come to me?"

"No." I looked into her face. A rare tear had escaped and was careening down her cheek. *Mejilla.*

THIRTY

WITH HIS BACK as girder straight as a toy soldier, Juan's ebony eyes filled. He said goodbye to Carlos with a child's pain. Carlos had his assignment. He would be going to Bogotá to teach. Juan's voice groped for answers as to why Carlos must leave. There was love for Carlos in Mexico. We had no answers.

I left the two of them on a bench in Chapultepec Park. I wandered back slowly, deciding to take the long way past the lake. I ventured over to the water's cuticle. Squinting, I recognized Señor Hermann. He was placing his jacket into a rowboat he'd rented. My anger against him gave way to amusement at a joke Carlos had told me. Carlos said we weren't certain if he was Nazi, but he was a grumpy German. That made him a *sour kraut*, Carlos roared. I had also roared. Now, watching Hermann, my anger returned. He looked up at me and waved.

"Señor," I called. "I didn't know you liked boating."

"Miss Benjamin. You must join me." He beckoned me near the water as he steadied the boat. "It is important to enjoy the sunshine, along with a boat ride each day."

I quickly debated with myself about the boat ride. I finally agreed. My compulsion to explore character was overwhelming. With a stiffly reserved formality to my voice, I muttered, "I do love boats."

"I also have a love of boating. In Potsdam, I was a

member of the sculling team. Before the war."

"Yes." Bitterness edged my words. "I imagine many Germans were forced to give up their boating." I situated myself in the rocking boat.

"The Señora tells me you are of Jewish heritage."

"My father is Jewish. Along with the humanitarian reason for hating what the Germans did to the Jews, there is the personal one of being Jewish." My glare was a censuring one. I wondered how he dared to even bring it up. "I still am revolted by Germans, in general. And Nazis, in particular."

"It was Schopenhauer who said that hatred comes from the heart and contempt from the head. And neither feeling is within our control. Some anger is healthy, but not hatred. That must be released, my dear young woman, before it injures you."

"I'm delighted there was enough anger to execute Adolf Eichmann. And the rest of those murderers should also be hung from the nearest tree." His eyes darted from my querulous words.

Dipping one oar into the water, he pivoted. "We must learn forgiveness," he lectured.

"I don't think so," I refuted. With an acrimonious disclaimer in my eyes, I added, "In fact, I think we should chase every war criminal down with all our energy."

As we glided, he studied my face. And I confronted his. "Well, I should get more exercise. I shall row faster. It won't frighten you?"

"No. I have enough sense to be angry, but not enough to be frightened."

"Excellent." He unbuttoned his shirt sleeves, twisting them upward. He then began heaving the oars.

With a start, my glance collided with his inner arm. Dazed, I stared down at the tattooed numerals. When his arm came forward, I leaned and touched the indigo numbers on his skin. With a feeble stammer, I asked, "You were in a concentration camp?"

"Yes. I was imprisoned and sent to a camp. For I had hidden my Jewish wife and our son. An infant, like you, he was half Jewish. He was a fine, healthy child." His glance lowered. "When he was born, I was so pleased he had his mother's dark skin and radiant bronze eyes. But it turned out to be most unfortunate. Perhaps he might have been spared if he would have had my lighter coloring. He was so like my beautiful wife. I have been alone since that time when we were separated." Then the señor looked back at me, his glance aimed for my heart. "If my son would have lived, I would hope he would not have live with hatred. For that is a crime against one's self."

Hermann continued to vigorously row across the lake. I sat mute. My mind spun with the realization of my miscalculation. I wondered if his anger at the Nazis had been exercised off through rowing. Or perhaps the years had melted hatred away. For many moments, my eyes were sealed shut. My thoughts dispatched. Maybe forgiveness had taken over his life because living would have been impossible without it.

* * * * *

THE ATMOSPHERE WAS mellow academia. Carlos's goodbye party was held at the apartment of one of the younger history professors. Rippling with conversation, booze, grass, and hashish, the mood was better than mellow. It was nearly catatonic.

I felt Carlos sliding his arm around my waist. He whispered, "Kel, Leigh said Nora will be here and that she's bringing Michel, Eduardo, and Frenchy. And you told Nora it was okay to bring Renee."

"Why not." I took a drag from his reefer and then handed it back to him.

"Nora will shit when she sees dopers."

"Nah. She's even tried it. Bacchantes and Satyres. Anyway, this is something out of Colette's *La Vagabone*. I love lunatic fringe."

Carlos frowned. "Will you be okay with Eduardo being here?"

"He could never forgive me my trespasses. So screw him."

"It sounds as though you've made up your mind about who you are."

"Carlos, I would rather endure the hatred and jokes that come with being Sapphic, than to put up with the bullshit of being hostage to some egocentric, manipulative man. Ball and chain. Not for me."

"Whew! A couple more puffs and you'll become a true advocate."

I pried the marijuana from his fingers. "Hell, yes. I've really had it with the male ego. Present company excluded."

"A feeding at the lioness cage," he teased.

"I'll miss you, Carlos." I looked over at Tom. He was stumbling down drunk. "Tom is acting as though he were under-resuscitated once too often."

"Kel, he's an asshole, but we go back. Mind calling him once in a while to check on him?"

"I'm not AA, but I'll do my best. For you."

"Thanks." Carlos nodded toward the door. "Aw, shit."

I rotated around. Nora, Michel, Renee with her little porcelain doll face and Eduardo with his little porcelain scowl, entered. Our eyes tapped briefly. For the next half hour, I ignored Eduardo. I milled. Thurston told me there was still no word on my scholarship.

Then, when Renee went out to powder her little porcelain face, Eduardo was over like a shot. With a softened, contrite timbre to his voice, he questioned, "How are you this evening?"

"Sad that my dear friend Carlos will be leaving."

"You will no doubt get over him. As you got over me."

"Don't start," I admonished.

"Kelly, I came here to tell you I should not have said the things I said. You were being honest with me. I should have accepted that."

I recalled the feeling I had when I'd misjudged Hermann. I thought about how Eduardo must be feeling for inspection of his eyes told me of his retching pain. I knew there was still love. I didn't want him feeling guilt. For even if our parting was certain, we had once matched up. And even if the magic dies, it need not be snarled beyond friendship. Though the catalyst of chemistry had been clipped, I wished him no harm. "Don't worry about it, Eduardo. We both said things. It's in the past."

"As long as you know how truly sorry I am."

I hushed him. "*Esas cosas ocurren mucho.*" Those things happen said the Kamikaze cupid that was imitating me.

"I never meant to hurt you."

"You didn't," I murmured with a touch. "I promise you didn't. I was only sorry a friendship wasn't possible."

* * * * *

"THE MOON IS bright coral tonight and it's huge," I lulled.

Cresida pulled the covers up around us. "Yes. Although I prefer the moon's brightness and color in Cuernavaca, it is lovely now, also. I missed you last weekend. The villa was lonely."

"I thought about you often. But I couldn't miss the party for Carlos."

I was glad to be back with Cres. I glanced around her bedroom and realized how comfortable it felt. I felt even more at home at her villa.

She pressed back against the pillows and pulled me nearer her warmth. "You bring me so much joy. But I do know how much Carlos means to you. He sounds like a wonderful young man. And spending time with him is important since he'll soon be leaving."

"Tuesday he flies out. Gran sent some money to spend on something special. I decided to spend half to take Carlos to lunch at *Delmonico's* on Tuesday before he leaves."

"That is a lovely gesture."

"I love you both. Carlos as a friend and you as a lover."

"Kelly," she spoke softly, and then cleared her throat. "You've said you don't want my assistance, but perhaps we could have an agreement. I have never considered living with another woman because of the social stigma. But I have thought of a way of solving both problems. And being near you."

"Near?"

"Yes. Over the weekend, in Cuernavaca, Vincente told me how tenderly you worked with the plants. And that you beamed with love of them. It occurred to me perhaps we could have an arrangement that would benefit us both. Here, at my home, the gardener is excellent at the laborious work. But he does not give the plants and flowers the loving care Vincente gives in Cuernavaca. That takes a skill, as well as a love of flowers. If you could live here with me, and supervise the gardens, it would brighten the grounds. It would also be a perfect arrangement because it would afford us both an explanation for your living here. You would be able to stay in

Mexico and complete your education. And my gardens would be more lovely than ever."

"Cres, it's a magnanimous offer, and I'm grateful. But I'm not sure it would work."

As if reading my mind, she spoke. "It would be an independent arrangement. I would not interfere with your freedom. As you are aware, I maintain a most harmonious atmosphere. It would be conducive to your studies, as well as your writing."

"I would be frightened of being obligated."

Her eyes lowered. "I am happier with you in my life than without you. You bring me warmth, happiness, and laughter." She drew me near. "Kelly, the first night we were together, I realized your capacity for love. You wanted to please me, and so you did. You weren't pretending. And have not pretended since."

"I've never needed to pretend about my feelings for you." I leaned to her, inhaling the powdery fragrances that lifted. "I wasn't certain at the time why it would have been impossible to pretend," as her arms gathered me in, I added, "but I am certain now."

* * * * *

MY RANGY, PRINCELY pal was seated on his suitcase across from me. Holding both of my hands, he gazed into my sorrow. As the moments were whittled away, I thought about the day. I'd known we would one day be sitting in the airport, but this seemed so very soon. The days had passed too quickly.

After completing morning classes, I went by to pick up Carlos. He had awakened only half an hour before I arrived, and his chock of unruly hair gave him the appearance of a fluffed eaglet. He'd held me in his arms, and I recalled the one time we made love. It had been an experiment—a challenge to my feelings for the doctora. It had been to reinstate my sexuality. It had somehow cemented our hearts in friendship. Nothing more. And nothing less.

Memories scampered by. I thought of the day he'd purchased flowers in order to be out of context. Our visits to the *ostironerias*. Our trip up to the States over Christmas vacation.

And this noon I'd surprised him with the news of taking him to *Delmonico's* for lunch. We hadn't been there since he'd relinquished his watch to pay the tab.

He warned me if we were lunching at *Delmonico's*, I should take my watch. Then he lifted my watch and whistled. I told him it was a special day, so I'd worn the timepiece given me by the doctora. He said we could dine free for a month with that watch. Grinning, ear to ear, he added it would be wonderful to have our farewell luncheon in a place where the first course wasn't served in Petrie dishes.

Lunch had been superb. Our conversation strayed from parting. With a rambunctious grin, he vowed that we would one day reunite and have a wild fling across Europe. We frolicked with our memories of intimacy and love. The luminescent glow of his summer-sky-blue eyes reflected kindness. We also talked about his excitement about Bogotá.

After a final sip of coffee, I requested the bill. The waiter replied that it had been taken care of. My eyes darted to Carlos. He shrugged. There had only been one person who knew of my plans. It was the doctora. We toasted her class with a final glass of wine.

The return cab trip back to his apartment was a slow paced one. We would be meeting Tom, and he would drive us to the airport. I told Carlos that Cres had invited me to live with her. I confided that I was skeptical. Although she was more special to me than any other friend or lover, I worried about post-honeymoon blues. Carlos inquired if I loved her. Yes, I admitted. She inspired me. For I had finished numerous projects while wrapped in her tranquility. Even my latest, *Boat Ride*, was drafted rapidly and precisely while with the doctora. It was a novelette about my rowboat confession on prejudice.

Carlos kidded that being with Cresida was similar to being in the lap of a goddess, perhaps the Muse. And if she didn't want to leash me, why not live with her. Be happy. Life and love, he claimed, are patchworks at best. My sweet Carlos stated that life offered great lessons. And the heavy linen on the table would teach me to live as royalty.

I'd laughed. I was considering the plan for many reasons. Linen on the table wasn't one of them, I replied.

Carlos encouraged me to make *life* my true lover. And, he added, wild pagan love was a part of life no one should miss.

After returning to his apartment, we rapidly finished packing his luggage. The bags were then piled into Tom's worn Chevy. As that Chevy roved the asphalt canyons of the city, Carlos squeezed my hand. Cabs were armadillo tanks aiming for us. But we soon arrived, walked through the airport, hand in hand, and wished for additional time. Tom, in his straw hat and smoking a Panama cigar, was as sober as I'd ever seen him. Curls of smoke trailed after him.

Then we sat. When the flight was called, Carlos pensively stood. Tom grabbed him and gave him a bear hug. "Get out of town," Tom snorted.

Carlos grinned. It was a large, curving smile. "Hey, Polyclitus, get on your own side of the street. And don't let me catch you in Bogotá without my say so." Turning to me, Carlos leaned down into my kiss. He looked tall, charming, and kindly. He would ask not what his country could do for him. He would ask what he could do to promote kindness in the world.

"Question," I murmured. "Am I a Madonna or prima donna?"

"Kel, you're fifty-one percent of one and forty-nine percent of the other."

"And you're not saying which is which?"

"I've always loved a good cliffhanger. That will ensure a future meeting. Kel, you've made my life richer. We'll meet again."

He turned, walking away. He was embarking on a special mission. I loved his dedication. And I loved Carlos.

Tom and I made our way back to the Chevy. Tom reached into the glove compartment and pulled out Ovid's *The Art of Love*. Carlos had instructed him to give me the book after he'd left.

Thumbing through, I noticed he'd underlined something for me. A message. Carlos had underscored his philosophy of love. I read aloud, "I don't consider it love if it can't hurt me at all."

I smiled. And Carlos *claimed* not to be a romantic.

THIRTY-ONE

MY THREE-DAY SECLUSION was finally broken. Between classes and devoted hours to my pet typewriter, I needed time off for good behavior. It was a pause to refresh my body and replenish my mind.

After all, it had also been a stressful time. I had said goodbye to my loving friend, Carlos. There were decisions to make. One I had made. I would go on the Spring break Yucatan trip with Leigh and Lindy. That particular coin-flip had been in the air for weeks.

And now, I was to be rewarded. I had been anticipating a concert with Cresida. But I wanted to talk with her before the performance. I'd phoned her office, requesting we have a conversation before going out. She agreed, suggesting we meet at her office where we could go on from there.

Having never visited her office, I was delighted. The reception area was done in restful roses, lavenders, and dolphin grays. I smiled back at the receptionist as she led me into Cresida's luxurious, plant-filled office. Cres closed the door and motioned for me to be seated in a chair across from her desk. With a professional ambiance, she remarked, "Miss Benjamin, I've been looking forward to this evening."

"Doctora Valdez, I have been hungering for this evening."

We both beamed. We were together again. "It will be marvelous."

"Yes. First, let me thank you for the lunch. Carlos said he really appreciated it and to thank you. He also said you are one classy lady. And to ask that you take good care of me."

"My darling, I shall make every attempt to live up to his request. I enjoy doing things for you and I'm glad it pleased you. It was my pleasure."

I frisked my mind for a beginning to what I was going to tell her. I looked away, and then my voice began to quiver. "Cres, you know I cherish you."

"As I do you, my *chere petite*."

"I've been considering your offer carefully."

"Kelly, I understand your reticence. And the fact that it takes time to make a correct decision. You needed time to consider your options. That is precisely why I haven't mentioned it." She leaned forward, placing her elbows on the desk and folding her fingers.

"I appreciate that. But the way you suggested seems lopsided. I wouldn't feel right about living with you under the terms of being a free agent."

She inspected my face. "But, darling, I've told you that you can be responsible for the grounds. And I shall do nothing to impede your social life. Assuming *free agent* means no ties on your freedom."

"That's exactly what I've been taking into consideration. Cres, this is too important to me to do by halves. I can't be a part-time lover. You deserve more. You deserve loyalty with love. And so do I. The only way I would consider moving in with you is if we were to become permanent and completely devoted lovers. I'm not certain that's what you want. According to my sources, you have always demanded *your* independence."

Her lips moved slowly. "You wish to become my *exclusive* lover?"

"That frightens you?"

"No, Kelly." Her gaze went to the ceiling. "The age difference does concern me though. Although we banter about it, I have never been with anyone less than a decade younger or older."

"So I'm two decades younger. You've got plenty of room in your spacious home. Surely there's room for my bassinet."

She smiled. "Kelly, you must know how I feel about you. I do want you near me. And this is the first time I've ever shared my home with a lover. But do you think it's wise to limit yourself? You're so young."

"When you're a youthful ninety-nine, I'll be a well-aged seventy-nine. It won't seem like much of a gap at all." I swallowed. "Cres, I have thought about it. We make one another happy. Maybe we can't promise forever, but we can promise this time. And we can plan forever."

She walked to my side of the desk. Leaning back against the desk's top, her gaze was directly in my eyes. Inquiring in a dubious tone, she quizzed, "Do you understand what it is you're recommending?"

"Not some namby-pamby roommate situation. You're suggesting a devoted love affair. Cres, deep down I've come to realize I love you with an intensity that makes it unimaginable not to be faithful to you. I couldn't promise Eduardo that. I can promise you. He required and expected it of me. You've never demanded it."

"Our lives would be wonderful together. But it would be enormously difficult. You would be giving up so much. It is complicated as far as the people in our lives are concerned. I am not only an inappropriate age, but also the wrong gender for acceptance in your world. The lifestyle of being lesbian is very restrictive. It would not meet with the approval of your friends and family. Our love would need to be shrouded by untruths. One must practice deception in order to protect ourselves, and those we love from vicious bigotry. Are you prepared to possibly lose the love and respect of your family and friends should it be discovered?"

"Life is too short to live for other people's approval. And I know being cautious about our reputations is important. Particularly for you. Actually," I added with a slight grin, "being a lesbian is great press for poets."

She laughed. "But probably not for your family and friends in Kansas."

"I would think not," I teased. I then stiffened. "You keep bringing up negatives. If you want out of it, please say so. Now isn't the time to play Pinocchio."

"No. It is a time to watch carefully to see if one another's noses are growing." Her amusement dwindled. She ratified, "Kelly, we could make one another wondrously happy. Perhaps, if I am honest, it is something I've only dared dream about... but I am concerned for you."

"I can withstand anything if I can count on you not to abandon me."

She grasped my hand. Her eyes dispelled my insecurity. "I want to be your only lover, as you will be mine. Rodolfo can assist you with the move at your earliest convenience."

"I have exams and my novelette to complete next week. I'd rather not disrupt my routine until they're finished. Also, the following week, I've promised Leigh to go on the Spring break dig with her. I could move in the day I return."

"It will be splendid. So, now we have made our decision. Will you be able to accompany me to Cuernavaca in the morning? I shall make you study the entire weekend, I promise."

"I took the liberty to bring my books and toothbrush," I chided. "Hope it wasn't too presumptive to bring a toothbrush?"

"And not too presumptuous of me to have packed an extra?" she teased. She then swung her handbag over her shoulder. We walked to the elevator. When the doors had closed and we were alone, she asked, "After I had offered you the freedom I'd assumed your youth requires, why had you made this determination?"

"Because you didn't issue ultimatums. And because I've fallen in love with you."

"I see."

"I was hoping you'd tell me you're in love with me, too."

Her mouth opened as the elevator doors slid apart. She surreptitiously remarked as the two men entered, "You know how I feel about you." She then whispered, "You see how this life is one of concealment?"

"But the benefits are wonderful."

"Kelly, I do adore you."

"I adore my geode, Shakespeare, Bach and walks in the park."

"And?"

"And I am in love with you-know-who. And sunshine, roses, the ocean, and this moment."

"As I supposed," she bantered. "You are fickle, no?"

* * * * *

SANCHEZ SPUTTERED AS if incarceration was way too good for me. I then told her she could keep the deposit and didn't need to return my advanced month's rent. And I was attempting to find her another roomer. Leigh was practically already moved in with Lindy, and she had given notice that she would be rooming with her. So the señora was not thrilled. But, I informed her, if not for the move and job, I would need to be returning to the States anyway.

I retreated to my room to study. Leigh interrupted me when she stormed in like a full-force tidal wave. She had dropped by to pick up some of her mail that was still dribbling in. She had been told by Sanchez I was moving in with a doctora when I returned from the Yucatan.

"You must have the farkling I.Q. of a geranium! I told you about what happened with the ballerina."

"Leigh, she told me what happened. It wasn't her fault. The fact, we'll be living together as a symbol of her love," I barked back.

Chaffing, Leigh grunted, "I don't know what got into me. I thought I was your friend. I tried to warn you."

"And I appreciate that. But she won't hurt me. Truce?" I held out my hand.

"Sure." Leigh gave a hasty shake. "Hell, I've been short-fused lately with work on the trip preparations. I'll drop the camera gear by tomorrow. I borrowed a backpack along with some camping equipment for you."

"I don't want to encounter any snakes or *mala mujere*."

"Yeah. Nobody wants to roll over on a bad woman. Those old Toltecs loved rubbing their little woman's pussy in *mala mujere* if they were unfaithful," she snickered. "Probably enjoyed it better than carving up their sacrificial virgins."

"Poor little tarts." I giggled, adding, "I hope Nora is away with Michel when I move in with Cresida. She'll order out an entire crop of *mala mujere* for my indiscretion."

Leigh's eyes dulled. She became serious. "And you'd be amazed how many people would offer to hold you down while Nora treated you with the old Indian cure. Kelly, sometimes this life hurts like hell."

"You do mean *really*, don't you?"

"I mean *really*."

* * * * *

CARLOS HAD TOLD me not to worry about my final examinations. Tests, he lectured, were designed to assist a person in masturbating one's mind. It was not corporal punishment. But it felt as though the ax might be heading for the chopping block. Pun intended. I was confident I'd give a terrific academic performance, but I couldn't be certain until test papers were returned.

What was most important to me was my novelette's evaluation. Thurston asked how I felt about *Boat Ride*. I explained I'd carved apart my soul. A cell at a time. Thurston wryly smiled. His smile told me that was the true requirement. He then announced my scholarship had gone through. Ecstatically, I gave him a hug before realizing what I'd done. I quickly stood back to apologize for my brashness. He told me he deserved an additional hug. He'd corresponded with one of his publisher friends in New York recommending he read my short story, *Mere Pioneer*. His friend agreed, and the story had been mailed. He would let me know the results.

My eyes went like saucers as I thanked him.

I rushed to the telephone to exclaim to Cres that the scholarship had gone through. I babbled, "And Professor Thurston sent my story about Gran's mother to a magazine publisher in New York. There may be a market for it."

Her mood was suddenly glum. "I'm pleased with your good news. Does this mean you won't be moving in with me?"

I was taken aback. My throat jammed. "Cres, I want to be with you. Unless you issued the invitation because you thought I was a charity case."

"Darling, of course I want you with me. I didn't mean it that way. I, naturally, was hoping nothing would change our plans."

"I have an idea. Now that I'm flush, why don't I support us? I could afford a little garret."

"Today I would welcome the prospect of being kept in a garret. May I bring my staff?"

I chuckled. "What's a garret without servants?" I sensed her withdrawal. "Anything bothering you?"

"Forgive me. I have finished with a difficult session. A breakthrough. It was emotional. At times, my profession drains me. Perhaps that is why I so value you in my life. It all seems much better when you're at my side." She paused. "When you return from Yucatan, we shall celebrate your scholarship with a beach holiday."

"There goes the funds for the garret," I quipped.

"Perhaps I can take you to dinner tonight?"

"Nora planned a little party because roommates are going our separate ways. She wanted to get us all together. I hate that I won't see you before leaving on the trip in the morning."

"I know the Yucatan trip has been planned for some time, darling. You must have a wonderful learning experience. And tell me all about it when you return."

"Kris told me not to pick up any moving sticks. She dislikes snakes as much as I do."

"I would take her suggestion. Perhaps, if you aren't going to be too late tonight, you would like to stay over here?"

"Yes," I quickly agreed. "I'll leave the gathering early. I can tell Nora I need to pack. Then I can bring along my camping gear and leave from your home. If that meets with your approval?"

"Kelly, you do understand how this is a life of false statements. Covering over activities and pronouns."

"I realize that. I'll handle it."

"I feel as though I am most selfish. My way of living

creates a burden for you."

I swallowed. My throat felt a horrendous lump. "But *you* think it's worth it."

"Yes. And you?"

"I think you're worth anything in the world. But we'll see how you react to garret life."

* * * * *

IMMERSED IN THOUGHT about what I would tell Nora, I jauntily made my way toward the rotunda. We were meeting for our Friday torta lunch ritual. I'd attempted to get out of it by telling Nora we could catch up tonight at the get-together, but she was having none of it. That made me suspicious. She was going to grill me good.

"So let's jaw," I said as I lowered my weary body into a chair opposite her.

"Kelly, you're incorrigible. Honestly!" she chortled. "Why won't you tell me where you're going to live?"

She was getting right to the subject. "I've told you."

"Not everything. You can trust me. I won't tell Eduardo where you're staying."

Slipping off my bone-colored flats from my tired feet, I wiggled my toes. "There isn't really anything to tell." I fidgeted with the ribbed cuffs on my salmon-hued blouse. "I am doing the gardening in exchange for lodging."

"You're living with a man. I know you are."

"I'm not. The woman is a professor. Doctor, actually, in psychology—at the University. She also has her own practice." I guarded my words. "She needs a gardener. I need a room. I love gardening so it will work out great."

"What's her name?"

"Cresida. Nora, economically it's a good move for me. No

arcane mystery."

Her eyes narrowed. "Where did you meet her?"

My smile froze. I took a huge bite of torta, and then waved my fingers for her to wait until I swallowed. I chewed slowly. "Through Carlos," I finally reported.

"Carlos! So why can't I come visit you?"

"Maybe you can after I'm settled in. After all, I'm an employee. Not mistress of the home." With that statement, I had to glance away to keep from laughing. "Now, can we drop this line of questioning?"

There was a hush. I observed other couples. Hand in hand, they smiled their sweetheart smiles in broad daylight. Proudly. Out in the open. I was beginning to understand what Cresida had said about hiding out. There is a distancing from love's open truth. Sealed emotions were what prompted her warning about this life being intricately problematic.

"There's something fishy about this," Nora accused.

"Fishy as an aquarium. Fishy as the whole damned ocean! Look, you're interrogating me. Now, it's my turn. What's on tap for you and Michel over vacation?"

"We're leaving tomorrow morning. Taking Eduardo's car," she stumbled. "I shouldn't have mentioned that."

"It's okay," I consoled her. Nora could never hold back the details. She would make a piss-poor lesbian, I thought. "Nora, I really don't care about Eduardo any longer. Good luck to him and his."

"Well, gosh, I know you're probably hiding the fact that you're hurting. We're going to Acapulco. And you're going on that awful jungle trip with those lesbians."

"I don't mind."

"What?" her inquisitive glance scalded. "What did you mean by that?"

"I mean that it's an excellent learning opportunity. That's

all."

"Huh! They wear their crummy old army-surplus junk on those terrible digs." After a quick sip of Coke, she demanded, "I'd like to know. Tonight you're going home early to pack, but it looks like you're already packed. Why is that?"

"Nora, want a mint?" I questioned as I opened a roll of mints.

"Why would I want a mint while I'm still eating? I couldn't talk then."

"I would really like for you to have a mint."

THIRTY-TWO

HUNCHED DOWN, I focused the viewfinder as I squatted over several chunks of shard. When the frame was to my liking, I snapped the shutter. "One more bit of Chichen-Itza ruins saved for posterity," I commented to Leigh.

She was down on both knees leaning over a layer of debris. "Don't forget to catalogue the photos. Exposure and site number, date, and a *brief* description. Don't chock it full of flowery poetic shit," Leigh directed. She leaned back and squinted into the sun as she adjusted her Aussie hat. "What a flimsy cache. A farkling pile of rubble. Listen, don't forget to ask the profs plenty of mindless questions. I told them you're interested in field work."

"Actually, I do think it's fascinating."

She smacked her lips. "Sure you do, Benj." She scrapped away earth with a dental tool and then brushed with a small paint brush. "Showbiz. I'm not an actress, but this is even better. We try to make a dull topic look entertaining. The audience members are assholes. They think we're batty to sit around sifting garbage. But we generate excitement. Look at that coccyx!"

I chuckled, and then refuted, "You love it and you know you do."

Leigh inspected the potsherd. "Mayans painted their shit pots." The glyphs on the sides are a warning not to drink out of it. You poets say it was an artistic expression. What bunk! The expression was simple. This pot hauls turds. Simple as that."

"You've got such a way with words. I won't tell Lindy what you said."

Her gloved hand examined a clod of earth. She chipped it apart with an ice pick. "Up your datum point, Benjamin. I've got the kid convinced my mouth is immaculate."

"There isn't that much mouthwash in the universe." I stood and began to walk away.

"Benj, where you going?"

"A tour to better acquaint me with the area. On a trek across a Mayan memory. I'll scout the legacy of those monstrous warriors of old. I'll return to the days of Mesoamerican greatness. Here in this tropical woodland, this forest housed a great and famous ancient heritage. Vanished now, but their culture yet unfolds."

"Let me write the descriptions."

"See you back at camp."

* * * * *

I WAS IN my element. Action, excitement, and interesting characters to boot, I considered. Immediately upon our arrival at Chichen-Itza, we had met a major performer in the great production of ruins. Pablo Patron was a tour guide. In his rumpled, ivory-tinted garb, and wide-brimmed straw hat, he captured our attention. We guessed he must be in the vicinity of thirty years of age. With straggly sepia hair and jet black eyes, his stony face resembled a stone Olmec head. Stout, no taller than I, his carriage was a nudged agility. We wiped beads of sweat as he climbed steep, narrow steps with sure, effortless footing. His high-wire balancing act was coded in by his heritage, and his equilibrium was calculated.

Because I was constantly being shifted from place to

place, he acquainted me with the setup. He also gave me insight into the citadels that I could never have gleaned on my own. To Pablo, the atavistic ghosts were always on duty. He understood the morose cruelty in the gods' names. For this emblazoned city, wrapped in loden green and somber shadings, was part of his own spiritual encounter. He was aware when the bronzed sun set against a multihued skyline, the gods were getting their shuteye.

In short, Pablo was the type of character with whom I could hook up in a heartbeat. Wandering the mute grandeur of Chichen-Itza had gifted us with mutual friendships. I learned his boyhood was spent in the jungles. He had a girlfriend in another area and visited her often. Her name was Susana and she was his goddess. They would soon be married, and he divulged he would then become a fisherman. He would go into business with her uncle.

From the mist of morning through the shadowy haze of late afternoon, I explored and shot photos. Pablo explained Yucatan is a vast, flat sheet of limestone with low hills. The land is porous and rivers are fed through thunderstorms. This causes water to run underground, pockmarking the abrasive bedrock. The end product is hundreds of perfectly cylindrical sinkholes. Those deep natural wells are known as cenotes and were famous when this place was up and running, and are still famous now. Or infamous. The Well of Sacrifice sinks sixty feet below its rim at forest level.

A cenotes past was one of ritualistic brutality. Lovely young virgins were decorated, consecrated, anesthetized, and then fed to the gods. The women were hurled into the wells, along with treasures of the tribe. And if, Pablo expatiated, the splash into the water did not kill her, and she kept afloat until noon the next day, the woman was hauled out. Fished out to become a venerated saint, he explained.

Recently, the Well of Sacrifice was dredged for a second time. It yielded new treasures. Those treasures and those virgins once appeased the rain gods known as Chacs. Pablo let me know the gods had an insatiable hunger for young women. I supposed it was to let me know how virile his ancestral deities were. Horny was in the blood, Leigh had explained to me.

As Pablo reviewed the area, I studied the landscape's dense vegetation. The air was heavy with mist. Balmy and rancid, I found the area pungent. Pablo inhaled deeply. He closed his eyes and his lips moved in sainted prayer. There were also the sounds of hypnotic buzzing insects mingling with Pablo's scurrying words.

Then Pablo continued his tour. He led me through the Castillo. Inside the hundred-foot pyramid was the Maya-Toltec calendar. We climbed up the steamy hot double chamber. The steep steps were menacing, but I wanted to see the famed Chac Mool. The sacred red stone jaguar was well worth the trip but would not have been if I were claustrophobic.

My personal favorite hangout was El Caracol, the conch. I was enthralled by the cylindrical observatory. Its tower stood forty feet. I was fascinated by the inside circular staircase that elevated to a room where the walls were slotted for observing the heavens.

When I told Pablo how I felt the magnetism to the structure, he said it was simple to understand. Places and things, as well as people, affix a mystical fingerprint upon one's heart.

And so my days were filled with this wondrous land and its treasures. Attempting to not only make notes of each event, I also enjoyed the moments of being. There was tranquility— and it made time for thought.

On the final evening of the digs, we had invited Pablo to

join us for dinner at a small restaurant not far from the dig. We began with wine. Pablo informed me the ancient Mayans called wine *balche*. After a couple glasses of *balche*, we ordered. The restaurant's special of the day was *papules*. This, I discovered, was a meal of tortillas stuffed with eggs and covered with pumpkin seeds and sauces. Leigh ordered the *cazon el echiles xcatiks*, another Mayan meal. Hers was chiles stuffed with baby shark.

I joked about how baby shark wasn't appealing to a Kansan. Pablo bragged that all foods were best prepared on the Isle *Mujeres*, Isle of Women. That got Leigh's attention. The Isle is where his Susana lives, he told us. "You come with me to visit the island, and you can see it is best for food and for beach. It is North of Puerto Juarez. Very quiet beaches. The most beautiful in the world," he boasted. Kissing the tips of his fingers, he let them fly. "I have my truck, so you can come with me."

"We'd better not," I declined.

"Not so fast, Benj," Leigh said as she leaned toward Pablo. "When are you returning to Chichen-Itza?"

"Sunday. And it is free," he replied. "You can place your sleeping bags on cots at my Susana's house. It is all free."

"Pablo," Leigh schemed, "if we pay for the gas, would you take us to the airport in Merida? We need to be there by three on Sunday."

"It would take only a few hours from Puerto Juarez to Merida," he computed. "And the ferry ride takes not so much time. We would not have to leave Isle until ten on Sunday morning. You are free tomorrow after the noon. We could be there in time for dinner tomorrow night."

Bubbling, Lindy declared. "Luv, it would be an adventure. Merida is a bore. Spending all that spare time, there would be a misery."

"She's right," Leigh agreed. "Merida would be a drag. All weekend there—who needs it. I opt for the Isle of Women."

"Why doesn't that amaze me?" I said dryly.

"Come on, Benj. Water, beaches, sunshine, great food, and free lodging."

"I'm in," I concluded with a slight grin.

"Wonderful decision, luv," Lindy teased. "A bit of sun couldn't harm you two palefaces."

* * * * *

AFTER A SPRINGY ride in the bed of Pablo's battered truck, we arrived at our embarkation point of Puerto Juarez. It was little more than a cluster of shacks. I voiced my misgivings as we waited for the freighter that would take us to the Isle of Women. Again, Pablo loaded promises of supreme beauty.

During the ferry ride, Leigh and Pablo huddled together talking about the corners and caverns of various Mayan ruins. Lindy and I discussed black blues singers. We'd walked to the opposite side of the ferry making ourselves comfortable on some old mounds of netting. It was the only time I had been alone with Lindy since the trip began. This gave me the opportunity to grill Lindy about Leigh. I could never get straight answers from Leigh. My chances might be better with her lover.

My question about Leigh's attitudes was a direct hit. Lindy glanced back into my face with a burdensome frown. She motioned me near. Leigh is healing, she confided with empathy. She then told me Billie Holliday never sang a note while in prison. Do you understand, she questioned. Yes, I murmured. I had believed Leigh must have told Lindy the truth. Now, I was certain of it. And I was just as certain Lindy would keep her confidence. I didn't bother prying further.

We returned to Leigh and Pablo in time to view the shoreline. Sands coruscated under the afternoon's bright sun. My fears were dispelled when I saw the palm-covered island. From toe to toe, it was only seven miles long, and one mile wide. And it was breathtaking. Leigh said it was the best fucking place she'd ever seen. She got an immediate reprimand from Lindy. Leigh explained that when on vacation, she should be able to slip in an odd curse word or two. She got an additional look.

Pablo's Susana was light-colored with deep golden eyes and an exotic charm. She welcomed us into the cramped, thatch-roofed hut. Her superb hospitality was in context with the Latin spirit of generosity. And she was definitely in love with Pablo. She had been awaiting his arrival. She'd fixed delectable crab and shark tamales. They steamed away on an outside grill.

Lindy had been suffering with the trots since midweek, but she couldn't resist the tempting bill of fare. Leigh said it wouldn't do her any harm if she washed it down with *aruardiente*. That, I learned upon tasting, was a homemade brandy distilled from sugarcane sap. Tasty and strong, Pablo declared as he toasted.

He was correct. For we slept soundly on our bedrolls that had been placed on cots across the living room. The edges of our cots touched. I could feel the vibrations of Leigh and Lindy cuddling. Between them, and the heavy breathing coming from Susana's bedroom, I was glad I drifted to sleep quickly. My dreams were of Cresida.

Within moments of waking the next morning, I had donned my swimming suit and rushed out to the beach. Sleuthing the *Isle Mujeres* beaches for beauty didn't take any effort. The enchantment of this palm-crested island was captivating. Only the sounds of an occasional rustling palm could break such tranquility. Or enhance it, actually. I heard the crunch of sand as my bikini clad frame walked toward the water. Tiny silica and mica flecks glistened. I turned to view the powdery, ivory beaches. The calm, limpid waters that glided up on the beaches seemed crystalline.

I immersed my body in the ocean. It felt heavenly, and I was pleased we'd opted for the island. After a long swim, I explored crustaceans. Piles of coral rubble and reefs blended with the vivid, florid tropical fish. They flashed their rainbow iridescence. In their small, turquoise jetties, they swam in wonderful waves of splendor.

My hypnotic gaze broke. I returned to where I'd left my towel. Patting dry my dripping suit and skin, I scanned my tan markings. I reclined against a palm tree, breathing the lush, floral salt air. I sighed as my body relaxed on the cushion of sand. Experiencing the warmth of the morning sun was allowing me to construct poetry in my brain, jamming my senses, I mused.

"Enjoying?" Leigh broke into my thoughts. "Here." She handed me a rum-laced fruit drink. "This will complete your luxury."

I sipped. "Terrific."

She eased down beside me as she fiddled with her bikini straps. "I told you it would be great here."

"For a change you were right. Where's Lindy?"

"Went to find a crapper. I told her to take a shit on the shore. Let the ocean do the flushing. She imitated Nora's 'Oh pooh!' routine and off she went."

"Hope she's feeling okay today."

"Musta been something she ate. She's been eating a bunch of junk lately."

Unable to pass up a vicious rejoinder, I remarked, "Leigh, you shouldn't be so hard on yourself."

She sputtered, "Benj, that wasn't bad. For you, anyway. It was below the belt," she gasped for air.

"Don't tell Lindy what I said."

"No way," Leigh agreed.

Glancing up, I spotted Lindy and Pablo ambling toward us. "Lindy," I asked, "are you okay?"

"I'm doing fine. And," she clamored, "we have another opportunity."

"Opportunity?" we delved.

"Wait until you hear this." Her arm sprung back for Pablo's announcement.

"Susana's uncle, he is going on a delivery trip tonight. To another island. On this island, there will be a party. A ritual." His straw hat tipped back on his head. He looked enormously pleased with himself. "Uncle Ignacio will take us on his fishing boat. There will be calypso music and a barbecue. Much good times."

"Ritual?" I repeated.

"Yes, luv," Lindy disclosed. "We can see an actual voodoo ritual." Sucking for breath, her excitement brimmed. "I've studied the practices, but never expected this opportunity. The two of you can determine if you want to go, but I'm going."

"Not without me," Leigh declared. "How about it, Benj?"

"The place, it isn't so far," Pablo said, encouragingly.

I had concern his voluble answer was reminiscent of Juan's *hardly any* and *nearly enough* responses. And everyone knows Mexican time runs by Chac Mool. Pablo sensed my reluctance. I quizzed, "Who will be going on this trip?"

"We go with Susana, her Uncle Ignacio, and his partner, Ricardo. For much fun—we all go."

"Benj," Leigh coaxed, "Pablo brought you here. This isn't half bad. Right?" She turned to Pablo. "Have you ever been to one of these shindigs?"

"Many times. They are much fun. Festive and good times."

"Well, there you have it," Lindy confirmed. "Good times. Crikey, I'm excited. A blooming festival!"

"Are there snakes?" I cautiously grilled.

"Not if they know you're coming," Leigh quipped. "So what's it gonna be?"

"Come along," Lindy rallied.

Reason was on the peripheral. But why hang my pusillanimity out for the world at large to view? Why not a barbecue and *bruja*? "Count me in." I shouldn't have answered, but who is ever to know the perils hidden within the future.

THIRTY-THREE

MOST HAZARDOUS JOURNEYS begin innocently.

Enthusiasm is contagious. Naturally, we were primping for our first voodoo ritual with the same vigor as when we preened for the senior prom. We readied ourselves for a unique experience. I folded back the collar of my khaki-tan, snap-front safari shirt. I told the others about Nora's assessment of *dig* clothing. We all laughed while I finished stuffing my belongings into the canvas pack.

Lindy had slipped into her clay-colored, sleeveless Yukon shirt, and Leigh was buttoning the final buttons on her teal brush shirt. We were all clad in similar stone-toned expedition shorts. Leigh had recommended the shorts for their deep, roomy pockets. Lindy stretched her leggy, athletic body then grabbed her snap-brim jungle hat and her rucksack. She gave the thumbs up sign.

We were on our way.

We crossed a swaying rickety plank and boarded Uncle Ignacio's boat. Susana, with a toss of her long, solar-bronze curls, assured us all was well. Her glowing cherubic face grinned with delight. *Tio* Ignacio and his jovial Sanche Panza, Ricardo, also seemed upbeat. They assured us they were not smugglers. Not that it would have made the slightest difference to Lindy, for whom a specimen coven awaited.

Rocking and weaving, the sluggish boat pitched across the waters while we sang Calypso. Bellefonte's 'Day-O' was repeated a dozen times. It left an echo in my mind. Uncle Ignacio was a squat, graying man in his mid-fifties. He would bellow songs as he steered his craft. He was nuttier than all of us put together so, naturally, I was drawn to him. I called my interest a *professional intrigue* character study. Wild corkscrew gray curls encircled his face. From a distance, his head looked like a Brillo pad. His loud cackle at nearly everything rose with operatic flair. He enjoyed being called *tio*, uncle, so we overloaded the conversations with our avuncular tags of respect.

Admittedly, he was a character. Lindy described him as a delightful *twit*. Leigh claimed he probably thought we were delightful twats. We ignored her as best we could.

Less gregarious, but equally vaudevillian, was Ricardo. He was slightly older than Ignacio. His smile was wrinkled, and several teeth were missing. He had a gimp leg. He boasted how he'd lost a chunk of his leg to a shark. Since that day, he had never again feasted on shark dinners. He feared he might eat the one that lunched on him. He insisted it would be second-hand cannibalism. Although more reserved than our *tio*, Ricardo had soon limped his way into our hearts.

Proudly, they had led us around the plywood interior. They pointed out the two dozen barrels of cargo that were securely tied together. They were proud of their sailor's knots. Inspecting the flimsy vessel, I hoped they could tie it together should the need be. I was consoled by the fact the old boat had made thousands of trips before. One more wasn't asking too much.

Lindy passed me a bottle of dark rum and motioned for me to take a swig. Probably to anesthetize me. We were all seated on pillows that had been tossed on the deck. I leaned back against my pack for support. I was glad I wasn't hauling the camera gear. It had been left behind with one of the professors.

That lightened my pack considerably; however, I would have enjoyed photographing *Isle Mujeres*.

As soon as our voices and conversation were spent, I realized with concern it was taking longer than I had anticipated. Mexican time prevailed. Susana said we would soon be there. And if we turned back, we would be lost. It made absolutely no sense to me, so I took an additional gulp of the rum, and then passed it around.

Lindy was giving a spiel on voodoo. She claimed it was an amalgam of Roman Catholicism and tribal religion of West Africa. The spirit, she recited, is called *loa*. The priest is a *hungan* and the priestess is *mambo*. Drumming, dancing, and singing bring the spirit *loa*. What happens then, I quizzed. Leigh grinned and told me the *mambo* puts a hex on the person with the lightest skin. Susana denied it in an attempt to ease my discomfort. Pablo told me the *hungan* and *mambo* enter a trance for good white magic. The snake is the symbol of the spirit, they informed.

Our story swap continued. I told of the time my sister had watched a TV special on snakes. She feared them as much as I did. She'd gone to bed and was dreaming about the fanged and coiled serpents. Toward morning, Prince had given her a lick on the face. Kris nearly put a skylight in her room.

Glancing up, and to my relief, I spied a large area of land. We headed up through the narrow isthmus toward a tire-wrapped dock. I was ecstatic we'd arrived. I waved to the colorfully dressed woman on shore. Ricardo pitched a rope and the woman hitched us to a piling.

"Benj, stop grimacing," Leigh directed. "You look as though you're about to be lynched by the locals."

"You don't have the good sense to be concerned, so it's up to me," I retaliated.

"Sense!" she clamored. "You poets all need to be run in

and checked out under the hood."

"Nora is correct about one thing," I confirmed.

"What?" Leigh's hands were on her hips as she confronted me.

"She says you've got a goofy streak a mile long."

"Benj, fuck you. Her too, for that matter."

We looked at one another as laughter spurt. "I wouldn't try Nora if I were you. Unless you have a death wish."

"I wouldn't try Nora unless I had one hefty dildo."

"Leigh!" Lindy scolded. "Stop talking like that."

Leigh gave a final grin and then padded after Lindy. "Coming, dear."

"Milquetoast," I called after her. She pretended not to hear.

* * * * *

WHILE THE MEN made great theatre of unloading the barrels, we followed a dirt path until we were enveloped in a jungle mecca. A couple hundred people milled the rich tropical vegetation of palms, majague, and decorative citrus trees. Near a patch of sugar cane was a strangely shaped tree. It was decorated to the max. Lindy explained it was the sacred temple tree.

I walked around a swarm of mosquitoes toward where women were standing beside a plume of smoke that puffed from a stone pit. Inside was roasting pork wrapped in banana leafs. It sizzled and spit.

While dinner cooked, I wandered. I was astounded by the multitude of colors, images, sounds, and aromas. They clearly were imprinting new impressions on my mind. Someone handed me a fresh sugar cane to chew. I'd never even seen one. My teeth crunched the fibrous cane. I quickly nodded approval to Lindy and Leigh. When they gave us each a platter of barbecued pork, spiced vegetables, and fruits, we again nodded. We were too famished to vocalize our delight at the food. Susana passed us each a melon drink that came from a clear bottle with a corn cob stopper. Leigh poured rum into the beverage, and we toasted.

After dinner, we again wandered around curiously gawking at the interesting sights and sounds. Rhythmic maracas, tambourines, drums, and chanting continued. The scantily dressed drummer's eyes were transfixed on the evening's flush of a full moon. People sang, clapped, and puffed their ritual pipes. Although I hadn't wanted to pull out my spiral journal and pretend to be a reporter, I knew there was no way of forgetting the spectacle. Shining, oiled bodies pranced with writhing celebratory motions. They were on display under the moon. That moon appeared to expand as the music's piercing beat increased.

With moon, stars, and candles glinting, the nocturnal jungle seemed to transport me to another dimension. Umbra shadings from acanthine, tangled images snarled around us. The crowd danced on spongy earth, and their motion created crawling shadows. The sylvan pilgrimage, with its cascading chants, was eerie. Spooky, but we were under an umbrella of exuberance that protected us from the rites. With festive, primitive idolatry, the event took hold of us—grasped us tightly in its grip.

I nudged Leigh. "I drank too much juice. Where's the lavatory?"

"Lav?" she howled. "Benj, think of the jungle as your private outhouse. Just don't wipe with *mala mujere*," she said with a snicker.

"Don't make me laugh or I'll need a change of panties as well," I admonished. Lindy stuck a handful of tissues in my palm as I passed by.

"Thanks. I'd really rather blow my nose with *mala mujere* than wipe with it," I issued with a giggle.

Upon returning to camp, I noticed a tension. "Back from the loo in time," Lindy remarked.

"Why are they chanting more quietly?"

Leigh whispered, "They found out you were pissing on the earth they love. They're deciding which end to hang you from—head or tail. One's as useless as the other, so it's a tossup."

Susana corrected, "The ceremony is beginning."

Inertia seemed suspended. I figured the old *loa* was about to pounce. Center stage was the *hungan*. Bare-chested, moving in circles, the sorcerer's brown body gleamed. His feet stamped to the beat of the drum. A younger man rotated a machete in one hand. He flagged a live chicken with the other.

Tapping my arm, Lindy warned, "Kelly, if you're squeamish, you'd best close your eyes."

"Benj won't even go to bullfights," Leigh tattled.

I took another sip of rum, turned my head, and bolted my eyes shut. I heard a snap and fluttering feathers. I looked up to see blood threading down the *hungan's* body. He was still chanting while being anointed with sacrificial chicken blood.

My face must have been bone white because Susana asked twice if I was okay. I nodded, telling her fine. I reached for the bottle again.

Although I'd braced myself for the *mambo's* act, I figured it would be much tamer. She danced her way to the sacred tree and then bowed before the exposed roots. She offered a large folded leopard skin bundle. Atop of it, she placed a human skull. Again, she bowed to the holy tree. Then she prostrated her glistening body. She was clad only in thin leather straps around her buttocks and a bikini-skimp matching leather top.

Her black flesh was exposed and her breasts heaved with the drumbeat. An amulet swayed from her neck. It tangled with a chain of coral, teeth and pierced stones. The upper portion of her arms was bedecked with twining golden bands that matched her gleaming diadem. Her face was dusted with ash, and her eyes were piercing bronze.

Swaying, the *mambo* encouraged the crowd's clapping. Methodically, she placed candles on either side of the skull that rested on its elevated altar of leopard skin. From beneath the skin, she took several sets of beads and shell necklaces. As she stood, she began whirling them. Her bare feet tapped the earth as she approached the crowd. She neared us, twisting a strand of shells around Lindy's arm. Lindy participated by twirling the beads to the low rumbling sound of drums. Then the *mambo* anointed an old man with a pungent curative mixture of oil and ash. After she had signed him, she gave a swift snap of her palm against his forehead. He fell to the ground and began slithering like a snake. When he reached the edge of the circling crowd, his body went limp.

Mambo took the glowing candles from her altar. She began rolling them over her skin. She seemed to be bathing her flesh in fire, but she didn't flinch. She handed one to an onlooker. She then began rotating against the torch. When she moved toward me, she protracted the other candle in my direction. My throat was Death Valley dry. She placed the candle in my hand. It fell through my fingers. Lindy quickly retrieved the smoldering candle, extending it toward the *mambo*. The *mambo* waved her hand re-lighting the candle wick as her fingers sprouted open.

I was transfixed. As she moved away, I delved, "How did she do that?" My eyes were on stalks.

"I haven't a clue," Leigh replied. "I *do* know you never would have made acolyte tryouts."

A nimbus of light accompanied the *mambo* back to her altar. She held up the skull ceremoniously, and then placed it behind the leopard skin. Kneeling, she leaned over the bundled skin. While she unfolded it, she continued performing erotic gyrations. As it was unwrapped, I caught a glimpse of movement from within. I was tagged by a simple guess.

"There's a snake in there, right?"

"Right. Not to worry," Lindy confided. "The *mambo* has perfect control over her *loa*."

The snake poked upward. It then spiraled into the air. The coiling boa constrictor wound around the *mambo's* dancing body. With a curlicuing motion, the snake convoluted with the *mambo's* choreographed gestures.

Then a mystical drumming began to dwindle until it was barely audible. The *mambo* was on her knees directly in front of the snake. Snake and woman dipped and weaved as their heads neared. The *mambo's* mouth opened widely. The reptile poked its way several inches down her throat. Moments later, it retracted from her mouth. Drums intensified.

I felt revulsion, but I was mesmerized. My eyes would not shut. "That's the damnedest thing I've ever witnessed," I murmured.

Leigh turned to me, laughing. "Yes, Benj, but these people would probably roll on the floor if they saw a batch of old bearded men with skull caps blubbering at a wall or some doctor carving off the skin of a prick. Or how about a troop of clowns wearing shamrocks and leaning off a cliff to kiss a farkling stone? Now that is pure goofy."

Glaring, I questioned, "Do you have one shred of empathy for people and their tradition? Isn't there anything you respect?"

"I respect knowledge, and Lindy."

"I couldn't help notice you didn't include yourself in that

brief list."

She diverted her glance from mine. "Benj, there are times you act like a sack of sugar, and I'd like to feed you to that farkling snake."

I didn't laugh. When she cast her eyes back at me, I saw an entire spectrum of pain in them. If it was a victory to have pushed her button, it was indeed a victory by default. And an empty win. There was nothing I could do to turn her hatred around.

* * * * *

"SO WHEN DO we leave?" I questioned Pablo. He had returned from checking *Tio* Ignacio's barrel's bill of lading.

"Not yet," he replied with a shrug.

"My uncle," Susana explained, "tells us it is too dangerous until the sun is up."

"Dangerous?" I grilled.

"He is frightened," Pablo yielded. "He sees the *soldados*. He is frightened they might not see that his is only a fishing boat. They might shoot."

"*Soldados?*" I questioned Leigh, who was now extremely serious.

"What soldiers?" she asked with an agitated sharpness. "You mean coast guard?"

"Soldiers," he confirmed with another shrug.

Pivoting to Lindy, Leigh clamored, "You don't suppose...."

Lindy calculated, "We were in the water at least four or five hours. Maybe going thirty miles per hour. We aren't in Kingston."

"Cuba," I enunciated slowly. My spirits suddenly went to my socks.

"*Sí*," answered Susana. "But only a remote area. Here the Cubanos like us."

Leigh took charge. "You two have your passports?"

We nodded affirmatively. Lindy answered, "I've both mine. Brit and Yankee."

"If we get stopped, you deep-six the American one. Good thing you're only twenty," Leigh snapped. Maybe if we get in a pickle, they'll let you go."

I grumbled, "If Gran knew I was in a commy country, she'd disown me."

"We aren't going to tell Granny, are we?" Leigh spread a healthy dose of sarcasm. "We're not going to tell anyone." She glanced at Pablo. "When will it be safe to leave?"

"When there is sun. For now, you can follow me. I'll show you where there are hammocks and mosquito nets. We can be much comfortable."

"Pablo, we're Americans," Leigh grunted. "Nets and henequen hammocks are not terribly reassuring to us."

We glanced at one another as we were led to a shanty. We knew this was a test of womanhood and must be defined by our stamina to believe it would turn out okay. Someone said that one's last gasp is probably the loudest. I'd had my near-fatal romps with death. Both from 'chancy acts.' This act of chance and stupidity, I meditated, could be the final sticker price costing me my life. If there was a joke anywhere in this, three strikes and you really are out. Stupid doesn't continue to redeem itself. Sometimes it sticks.

We walked past a row of lean-tos and at the end was a dark shanty. Inside a line of hammocks were strung. Netting draped down from bent nails on ceiling boards. We slid into three vacant hammocks beyond the half dozen occupied ones. Whistling snores annoyed me as I wiggled my body into a nearly comfortable position.

"You realize, if they catch us, they could shoot us and no one would ever know," I complained.

Leigh's arm pierced through the netting. She thrust a bottle of rum at me. "This will help get your mind off being shot."

Unscrewing the cap, I sighed. "Thanks." I took a large gulp.

"If anything happens to us, it's my fault," Lindy blamed herself. "I've made a dog's dinner out of this trip."

"That's crap," I vetoed her guilt. "Don't worry, it will be okay." My pessimism was going undercover. I bridged the quart of rum toward Lindy. "Here, have yourself a little nightcap. Leigh claims it will get our minds of off being murdered while on our tour of Cuba."

* * * * *

"THEY'VE GOT GUNS," I mumbled as we obligingly put our hands behind our heads. Per request. The only motion was the rocking of the boat, and the only sound was its thump as it hit the dock."

"*No dispare usted!*" Pablo bellowed for them not to shoot us.

Leigh whispered, "Kelly, don't open your mouth. Your Spanish could get you in a world of trouble." She sighed. "And we were almost ready to leave."

We'd packed up very early and boarded for our escape. But it wasn't in time.

"She's right," Lindy cautioned. "Pretend not to understand a thing they say."

"We are being detained," Pablo confirmed as the dozen soldiers swarmed the vessel. "He wants your passports." Pablo then tried his best to reason with them. But to no avail. The others were led to the other side of the boat while we Americans were surrounded.

We dug into our packs, searching hastily. The soldiers watched. They were dressed in filthy guerrilla fatigues. Their rifles were strategically aimed at us. I was paralyzed with fear. My fingers fumbled with great inaccuracy. Finally, I handed my passport to a short, stocky leader. His scowl was heavily starched.

"Jankee pigs," he spat. He slid our passports in his chest pocket.

Without thinking, I protested. "Hey, those belong to us."

He reeled around. His black crocodile eyes glared. He gave me a shove before ordering us to be quiet.

Two guards held us at bay while the other soldiers searched the boat for contraband. "Benj," Leigh said out of the side of her mouth, "let's proceed under the assumption that they aren't as dumb as they look. Cooperate. It's our only chance."

"Can we put our hands down now?" I inquired. "They've already frisked us."

"Benj, I wouldn't do that. Something tells me the porky jerk-off moonlights as a mortician," Leigh answered. "Don't go into your desperado routine here."

Waving his gun, the guard shouted, "We mordur jankees. Throw them in water."

I might as well have tossed myself into the Well of Sacrifice, I thought. I grimaced to Lindy. The leader continued looking at our passports. Leigh chastised Lindy, "I told you to use the Brit one."

"Luv, we're in this together," Lindy whispered back.

They began rummaging through our packs. One of them pulled my notebook out. I made a grab for it. My arms were grasped tightly as he pitched me back. He put his face right up into mine. With a menacing scream, he sprayed orders not to move. Leigh quickly retrieved the notebook that had been dropped in the skirmish. She handed it to the leader.

No maps, she answered. He thumbed through it, and then told her to translate some of it. Poetry only, she said, reading a few passages. She then extended it to him for additional scrutiny. When he was satisfied that it held no secrets, he gave a surly mumble, then hurled it at me.

"What did he say?" I asked.

Leigh grimly reported, "He said it was artsy-fartsy shit and not worth his effort."

Objecting, I countered, "He never did. I heard the word *Yankee*."

Lindy translated, "He called it stupid Yankee imperialistic propaganda."

"Same thing," Leigh grumbled.

"Everyone's a critic!" I sulked.

The leader walked to me. He surveyed my grimy, mosquito bitten body. Then he touched my necklace that had been a gift from Eduardo. Figuring he wanted *mordida*, the bite, or bribery, I took it off and handed it to him. He tucked it into his pocket. He then grabbed my elbow and began leading me to his cruiser. Lindy bolted, and her grasp locked his arm. The second in command gave her a poke with the butt of his gun. She grabbed her ribs as she buckled.

Pablo heard the commotion and broke away. He rushed to us, rapidly speeding his words. The leader dropped my arm. He nodded to his followers. They made their way back to their military cruiser.

Leigh dropped down to lean over Lindy. "The dumb shit," she seethed.

"You okay?" I asked as I knelt on the deck.

"Fine, luvs." She caught her breath, and then stood.

When the soldiers sped off, full throttle, I felt as though life's reset button had been pushed for the third time. I asked Pablo what he'd said to them.

"I say that your grandfather, he is head of the socialist party in America. And you will report back to them that the Cuban comrades are brave. And I tell him your uncle, he is a cardinal in Rome, and he prays for Castro each day."

I commended his quick thinking and his acting ability. Then I inquired, "So how do we get our passports back?"

Leigh scowled. "Castro will hand deliver yours. Because I'm certain those fuckers will tell him how upset you were. And now that they realize you don't like lending it out, I'm sure you can expect it back soon."

"Seriously, what will we do?"

"Benj, we'll tell the Consulate that they were all in one bag and were stolen. You'd better rehearse the lines. I don't want you getting mixed up with some far-fetched plot you're writing. We'll report it to the Consulate first thing upon arriving back in D.F. We need to swear to secrecy. And Benj, don't tell Nora. I don't want her to know that while in my custody, you were nearly shot to death."

"Telling anyone hadn't crossed my mind." This secret, I vowed, would be set into cold storage with due haste.

"Sorry about your necklace," Lindy said.

"I was going to take it off when I move in with Cres anyway. I'm concerned about the crack in the ribs you got. Thanks for coming to my rescue." Glimpsing over at Leigh, I added, "You sure froze."

"I'm not good with these kinds of things." She turned, walking to the opposite side of the boat.

Lindy motioned for me to be silent. "Not now," she whispered. "Look, it's my fault you're here. It was my idea to see the ritual. I'm the berk."

I gave her a gentle, playful shove. "Nah. Nobody put a gun to my head to make me come here. Only to make me leave." When Leigh approached, her face was sullen. I wanted to cheer her up. "Leigh, don't you think they could have given us a flipping cigar for the trouble?"

"I'm glad you didn't get hauled to the cruiser and sampled by the entire Cuban army," Leigh muttered. "They love washed-out blondes."

We laughed as the patrol cruiser left our field of vision. Uncle Ignacio and the crew started up the engines. The three of us eased down onto the deck. With numb faces, we gazed out to sea. I declared, "Seriously, I'm glad they didn't shoot us."

Leigh scoffed. "The little fucker didn't even have his finger on the trigger. It's tough to pick your nose and shoot a rifle at the same time." She quickly retracted her language, "I take it all back, Lindy. I mean to say, the little dickens."

"Luv, you get it all out of your system. You'll feel better. I give you dispensation."

"That little mother fucking, cock-sucking, *cabrone*, son of a bitching suck, *chingad*, pisser, prick." Leigh's tirade trailed. "Well, aren't you going to scold me?"

"Not at all, luv. I'm glad if it made you feel better." Lindy blew Leigh a kiss. "I couldn't be more in agreement with what you called him. Sod the bloody fucker."

Leigh goggled at me. My eyes popped wide open. We then burst into laughter. Astounded, I asked, "Leigh, you taught her all that in these few months?"

Leigh replaced her sunglasses. She leaned back as the boat rocked. She tipped her hat forward. "I also taught you plenty, Benjamin." Folding her arms, she made her pronouncement. "I think you'll agree—there is *no* fucking business like show business."

THIRTY-FOUR

FAREWELLS ALWAYS GET me down. And the day was brimming with them.

Pablo loaded the truck in haste. We had our goodbyes with *Tio* Ignacio, Ricardo, and Susana earlier. Then there was a ferry ride back to Puerto Juarez. While Pablo worked on the clattering truck engine, we went skinny-dipping. That was to make us feel somewhat bathed.

The truck chugged along at record speed, getting us to the airport in time to catch our flight. Then we said our farewells to our friend, Pablo.

Having slept in the truck on the way to Merida, we were wide awake on the plane. The other students zonked out immediately upon liftoff. We visited, and then Lindy divulged that she now knew how her favorite aunt felt when she'd been captured in Singapore. Her mother's sister had been a medic. She was held captive by the Japanese for nearly three years. Lindy contended that she would probably still be there, or dead, had the bombs not been dropped on Japan. That horrendous event had saved the women and children held in prison camps throughout the islands, Lindy claimed.

My thoughts twisted to my Grandfather Benjamin. I continued thumbing through an old *Life* magazine. I was thinking how many perished because of the bomb, but many were also saved. Sadly, it had been a man-made exchange of life for life. Lindy's revelation was significant. I hadn't thought about it in those terms. Why, I questioned, need there be anyone obliterated by war? That remained my final consideration.

When we arrived back in Mexico City, I scrambled to the apartment. Nora was out and that pleased me. There would be no inquisition. A burden I didn't need. Waking in a humid jungle, glowering down the barrels of a dozen loaded rifles, riding in a truck with pogo stick springs, and an airplane ride that played leapfrog with headwinds was more than enough excitement for one day. Nora would have put the day over the ledge.

I took a leisurely shower, called Cresida, and then made plans for a getaway. My packing was complete. I said goodbye to Erika, Sanchez, and Lupe. I told Lupe that visiting her village had given me a great gift. She knew what I meant.

I squeezed into a cab beside my suitcases, a box of books, my typewriter, and assorted belongings. Cresida had wanted to send Rodolfo, but I insisted it would be much easier and quicker to taxi to her home. Our home, she corrected. That made me consider the declaration I was making.

For now, my day of bidding farewell was nearing an end. I would convert to an evening of greeting the doctora and my new life. There was an apprehension about moving in with her. But the queasiness evaporated when she folded her arms protectively around me.

"I've missed you," I crooned in her ear.

"Welcome home, my darling. A special festive dinner has been prepared. All your favorites."

"I'm famished."

"And dinner is served," she said with a smile.

While eating, I related the events of the dig. She laughed, and her eyes sparkled. "It sounds a wonderful trip," she commented.

"Cres, I'm so glad to be back here with you."

"And I'm glad that you've returned."

Lifting a glass of wine, I toasted, "Yes. I've returned to you."

She reached across the table, caressing my hand. "You make me so happy. You look weary. Are you well?"

"I'm fine now. Spending the last couple of days with Pablo, the master of disaster was nerve-wracking," I joked. "The guy knows how to lean into a punch."

"They all sound delightful," she said with a laugh in her voice. "I'm glad you had such adventures that you'll always remember."

"I'm glad I have a shrink nearby." I squeezed her fingers. "After only being a few feet from a boa constrictor, I'll be dreaming of snakes for weeks. It was not my idea of entertainment."

"But it sounds as though you enjoyed your travels."

"Most of the time. The snake ritual was bizarre. And there were a few tentative moments."

"Tentative?"

"Well, a tad dangerous."

"Dangerous moments?" Her eyes zeroed in on me.

"We got into some difficulties." I took a quick sip of wine. "The white magic ceremony was in Cuba."

"My darling, an American should not be there." Her words were stern. Her eyes riveted to me. "Why ever would you visit Cuba?"

"We had no idea where we were going. They said only that it was a beach on a remote island."

"You encountered problems?"

"We were caught. Detained. Just as we were leaving, soldiers boarded our boat. It was frightening. They had guns. Pablo talked them out of harming us. They did take our passports. Leigh said we need to tell the Consulate they were lost."

Her look of distress had turned to one of alarm. "Kelly, you took a terrible chance. Please promise you'll never endanger yourself again." Placing her napkin on the table, she reached for my hand. "I don't know what I'd do without you."

"When they pointed the guns at us, I was worried I might never see you again. I was thinking of you. Of us." I lifted her hand to kiss her fingers. They tenderly caressed my lips. "I was thinking of how much I love you."

"That means a great deal to me. Kelly, often it is most difficult to express my love. I hope you understand."

"Yes. When I express my love, I don't expect words back in kind. I'm aware how the tragedy with your ballerina friend devastated you. I understand your reticence to say all the words."

Her glance lowered. "Although I rented a lovely apartment for her and tried to share as much time as possible, it was never enough. I did attempt to make her happy. I failed. She thought we were emotionally estranged because we lived apart. It was a great deal more complicated than that." Her eyes filled with teardrops. She sipped at her wine slowly, pensively. "I shall make an effort to be less isolated."

"Cres, you're in my heart. I don't need outward expressions of your love. You make me feel your love when we touch."

She opened her mouth. Her lips began to forge words. Maria appeared, and Cres smiled her love to me. "The mousse de mandarine looks excellent, Maria. My compliments."

The beautiful tangerine mousse was garnished with almond slivers, powdered sugar, and decorated with a wreath of kumquats. Its faint scent of citrus was marvelous.

When Maria had exited, I stood, picking up the silver

platter holding the exquisite desert. With the mousse in one hand, I grabbed two spoons with the other. "Hey, Cres, you said you wish to make me happy. So would you please bring the coffee and let's have dessert in bed."

She followed instructions with a perplexed grin. She stacked two coffee cups and with her free hand looped her fingers around the handle of the silver coffee server. "Mousse de mandarine in bed?"

"Absolutely." I winked. "You don't mind a little adventure?" I placed the dessert on the nightstand, then poured coffee for us.

She tightly clamped shut the door. Her eyes questioned. "Are we to share this adventure?"

With a cushiony, slow touch, I unfastened the buttons of her silk blouse. When it slipped from her shoulder, my mouth trailed from her shoulder to the upper portion of her neck. My lips rested below her ear. I whispered my request. "Please lean back and close your eyes."

After our clothing had been removed, she reclined against the billowing pillows. Her eyes shut. I moved to her, inhaling the jasmine scent of her body lotion. My heart rate accelerated. I took a heaping spoonful of mousse and carefully smoothed it on her stomach. With deliberation, my mouth traveled across her skin, tasting the mousse. "Delicious," I murmured. My cravings had never been so tangerine oriented.

When I repeated the spreading of mousse on her breasts, I heard her moan slowly. My lips moved from one breast to the next, gently feasting from her swelling nipples.

This, I thought, was the grand desert appetizer. We would both enjoy the final course. I never would have guessed tangerines and jasmine blended so beautifully. The entire banquet was conducted with eloquence and with steamy grandeur. Love felt splendid. Of course, tangerine and jasmine were only the seasonings.

Some things, I determined, must be tried to be believed.

* * * * *

I HAD BEEN cracking the spines of my new textbooks in amplified fashion. Study was an anthem.

Deciding to drop by Professor Thurston's office was part of the procedure of gaining even more knowledge. He recommended the best of literature. When I saw he was on the phone, I turned to leave. He beckoned me in, covering the telephone receiver and whispering it was Kirk Underwood. Kirk had been searching for me and found I had moved. Thurston held out the phone, asking if I wished to talk with Kirk.

My answer would have been negative, but I didn't want to draw attention to my displeasure with Kirk. Reluctantly, I took the phone. Kirk explained that he would be in D.F. to give a lecture at the college. His new book sales figures were reaching new heights. He would be sailing his yacht down Baja. He wanted me to meet him in Guaymas, suggesting we sail the rest of the way together.

I politely declined, and then curtly changed subjects. I asked him what he would include in his lecture. He would, he declared, tell students to read Rabelais and Marquez, then return to the United States and sell out. His sarcasm was in full bloom.

He asked how my love life was going. I responded by telling him I'd found someone special. He said he intended to steal me away from my new love. I laughed. Kirk asked if *he* was a prizefighter. No, I replied. However, a prize was my repartee.

When I hung up, I shrugged. Thurston understood my

discomfort completely. "Kirk's a true playboy. We weren't meant for one another," I joked.

"I miss our young Carlos," Thurston remarked. With piercing inspection through his lowered spectacles, he quizzed, "Don't you?"

"I miss Carlos a bunch," I confirmed. "He's one of my best friends in the world."

"I'm glad you stopped by, Miss Benjamin. I wanted to inform you about your story. Young lady, it has been accepted for publications. Details will follow, but I'm certain terms will be most generous, and to your satisfaction."

Beaming, I felt my excitement brimming. "That's wonderful! Thank you, sir. I owe you so much. I want you to know how appreciative I am of your assistance."

"Please don't neglect your poetry. You must never forget your primary passion."

"I won't, sir."

Rushing across campus, I spied Leigh and yelled for her to slow down her galloping pace. I blurted, "Leigh, my story was accepted!"

"Whoopee shit," she grumbled. "Our passports were returned to the U.S. Consulate. *La embajado Americana.* They thought we'd been captured. The American Embassy will be scoping us now. The university reassured them that we're safe. We could have created an international incident. Now, everyone's pissed off over the deal. There's a message at your place telling you that we're to meet with the college president. We've got to go down to the consulate's office and *personally* pick up our passports. Crap."

"You think they suspect we were actually in Cuba?"

"You think birds shit on statues. Of course, they know, simpleton! The jerk-off soldier probably told them we were involved in some dastardly espionage against Castro. The little fucker."

"All we need to do is stick with our story," I schemed. "It's our word against theirs. So what does Lindy say?"

"She thinks the entire brouhaha is her fault."

"We all went voluntarily."

"So what's this story business?"

"The magazine is buying the story about Gran's pioneer stepmother. Cres will be pleased. It was so terrific returning to her."

"She was laying women when you were in your sperm-and-egg days."

"Leigh, why is your attitude so goddamn rotten? She isn't the type of person to *lay* a woman." I paused, then disclosed, "For the first time in my life, I feel loved and sheltered. It's as though I truly belong. No drunkenness. No silly high school games of jealousy. It's a pure, mature love."

"It's mature all right. Hell, Benj, when you get miffed, she probably asks if you got up on the wrong side of the cradle."

"Look, I don't mind your nut-cutting when it comes to guys in my life, but leave her alone."

"Hey, I'm in a crappy mood." She pushed the straggles of her hair from her eyes. "I only pulled a B in one of the classes I was certain should have been an A. Then with this fucking passport business, Lindy is in tears. She thinks you're irked with her."

"I'm not irked. It wasn't her fault. I'll call her tonight. Find out how her ribs are doing and give her complete absolution. Okay?"

"Sure. Benj, during the Easter celebration in Mexico they have this effigy called Judas. It's usually a skeleton replica made of papier-mâché. It hangs from a tree or post. There are these fireworks attached, see. Well, anyway, people write the names of their enemies and stuff the note into the Judas dummy. During festivities, they light the sonofabitch. Judas is blown all to hell, and that's the wish for a person's enemies. Well, next Easter, I'm putting those fucking Cuban soldier's description in Judas. I'll stuff a ream of paper up the old bugger's ass. Wads."

"Great gesture. Doubt if it will cause the soldier's much discomfort though."

"But it will do me infinite good."

I rubbed my temple. "It's over. Let's forget about it."

"I don't forget fuckers like that."

"We're safe. Why are you so still so angry?"

Her eyes were sharpened daggers. "I have an angry heart."

"I don't think so." I grinned widely, and then added, "But I could be wrong."

She countered with a scowl. "I may place a slip of paper with your name on it up the butt of old Judas." She then giggled. "But the old fart would probably shit the note back out."

"That is what I call the ultimate of rejection slips."

* * * * *

DURING OUR FRIDAY torta luncheon, Nora told me of her Acapulco holiday. I had to admit, it was much more exciting than being held at bay by Cubans.

She called her holiday a sordid affair. And so it was. Eduardo had been sullen. Ah, I remember it well. Renee cried on Michel's shoulder. Middle of the night, Nora woke to find that Michel was not tucked in beside her. She stalked the hotel halls, prowling the area for her lost lover. Finally, she discovered Renee and Michel out on a small fire escape landing.

Renee, with her back to the wall, had her legs wrapped

around Michel's midsection. Her nightgown was hiked up, and Renee was moving up and down like a roaring piston. Michel's p.j.s ended up down around his ankles. Renee was pinned to the wall with pleasure. Nora gasped, returning quickly to the room and she then bolted the door.

It was a quiet ride back to D.F.

I was tap dancing on quicksand when I inquired what else happened at the house of Sanchez.

"Erika's dating an Italian singer. He claims he can't dump his wife."

"They all give you that baloney."

Nora gave a hesitant nod. Accompanying the nod was a nervous laugh. She then confessed, "Kelly, I can confide in you. I'm seeing a married man. He's one of the professors. Please don't say anything."

"You know I can keep a secret. I won't tell a soul."

With a confirming nod, she said, "So can I. So tell me about your special man."

"Nora, there isn't a special man."

"Come on. Who is your mystery man and why can't I meet him," she cajoled.

"It wouldn't work, Nora," I stealthily replied. I took another quick bite. "So is Eduardo heartbroken over Renee?"

"He acts as if he could care less. Kelly, stop trying to change the subject. I want to know about your mystery man. You're ashamed of him, aren't you?"

"Let's not talk about it," I said with a flush.

"What are you ashamed of?"

"Nora, I'm not ashamed. There are things you couldn't handle. So back off."

Her face was becoming redder than a mid-summer tomato. "If you're my friend, you'll tell me."

"Maybe because you're my friend, I won't."

"That doesn't make sense. Oh, please, Kelly, you can trust me."

"I'm living with a woman."

"You told me that."

"The woman is a lesbian."

Her face was immobile for many moments. "What if she made a pass at you?"

"She has."

"Did you slap her?"

I looked away. "No."

"Kelly, how could you ever live with that kind of woman?"

"Nora, I'm having an affair with her. Actually, it's much more meaningful than an affair." Nora's face reflected shock and disdain. "I lied to you about meeting her through Carlos. I met her at a party in Acapulco. I was with Leigh." I picked up my soft drink to sip. Nora was speechless. I rather enjoyed that. "Well?"

"Kelly!"

"Hold the confetti. I'm not exactly an official Lesbian Hall of Famer."

With a delayed reaction, she wailed, "My God, Kelly, no. Why?"

"I don't know why. I know I love her."

"Honestly! What can two women do together?" Her gasp was one of repulsion.

"I knew I couldn't tell you without a big scene."

"You didn't answer—what can two women do?"

Attempting to quell my anger, I asked, "What do you mean, what can two women do. Are you talking about in bed or emotionally? What the hell are you asking? Is a few inches of prick all there is to love and romance? Are you asking how I can get by without that magic flesh wand? Have you no imagination?"

"I just asked you to tell me what you do?"

"For starters, two women can have trust. I can be assured I won't catch her fucking someone else out on a fire escape."

"I didn't need to hear that."

"Nora, I'm trying to tell you how I feel. I'm being honest with you. I am faithful to her. I am loved by a wonderful, kind, decent, well-educated woman. Now, if you are truly my friend, you'll accept that."

"I'm sorry for you. It's all that darned Leigh's fault."

"Not hardly," I disputed.

"I still want you as my friend," Nora finally stated with measured enthusiasm.

"Good." I returned her smile of reticence. "Because I haven't changed from the person I was when I sat down here an hour ago. I'm still Kelly Benjamin." With a slippery grin, I teased, "I add D-Y-K-E after my name now." Why not, I considered? I had my advanced degree in Sapphism. "Next time you hear a blue joke about queers, you can say one of your best friends is gay. Cheer up, Nora. Liberalism is in."

An unexpected laugh spurted from her gaping lips. "Oh Kelly, you'll never change! You're still outrageous."

* * * * *

THE DAY WAS filled to the brim with pure malarkey.

Sitting in the principal's office, actually the University president's digs, was a tough pill to swallow. Leigh, Lindy, and I ended up compromising our deviousness by telling the truth. We had no earthly idea where we were going. After a cautionary lecture, we were allowed to go down and pick up our passports. Another cautionary lecture later, and we had our passports back.

Touring Kelly's Poem

I stopped by to pick up the final remnants of mail that had arrived after I left. Lo and behold, Eduardo was there. He'd left messages for me, and when Sanchez told him I'd be stopping by for mail, he appeared. Said he was passing by. Yes. And donkeys fly through the air with the greatest of ease.

I resisted the urge to ask how his little fire escape *puta* was doing. I didn't mention that she must feel like a hot potato being passed around like that. She was acting the part of a pastured cow out sniffing the bulls—or balls. I wouldn't have been so resentful, but he continued to bring up my past. One he knew nothing about. After he had made several comments—like he was willing to forgive me, I told him I wasn't the one needing to be drug through the disinfectant. He got the message. He exited in a huff.

I sorted my mail. One letter was from the magazine with a contract offering me two-hundred and fifty dollars for my short story. My buoyant cheer returned.

I waited a few more minutes before leaving so I wouldn't run into Eduardo on the street. I chatted with Sanchez and Lupe before calling Rodolfo. He would be by to collect me in half an hour. I didn't want to run late since Cresida and I had planned to attend a concert later. I was anxious about it. I dashed out to purchase a dozen helium balloons to place in the doctora's bedroom. The balloon bouquet with attached card told her of the short story sale and of my love for her.

After tying the balloon's strings to her bedpost, I decided what I would wear to the concert. I was looking forward to being out with her. After I showered and dressed, I studied. Then I realized it had been some time since filling her fountain pen with black ink. It was one of those rituals that made me feel good to be able to do something, however small, for her. After completing the task, I prepared her bath. I continued to check the time, which was passing all too rapidly.

Cresida arrived late, carrying her briefcase, and looking tired. I greeted her with a hug. "You look weary. The concert will relax us both."

"I still have reports to prepare. I'm very sorry, but I won't be able to attend the concert tonight. Another night, I promise."

"Cres," I began pleading my case, "I've been waiting all week to get out."

"Darling, if you wish to attend, you may do so without me. Rodolfo will take you and pick you up."

"I wanted to be with you. Near you."

"I can't neglect my duties," she said with a censure. Her stern look lasted several moments, and finally eased. "But please feel free to go alone. I'll be busy all evening anyway."

With the combustible temper of a storming ocelot, I raged, "Fine. I'll go without you. You haven't had time to relax all week. So keep working if you insist. You'll end up sick or with a breakdown. Well, don't expect me to sit around in a detention center and wait for you to collapse."

Cres had left a ticket on the table and had retreated to her private office. There she would seal herself away. Along with her file cabinets filled with classified, confidential studies. I usually didn't mind when she barricaded herself. It afforded me time to write and study. But tonight I had good news. I wanted to celebrate my story. I brooded. *And* I wanted to be near her. She looked so tired, and I figured I could cheer her up. Ease her tension.

Rodolfo escorted me to the car. When we arrived at the *Bellas Artes*, he announced he would return for me when the concert ended. In I went, alone. I was assuredly asserting my independence.

As I began my ascent to the mezzanine, I heard Joy's boisterous whine. "Kelly," she called to me as she drifted nearer. "Where is Cresida tonight?"

"She needed to work this evening."

Her mauve lipstick was reflective enough to blind a rabbit at a hundred yards. Her voice oozed with sugar sap. "Give her my best."

"I shall," I said congenially. "And how have you been?"

"Marvelous. Brenda popped out for a cigarette, but she'll be sorry she missed you."

"Tell her hello for me."

"I hear you've moved in with Cresida. And is it working out?" she queried with a mewing voice.

"Yes. It is." We said our farewells, and the entire ordeal had gone without a hitch. Our last little conversation must have been a take.

We went in separate directions, and I was glad we weren't sharing box seats. I went to my seat, realizing how miserable I was without Cresida. Glancing at the empty seat next to mine made me incredibly sad. As I watched, I thought of all the crazy little stories I always told her. They never failed to amuse her. Now the stories were being wasted in my brain. Stillborn tales and dormant descriptions were only mental debris, spoiling and rotting away within my head. They were lost and useless if not making Cres laugh.

My stand of independence was only making me melancholy. I was trying to prove I was self-reliant. And I missed her.

By intermission, I was miserable. I strolled down to the lobby. When I reached the entrance, I looked up. Staring across the room, with her romping hint of a smile, was the doctora. I met her half way.

"Kelly, I didn't want you to be alone."

"I'm glad you're here. I was wishing Rodolfo hadn't left. I was ready to return." My own smile sprouted as I viewed her alluring eyes. I squeezed her hand quickly, as we made our way to the seats.

"My darling," she whispered, "I'm so happy about your story. Congratulations, I'm pleased for you."

"Cres, more than anything, I want to make my grandmother proud of me, and I want to please you."

"You do. I'm enormously pleased." She paused, inspecting my face. "Is there anything troubling you?"

"No. Not any longer." I reached to touch her hand. "I have some stories to tell you."

THIRTY-FIVE

WE WERE BOUND for the luxuriant embrace of a Cuernavacan Sunday morning.

Even our gestures were done with Raggedy Ann lounging motions. We had spent most of the morning swimming, as well as relaxing on plush chaise lounges. Cresida tipped back her sunglasses. They rested on her head. Blazing sunlight gave a satin sheen to her hair. She turned onto her stomach. I joined her, sitting on the edge of her lounge. I began rubbing her shoulders with lotion. Leaning near, I carefully stole a kiss. She cautioned me to take care. Pointing to Vincente in his straw bird nest hat, she gave me the hush sign. She then winked. When she lifted her torso, her soft cleavage made me wish we were alone.

"You've done wonders for the flowers, in both D.F. and here," she commented.

"I'd love to do wonders for my most beloved flower. I would love to kiss your lips."

She turned over, squinting to see me clearly. Her hand lifted to her forehead as she smiled a full-impact smile. "We shall have all afternoon and tonight for kisses," she offered.

"I even composed a poem for you." Her expressive eyes were inquiring. "Cres, my love for you is so deep inside my heart; it seems to have virtually gone through my very center core. I guess that's what I try to say in the poem."

"May I see it?"

"I'm still polishing. Maybe later."

When I rested my hand on her chin, she playfully nipped at my fingers. "You tantalize me too much, my darling," she teasingly chastised.

I moved back when I heard Isabel behind us, approaching quickly. She was clamoring for the doctora to take an emergency telephone call. I was hopeful it was something that could be handled without her leaving. She was finally beginning to be rested.

I strode to the garden's edge. I had deadheaded the roses earlier, and so I reached to touch a bloom's petals with the love of a guardian. Looking up, I saw the splendid panorama. Beyond a wrought-iron gate were the other lovely colonial homes surrounded by sherbet-colored walls. There were flower-boxed balconies trimmed with a profusion of shimmering pink blossoms. Decorated yards were flamboyant with flaming woody vines filled with clinging tendrils and bracts of purple bougainvillea blossoms.

Vincente had schooled me on the bougainvillea and other flowers native to Mexico. He didn't resent my helping with the gardening. Thankfully, he welcomed my help and was acting as my mentor. He enjoyed the part of being my botanical tutor.

There was a feeling of great fortune. I looked up with awe at the pure white clouds scrolled in silver. I felt a warm gust from a trough of soft wind. The balmy tropical weather of Cuernavaca always inspired me. As did the doctora.

Turning, I gazed back at the gardens. Small trapezing lizards scattered with their leaping gymnastics. Legions of hummingbirds with hiccupping motion surrounded hibiscus bells of crimson and alabaster. And to my side, a caravan of marmalade-hued butterflies busily sought their territory on gardenias. This paradise, I considered, was where my heart felt most at home. Other than when in the embrace of my Goddess and Muse.

I hoped by the time I returned to the terrace, Cres would be there. That was not the case. I was summoned by a distraught Isabel. She told me the doctora wished to see me immediately in the study. I entered in haste, sensing an emergency. Cres sat frozen, her face numb. She was on an over-stuffed leather chair, sitting as if she were in shock. Her eyes misted.

"Cres, what's wrong?"

"From Spain they have called to tell me my father has died. I shall be required to return at once."

I knelt beside her, taking her into my arms. Her head sunk against my shoulder. She clutched me. "Cres, I'm so sorry."

"We shall leave at once for Mexico City. I'll fly to Madrid tonight." She stood. Her shoulders lifted momentarily. She walked to the sofa. As if her legs buckled, she sat. "Although we were not as close as most fathers and daughters, there was love."

I poured her a glass of brandy, and then sat beside her. "Cres, is there anything I can do?"

"No. Only wait for my return." She gazed helplessly out the French doors onto the terrace. Dazed, she divulged, "When I was small, I would see him in his gold-trimmed uniform. He was so stately and proper. I remember always wanting to touch the many medals on his jacket." Her eyes were brimming with teardrops. "When I visited his office, he would pin a peace rose on my chest—as if he were giving me a commendation. He would then salute. And I would return his salute." A tear spilled. "That was before his empurpled exile."

"Would you like for me to accompany you?"

"You must not leave your studies. I shall have my mother and brother. My brother has undoubtedly planned the funeral." She finished her drink. "I shall now pack for our return to

Mexico City."

The trip to D.F. was rapid. We rushed to the airport. I dreaded our parting. I slipped my unfinished poem into her hand. I requested that she wait to read it on the plane. I knew it by heart:

My fated soul roams toward your caress,
Astounding my sensations, I confess.
Awakened, I'm aware of being lost.
Yet I accept the bridge I've crossed.
Within your romance, I am bound
By crystal love, where I've been found.

She tucked it carefully into her handbag, and then gave me a parting *abrazo*. "I shall miss you."

"My heart will be with you, Cres."

As if reminiscing, she murmured, "I once asked my father if the rumors stated by other children were true. They had accused him of being a cruel leader. He quoted Goethe. 'To rule is easy, to govern difficult.' I was never to approach that question with him again."

We heard the loudspeaker booming a last call for boarding. I watched her disappear down the jet-way. Even after her plane was airborne, I didn't want to leave.

* * * * *

CRES WAS IN Spain, and other than the hired help, I was alone. Leigh and Lindy decided to have a celebration dinner. They titled the party, *Thank Gosh We Have Our Passports Back.* They suggested I stay at their apartment overnight so we could leave directly for the university in the morning.

I had time after my classes were finished to stop by the park. Leigh and Lindy weren't expecting me until five that afternoon, so I dawdled. On my way to the park, I decided to pick up a couple of magazines. I began browsing. My glance was snared by the leading Spanish publication. On the cover was an inset photo of Cres, her mother, and brother. Displayed on the cover, in full regimental regalia, was her father's photo. I purchased the magazine, and then rushed to the park where I sat reading the article.

With my limited command of Spanish, which was between barely none and hardly any, I attempted to decipher his lengthy obituary. While in power, there had been numerous assassination attempts. He was beloved by many. He was despised by as many. He was accused of leaving his land with empty coffers. The charges of filched booty were underscored by a list of the family's wealth. Much of the money had gone toward staging a Latin bloodbath to instate a dictatorship for his son. Only a few sentences were devoted to Cresida. It reported that she was a *medica* in Mexico. It listed some of her academic and literary honors.

I scrutinized the corner photo. An elderly, aristocratic widow was being helped by her grown children. The old woman was thin and drawn. At her mother's side, Cres held her mother's arm. Barely recognizable, Cres wore dark glasses and black netting draped down from her hat. Her face was blurred. Her dictator brother was at his mother's other side. His face reflected great gloom.

The doctora's image appeared to be out of focus. Her expression could not be read, but I felt her pain. I lovingly touched the magazine photo of her.

Folding the magazine, I stuffed it into my tote. I didn't want to be late for a quick meeting with Juan. I'd seen him at the bus stop and told him I was planning to be at Chapultepec later. I was in for two shockers.

One, Juan was pulling down a deal when I approached him. He was no longer in the shoeshine business, but now in the prophylactic business. Doddering old grouch as I may have appeared to him, I scolded. He offered me a few rubber samples after I claimed he was selling cheap products. He boasted he could always go back to the shoeshine business if the market on protection crashed.

The second shocker was when Eduardo arrived. He was wearing a blue blazer and a contrite demeanor. I scowled at Juan for tattling to Eduardo that I would be at the park. Juan high-tailed it out of there in a hurry, leaving Eduardo.

Promptly, he invited me to dinner. I told him I was dining with friends. With a spike to my voice, I told him I didn't think it was a good idea to see one another again. It could certainly never be as it had been. And he assuredly would settle for nothing less—for instance, friendship. He continued to follow after me, arguing that we should start again. I wheeled around, facing him. I told him there was someone new in my life and I was being faithful. I encouraged him to forget about me. Again, I asked if we could be friends. He, again, said that would be impossible. I told him I was sorry. And I was.

By the time I arrived at Leigh and Lindy's apartment, I was in need of the *Carta Blanca* Lindy eased into my hand. Their apartment was homey, modern, and obviously decorated by Lindy, who had natural flair.

As a special liberation treat, Lindy announced the menu was purely *Jankee*. A feast of steak, french fries, cornbread, and apple pie. I helped peel potatoes while Lindy whisked cornbread. Leigh was in charge of the steak. We refrained from making any jokes about *meat*.

"Juan has a sideline," I announced. "He's hawking rubbers."

Leigh roared. "I know. He offered me a two-for-one special. He'll go broke if he waits for that sale."

"I had lunch with Nora. It's over for good this time with

Michel," I confided.

"What happened?" Leigh quizzed.

"While in Acapulco, Michel and Renee were diddling on the fire escape."

"Shit! I mean sugar," Leigh corrected with a side-glance in Lindy's direction. "This Renee is a little popsy."

"A bit of fluff," confirmed Lindy. "I feel sorry for Nora," Lindy said.

"She'll bounce back," Leigh commented with a snort. "She's probably bouncing right now. So who is she seeing?"

"Maybe she'll try it alone for a while," I replied.

Leigh scoffed. "I suggested she try it *alone* once. Said there would be no need to fear unwanted pregnancy."

"What did she say?"

"She picked up Lupe's egg beater and threatened me with it," Leigh answered. She grinned. "I told her it was a little sizey for a French tickler. She had no idea what I was talking about."

"Nora is okay," I defended.

Toasting, Leigh lifted her beer. "To our freedom, our passports that have come home, and a new sausage for Nora!"

With a quick sip, I added, "She'll be fine."

"I mean, really," Leigh said with a cackle. "No chance of her knees growing together."

* * * * *

THERE IS GREAT intimacy in secret sharing. My reunion with Cresida reinforced it conclusively.

My arms formed a ring around her waist. I snuggled against her back as we slept. Cres had arrived late. She undressed with a somber slowness. When she slipped into bed, I awoke. My limbs corded with hers. I felt a joy that she'd returned. I kissed the back of her neck and whispered, "I missed you."

There was a moment's silence as she turned over. "I suppose you've read the accounts of my father's life?"

"Cres, I'd heard the rumors before I fell in love with you."

She leaned up on her elbow. "They were not rumors."

"That has nothing to do with your honor."

"The sins of the father."

"Cres, you are a fine, decent human being." My arms slid around her neck. "We can't be expected to pay for what our parents or grandparents did."

She lifted my chin, and then kissed me with the softness of a fresh rose petal fluttering against satin. Her body tensed. "You know that my father was called a dictator and a thief."

"I know the guilt you're going through."

With an astringent snap, she replied, "I think you cannot know. But I wish for you to know that I have asked my bequest be returned to my country's poor. Just as my trusts had been. Perhaps you think I'm a great deal wealthier than I am. My education was paid for by a legacy given me by my maternal grandparents in Spain. They were well-to-do merchants. I have relinquished all rights to my parent's wealth. I own no land in my native country, no businesses or investments. Any investments I have, I have paid for with my earnings, writings, lectures, and teaching. I have this home, and my villa and a thriving practice."

"You can be proud of what you've done."

"Two days ago, I signed a document requesting that the entire bulk of my inheritance be returned to my homeland. From the estate, I shall be given two of my father's medals and a portrait of myself as a child. Do you think I'm mad?"

"I think I'm a good judge of character. Maybe you should inspect my heart. I love you more and respect you even more, for returning the money."

"As long as you're aware of my heritage."

"Cres, I'm only concerned with you. Not your parents. My father is a drunk. That doesn't enter into how you feel about me."

With an irritation, she responded quickly, "Your father may be an alcoholic, but I would doubt that he is responsible for the deaths of thousands of his enemies."

I swallowed. "I was not going to ever mention something. However, I feel I should reveal my own family secret. I want to share everything I am with you." I pulled my robe over my nude body and went into my bedroom. I dug through my desk drawer and took my Grandfather Benjamin's journal.

When I returned, Cres was seated on the bed. She'd turned on the nightstand's lamp. "It's important," I began, "so you know I have an insight into how you're feeling. The sins of the father. The grandfather." I extended the journal.

"What is this?" she queried as she began thumbing through it.

"It's my grandfather's diary. Journal really. He was a scientist. Where the marker is placed, you'll find his recollections of the day the atomic bomb was detonated. The bomb he assisted in building."

I sat beside her, watching as she scanned the pages. My own secret had been exposed. I had unveiled my own sense of handed-down guilt. "That bomb's offspring may end the world. The horrific verdict isn't in on that one. However, there were thousands of deaths. Yes. And when the bombs were released on Japan, innocent people were sacrificed. Not only enemies. Not only warriors. But children, infants, people who had no involvement at all in the ugliness of man's hate."

"World War II," she stated as she looked up into my face.

"Yes. I have to accept what my grandfather did. He did it

for his own reasons. It had nothing to do with me. If I would allow this knowledge to impact me, I could be destroyed like my father. We can't carry another person's guilt. It's far too heavy a burden."

"I had no idea about your family."

"Cres, the thing is—I recently had another insight. Lindy's aunt had been an English prisoner in Singapore. Had the bombs not been dropped, she would have lived in captivity and died in captivity. And many more lives might have been taken if the bomb would not have been dropped. The same with your father. We don't know if it took force to save his country. We don't know what was in his heart. We only know what is in our own hearts."

"I know there is goodness in your heart."

I took her hand in mine. "You're only a shrink. I'm only a poet. We don't kill. We only attempt to make the world better."

There was a pause. She then placed the journal on the nightstand. She leaned to kiss my temple. "You have offered to share my pain with your disclosure. I understand that your love for me doesn't involve my father's treachery. And mine for you doesn't involve your grandfather." Her lips lifted into a trembling smile.

She eased me into the thicket of her arms. Her cheek grazed mine. We clung together. I speculated that my revelation had done the opposite of making me vulnerable. It had sewn a portion of our hearts together that would never be pulled apart by time.

PART V—IN MASKS OUTRAGEOUS AND AUSTERE

In Masks outrageous and austere
The years go by in single file;
But none has merited my fear,
And none has quite escaped my smile.
- Elinor Wylie
"Let No Charitable Hope"
(*Collected Poems of Elinor Wylie*,
Alfred A Knopf, Inc. 1932)

THIRTY-SIX

WHITMAN WROTE, 'I am the poem of earth, said the voice of rain.'

The months of living with Cresida had been my earth poem. That line and the acknowledgment came to mind while preparing for the *Cinco de Mayo* celebration. Cres realized it was time to break from mourning. She suggested a May 5th soiree. It was to be held at the villa in Cuernavaca.

The afternoon skies drooled, cleaning the air. The rains left an intensified verdant landscape. Purple collages were formed from Bougainvillea petals having fallen to the pavement.

It was the first party we'd given. That made it more special than I could believe. Cres had invited several people I hadn't met. Those I knew included Joy, Brenda, and Roberto. My guest list was short. Leigh, Lindy, Paul, Jose, and Nora had all RSVP'd. Erika was included, but she had plans.

Rodolfo, with his wool side-whiskers and narrow smile, had roamed the premises and determined all was well. When the guests began to arrive, I doubt he was so sure. Leigh, Lindy, and Nora arrived with Paul and Jose. Nora observed carefully. Her face displayed the anguish of severe hemorrhoid distress.

"Glad you're here," I greeted her warmly.

"Oh, Kelly, I'm a fish out of water."

"Have a cocktail, Nora. Leigh and Lindy are over there

getting something to eat. Want to grab a plate?" I pointed to the table. It was lined with platters of shrimp Empanadas, guacamole, and a fish in pastry shell dish called *conchas de pencado*, roasted squab, and viceroy's cake. The cake looked lovely. Layers of cake, custard, and macerated fruit made a colorful splash to the table decor. "You'll enjoy the food."

"Honestly, Kelly, I don't know why I was talked into coming here." Her face was pinched—her expression stricken.

"Enjoy. Everyone is nice. You'll like Cres. Everyone does."

We had joined Leigh and Lindy before Nora had a chance to continue grumbling about feeling out of place. Nora piled her plate, and I poured her a drink. While I was at the bar, I poured Cres a scotch and held it up. She made her way to us.

"My darling," she said as she took the drink, "thank you." She had earlier talked with Leigh and Lindy, so she smiled at them. She was gracious when introduced to a dubious Nora. "Your friends are delightful," she commented. "It is no wonder you had such a good time in Yucatan."

"Yes," I ratified. A side glance told of Nora's disapproval.

Leigh broke the ice when she made a point of examining the new dress Cresida was wrapped in. It was an almond crepe with sapphire floral designs. It molded to her exquisitely formed body. Cres was stunning. Her allure had captivated Leigh, who was always on what she laughingly called *pussy patrol*. Naturally, Lindy would not have heard of Leigh's avocation.

Leigh lulled to Cres, "Goddess sakes, you're even better looking up close."

With a shy formality, Cres murmured, "Thank you."

My smile unwound. "And with a magnifying glass, it only gets better."

"My darling," Cres uttered with a grin, "I must mingle."

She gave my hand a squeeze.

When she left, Leigh poked Nora. "Well, you have to admit, she's gorgeous. And she's really, really classy."

Nora countered, "She's a woman."

"Is she ever," Leigh continued.

"She's all women," I teasingly verified. "Nora may not understand all this, but I give her high marks for being here and attempting to accept." I lifted my glass of punch. "To Nora."

Nora muttered her embarrassed-for-show thanks. She seemed to settle back and enjoy a bit more. She then spotted Joy and Brenda.

I knew an out-and-out inquiry would begin. So I jumped right in. "The goofball is named Joy. The woman with her is a model named Brenda. Brenda seems nice."

"Model!" Lindy clamored. "That's why she looked so familiar. Yes. She's a cover girl. I've been trying to place where I might have seen her. On the cover of fashion magazines."

"Mystery solved," I said. "I met them at a concert. As I said, Joy is a pain. But Brenda has always been congenial. She's an extraordinarily intriguing woman."

I couldn't help wondering what she was doing with Joy. Brenda was in her late twenties and certainly had her share of success. Her sultry, yet yielding expression had put her on the cover of major magazines throughout the world. Her auburn hair was angel-fluffed now, but I'd seen it pulled back into a bun for some glamor shots. Her angular face would flash that famous semi-frolicsome smile that showed off her milky white teeth. Her long-limbed, seductive body was now tucked into a saffron cocktail dress. There was a lethargic drowsiness to her sexual ambiance. I had no idea that her droopy eyed sensuality was caused by drugs until I heard Joy mention something to

Cresida about her being stoned.

When I asked Cres about what Brenda saw in Joy, she cited Sappho's words that love makes a poet out of a bore. I delved for an answer, saying there had to be more than that. Cres explained about Brenda's drug dependency. Joy was a supplier to the young woman. Joy provided money, power, fame, *and availability of* drugs. One-stop shopping with access to the rich and famous. And, I came to understand, Cres was in a sobriety struggle for Brenda's salvation.

After Joy and Brenda had made their third visit to Joy's limousine, Cres must have decided she was losing her battle to help Brenda. From the somber expression Cresida was wearing, my guess must have been correct.

* * * * *

WITH ALL THE anticipation of the Cuernavaca party, I had to admit it was luster and elegance, and it was certainly enjoyed by the guests. Even by Nora.

But as much as I had anticipated the party, I was apprehensive about the party following the author's lecture program series had been unpleasant. From time immemorial, it was customary to have a small gathering after the lecture. This gave students and faculty a chance to get to know the guest lecturer. Kirk Underwood was having his day in the sun. Actually, it was his evening basking in celebration after the program. The intimate party was held at a professor's apartment. Paul and I went together.

I recalled how Kirk and the others were in clusters. When he saw me, he waved. I gave a weak return wave. He made his way toward the makeshift bar to beef up his drink. I dashed the opposite direction to see Professor Thurston. I tucked into a corner for dynamic conversation with my mentor.

But my luck obviously didn't hold. Kirk approached, and Thurston gravitated away. Thurston was always being buttonholed by my fellow students. Kirk handed me a glass of Chablis.

"Thanks, Kirk." I took a quick sip. "I see you're still venting your anger about censorship and gutless publishers. Talk about chomping the hand that feeds you."

"And I'm also still wild about getting you in bed."

"Boggles my mind. I'm astonished you're attracted to me." I tried to make my laugh superficial enough to match his grin. "You've got all the starlets you can handle. I'm a thin, semi-attractive hick from Kansas."

"I'm crazy about you."

"I'll bet," I dryly commented.

He slugged down straight booze. "I have my yacht waiting. We can fly to Mazatlan. Board. Sail to San Diego. You can fly back to Kansas from there. It would be a nice summer vacation.

"I've enrolled in summer session."

"Then I'll buy you a return ticket to Mexico City. I could introduce you to people who could open doors for your career. You name it."

"Kirk, I realize I'm a silly girl from the sticks, and I should be overwhelmed with your offer, but I'm not. It's as simple as that." My glance was meant to scorch.

"Don't give me that crap." He leaned back, tipping on his heels. "You probably have plans with some sweaty-palmed punk who will make you haul your own luggage. He'll ball you in a cheap hotel, and then never call you again."

Turning, I walked across the room. He followed. Over my shoulder, I jabbed, "Kirk, I don't find you intellectually stimulating."

"I'd like to know what you do find stimulating." His upper

lip curled. "Or who?"

"Not you. Look, you're getting soused. I'm leaving. *Hasta luego.*"

"Kelly, I'm sorry." As we passed by the table, he grabbed a bottle, pouring as we walked. "You bring out the worst in me. I can only apologize."

I motioned for Paul to get our coats. "Kirk, if you don't stop drinking, the top of the curb is going to be way over your head."

"What's up with you and that faggot?"

"Well, the secret is out. I must be attracted to a sensitive, bright man with a sense of humor. Fancy that."

I walked to the door, ignoring his request to stop. He circled around, stepping in front of me. "I brought my yacht down for you. You know what that means?"

"It means that you're going to be chumming for a new woman to take back with you."

"Kelly, do you have any idea what you're passing up? I know important people. You want to be a writer. Well, ever heard the expression it isn't what you know, but who you know?"

"I've heard it. I never believed it. Until now." I gored him with my glance.

He straightened his tie. "Is that your final word?"

"Two words. In keeping with your penchant for the nautical. Shove off."

His face went lily white. "You may live to regret talking to me like that."

"And I may not," I disputed.

* * * * *

ENTERING THE LIBRARY, I watched Cres listening intently to

the telephone. "Yes, Mrs. Kelly. I am in agreement. Your granddaughter is a fine young American." She explained, "No, I'm not British. I went to university in Great Britain. I'm originally from Latin America." Her lips curved. "Kelly has arrived, so I shall hand the phone to her at this time." She held the receiver out to me. "Maria called me to assist with your grandmother's translation."

"Gran?" I spoke into the mouthpiece.

"Kelly Anne. I thought I had the wrong place. That woman doctor got it all figured out. You aren't sick, are you?"

"No. I'm fine. It's her home. I'm working for her."

"She's your boss?"

"Yes. I help care for the doctora's gardens."

"Good thing you've been helping your mother all these years. Now you're like a gardener. Kelly Anne, you come a long way down the road quickly. You got time for your writing?"

"Yes. And I have a surprise for you. Gran, as soon as I get the surprise, I'll send it to you." I thought of how pleased she would be with the short story. "How is everyone?"

"My old carcass is falling to pieces. Kris and your mom are fine. Your father is chewing clove gum."

My father chewed clove gum to hide the smell of alcohol on his breath. "Oh," I answered with a sigh in my heart. "I should be up there to help."

"When are you coming home?"

I felt as though I had waxed my mustache and was getting ready to tie fair maidens to the track. "Gran, I'm going to take a short session this summer. I want to get extra credit. So it will be mid-August. I can stay with you until mid-September."

"Mid-August!" she growled. "Girl, you're talking in my bad ear."

"It's only an extra month. How's Rod?"

"He's home in America." Her answer was accusing. "He tells me his car can go over a hundred-and-ten miles-per-hour. Then tells me he's never driven that fast. It's an estimate. He must think I grew these wrinkles yesterday." There were muffled voices in the background. Gran barked, "Kris wants to talk with you now. I'll be saying goodbye. I'm disappointed in your decision to stay down there."

"I'll be there when I can. Please take care of yourself, Gran."

"Don't worry about me. I'm staying awhile. I'm way underdressed for heaven anyways, so I can't be dying off."

I heard her chuckle. "I love you, Gran," I murmured. I closed my eyes so I could see her piercing blue eyes, the cobwebbed skein of loose gray hair, and her soft wisp of a smile when she joked. Words were wrenched from my throat. "Gran, I wish I could bring you down here to see Mexico and meet my friends."

"One thing I can tell you, Kelly Anne. The world shrinks with age. I'm nearly out of friends. So you treasure all your chums. Now then, take care yourself. And for goodness sakes, be thinking over your cockamamie idea of staying down there this summer."

I experienced the heavily-muscled ache of loneliness. There was a moment of expulsion from paradise. I heard Kris as she scooped up the phone. "Kelly," Kris shrieked. "I got back from walking Prince. We went by a garage sale and he wee-weed on a lamp."

I snickered. "Left in a hurry, did you?"

"Left like a rocket pulling a chunky little four-legged satellite. Prince hasn't lost an ounce since Christmas. If it's good enough for people to eat, it's good enough for Prince."

"And how's your dating career going?"

"I might as well join a convent. Kelly, Mom watches me

like a hawk."

"Only because she doesn't want you ending up like she did. Tied down."

There was a brief pause. "I'd never end up with an alcoholic."

"Sometimes people change. I doubt if there were signs when Mom and Dad met."

"Well, if I married an alchy, I would divorce. No matter what the church says. How about you?"

"Kris, I'd fly the coop, too." I expelled a deep sigh. "Is Gran okay?"

"She's fit to be tied because you're not coming home until August. She said it sounds like you've thrown in with the Mexicans for good."

"Please tell her I'm looking forward to seeing her. And I love you all."

Hanging up the phone with my eyes closed, I was being halved with a knife sharpened on guilt. I went into the doctora's office. Plunging down on the chair across from Cres, I gave an enormous sigh.

"Your grandmother is delightful. You really must call her more often. I promised her that you would call twice a week from here on. It would greatly ease my conscience if you would. Kelly, I seem to be stealing you away from your family."

"I don't want to be there. Not with my father drinking."

"What did your grandmother say?"

"She told me to tell my boss to make me do as I'm told."

With amusement, she quizzed, "And how did you reply to that?"

"That I usually do behave." I reached for Cres and clasped her hand. "And what did she say to you?"

With mirth in her eyes, Cres teased, "She told me that if

she ever found out her granddaughter went to Cuba, she would put that granddaughter in leg restraints and chains forever more."

"That's my gran," I confirmed with a wink. "She was not best pleased about my staying. But she knows it's what I want."

"Someone I once loved said that love equals hurt. It is painful to be away from those we love."

"Gran didn't like my coming down here to begin with. I guess by now she probably thinks my heart is a stone. And it's big enough and dense enough to carve a Chac Mool on it."

Cresida stood, walked around the desk, and leaned down to kiss my cheek. Her lips eased toward mine. "Would you care to fly back and see them for a few days? I can easily arrange it."

"No. She'd only want me to stay." I returned her kiss. My arms wound around her neck. "And I don't want to leave you."

THIRTY-SEVEN

DAYS WERE TICKING away.

There was a pulsing energy in the air as the school year was ending. We had extrapolated our own wisdom from that year. Certainly, I had changed my impressions of life as well as literature. Experience and living's emotive fervency had expanded my knowledge and understanding of the world—of me.

The countdown was approaching. Our apartment had yielded four friends from different corners of the world. We came together as strangers and were strangers no longer. A sendoff was required. And so was planned. Nora was the social coordinator. That went without saying. Experience had primed her for the job.

Nora would be returning to Portland for her summer. Leigh would be off to Peru on a university sponsored dig. The second part of her summer would be spent visiting Lindy in Georgia, upon Lindy's return from visiting her mother in England. I wouldn't have minded spying on that drama. Leigh in Georgia! Erika would be off to live with her half-sister in Hong Kong for as long as fortune lasted. Cres and I had decided to have a beach holiday during class break. I would savor the moments—effervescent glory. That's what I would name a poem. I would cherish the woman of my astonishment—Cresida.

I was the first to arrive back at the house of Sanchez. Nora rushed in. I sat on the bed watching her squirm into a mint-hued sheath. She squinted as she sat beside me. "Kelly, Texans moved in after you left. Lock, stock, and barrel. They told Sanchez that she could cram her list where the sun doesn't shine."

"The lists are gone?" My eyebrows shot up. "You mean it was that easy?"

"Every list. Gone. Gone. They tore them, burned them, and ridiculed them in front of her. These women are very rough women. Keep their rooms like pigsties. Thank goodness, I didn't get stuck with them. Erika moved in with me. She's bad enough with her cavorting. But honestly, nothing like those two from Houston. Well, I doubt if they'll elect to stay here next year. I certainly don't have anything to do with them. I've been so busy."

"With the prof?" I launched my investigation.

"That's over. He's taking a post in Europe. Huh! It wasn't a great relationship. Anyway, I ran into Gab the other day. He's taking me to the airport. So who knows? I haven't heard from that weasel, Michel. Eduardo dropped by a couple weeks ago saying you ran him off. He's dating a friend of Renee's. Isn't *that* the berries?"

"At least, when Renee makes dating recommendations, she knows of what she speaks."

"And how are you and that *woman* lesbian?" she frostily asked.

"Fine. And assuming we're both back here next year, I hope you'll get to know her. She's really wonderful."

"She's so much older than you. I mean, she doesn't look forty, but she's still much older. I mean, where is it going?"

"To the edge of forever."

"Oh, Kelly," she whined. "You're going through a phase. You aren't really like this. I told Leigh that you'd snap out of it when you meet a really nice guy. She said to kiss both sides. I knew what she meant. It made me feel like throwing up." She snorted. "*Honestly!*"

"We may need to put Leigh on a short leash tonight."

"Kelly, I know you'll turn around."

"Nora, I appreciate your friendship. Your acceptance. But don't expect me to become straight. I don't expect you to become lesbian. Maybe I knew it all along but repressed my sexuality. Some moral obligation forced me to explore with men. But it isn't the same."

Nora's frown was deeply etched. "Why?"

"Men think intimacy begins in the bedroom. Women know it ends in the bedroom."

"And that's it? So why would it be so difficult to convert back?"

"I wouldn't expect you to zigzag, so why should you expect it of me? I'm comfortable being myself. Maybe for the first time I'm accepting myself. Dunking stools are out of fashion."

Nora chuckled. "Other than on Lesbos, your lifestyle has never been in fashion."

"My feelings for Cres have never wavered," I said with a good-natured grin. "And they won't change. I won't change."

"I'm going to miss you. We had some great times together."

"We sure did." And then, without realizing it, we hugged. For the first time since the revelation about my sexual *misconduct* had been announced. I gave an extra squeeze. "And we'll have more great times. I thrive on your condemnation about my perversion," I teased.

Moving back, she questioned, "Think we'll ever be like we were?"

"All we're doing by our parting is leaving something for

another time."

"Oh, Kelly, I hope so. When we doubled, you were always so funny."

Blithely, I swallowed my smile before promising, "I'm not out of punch-lines yet."

"You really care for this woman?"

"Yes. Nora, she's the greatest occasion of my life." I stopped short of telling her the rest of the truth. At times, I felt if I let go of Cres, my oxygen supply would be cut off. I was glad when I heard the door slam. "I'm shamelessly in love with her."

Erika scampered up the hall. "Vel, I getz my lipstikz and we goez," she babbled.

Leigh ambled in, following after Erika. She carried a tote bag. "I have a little something for everyone," she announced to us. She pulled a small onyx unicorn and handed it to Nora. "For the only woman I know who smiles when she sits on the head of a unicorn."

Nora gasped. "Oh, pooh!" She then joined in our giggles.

Leigh handed Erika a rolled wad of oriental currency. "You're the only woman I know who wants to go to Hong Kong because of a yen."

Erika unrolled the rubber band that held the money. The bills expanded, and then fluttered from her hand. She quickly retrieved them, jamming money down her blouse. "It takz many sackfuls to buy ze loaf of bread. So thiz is ze donut."

Leigh peered into the sack. She looked back up, surveying my pensive expression. I was bracing for the worst. She pulled out a cupcake baking tray. "We all know where the cupcake went. You escaped from the bakery, huh, Benj?"

"I did." I clutched the tray. "Thanks."

"Kansas wholesome is a thing of the past," Leigh expressed. "I like you better now that you're public enemy number one."

"I'll bet."

Leigh ignored my momentary glare. She rotated to Erika. "I was going to get you a cheese board for Edith's cheese, but since you'll be moving, I decided on the couple bucks worth of yen."

We howled in unison as we left the apartment together. Arm in arm in arm in arm, we hit the landing. "Erika," I inquired, "did you steal the cheese?"

"Yah!"

Leigh bellowed, "I was beginning to think it was a farkling mouse."

"You were the mouse?" Nora grilled Erika with disbelief.

"Yah!" she confessed again.

* * * * *

MEMORIES WERE LAUGHTER-COATED.

Recollections took us through our meal, and we had toasted them all. The final fringe of the sash was slipping through our fingertips. We gave one another each an *abrazo*. Nora and Erika caught a cab back to their apartment. Leigh suggested we have one more nightcap before leaving *Chipps*. I had planned to call Rodolfo to pick us up there, and then drop Leigh off at her apartment on the way back to *Jardines del Pedregal*.

Leigh and I sat at a small table for two. Leigh was loaded. She held her amber glass up to the light. "Life," she drawled, "begins with the premise that nothing makes sense. Isadora Duncan's lady, Mary-somebody-or-other, gave her the scarf that choked Isadora to death. I mean, really, that's fucking nonsensical."

"Life doesn't promise reason. It would be too boring if

reason actually prevailed."

"Prevailed," Leigh grunted. "You always sound like you swallowed a dictionary and you're trying to barf it back up."

"Farkle you," I chided.

"I was saying life makes no sense."

"Leigh, are you ever going to let down the barricades?"

Her elbow props began to slide. She sat back to dispute my allegations. "No barricades."

"Sure, you've got them. What's really nonsensical is that you can't trust anyone."

Her half-mast eyes batted. "It's all slipping away."

"Tell me about slipping away. Tell me about your sister. The *truth* this time."

Her immutable expression crumbled. Suddenly, dime-sized droplets were being squeezed from her eyes. "I lied to you. I didn't know how to tell you about what happened."

"What is the truth?"

Her resistance was being shoveled away. She blinked her waxy lashes free of tears. "Truth?"

"There was no death record for any twelve-year-old named Cindy James in Colorado Springs the approximate year you were eleven."

"No."

"So why did you lie to me?"

"My sister and I were walking home, and…." she broke. Swatting tears, she scowled at me. "Why did you check?"

"You started to tell me. I think you wanted to confide in me. And I checked because I'm your friend. I wanted to know why you're hurt. Leigh, I think it's important for you to talk about it. Tell me the truth."

She wiped her eyes with a cocktail napkin. Her stare was planted on the table. It squinted into a drunken focus. She repeated, "The truth."

"Tell me."

"Cindy and I had walked to a corner shop. We'd been walking home. Two men in a car grabbed us. We fought. I broke loose. I ran, yelling for help. Cindy screamed as they were putting her in the car. People were watching. Watching, for fuck sakes. They wouldn't help me. I pleaded with someone to help me. The car drove off. They didn't want to get involved, they said later."

"God," I murmured.

"I should have tried to fight them. I shouldn't have run. Don't you see? It's my fault." She sniffed as her head fell into her hands. "Maybe I could have stopped them. I got their license plate number, but the car was stolen."

Reaching, I took one of her hands in mine. "Leigh, you were only eleven. What chance did you have against two grown men? They would have only abducted you, too."

"They drug her away." She wept inaudibly. "You see, it was my fault."

"It wasn't your fault. You were a child. They were adults. You didn't have a chance. The best you could do was to escape and get the license number. You did that."

"It was my fault. Kelly, I forgot the change. I left the money on the counter in the store. We had to go back for the fucking money. If we wouldn't have had to go back…"

"Leigh, they were probably following you. A few minutes wouldn't have mattered. You didn't do anything wrong."

"She's gone. I must have done something wrong. The damned money!"

"Leigh, don't do this to yourself." I hesitated. I wanted to dismantle her guilt. My heart seemed silent. Years distilled everything for her except the unknown. "Leigh, you know they were probably waiting for you. Nothing would have mattered. The abduction would have taken place anyway. And a child doesn't have the strength an adult has. It wasn't a fair fight. You couldn't help that."

"I lied about Cindy being dead because I have no way of knowing if she's dead or not. When I think about how she might have suffered if she did live, it makes it easier. I say she's dead. I fight with my mind not to resurrect her. I don't want to know how terrible it could have been if she'd lived."

"It could have happened to anyone, Leigh. I know you did all you could. You did all the right things."

"No. Because I'm not with her."

"No, you aren't with her." I took a deep breath. "That leaves the entire responsibility of another type on you, Leigh. Stop your fucking around trying to hurt everyone else. What you say about people's faith, their nationalities, about them—it hurts. You're the survivor. So, damn it, be responsible for building people up rather than tearing them down. Show them kindness. Do you think Cindy would have wanted you to alienate others? Calling people names and invading on their feelings? Hell, no. You should realize she wouldn't want you hurting others, any more than she'd want you hurting yourself. It's time you stop the hurt."

Her eyes focused, her expression was harsher than if I'd slammed a baseball bat across her face. She suddenly looked away. "Sometimes I can't help striking out."

Lifting her hand, I squeezed it. "At first, I thought you made your vile remarks for shock value. But you want others to hurt as much as you do. The ironic part is that you aren't to blame. And you shouldn't be hurting. And you shouldn't hurt others."

My mind stumbled backward. How often I had taken Kris by the hand and walked her to the Ben Franklin Five & Dime. How often I'd slapped the money on the counter for our purchases and forgotten to pick up the change. We were too busy dividing licorice whips, jawbreakers, bubble gum, and other assorted candy of the day. How often I'd been too absorbed, too distracted, in a comic book to notice Kris had wandered away. I always found her roaming down another aisle.

How easily Kris could have been lost. A stab went through me. I recalled my childhood exasperation with a slowpoke kid sister. Kris was the little girl I had to drag along with me on my jaunts. Tears formed in the corners of my eyes. I couldn't bear to think about how I would have handled the years without Kris since I was eleven. If those years had been pirated, life would be bleak. Impossible. Kris could always make me laugh. We knew one another's history. We shared that history of youth.

I wanted desperately to call Kris. To tell her how much she has meant to me those many years. I would write her in the morning to tell her that I treasure her. If she had abducted, I would have outdone Leigh in the bitterness department.

Her lips bobbled before she mumbled, "Kel, I'll try to be better."

"Come on, I'll get you home," I said as I stood to steady my friend. "Leigh, now I understand why you're so angry. I'd be angry, too."

And without a doubt, I would no longer be young.

THIRTY-EIGHT

WEEKS PARADED DOWN times path. The days, marching in single file, had fled into yesterdays. Cresida and I had returned from a wonderful holiday in Puerto Vallarta. Before I knew it, summer sessions were nearly completed. Even with intense studying, it was the best summer I'd ever had. Most of my classes pertained to writing, so they were enjoyable, as well as inspiring. I was productively writing and being swept away by a love of language.

Also, I had never known such tranquility and tenderness in my life. Each time the doctora's throaty laugh curled around a joke, my heart lit up. Our evenings were shared with warmth. We would swap events of the day. We would mull the discourse, the information, the knowledge, and the wisdom.

Nights were spent nestling. Our bodies merged with each cherished word and embrace. Love was my feast. The taste of her minty lips, her honeyed skin, and the scent of her was my enticement. My fingers warmed with her touch. The calm of silent nearness after making love allowed my spirit a glimpse of eternity. It was an observation of what heaven might be all about.

There were times when I would gaze across the table into her eyes, admitting how I was consumed by love of her. I had consecrated her entirely. Love was holy. It was an ever-increasing reverential adoration of this woman. Her gentleness healed my fears. When I was in her company, all things were possible, and all love was probable. I'd even come to terms with the label I would need to endure. The tag attached to our selected love would forever be mine.

So I awoke and watched her sleep. Her eyes blinked several times. She stirred. Stretching, she turned and looked into my face. "My darling, what is it you're thinking?"

"Of my overwhelming love for you. How I can trust your love." Kissing her forehead, I then grinned. "Making love last night. At times, I wonder if you can tell what I'm thinking."

"Perhaps." She sat up against her pillow. I leaned against her shoulder, snuggling into her warmth. "However, in retrospect, Kelly, I realize that I may have miscalculated some of my initial thoughts about you."

"Oh?"

"There is an anxiety within you. We spoke of it before. I may have misinterpreted your risk-taking zest for life."

"When you asked about my quest for adventure being a fear of death?"

"Yes. I now think it may be caused by transference."

"Transference?" I quizzically repeated.

"Yes, darling. You have an extraordinary nearness with your grandmother. She is elderly and in poor health. A person of that age becomes mentally poised for accepting their mortality. It isn't unusual for that feeling to become transferred to someone with whom the person has a special closeness."

"That must be it," I replied with solemnity. "I must be frightened I won't have time to gain enough experience to write all the books I want to write. I also wish to have a thousand more nights like we had last night." My rasp lifted to a laugh. "You are incredible. I'd like nothing better than to end my days in your arms. And to be a respected poetess."

"There is an old saying that success is a journey. Not a destination."

"Journey. Even the word evokes a wondrous connotation. The middle-English word is *journe*. I like that."

"Yes. My journey with you is wonderful, Kelly."

"There's a poetess named Marina Tsvetayeve and she wrote a couple lines that make me think of you. Of how I feel about you. She says she's crying out and offering words of homage and that she's the shell and the ocean is the sound. Well, that's how I view our love."

"You find our lovemaking analogous to the sea?"

"Sort of, yes. Last night I thought about that."

"I'm most fortunate that you've entered my life."

"Cres, you set me ablaze inside. I don't feel that way with anyone else."

"There are times we cross from sensual to erotic." She kissed my cheek. Her lips lingered for a few moments. "My hunger for you overwhelms me. Do you ever find anything we do objectionable?"

I questioned, "Objectionable?"

"Because I want you completely."

"If it isn't painful, it isn't objectionable. Why?"

"As I've mentioned before, you're from a conservative area."

"Cres, I would do anything to please you. For the first time in my life, I feel as though it's safe to love. I trust you. I can throw away my amulet filled with good luck charms. I don't think you'd ever harm me. And there's nothing in the world I wouldn't do to make you happy."

"I shall never harm you, my darling," her satiny pledge assured me.

* * * * *

CRAMMING FOR FINALS and preparing to return to Kansas were

the order of the day. I had purchased a return ticket home and was experiencing the tug of Mexico. There was a magnetization that I knew would never go away. I didn't want to leave the doctora, my friends, and professors, *or* the land to which I now belonged. Knowing I would return for my senior year would keep me going with its promise.

Flipside, there was a yearning to see my family. I wanted to feel Gran's hug and to laugh at Kris when she blew the punchline of a joke. I knew seeing my father again would be strained. I'd hand him back my grandfather's journal and tell my father it had nothing to do with me He could take it to his grave with him. For my part, I had inherited my grandfather's love of knowledge. He was a good man doing his best in a bad time. Nothing more and nothing less.

I'd just arrived on campus when a student told me Professor Thurston was looking for me. I made my way to the creative writing center. Streamers of students were trailing out as I edged my way inside. "You wanted to see me, sir?"

"Yes, Miss Benjamin. I've received something of great importance."

"My short story?"

"Indeed." He dug into his briefcase, then handed me an envelope. "They sent along five copies. My friend also sent me one, which I had requested for my own files."

I cradled the envelope a moment, and then pulled out one of the magazines. My eyes searched the table of contents. I confessed, "I'm ink crazed, and I admit it." Rapidly I thumbed through the pages until I saw the illustration of a prairie woman. Her hair was pulled back into a bun. A small girl with a long skirt clutched her frontier mother. In her hair were the pale blue ribbons my grandmother had described to me. The title was in pioneer typeface. My heart gave a wild spring when I saw the byline. By Kelly A. Benjamin. I tried to swallow the feeling of being socked in the throat with an enormous sense of amazement. This was my first major market effort. My voice strained. "Gran is going to be thrilled."

"As was I." A smile formed on his mouth.

"Sir, if I come to anything as a writer, I want you to know it's because of Gran's feeding my soul good literature, and because of you. You're inspiring me. And...." I said, feeling my voice quake, "I respect and love you, sir."

"I don't believe I ever had a student tell me that. Thank you. Yes. Thank you very much."

I hugged the magazines. "I'm going to take Gran's copy to her. Surprise her."

"She'll be most pleased. And proud. And the other copies?"

"One will go to a friend. I'm staying with her. One I'll send to Carlos. One for my sister, and I'll keep the other copy as my file copy."

"I sense from your writing you're much more settled now. Am I correct?"

"Yes, sir. You can actually tell from my prose and poetry?"

"Certainly. Your last efforts were more fluid and relaxed. More assured and confident."

I glanced up at the door as Professor Roberts entered. Thurston greeted him. "Nathan, Miss Benjamin's story has arrived."

"Ah, yes. So it has." He examined it. With a half hum and half grumble, he conceded, "Very well done. You officially have now received a good, solid A."

"So *that's* what it takes to get an A," I exclaimed. With a query and a chuckle, I asked, "So what *does* it take to get an A+?"

Handing the magazine back, he replied, "Miss Benjamin,

the A+ is given if your readers and critics are wild about your work. And are wild about it for a *very long* time."

* * * * *

ARRIVING HOME EARLY, and with energy exploding, I felt I'd signed a promissory note with the world of literature. I donned my gray oxford baseball jersey, faded cutoffs, and tennis shoes, and then headed for the garden.

I had phoned Cresida to tell her my story had arrived. I couldn't wait for her to get home so I could show her the magazine. I decided time would pass more quickly if I busily trimmed out a section of briary shrubs I'd wanted to tame. After which, I stood back, unbundled my fingers from the bulky gardener's gloves, and felt the sun on my face.

"My darling, we must celebrate your story!" the doctora exclaimed. She approached, giving me a hug. "You shouldn't be out here working today."

"I needed to burn off energy."

"Well, we shall go out for a special dinner honoring the occasion. Gardening duties can wait. We shall celebrate in style."

"Cres, I wanted to be in the garden today. I was thinking about flowers. Carlos. One time he bought me an armload of flowers. He said he did it because it was to be totally out of character. He claims not to be a romantic."

She smiled. "He is on your mind today?"

"Yes. It's his birthday."

"Come," she ordered. "You must call him. You can wish him happy birthday and tell him of your good news."

Apprehensively, I followed her to the library. She assisted me in getting the call through and then turned to leave. "Please stay, Cres. He's part of both of our lives now."

"As you wish." She sat at my side.

"Carlos, *feliz cumpleanos!*"

"Kel," he bellowed. "Been keeping that fifty-one percent in line?"

"I'm glad you didn't say in a *straight* line," I teased. Winking in the doctora's direction, I announced, "I've never been happier. Cres makes me deliriously happy."

"Oh, before I forget. I have an update. Got a birthday card from my buddy. The journalist. He unearthed a really bizarre twist to the information about Leigh he was working on. Seems there was a kid, Cynthia James. From Colorado Springs. She'd been abducted. The kidnapping was in broad daylight. Another article said there had been no attempt to contact the family for ransom."

"Leigh finally told me about it. Explains why she's so angry. At least she knows I'm on her team and will listen whenever she needs to talk. I'll give you the skinny on it in a letter. Also some great news. I got my published story. I'll put a copy of the magazine in the mail for you."

"Terrific. I'm really happy for you. I haven't been able to do much more than scribble a few human interest things. Only one made the wires. I'll send it when I get it."

"Are you okay?"

"I love it here, Kel. Need a bodyguard to keep the women away. And how's your lovely woman?"

"My lovely woman is right here with me. It was her idea to call."

"Kel, give her my love. Wish I could give it to her in person," he joked.

"I'll tell her you're waiting in line."

"Unfortunately, I don't think she's interested."

"Fortunately, I'm sure she isn't. We're going to dinner tonight to celebrate. We'll toast your birthday."

"Kel, thanks for the call. I didn't think you'd remember."

"You'll always be my prince of print."

"And you'll always be my princess of poetry. Poetry, you remember the heart-junk that teases the pleasures of humanity. Words that stand in for horse manure and the true emotion of us all."

"What do you know about emotions?" I jabbed with a laugh.

"I know you're special to me, Kel."

"Sounds like hormonal poetry."

"Don't ever change, Kel."

"No."

"Kel, life is an internationalized experience. Love is the opposite. I'm glad you're happy. I hear it in your voice."

"Yes. Well, keep up your reprobate standing. I miss you." I hung up. I turned to the doctora. "Cres, thanks."

"He is a special young man."

"Cres, he accepts me."

"Very special, indeed."

* * * * *

"*CETTE ROBE VOUS va bien*," Cres lulled as I gave a whirl.

"And your dress is also magnificent," I said. Looking into her eyes, I smiled. We had shared a tender and sensuous bath. Our eyes anchored. I asked, "Do you suppose that we could postpone the celebration dinner until another night?" Romance was written all over our faces.

"I'm certain Maria would not object to fixing us a quick *merienda* later."

My hands slid around her waist. I unzipped the black taffeta cocktail dress. It glided slowly down her body, exposing a strapless black bra. I unfastened the hooks. "My appetite has changed directions." My kiss began on her neck, ending on her shoulders. "I love you with everything I am."

She unzipped my dress. Her embrace seared as our skin touched. She whispered, "*Esta noche.* We shall share our entirety."

"Anything," I consented. "Anything you want—need. Everything I have. I am. Is yours."

* * * * *

"END OF THE line, kiddo," I told Juan. I would be leaving for the United States of North America after tests next week. I hated saying goodbye to Juan, even for a month. We strolled the park, licked ice cream cones, and chatted. Juan's small frame was wrapped in a frayed slate-colored jacket. I straightened his collar as I lectured, "Now, you study hard while I'm gone. Okay?"

"I study hard. You come back, no?" His huge, dark eyes flinched.

"Absolutely. I'll return. In a month."

"Take me?" he clamored. He threw his arms around my waist. "Please."

"Honey, I can't. They have laws. You need papers to leave the country."

"I can write papers. The government likes me." He puffed his chest out. He exhaled and his chest deflated. "You will be like my mother. You don't come back."

"Juan," I uttered, leaning down and pulling him into my arms. "I'll be back. You're a terrific kid." I cupped his chin. "I don't want to disappoint you. I'll bet your mother didn't want to make you sad by disappointing you. Things sometimes happen that make it impossible to keep promises."

"Nobody here wants me. I could be your boy." His

disarming eyes blinked.

"And I would be proud of you. But you have to stay here. This is your country. It's a magical country."

He reached into his pocket. He scoop-shoveled his PT clip. "For you. You take."

"No," I declined. I rolled his fingers back around it. "You've got to keep it always. It's a reminder of how wonderful you are. Kennedy thought you were special. He gave it to you. I think you're special, too. Now, make both of us proud of you."

Juan accompanied me to the apartment with his hand in mine. I wanted to stop off and say my farewells to Sanchez and Lupe. I knew next week would be busy. Before going up, I pulled the bill of Juan's baseball cap over his eyes, then gave him a hug and told him to behave. And to continue being brave. His smile was there along with his sorrow.

Lupe opened the door and motioned for me to enter. When Edith Sanchez appeared, she gave me a hug.

"I wanted to stop by to thank you for everything."

"Now, dear, if you haven't made arrangements with your doctor friend, you're certainly welcome to return here."

"Thanks. I plan to be staying there again when I return in September. But I'll stop by so I can see how you're doing."

"Everyone is going their own ways. Even our Lupe is marrying her *novio*. Nora will be returning. But those women from Texas won't be returning. I've told them I'd rather they not stay with me. They are rude and vulgar. You know the type."

"Yes. I know the type." I could imagine Señora Edith Sanchez up all night making new lists the day after they left. With *abrazo*, I said goodbye to Sanchez and Lupe. I told Lupe how much visiting her village meant to me. *Mil gracias,* I thanked her a thousand thanks.

THIRTY-NINE

I CLUTCHED MY Spanish textbook as I passed through the hallway. Noticing that Cresida's office door was open, I rushed in. Joy had called earlier, so I wanted to give Cres the message.

When I entered, Cres smiled up at me. I gave her Joy's message to call. She told me she didn't want to disturb my studies when she arrived, so began making notations. There was a stack of files on her desktop. She then promised we would spend the remainder of the afternoon together.

The phone rang as I leaned down to kiss her forehead. After hanging up, she apologized, telling me that she would need to leave. There was an emergency at the hospital involving a seriously troubled patient. She grabbed her purse, called for Rodolfo to bring the car around, and made her way to the door.

I promised to put the time to good use by studying hard while she was away. I went into my bedroom, and then realized I'd left my Spanish book in her office. I scooted down the hall.

Entering, I grabbed my books. She had left so hurriedly, she'd forgotten her fountain pen. Because of my studying for finals, I'd been neglecting my ritual of filling her pen for her. I unscrewed the cap as I walked around to sit at the desk. The inkwell was off to the side, so I pushed the slightly fanned out files across the desk. I hadn't wanted to chance spilling ink on them.

Suddenly, my eyes hooked on one of the tabs. I was stunned when I saw my name written. K. BENJAMIN. With a mechanically lame, nearly debilitating effort, I pulled it from the stack. My stomach pitched. Tabulated, by date, was a stilted vignette of medical data. She had tapped into my deepest secrets, fears and fantasies—all of me that I'd shared with only her. Perched on the edge of the chair, I felt a suspension of numbness invade my entire body.

I perused data about my arousal level, sexual stimuli, erogenous areas, and a smattering of esoteric directives. My sexual entity was recorded on those pages. My thoughts, my writing, my life, it was all there. Love was not mentioned. I shut the file that housed my psychosexual charting. A broad sweep of pain covered me. I preferred Leigh's vocabulary. Those words were an improvement over the cold, clinically blueprinted, genital geography that the doctora had written.

Covering my eyes, I wept. My mind, as well as my emotion, had been raped. She had ravished my soul. A sickness was twisting my insides. I caught my breath, for it felt as though it was being vacuumed out of me.

Sluggishly, with file in hand, I began to stand.

The phone rang. I answered it. Joy's familiar drone blasted, "Your lover hasn't returned my call. Did you tell her to call me?"

"Yes. She left on an emergency. And she is no longer my lover."

"You've broken up?"

I answered, "Yes."

"What are you still doing there?"

"Joy, I just this moment decided to leave. I'm going to pack now. So I don't have time to talk with you."

"Someone new?"

There was disgust in my answer. "Of course not. I really

can't talk now."

"Where are you going?"

"All my friends are away for summer. I have no idea."

"Get your things together. Come over here. There's loads of room in my penthouse. An extra bedroom. You can have a little wine. Talk. I'll listen to your troubles. I'm not such a terrible person. Brenda is here, too."

"I'm confused right now." I was dubious of Joy's reliance.

Her voice had become sincere. Serious. "All the more reason to get away. Clear your head. Come on over and tell me where it hurts."

I paused. Considering that I had nowhere else to go anyway, I answered, "Okay. I'll call a cab." I took down her address, and then packed. I felt outraged—however, I was as weak as I ever remember having been. I shut the suitcase, filled my tote with textbooks, and notes, then glanced at the file on my nightstand. I had the urge to shred it or in some way mutilate it. But my moist eyes only spewed tears. I looked away.

I heard my door open. "No actual emergency at all. It was only a mild reaction to a medication given for migraines." Cresida entered. She stood frozen, leaning back against the doorway. She had spotted both suitcase and my file. "Kelly, this isn't how it might appear."

"I'd left my Spanish textbook in your office. I decided to fill your pen while I was there." My expression mirrored my despair. My voice limped. "I saw the tab on the file. I was moving the files so I wouldn't get ink splatters on them. My file was out, so you must have needed to jot down last night's session. Measure my clitoral stimulation."

"Kelly, we must talk." She sat on the bed beside me. She reached for my hand, but then eased her own arm back.

"I asked you if the rumors were true. You denied them.

You told me you didn't keep records on lovers. Told me I wasn't a study. I believed you."

"I would like the opportunity to explain."

"Explain! Love wasn't mentioned in your documentation. No damned wonder you were reticent to say the words. I believed that you did love me. But no one could betray a lover as you did me and *love* them."

"This isn't meant to be a betrayal."

"You took my love and put it onto a glass slide. You put my soul under a microscope. My sex life was on display. Your colleagues can press their faces against the window of my personal expression. It's scientific voyeurism. You violated my trust."

"I must tell you my reason."

"I don't want to listen to any more lies. I've heard enough of them."

She paused. Her face was haggard. "I understand your anger."

"No. I don't think you do. You have no earthly idea what I'm feeling right now," I disputed.

"Kelly, please," she said as she reached for my hand.

I pulled away. "Don't ever touch me again." I walked to my suitcase, and then lifted it. "I'll be back for the rest of my clothing and books. I don't plan to take anything you bought for me with the exception of one thing. I'm taking my half of the geode. Only because I don't want you to have it. Our love isn't a circle. It's ended. And I want it as a reminder to never again forfeit my love. Not ever," I spoke acrimoniously.

"You shouldn't be alone."

"I won't be." I felt lame. "Your friend, Joy, called back. She's invited me to stay with her."

"No. She'll hurt you." Tears swamped her eyes. Her lashes flood. "Please don't. You don't understand what she's capable of doing. She can tear a troubled woman apart. Let me find you a place. Please, not with her. She can ruin a woman."

"I can't be any more destroyed than I am now." I swung my tote over my shoulder.

"I would never have harmed you, Kelly." Tears pressed past her eyelids. "I don't want to lose you."

My lips quivered. "For what it's worth, I've never been hurt this deeply. Not by anyone in my life."

"You must listen. You were *not* a study. You have an unresolved problem. I wanted to protect you from facing it alone."

Maria called out that the cab had arrived. "When I return for my things, I'd rather it be when you're working. I don't want to ever see you again."

"Kelly," she pleaded, "I have never begged anyone for anything in my life. I'm a proud person. But I'm begging you, please don't leave me. I am sorry I've hurt you. Please allow me to get you a hotel room if you wish. Or stay here and I won't even talk to you. Please don't leave me."

"You've left me no choice." I pointed down to the file. "Maybe *that* will keep you warm tonight."

While walking to the cab, I wondered if I could ever again feel. There was an emptiness that made my spirit barren and devoid.

The odds and ends of a dying affair had never concerned me. I had never anticipated the death that happens to a corner of one's heart where romance is stored. I had left behind the part of myself that allowed me to see who I am through the doctora's eyes. I had believed them to be the true eyes of love. *Ojos de amor.*

Now, I would be attempting to extinguish pain in any way that I might. I wouldn't be too fussy about ending the torment. No matter what the remedy might be, as long as it promised release from this excruciating moment. I wanted to extricate the agony—the throbbing loneliness. For it was trampling me under. I wanted to close down all memories. I didn't care how it was to be done.

I gave the driver Joy's address.

FORTY

I WAS NO longer on the sidelines. I was a player attempting to intercept loneliness. Plans were to make my own script changes. I was going from the arms of an erudite doctora to a depraved socialite in no longer that it takes a cab to navigate the city's interior.

The cord of my greatest love had been clipped. I was desensitized enough to pretend a stranger in a penthouse could ease my pain. Why shouldn't a junkie swinger be able to patch up my pride? Eduardo's love impeached me. Cresida delved my brain and probed the contents of my heart. She took what she needed for her research then stuffed the remainder of my cerebellar matter back into my skull. She told me not to worry about the exploratory. It was for my own good. In the process, my soul was pounded by the iron knuckle of reality. If I couldn't trust someone I loved that much, how could I trust anyone?

Obviously, I hadn't been prepared to match wits with a renowned love tech goddess doctora.

* * * * *

AND I CERTAINLY hadn't been prepared, in any way, for Joy's penthouse therapy.

"Kelly, sweetheart, come in." Joy greeted me with a vamp like grin. Her emerald-colored, satin day-pajamas crinkled as she walked. She escorted me into the lavish, avant-garde penthouse. The fragrance of spice was meant to mask the odor of drugs. I recognized the sweet smell of marijuana.

"I need a place to stay for the night," I said, trying to sound relaxed and casual.

"Brenda is in the bedroom. Come have a glass of wine with us."

I followed Joy into a spacious bedroom. Brenda was reclining on the largest bed I'd ever seen. It was at least twelve feet across and heart-shaped. Melon-pink satin sheets and covers were bunched and bundled around Brenda. She was wearing a see-through flesh colored nightgown. It drooped from off her one shoulder. Taking a drag from her carb pipe, she issued a huge smile my way. I guessed it must be filled with hashish, but for all I knew, it could have been opium.

"Hi, baby," Brenda greeted me.

"Bren, we've got a new playmate for the night," Joy said with a glimmer in her eyes. "I'll get some more wine. You be a good girl and share your smoke with Kelly."

Brenda patted the bed. I sat. Her eyes were at half-mast. Their glow told me she was higher than a Georgia pine. She extended her pipe. "Have a puff. Puff the magic dragon," she sang with a giggle.

I took a quick puff. "I'm really not used to drugs. I've tried it a couple of times though."

"You don't need to be used to it. It gets used to you," she purred.

Joy returned carrying a tray with tulip glasses and a bottle of light wine. She poured and we each took one. She then flung her body onto the bed. "To new friendships," she toasted.

"Yes," I agreed. I lifted the glass to my lips. With only a couple of puffs from the pipe, I was already feeling drowsy. After emptying the glass, I began to protest when Joy refilled it. "I shouldn't be drinking. I've got tests tomorrow."

Joy continued pouring. "We're the world's best teachers. Relax and enjoy, sweetheart. You'll pass your tests with flying colors."

Brenda's head hurled back with her laugh. She sputtered, "You can teach her about tests, but not testes."

Joy's fingers ran the length of my leg. She noticed my displeasure and lifted her hand. "Give her another hit," she barked at Brenda. "She needs a good time." Her lock-jawed speech produced nasality in her dramatic vowels. "A *good* time."

"I'm already getting high," I complained.

Joy rummaged through a tray of pill bottles on a nightstand. As if selecting marbles to shoot with, she sorted them out. She handed me a couple. "Try these. They'll clear your head."

"Looks like a drugstore," I marveled. "Where did you get such a vast array of pharmaceuticals?"

"Not from Cresida, that's for sure," Joy muttered with a grimace. "Doctora Valdez is stingy about giving out prescriptions."

"She should have been so parsimonious with her analysis," I blurted.

Joy folded my fingers around the assortment of pills. "These will settle your nerves," she assured me. "Now, sip your wine, try the pills, and you'll feel marvelous." She guided my hand to my mouth. "Sample a little bit of heaven on earth."

"A little bit of heaven." I took one, and then pressed the remainder back onto the tray. Gran always recommended tiptoeing toward the untried.

The women expropriated the drugs with cliquish intoxication. I thought of a Keat's quote I'd learned in high school. 'And this is why I sojourn here alone and palely loitering, though the sedge has withered from the lake, and no bird sings.' I thought of Lindy telling me about Lady Day. I quickly forced down another swallow of wine. I knew my reasoning capability was deteriorating, and I allowed myself to be in the center of that oblivion. I relished relinquishing my reality. I laughed at my alliteration. Even my thoughts were funny.

"Now, isn't that better?" Brenda queried.

"Yes." I giggled.

A flourish of giggles sprouted. My mind was skirmishing. I realized that time was a patchwork. A violently brilliant explosion of colors produced a spastic escape. The frenzied pursuit of strident jazz sounds came from Joy's expensive high fidelity equipment. The music chased me and captured me with every note. I emptied the glass again, and it was dutifully refilled by Joy.

The pill, booze, and the contents of the pipe had chipped away at my coherency. I wasn't certain what the pill was, but I was glad I hadn't taken the entire handful.

Joy's image seemed to float toward me. She chided, "Come on, Hemingway." Her voice gave me chills as she coaxed. "Let's give the writer from Kansas something to write about." She stood, tripped out of her pajamas, and her arm waved toward the bed. Brenda tipped slightly as she stood. She unfastened her gown. Gravity disrobed her. When the cloth had fallen, I saw why she was the top glamor model, swimwear included. She poised with elegance and with availability.

"You do want us?" Joy inquired with a smirk.

Slowly, I began to unbutton my blouse. I felt my bikini bra being unfastened by tingling fingers. I stood, stepping away from the mound of clothing piled around my ankles.

Joy's arms circled my nudity. I coasted down onto the satin sheets. "Relax, baby," Brenda instructed as she tossed my hair. "You are such a baby."

"Yeah," Joy inveigled, "loosen up. Life is yours for the living. Don't end up some boring old pundit like the doc." Her husky laugh rose to a shrill sonata. Then, as if broken, it ended. She wiped the tears that had filled my eyes. "I shouldn't have mentioned Cresida."

"No." I squeezed my eyes shut. When they began touching me, they became grafted caricatures adhering to my skin. Their touches began whispering over my limbs. I began hyperventilating. A vertiginous sensation sprang throughout my insides. I gasped for air, desperately attempting to pump breath back into my lungs. My racked limbs quaked. My flesh felt waves. My mind was clotting by spare images. I grappled with realism.

"Settle down," Joy insisted with a cruel laugh.

"My God," I shouted with a choke. "Stop," I begged, gasping, "Please, stop."

"I'll get some more wine. Maybe that will help," Joy said as she got up.

When she'd left the room, Brenda softly soothed my temples with a series of kisses. "Joy gets carried away sometimes. Baby, are you gonna be okay?"

"I want to leave."

"I'll tell her to knock it off."

"I need to leave, please."

"Baby, I'll make her cool it. Stay so we can sample you."

Looking up, I saw Joy in the doorway. In one hand, she had a bottle, in the other a syringe. Her eyes targeted me with both lust and hatred. She sat on the edge of the bed. Grabbing my arm, she seethed, "Stop struggling."

My own withdrawal was more of a convulsive tug as I struggled to move away from her. My limbs were heavy. I felt powerless. "No," I shouted. The series of screams hollowed me out. They reverberated from my mouth to the tip of my skull. I heard my own strangled cry. It came from the entire world. A bomb was falling. My flesh was burning away from my bones. Explosive flashes melted me away—melted humanity away.

I could barely decipher Brenda's voice. "Joy, knock it off. Stop. Leave her alone. The kid doesn't want any of this. I'll shoot you up. You'd like that."

My eyes eased back open. I watched as Brenda took the syringe. With a ritualistic motion, she tied Joy's upper arm. She then slipped the needle into her vessel. Joy's face went numb. Her eyelids lowered. "Oh, yes," she said as she drifted away.

I attempted to stabilize my mind. Barely cognizant of what was happening, I did know that I had been spared. Although wilting, my spurts of breath helped me fight for reentry. My head was filled with dueling hatchets as my brain rushed, flushing inside.

I sobbed when I realized I was being cradled in Brenda's arms. My neck went limp as my head pressed against her shoulder.

"Help me," I uttered.

"Your first time in a swing?" she rhetorically quizzed. "I'm sorry, baby. She shouldn't have tried anything." She shook her head a couple of time, attempting to return from the effect of drugs. "She gets out of hand. I'm sorry."

"Please, help me," I begged. "I don't want to do this. I don't want to be with either of you."

"I'm sorry." She rocked me a moment. She pushed Joy's unconscious body to the other side of the bed. Joy yawned as she curled in a ball. "She's out for the count. Joy's head is so fucked up. Tomorrow, she will barely remember trying to rape you."

Brenda led me to the bath and filled the huge sunken

cranberry tub. She helped me into the tub. She pushed my hair from my face. Lathering, soaping my cardboard body, she tenderly rinsed the suds. As if she were cleaning me of my sin, absolving me, her touch was fleecy.

"You'll be okay, kid."

"I don't understand. Joy has everything," I mulled. "Why is she so screwed up?"

"Her childhood was strange. That's all I can say. It's always some fucking man that ruins us big time. Always."

"Some men are gentlemen." I remained aloof, my pallid, expressionless face was unable to comprehend or communicate my emotions. A residual tremor undulated through my body when Brenda began drying my still body.

"Baby, I'll get you out of here. We'll walk. Wear off the dope and booze. I'll get you settled in a hotel room. Safe."

"Why are you being nice to me?"

"Kid, sometimes a lover isn't enough. You need a friend. I'll be your friend." She could read the skepticism in my eyes, she added, "You'll need to trust again one day."

Subdued, my eyes contacted hers. That simple glance broke a small barrier. It wasn't by choice, but by need. There were no alternatives. I was alone behind a mesh curtain. It was an impossible veil to lift by myself. I had deliberated before I returned her million-dollar smile.

It was a start at healing.

* * * * *

A FILMY AFTERNOON haze covered the city. Our cab ride toward the Alameda Hotel was silent. Thoughts were still choppy, but my body was steadier than it had been an hour ago. I evaluated my problems. Final exams began in the morning. And my heart, I conceded, was smashed nearly to oblivion.

Brenda sensed my need for silence. After she'd checked me into the hotel, and put my suitcase and books in the room, she suggested we go for a walk in the park. The exercise would help, she said. And she insisted I shouldn't be alone. After a stroll through the park, we could stop at an outdoor café for coffee and pastry. She promised the walk and food would help settle my quivering mind and shivering body.

Her coppery head rotated toward me. "You're a real kitten, baby." Her lips curved. "You're safe now. You can get some sleep tonight. Get through your examinations. Block all this out."

"Block today out?"

"Baby, I do it all the time. I'm basically a blue chip screw. What I'm saying is that people pay my way. Sure, I've got money from modeling. But with my lifestyle, I go through it like water. I'm a classy hook. I've slept with presidents, royalty, movie stars, and spoiled rich girls. I jet to the Bahamas, have a place there. I have apartments in Paris, New York, and L.A. And a horse ranch in Arizona. I go there to clean up once in a while."

A frown accompanied my question. "But why the drugs?"

"Makes blocking it out easier."

"Why did you start taking them?"

"Because I hurt. Just like you hurt this afternoon. I've hurt my entire life."

"But why?" I cross-examined.

She threw her head back and laughed. "Because I was too luscious." With a somber blink, she added, "I developed early. My old man was bedding me by the time I was twelve. If he hadn't, someone else would have. By the time I was fifteen, I was on the road. And on my own."

"I'm sorry."

"I left a trail of mistakes behind. I've attempted suicide several times over the years. Maybe if I can help you, it will give me a chance to pay Cresida back. Your doctora saved my life. Over and over. She's the only one in the world who never gives up on me."

"You're her patient?"

"Yes. Never lovers. If that was what you were wondering. She's the one who taught me that lovers aren't enough." Brenda scoured my face. "I know what you're thinking. And you're right. I wouldn't have minded bedding the doc. But I was her patient. She never would have touched me. She made that crystal clear."

"She truly separates business and pleasure?"

"Baby, she's got too much integrity to mess with her patients."

My voice was brittle. "Maybe I was the exception. I found out she had a file on me."

Brenda continued her jaunty walk. "Baby, the doc has patients lined around the block. She's in demand. She's probably never told you this, but she's one of the most eminent shrinks on the continent. You think she goes out looking for a charity neurosis to cure?"

"I'm not sure."

She tossed her curls as her head swiveled back. She frowned at me. "You think she has nothing better to do than rescue some punk kid? She's too influential to need that.

"She charges more for an hour session than most people make in a week. What the hell does she need with you?" Her candor stung. "You may be a bright kid when it comes to learning smart, but you're a real dumbass when it comes to people."

"Early on she told me she didn't keep files on her lovers. So why did she have one on me?" My voice skidded. "I trusted her."

"You trusted her," she mimicked. "Get off your pity pot, baby." Brenda stopped to overlook a fountain. "Maybe you should come clean with yourself. You know that old adage about not trusting others because you don't trust yourself."

My throat was parched. "She said she was trying to help me."

Brenda grabbed my arm. "Think about it. There's a strong possibility she loves you and wants to help you. The doctora told me that without hope, life is difficult. With hope, life is easy. She helps me keep life simple enough to live. I'm struggling and may spend the rest of my life battling memories, but hope is a staggering ally."

We walked in silence to the outdoor café. After selecting a pastry from a cart and sipping cappuccino, the tension eased. When drinking a second cup, a dam of words exploded.

I would never know why we began talking from our hearts, but we did. I wondered if it might be the drugs wearing off that made us loquacious.

Or maybe it was our emotions.

We exposed our underneath, inside selves. As we related the symptoms of our existence, we laughed, wept, and poured out events that structured us. Our soul words were larcenous, straining, and finally, excruciatingly truthful. We shared intimate secrets of kindness and of villainy.

After a third cup of cappuccino, she questioned, "Baby, how are you really feeling about the doctora?"

My wet lashes felt of mildew, but they dampened again. "I love her. That's why it hurts."

"Don't you think you should tell her how you feel? Your love didn't go away. And why would it if it's really love? You wouldn't leave a poem unfinished. Tell her how you feel about her."

"After what happened at Joy's, she'll probably never want to see me again. She tried to warn me."

Brenda chuckled as she shook her head. "Baby, get on to this. In my favorite movie, *The African Queen*, there's a line that knocks me out. It says it all. 'Nature is what we're put in this world to rise above.' Think about that. Get out of your playpen. People aren't perfect. Cresida isn't perfect. She's got the same fears we all do. We expect her to understand human nature better than we do. But we can't expect more of her human nature than is humanly possible. You allowed your love for her to be smudged because she isn't perfect enough for you. And in her profession, she damn sure knows about human frailty. But she also knows forgiveness is part of the territory of getting well. She knows about forgiving."

We walked back across the park. Strand by strand, we had spilled our stories to one another. We were strangers, trading off our emotions, our pasts. No embellishing rhetoric. No bullshit. We emptied ourselves in a cathartic overture. We traded the ticking truth beneath our outer layers. We cleansed as we exposed our souls.

The sky was beginning to darken. Brenda hailed a cab. When we reached the hotel, she opened her purse and slipped a wad of money into my hand. "This will cover the hotel and your expenses until you're ready to leave for Kansas."

She leaned back against the cab's seat. I reached down, wrapped my arms around her, and whispered, "Thanks. You've been kind to me. This is one of those endings where the stranger rides in on a charger, saves the damsel, and off she goes. Nobody believes such a contrived conclusion." I allowed a quick laugh to escape. "I'm grateful." We remained gathered in one another's embrace for many moments.

She gave her fluffy hair a maverick flip. She winked. "Remember... *The African Queen*. Life doesn't expect perfection of us. That gives us a shot at improving." Her eyes became somber, intense. "And remember about hope. It means we're never more than one patch away from a complete recovery."

It was the most succinct definition of hope I'd ever heard.

FORTY-ONE

I MEANDERED THROUGH my mind's walkways.

Thoughts had often detoured during my first day of examinations. Questions thrashed. Many unrelated to university questionnaires. If I were to become a writer, I must understand human nature. I would be required to know how near vice and virtue align.

My first night in the hotel had been sleepless. The coffee had contributed to my awaking from the drugs and wine—but jolted, my nerves continued. In the desolation of a tenebrous room, I had jotted impressions. When morning invaded, my tap-dancing typewriter keys had transcribed the night's introspection. Words long ago buried were spilling. They frightened me.

I was a walking zombie during the next day's examinations. And when they were concluded, I decided to pick up the rest of my belongings at the doctora's house. I wanted to talk with her.

I now knew I must say goodbye to her.

The past twenty-four hours had taken me from the only security I'd ever really known to one of the greatest nightmares of my life. The bounce left me weak and confused. I wasn't certain if I was up to an encounter with Cresida. It would be an emotional confrontation. But I was certain it needed doing— regardless. I called and told her I wished to talk with her. And that I wanted to take my books and belongings.

When I arrived, facing Cres broke my heart. She had left her office earlier, returning home to meet with me. Her reddened eyes and weary face mirrored my own.

"Kelly, it is vital that we talk."

"Yes." I sat on her living room sofa, next to her.

"I deeply regret hurting you. I betrayed your trust. No matter how lofty and genuine I perceived my ideals to be, I realize it was wrong. For that, I apologize. I would like to explain how I viewed the files I kept on you."

"And I would like to try and understand."

"I kept no such file on my ballerina lover. If I had, perhaps I could have better assisted her. She was a sensitive, creative woman. Not unlike yourself. You are troubled. I saw some of the similar anxiety. I wanted desperately to avoid seeing you eventually go through the pain she did. Perhaps I was frightened of losing you."

"You gained entry to my thoughts, but you never really provided me with access to yours."

"I've maintained a file on myself. I would have provided it for your inspection. You may see it." She went to her office, returning with a thick file. As she handed it to me, then she said, "I have never meant to hide myself from you."

She poured drinks while I thumbed through her file. Along with clinical jargon, there were notations of her love for me. They had been documented from the first time she admitted she'd fallen in love with me. It was during our midnight swim in Cuernavaca.

I shut the file. When I looked up at her face, I questioned, "Why couldn't you have said these words to me? In all the months we were together, you only told me you loved me a couple of times."

"I know the scripting of creative people. The price of

creating is often self-involvement, often isolation. There is an enormous pressure brought about when love is verbalized. I didn't want to burden you with my words. But I attempted to make you experience my love through my actions."

A tear tumbled. "I'm a writer. Words are important to me."

"Eduardo's words cornered you."

"Yes."

"But you must have known of my love," she murmured. She reached for my hand, and then stopped. "Kelly, may I touch you?"

My eyes clamped shut. I felt self-revulsion. "After yesterday, I'm not certain you want to touch me again."

"Brenda called last night to tell me that you were safe. You could not have had any idea how truly troubled Joy is. I attempted to warn you. But, Kelly, it has nothing to do with my love for you." With a benign gentleness, she added, "Life is much larger than we often allow it to be. I'm only sorry you were hurt."

"Once you asked me if I would come to you if I needed you. I need you now." She wrapped me in her embrace. I whispered, "I need your love to cancel yesterday. To cleanse me." I sobbed against her shoulder.

"Yes. Yes, my darling. The *ovalness* of love. We all must learn to love again. Or perhaps more. You will stay with me tonight?"

"I'll stay. We'll be together one final time. I need you. And I do love you."

"And I am in love with you."

"Cres, tomorrow I'll leave. I'll be letting go with love."

"Will you return to me?"

"Life is a chain of farewells."

"You're very young to have learned that great lesson."

"It's a sad lesson, but also a wondrous lesson. Sad because it seems the nature of love makes it transitory. It is wondrous to have had one great love of my life."

We both knew the meaning of past tense.

* * * * *

OUR FINAL NIGHT together was a time of need, and of love, for both of us.

We cradled together. The tender lift of elation was to be my parting memory of this journey. Of that word, used in centuries past where romance belonged and I often thought I belonged—journey. And the great tour of my life was completing. A tour of me and of a poem that I am.

The doctora's need to tell me of her love, repeatedly, was our accompaniment. Through that last night, our bodies wrapped, spooned, and clung. We clutched one another's heartbeat. Our lovemaking was as if it had never before been. We didn't know if it was to be our last evening together. One never knows for certain. However, we treated it with the eloquence, resplendence, and adoration as if it were. As if this act could never again be equaled in warmth. No other night had compared or would compare. For that was how it was planned. And that is how it was.

Again, as in each time waking in Cresida's arms, I felt I'd swallowed a sunburst. It's glowing inside me never failed to astound me. I didn't know, and perhaps would never understand, the 'magnetization' that drew me to her. I didn't comprehend its magic. Nor was it important that I understood. Only that I accept the miracle of love's intent.

In the morning, our eyes followed one another until it was time for me to leave. She asked if I would call her if I ever needed her. Absolutely, I answered. Our faces were damp as we clung to one another. We both knew I couldn't promise to return. I could only promise that I would think of her each time I viewed an oval-like moon, a bursting sunset, a bright beach, a yellow rose, crystal, or a lovely woman.

In leaving, my voice strained. I told her of my love. I kissed her and gave her an absolute *abrazo*. She placed a copy of *Love Songs of Sappho* in my hands. She related that it had been a gift to her from her first lover. And the marker was in the same spot.

I got inside the cab. I felt her clasped hand easing from mine. And then the cab pulled out of her driveway. I unfolded the book to where the marker had been placed, and I read:

Sweet woman how you will remember always till you are old,

The things we did together in shining youth!

For many things we did then innocent and beautiful

And now that you go from here, my heart is breaking.

A flush of heat, along with the rolling of tears, nearly suffocated me. I buried my face in my arms. A hideous lump knotted behind my breastbone, deep within my chest. The pain intensified as blocks clicked away.

* * * * *

I TOOK A final stroll around my mountainside atelier. The lightness of my tote, normally weighted down with a dozen heavy books, reminded me that classes were over. I had a few minutes before the bus would take me from the campus, so I decided to call Eduardo. I wanted to tell him goodbye and that I would remember him always. We had shared a wide array of emotions. And we had shared many places in his wonderful land.

He insisted on driving me to the airport. It would be a

perfect symbolism—the circle was closing.

As the school bus weaved toward the city's heart, excitement built. It would be bittersweet for I wanted to see my family, but I knew this city would long be missed. Imprinted upon me was the knowledge, wisdom, and love imparted by those I'd come to know and to love. Great and gifted lessons were mine to take away.

Calvin Thurston had taught me to become a *toward* person. I would search for a fairer leaf. And, perhaps, I would one day dedicate a book to him. Nathan Roberts instructed me about what an A+ means and the attached challenge. Edith Sanchez had taught me that there was a type to know. Señor Hermann had educated me on the fact that there's no way of knowing who the type is. Nora coached me about friends not needing to understand. As long as they accepted. And at all costs, watch out for donkey doo-doo. Lindy enlightened me about Lady Day. She never sang while in prison. And she helped me to better understand a friend who was also not singing. Leigh acquainted me with the reality that not all children are young. Erika taught me to laugh at absurdity. Pablo guided me in knowing that if one could survive the Well of Sacrifice, canonization was promised. Tom tutored me about friends who sometimes need looking after. Kirk taught me about people who want to rope a dream. And can't. Joy acquainted me with the fact that drugs are ugly. And Brenda taught me that they are sad. And that hope is the anchor of existence. Juan taught me how to say and feel *agradecidisimo*. Rodolfo showed me how to allow questions to be answered by not asking them. Lupe trained me to sing her Aztec song: 'Our body is like a rose tree. Our hearts will grow green again.'

The glistening lesson-plan of love was also mine. Eduardo taught me the first shade in love's prism. He caressed my heart with youthful romance. Carlos inspired me to understand that it was fine to touch flesh without groping for a nerve. He taught that friends and lovers could be one and the same.

Cresida enlightened me about encircling warmth—and how to view crystals. She taught me how to properly pronounce *la femme* and everything I know about the passion of same.

She taught me who I am.

* * * * *

ARRIVING BACK AT the hotel, I finished packing. Then I clamped shut my suitcase. I checked my ticket and passport, and then plunged them into the bottom of my handbag. Finally, I rested on a tufted chair and gazed out of the window.

Attached was the loneliness of missing the city I so loved. Mexico City is where my soul longed to home. In only hours, an airplane would be taking me from the colonias, barrios, and those patches of city that became conducive to poetry. I would be going away from the mosaic stone tattooed tiles, the ring of brass bells, marimbas, and heart fiestas. Away from the gold-dipped angel, the fried egg *Bellas Artes*, the giant cypress where Cortez wept, the splashing Rivera murals, and flowered boats. Away from the misty rains of afternoon, raindrops softly dripping, away from stone fountains, bronzed statuary, arched walkways, laced churches, and tree-lined boulevards. Away from ancient pyramids, radiant beaches, and smiles of splendor.

A knock on the door jolted my ruminations. Eduardo embraced me. I smiled. "I couldn't leave without thanking you for sharing your country with me."

"I am also happy we met. And sad that we parted." He kissed my cheek, and then lifted my suitcase. He followed me to the elevator. "And will you return?"

"I've got some repair work to do. Some sorting. I'd like to return next year. But nothing is certain. Nothing."

"I know." He took my hand. We felt the whoosh of the elevator when he kissed my wrist. "And our love, can it one day be repaired?"

"Eduardo, it's difficult to renovate romance. But we can and should salvage our friendship."

"You have left the person with whom you were living?"

"With all my heart, I hope I haven't really left anyone." I mulled the brevity of life and the vacancy of leaving. "If we've loved, we leave memories." I considered my own words. My heart had set off to explore. My ensemble of lovers had given my heart an adventure. As poetry is only a rough draft until it's heard or read, love is empty until spirits twine. And that can never be undone.

We chatted about mundane events on the way to the airport. We had ended our perishable silence with important emotional release. Our indulgent forgiveness was traded. We laughed at jokes known only to us. And when my flight was called, I brushed his cheek with my lips.

"Kelly, may we say *hasta luego* and not *adios*?"

"Yes. I'd like to see you again."

"If only I would have given you time."

"Eduardo, I don't believe that would have been enough. I have to reach deeply to find my path. I've got to go away to determine my own mystery—and how I'm to live it."

"My mother says there is an old expression about angels. She says that we are angels with only one wing. We can fly only when we share *abrazos*—for that makes two wings."

I hugged him tightly. Our lips touched briefly. "I wish you happiness in your life." And then I turned to walk away from him.

From the plane's window, I could see the outline of his

frame as he watched. I could feel his pain. And mine. When the airplane lifted, I hoped that it had both wings, for I did not. And would not until I arrived back with my family. With Gran's hug, along with her lullaby, there would be two wings.

Mexico's embrace was slipping from my clasp. The Braniff sailed toward Dallas. During a half-hour layover in Dallas, I decided to check my makeup. I pulled out my compact. Glancing at my somber reflection, I spread makeup base across my weary face. There was little I could do about the limp, tawny hair, and baggy eyes. Lipstick was glided over my lips. I clearly looked as terrible as I felt, I thought. With that, I flushed. It was my first blush in nearly a year. I scoffed at my mirror image. Retrogressive cupcake! I accused.

While my handbag was still open, I checked to see if I still had American coins to phone my family when I got to Kansas City. As I rummaged, I pulled out the geode. I gazed at its crystal-toothed center. Transfixed, I watched the sparkle of the jeweled pinnacles. It somehow illuminated my heart. My head eased back against the pillow. I closed my eyes.

Drifting into a dream—I saw fresh, sparkling powder snow. It would assist me on my run. If I were to make the steep grade below me, I would need total abandon. I bent to secure my ski boot's binding. I studied the wood grain on my cross-country skis. Then I surveyed the steep incline that I had failed to make on my previous attempt. I plotted my run. Purple wax. I would leap a few meters before approaching that intimidating curve. It would require a rapid swinging wave of my skis. I lifted my poles. I jabbed the twinkling snow. Pushing away with resolve, I gained momentum. Aware of the perilous speed, I approached the base. I curved my angle. A swift, midair jump turned the earth beneath me. One ski hit before the other. I tottered as I regained my balance. Before me was a wide, clear trail. I saluted the glistening snow and my wrap of crystal mountain peaks.

With precision, I had gauged what the mountain had required of me. My confidence had not bolted. There had only been one sweaty-handed decision. I couldn't consider not making the run.

Gently nudging me awake was the flight attendant. We would be landing in Kansas City in a few minutes. I tried to swallow the dryness in my mouth. In my dream, I hadn't crumbled. I hadn't almost died in the actual skiing accident. In the dream, I had made it through the trail. With directive, guidance, and with trust, I had maintained my balance. Buck up, wonder waif, I chided myself. Without fear and with hope, survival had a chance.

After debarking, I felt like running to the baggage claim area. I paced my stride. Then with a start, as I lifted my suitcase, I saw Kris and Rod approaching me. I hugged them both. "Is Gran okay?"

"Kelly, we tried to contact you," Kris explained. "Doctor Valdez gave us your flight number. Gran's in the hospital."

"Will she be okay?"

"She got worse yesterday," Rod answered. "But she was determined to make it until you returned. Your mother said waiting for you might have gotten her through the worst part of the pneumonia."

Rod took my suitcase. Kris gave me a pat on the shoulders as we walked. "Kelly," Kris encouraged, "she's a tough old bird. She'll hang on. I know she will."

"I left immediately after tests."

We hastened to Rod's car. "Everyone went to the hospital," Rod said. "We'll go directly there."

"Thanks for coming to get me."

Kris suddenly blurted, "Kelly, Gran told me to tell you welcome back to America."

My eyes watered. I knew she would make it. All the women I ever needed had always been there for me. Gran was a fine-spun tapestry and we were stitches in her journey. As well as our own. Slender threads are the roads leading back toward one's natural habitat.

"We're all glad you're home, Kelly," Rod commented as he slid my suitcase into the back seat.

Kris disclosed, "There's something else. Gran said to give you a message. It doesn't make sense. She may have been hallucinating, but she said you would understand."

"Understand what?"

"She said to tell you welcome back to the bakery."

"Yes. I do know what she means." I wondered how she could possibly have known.

It was time to return to the bakery.

EPILOGUE

WHEN MY TRAVELS *began, back many decades ago, I only wished to experience youth and to know Mexico. Mine was a pilgrimage of realizing both objectives. As I began my adventure, I felt life had left me stranded—life was my night-long beast. I wanted to conquer what I couldn't understand. What I found, beneath the truth, or perhaps within the truth, was that there were no antagonists.*

There was no need to traverse the planet—wandering as a nomadic writer—poet. I wanted to write one memorable poem—perhaps this is that poem.

They say youth's love is not to be trusted. But what I felt might be as trusted as any other love I have known since. For it was love—assuredly. Time is a most random miracle. Time has intensified my ability to interpret through another's needs.

It was that trip that I took when turning twenty that most changed me. And I remain grateful. It was my tour—such an ascending and internalized path of words, which lead across my poem.

With Regards,
Kelly Anne Benjamin

TOURING KELLY'S POEM
THE WORDS — THE POETRY

AND ALL THE WORLD WAS MEXICO

When all the world was Mexico
The world, my world, was one.

We came and tore moonlit shores
Away from out-stretched Manila.
Dreams deflowered and went away
Drifting like shifting sands.

When all the world was Mexico
A world, my world, was grand.

Melancholy clouds came down
And lingered over-head,
Distraught drums kept rumbling
Sounding songs of the dead.

When all the world was Mexico
This world, of mine, was one.

And now comes silent tidings
From nature comes the call.
To find a place where this world
Is Mexico to all.

BUTTERFLY IN YELLOW

Chapters written to a striped Butterfly in Yellow
Palpitating with wings on debut.
Existence unfolding as it discovers a perch.
Its pillow has tiers of lemon petals and a flutter in bursting rose.
Mid-tropical winds give motion to its wings
A weightless Butterfly in Yellow timidly settles
                    to suckle honey flakes.
All penned in a book that lives only three moments.

LAGO DE CHAPULTEPEC

A castle over watches dwarfed boats
                making their path across the lake.
From the bridge cigarette butts
            float on the water's edge.
But view the whole of Mexico
            ignoring the pseudo-Mexican boarder.
That's what I do on a lunch break
            while feeding torta crusts to gleeful, smooth swans.
I look away from the twitching rhythms of a shallow proximity
                and see the splendor of a land.

Touring Kelly's Poem

When All the World Was Mexico

When all the world was Mexico
The world, my world was one.
Time came and tore moonlit shores
Away from outstretched hands.
Dreams diffused and went away,
Drifting like shifting sands.

When all the world was Mexico
A world, my world, was grand.
Melancholy clouds came down
And lingered overhead.
Distraught drums went rumbling
Sounding songs of the dead.

When all the world was Mexico
This world, of mine, was one.
And now comes silent tidings
From living comes the call.
To find a place where this world
Is Mexico to all.

Butterfly in Yellow

Chapters written to a striped butterfly in yellow:
Palpitating with wings on debut, it is.
Existence unfolds as it discovers a perch.
A pillow has tiers of lemon petals.
They are set a flutter in bursting rows.
Mid-tropical winds give motion to its wings.
A weightless butterfly in yellow timidly settles.

It suckles honey flakes.
All is penned in a book that lives
only three seconds.

Lago de Chapultepec

A castle watches over dwarfed boats
As they make their path across the lake.
From the bridge,
I view cigarette butts afloat on the water's edge.
But the view—
the whole view of Mexico must continue beyond the border.
Ignoring pseudo-Mexico—
that's what I do on a lunch break
while feeding torta crusts to gleeful, show-off swans.
I look away from the blinding,
shallow proximities and see the heart's splendor of a land.

Fisherman of Veracrus

Sea-filled breezes slap the face of a bronze fisherman.
He leans to spread his net across a Veracruz surf.
He sweats in the damp air as he strains to pull his net.
Sea spray splashes at him.
He periodically wipes perspiration with a quick arm.
He rocks and weaves with waves of shifting color.
Whitecaps roll to meet the glistening, beige sand.
And the fisherman's lips curve into a smile.
He whispers up a prayer.
Let there be fish plentiful.
Let him be paid for his labor.
Let the world smile.

Miramar Beach and Bocochibampo Bay

A mirror beach is sunlit as the shore receives the ocean.
A crystallized bay is topped with diamond waters.
Rippling, foaming waves slap shell-studded, pebbled sands.
All of this is called 'love' by all that is nature.

Parque de Chapultepec

Chapultepec Park is:
As dabbled with color as an artist's palate.
As plaid as a crisscrossed prism.
As flower-filled as a Fifth Avenue floral shop.
As free of over-splendor as a beautiful nun.
As packed with stone-carved monuments as saints in heaven.
As magnificently simple as a clear sky.
As spotted with brightly colored balloons on strings
as a polka dot factory.
As full of squeals as a three-year-olds birthday party.
As still and serene as a deathbed.
As new as the freshest yellow bud.
As old as the splintering palms.
As Mexico as any spot in the world.

Curtain Up

Mexico City has an opening night on every block.
Tree-shaded avenues and glorietas make a backdrop.
It's a show with such total catharsis that you are touched
by cotton clouds and parachute heavens.
Each paved street sends shivers of appreciation.
Faces are directed into action.
Women at corners, sitting on upturned pails,

concentrate on turning tostadas.
An old man collecting Coke bottles
in a bag around his shoulders—nods.
The sound of rubbing glass is a perfect sound effect.
Chicklet kids are selling packets of gum
that you don't really need but you purchase anyway.
They are a wardrobe mistress' dream.
Impromptu scenes and people are photographed
and stored in the memory for some lonely night like now.
I applaud. I stand. A complete ovation.

<u>Los Viejitos</u>
Little old dancing men leaning on canes
Feigning agedness, sickness, and pains.
Crook-backed dancing men smile a sneer.
Baby pants, clowning, and showing no fear.
Feeble dancing men, extend their arms.
Ribbons fall from sombreros with great charm.
Hunch-backed dancing men grinning a smirk
think up ways to get out of work.
Humped, old dancing men, legs spread apart,
leap and jump as if they are pulling a cart.
Festively dressed dancing men hobble and stall.
They hold tight to their canes so not to fall.
Little, old dancing men in embroidered pant legs
await the breaking open of kegs.
Happy, sad dancing men enjoy prancing
for a mystified audience who enjoys their dancing.

<u>Monumentos</u>
From Southern Winds to Eternal Spring,

I'm wanting to wander on.
Concealed pain bursts through all
– dusk, dark, and dawn.
An angel hovers—overlooking city streets
where castles, cathedrals, and palaces meet.
Brave warrior with a chieftain's shawl
proudly stands protecting with a valorous call.
Diana raises her bow from above
and arrows are aimed to touch perfect love.
Four arches greet the revolution's fight
and victory comes with a bloody night.
Shining great suns of day remain valorously bold.
Worlds of beauty exceed Inca gold.

Con un Abrozo

A sad farewell, I bid this land
as a dream slips through my hand.
Yet, parting abrozos won't correct the day.
I can't look back again or I might stay.
I would remain within my enchantment.
The moments that life has kindly lent.
But I must leave, my path is arranged.
My tour of love has been changed.
Lest the rest of my life be spent in only two places,
I'll continue to search for many other faces.
I won't be restricted to one part of earth.
I'll hope each land brings me this mirth.
And each farewell will be as sad as this.
For I treasure that here has been such bliss.
May I always have such treasured time
where I'll miss and long for its special rhyme.
Remembrances will fondly glance from where I go.

I'll never run away, my stroll will be slow.

Cresida
Amante.
Amiga mia, con todo mi amor.
Amor imposible?
Amor is possible
Todo amor.
Regalame este notche.
Destrozarle mi Corazon.
Cresida, you are as possible as your myth makes you.

—

Words for Cres

Effervescent Glory
It was a translucent soul I'd shared with her.
Newfound love, unforgettable romance—and us.
I danced on ledges of memories.
Perhaps it was only with her I felt safe.
And wasn't—for recollections of love rained down on me.
She'd gouged disappointment from my soul.
I still feel her lips and know the warmth of her kiss.
She guided me through to magic
until it annihilated me.
Then she dispatched the memory of when glory had been mine.

Final Words for Cres

My fated soul fell toward your caress,
Astounding my sensations, I confess.
Awakened, I'm aware of being lost.
Yet I accept this bridge I've crossed.
Within your romance, I was bound
By crystal love where we'd been found.
You'd waited for me, then you were here.
I'd searched for you, then you were near.
Love's rhapsody was mine in your embrace.
I'd watched existence within your face.
You'd directed me to the path I'm on.
The other romance was forgone.
Soft love—this gentle tour you've shown
Became the mystery all my own.
Your embrace taught me where I belong.
Your voice gave me the meaning of my song.
Now lyrics from my final words flow
Across the sky—like a pastel rainbow.
Can the question of decades ever release
The answer of my own eternal peace?
My gratitude—you opened my world for me –
My heart to beat, and my eyes and soul to see.
Agradecimiento, my lovely woman.
Para siempre, Cresida.

—

ABOUT THE AUTHOR

KIERAN YORK IS the author of the lesbian mystery series featuring Royce Madison. *Timber City Masks* and *Crystal Mountain Veils* were written and published in the mid-1990s and was reissued in 2014, and again in 2015 by Scarlet Clover Publishers LLC. She also wrote a collection of lesbian short stories entitled *Sugar With Spice*.

In 2012, York's book, *Appointment with a Smile*, was published and was a 2013 Lambda Literary Society Award Finalist in the Romance category. Her next novel, *Careful Flowers*, was released in 2013. Both books were published by Blue Feather Books.

In 2014, Scarlet Clover Publishers LLC released *Earthen Trinkets* and *Night Without Time*. *Loitering on the Frontier* is forthcoming.

York was also a contributor in *Sappho's Corner Poetry Series—Wet Violets. Volume 2; Roses Read, Volume 3;* and *Delectable Daisies, Volume 4.*

In 2014, her volume of poetry, *Blushing Aspen,* was published as the Sappho's Corner Solo Poet book of poetry.

Previously, during the seventies, and eighties, Kieran worked as a reporter and reviewer for both newspaper and magazine and was a newspaper publisher for three years. She also wrote and performed songs with a women's band. She has been a guest lecturer and panel member at various events, including Rocky Mountain Book Exhibition, Colorado Musicians Series, Sisters in Crime Mystery Writers, and Mystery Writers of America, Inc. She is a member of Lambda Literary Society and Golden Crown Literary Society.

She has written for *Journal of Mystery Readers International.* In addition, she has given numerous campus and coffeehouse poetry readings, as well as taught poetry and creative writing workshops.

She graduated from a Kansas university and attended Mexico's University of the Americas her junior year. She has done graduate work at the University of Colorado.

Kieran lives in the Rocky Mountain foothills of Colorado with her schnauzer, Clover. She enjoys gardening, music, literature, and art. She considers her valuables to include Clover and other family and friends, her library, her antique typewriter collection, her guitar, and her garden.

Additional information is available on her website. She has a blog—Embellish Your Smile at http://kieranyork.com. Current information on Scarlet Clover Publishers LLC can be found on http://scarletcloverpublishers.com.